Eighty-Nine Years and Still Evolving

Essays and Writings

D1519211

James Emerson Hough

ISBN 978-1-0980-5124-2 (paperback)
ISBN 978-1-0980-5125-9 (digital)

Christian Faith Publishing, Inc.
832 Park Avenue
Meadville, PA 16335
www.christianfaithpublishing.com

Printed in the United States of America

FOREWORD

There is no such thing as pure originality. A person's knowledge is the amassed thoughts and experiences of innumerable other minds.

We inherit language, science, mathematics, religion, opinion, imagination, ambition, country, tradition, custom, law, and the idea of what is proper and equitable. All these were already created, and we practice them.

An expressed factual thought makes ridiculous the critic who informs another person where such a thought had been written or said before. The words of some people we remember so well we often use them to express our thoughts.

The highest praise attributable to a writer is that they actually possessed the thoughts that inspire others.

This nonfiction book is a collection of thought-provoking essays and writings that will stimulate the reader's own introspective consideration of thoughts and emotions or augment their personal intellectual powers or spiritual resources.

The author's conservative philosophy is both an art and a science; a system of values by which he lives, the depth of which has grown unchanged with time and has thrust his relevance to God and God's universe into perspective.

It emphasizes the need for traditional values and moral order manifest through natural laws and laws of science to which a prudent society has the duty to perform.

In pursuit of wisdom, the author critically analyses assumptions and beliefs by intellectual means and moral self-discipline based on observation and experience, logical reasoning, and ethics and the nature of reality (relationship between mind and matter, substance, fact, and value) and the nature of knowledge (its presuppositions and foundations, extent, and validity).

Born 1930, the author possesses a strong patriotic obligation to honor America with service, commitment, courage, and integrity; was honorably discharged a disabled veteran, United States Army active duty 1953–1955; practiced more than forty-one years as licensed professional in the applied earth sciences; and is lecturer *emeritus*, University of Cincinnati Evening College.

CONTENTS

Chapter 1
My Physical, Mental, and Spiritual Maturity

August 29, 2019

My **body** grows older and tires easily, is shorter of breath and unsteady afoot; the daily four-mile walk in my awe-inspiring forest preserve with my dog Freedom is history.

My **mind** grows more mature and wisdom; the ability to discern what is true, right, or lasting is augmented.

My **soul** is created in God's image—unchangeable, immortal, infinite, eternal, neither matter nor energy, neither male nor female—and remains with me until my body and mind are near death or die, at which time God takes my soul.

My mind grows either more mature or remains immature. My body does not age; it gets older. Cheese and alcoholic beverages age. Good health and mental maturity allow me to physically and mentally relax, to listen, to hear what is said and not said, to respect other opinions (even opposing opinions held rigidly by others), and to reason clearly before speaking.

Spiritual maturity permits me to learn by eagerly seeking recondite information and to experience a divine presence in my forest preserve, outside of which fewer than five percent of my hours are spent. Spiritual maturity provides me peace of mind, joy in life, total lack of fear, depth of understanding, and compassion.

I give thanks to all the mature persons who have engendered in me by word and example the desire for a healthy mature life and the meaning of living life to its fullest.

THE TWELVE DISCIPLES

May 31, 2019

PETER. Galilean, uneducated, oldest teenager, married, fisherman, older brother of Andrew, the group spokesman, crucified head-down on cross AD 64 in Rome.

JAMES the older. Galilean, uneducated, teenager, fisherman, older brother of John, from well-to-do family, beheaded AD 44.

JOHN. Galilean, uneducated, age twelve when called by Jesus, younger brother of James the older, from well-to-do family, born AD 14, died age ninety-eight AD 112 of natural causes on the isle of Patmos.

ANDREW. Galilean, uneducated, teenager, fisherman, younger brother of Peter, crucified AD 69 in Greece.

BARTHOLOMEW NATHANAEL. Galilean, uneducated, teenager, of royal blood, sister was wife of David, killed by skinning using knives.

JAMES the younger. Galilean, uneducated, teenager, brother of Jude and Mathew.

JUDAS ISCARIOT. Galilean, uneducated, teenager, betrayed Jesus and afterward hung himself in the Temple of Jerusalem AD 29, replaced by Matthias who was stoned to death years later in modern-day Georgia.

JUDE. Judean, uneducated, teenager, brother of James the younger and Mathew, killed by arrows in Armenia.

MATHEW. Galilean, uneducated, second oldest teenager, tax collector, older brother of James the younger and Jude, martyred in Ethiopia.

PHILIP. Galilean, uneducated, teenager, fisherman, hanged in Egypt.

SIMON the zealot. Galilean, uneducated, teenager, fisherman, martyred in modern-day Turkey.

THOMAS. Galilean, uneducated, teenager, a skeptic, killed by a spear in India.

Except for Jude, all the disciples are Galilean, and all are uneducated Aramaic-speaking Jewish teenagers. The oldest is Peter who is married. The second oldest is Mathew. John is one of the youngest, if not the youngest. There are three sets of brothers; two sets of two and one set of three, comprising seven of the twelve. Five of the twelve are fishermen. None of the twelve ever recanted their belief that Jesus was who He claimed.

TIMELINE

The following dates and information are established and arranged in chronological order by officially recognized historians using three different calendars, each generally described as follows.

The Hebrew calendar is both solar- and lunar-based. A lunar month has about 29.5 days. Because the month is not divided into full days, the lunar months in the Hebrew calendar have either twenty-nine or thirty days. Hebrew days begin at nightfall. Twelve lunar months total only 354.4 days, whereas twelve solar months total 365.25 days. To account for the eleven-day difference and maintain a solar year, the lunar calendar has periodic leap years which add an extra thirty-day month to the end of the year. The leap year occurs about once every three years. Hebrew year 5779, before Rosh Hashana, corresponds to Gregorian year AD 2019. After Rosh Hashana, it is Hebrew year 5780 and Gregorian year AD 2020.

The Julian calendar is solar-based, introduced 46 BC by Julius Caesar, is divided into 12 months, 365 days, and a leap year of 366 days every fourth year.

The Gregorian calendar is solar-based, sponsored by Pope Gregory XIII AD 1582, is a corrected version of the Julian calendar and used worldwide today. Britain converted AD 1752. USSR converted AD 1918. Greece converted AD 1925.

1800 BC. Abraham alive
1660s BC. Writing of original Old Testament begins
1400 BC. Moses alive
587 BC. Babylonian conquest of Jerusalem
510 BC. Beginning of Roman Empire
400s BC. Writing of original Old Testament ends
145 BC. Book of Daniel written, final book of Hebrew Bible
63 BC. Conquest of Palestine by Romans
44 BC. Assassination of Julius Caesar by Cassius and Brutus
4 BC. Birth of John the Baptist, six months before Jesus
4 BC. **BIRTH OF JESUS**
4 BC. Herod, king of Jews, orders the killing of all males age two
    and under
4 BC. Mary and Joseph flee with baby Jesus to Egypt
4 BC. Death of Herod, king of the Jews
AD 6. Birth of Apostle Paul
AD 14. Birth of John
AD 8. Jesus age twelve visits the Temple in Jerusalem
AD 8–26. Jesus works, age twelve to thirty, as carpenter in Nazareth
AD 26. Jesus baptized in the River Jordan by John the Baptist
AD 26. Jesus in the Judean Wilderness
AD 26. Jesus hails fishermen Andrew, Simon, Philip, and Bartholomew
AD 26. Jesus turns water into wine and drives moneymakers from
    temple in Jerusalem
AD 27. Jesus's Sermon on the Mount
AD 27. Jesus's miracle of the leper
AD 27. Jesus calls Matthew
AD 27. Jesus and the imprisonment of John the Baptist
AD 27. Birth of Josephus, Jewish historian
AD 28. Jesus's miracle of the loaves and fishes
AD 28. Jesus walks on water
AD 28. Jesus foretells his death and resurrection
AD 28. Jesus questioned by the Jews

AD 29. Jesus and Lazarus

AD 29. Jesus tells of imminent betrayal

AD 29. Jesus on the Mount of Olives

AD 29. The Last Supper

AD 29. **JESUS CRUCIFIED**

AD 29. Judas Iscariot hung himself

AD 29. **JESUS RESURRECTED**

AD 29. Jesus after resurrection, Sea of Galilee

AD 29. The ascension

AD 33. Conversion of Apostle Paul

AD 44. James the elder beheaded

AD 64. Peter crucified

AD 64. Apostle Paul beheaded in Rome

AD 66. Writing of original Christian New Testament begins, based on **oral tradition**

AD 66–70. Writing Gospel of Mark by highly-educated Greek Christian

AD 69. Andrew crucified

AD 80–85. Writing Gospel of Luke by highly-educated Greek Christian, used Mark

AD 90–95. Writing Gospel of John by highly-educated Greek Christian, used Mark or Luke

AD 100. Death of Josephus, Jewish historian

AD 112. Death of John

A Treatise
Creation, Spirituality, Science, Religion

September 6, 2007; last revision October 15, 2019

The significance of God, the Eternal Being, I did not fully understand until after four years of studying geology; a near-death out-of-body experience when injured at age twenty-four during military service; two years graduate study of geology and engineering; six years professional applied earth science working experience; and twenty-two of thirty-five years in private professional practice of the applied earth sciences. I was fifty-six years of age at the time.

While practicing the applied earth sciences, I also studied metaphysics—the nature of reality including the relationship between mind and matter, substance, nature, fact, and value.

My analytical thinking asserts the existence of an ideal spirituality that goes beyond transcendent truths and is knowable through factual truths. My spirituality is based solely on truth my soul was created to have dominion; it is not based on a belief or a faith in any one or more sets of religious doctrines created by humans.

At the age of seventy-eight, as I watched my wife of fifty-two years quit breathing and her immortal soul taken, my life experiences altogether fully convinced me of the following seven major principles.

- God—with unlimited power, total knowledge, and simultaneous presence everywhere—created the universe and everything in it. God is outside of the universe and of real time, immortal, infinite, eternal, neither matter nor energy, neither male nor female, and unchangeable.
- God's perfection is represented by the perfect harmony of the universe.
- God created of human substance Jesus—a faithful Jew and subsequently an inspired prophet with a message of compassion, love, and truth—who was neither equal nor identical to the God who makes truth possible.
- God creates the soul in God's image—unchangeable, immortal, infinite, eternal, neither matter nor energy, neither male nor female.
- God creates the human body and mind and gives the mind a soul—the source of moral and ethical judgment—that remains until the body and mind are near death or die, at which time God takes the soul.
- God created in orderly manner conditions for good, bad, evil, atonement, and forgiveness, gives the mind free will, and monitors human behavior.
- God created in real time on planet earth the domain and conditions of biblical heaven and biblical hell.

The soul is not born, does not die, and is known only by direct human experience and sense perception that the mind cannot fully describe, conceptualize, or understand. Birth, growth, death, and decay leaving only carbon are inevitable for all biological and zoological life. Only that which is not born—the soul—does not die.

All creations, objects, and conditions in the universe are in a state of continual change, which is the answer to the mystery of creation; new forms arise out of the old, and each new form is determined by that which preceded it. The process of change is not chaotic; it's regulated by nature's universal law of cause and effect, which is unchanging, impersonal, and impartial.

All the constants and laws of nature that sustain science hold true. They are the hidden architecture of the universe. Even though the sun rises every day, there is no guarantee that it will rise tomorrow. The belief that it will rise tomorrow, that there indeed are dependable regularities in nature, is an act of faith indispensable to the progress of science.

Recognizing the existence of this kind of faith is an important step in bridging the artificial divide between science and religion. Science is the realm of certainty and verifiability while religion is a belief.

Science and spirituality sit within a similar intellectual framework. Just as faith is indispensable to science, so is reason essential to spirituality. The source of inspiration for science is in the realm of spirituality. To be spiritual is to sense that underlying anything experienced there is a sublime force touching a person indirectly; something the human mind cannot fully grasp. Science without spirituality is weak and ineffectual. Spirituality without science is sightless, without direction and based on faith alone.

The realm of science is to discover with certainty the truth. The domain of spirituality includes the soul's influence on human thoughts and actions about what is the truth. God's unlimited power, total knowledge, and simultaneous presence everywhere is beyond human comprehension. God seldom responds to selfish prayer or prayer only for oneself; God often responds to prayer for others.

Every effort of science to understand secrets of the universe reveals that behind the interrelations and discernible laws, there remains a subtle, intangible, and explicable force demanding profound respect and reverence beyond anything the human mind can comprehend.

This reverence can be likened to a young child entering a huge library filled with books written in many languages. The child knows someone must have written those books, does not know how, and does not understand the languages in which they were written. The child dimly suspects a mysterious order in the arrangement of the books but does not know what it is.

Nature is marvelously arranged and obeys natural laws, many of which are not well-understood by the human mind. Every human action in nature has an equal and opposite reaction; human failure to conform to natural laws imposes penalty.

Right human behavior is logical and moral, and it succeeds; contradictory human behavior is illogical and immoral, and it fails. Human conformity to natural laws is mandatory; nonconformity accounts for the chaos and deadly affairs of humans and societies. All human values and efforts without the complete undergirding of a God of justice and compassion are doomed to failure.

The order of things in human society is as good as the character of the population permits. People of virtue are the conscience of human society. When the soul breathes through intellect, it is character; when the soul floods through feelings, it is love; when the soul flows through free will, it is virtue.

The most wonderful state of consciousness a human can experience is to grasp the mysteries of the universe. It is the fundamental emotion present in all true science. Those to whom this feeling is a stranger or those who no longer wonder and stand rapt in awe are like snuffed-out candles.

Science is inspired with the aspiration for truth and understanding, seeking to uncover the unchangeable laws that govern reality. In so doing, science rejects the notion that God interferes with natural processes, a role that would violate creation's vast principle of cause and effect.

Science affirms positively the irreversibility of natural processes, the impossibility for something to arise out of nothing, the impossibility that everything already existed in the universe, and that a power outside the universe and real time created the universe and everything in it. That power is what humans call God.

Scientists have detected gravitational waves from a collision in deep space 5.88 trillion miles away. This finding confirms Einstein's theory about the ripple effect of space-time and has generated attributes to the achievements of human reason.

Astrophysicists know that the value of the four fundamental forces (gravity, strong nuclear force, weak nuclear force, and electromagnetic force) were unwavering less than one-millionth of a second after the so-called big bang. Alter any one of these values about ten-septillionth (1 followed by 21 zeros) of a second and the universe could not exist. The odds against the big bang, that it all just happened, defies common sense. It would be like tossing a coin and having it come-up heads ten quintillion times in a row.

England's Steven Hawking who coined the term big bang said that his atheism was "greatly shaken" at these developments. Hawking later wrote that "a common sense interpretation of the facts suggests that a super intellect has monkeyed with the physics, as well as with the chemistry and biology…the numbers one calculates from the facts it seems to me to be so overwhelming as to put this conclusion beyond question."

Theoretical physicists say, "The appearance of design is overwhelming." Mathematicians say, "The more we get to know about the universe, the more the hypothesis that there is a Creator gains in credibility as the best explanation of why we humans are here." The universe is the miracle of all miracles, one that inevitably points with the combined brightness of every star beyond itself to an Eternal Being.

*****

Genesis records that "the Lord rained on Sodom and Gomorrah brimstone and fire out of the heavens." An ancient clay tablet unearthed in the nineteenth century contains records dating 700 BC by a Sumerian astronomer observing an asteroid that fell on two cities.

Science notes that the description in Exodus of the Red Sea waters parting three thousand years ago indeed does have a basis in physical laws. A nineteenth-century documented case of the Nile Delta exists where a powerful wind pushed away about five feet of water and exposed dry land. Computer simulations prove that a sixty-three-mile-per-hour wind from the east, lasting thirteen hours, would have pushed back waters six feet deep, creating for at least four hours a dry land passage two miles long and three miles wide.

Science has established the Mt. Sinai that Moses trod was volcanically active. If an acacia bush happened to be above an open fissure, hot gasses would have burst out and the bush catch fire, turning it into charcoal. The flames could continue coming from the charcoal framework of the bush for a couple of hours before the bush would collapse. In fact, acacia bushes are common on Mt. Sinai today and are used by local residents for charcoal.

The story of Noah's flood has its origin in a cataclysmic event shown by science to have been sixty thousand square miles of Old Testament lands that were flooded about 5600 BC. This flooding resulted from sudden melting of polar glaciers, causing an onrush of ocean water into and from the Mediterranean Sea. The water cascaded through Turkey's narrow strait of Bosporus (dry land at the time) to the freshwater Black Sea, transforming it into a vast saltwater sea. As the water level rose by hundreds of feet during a period of not less than three hundred modern days, it triggered mass animal migration across Europe.

At least twenty-five cases of "Lazarus syndrome" have been recorded by medical science since 1983. In 2008, the heart of a West Virginia woman, Velma Thomas, stopped beating, and she was clinically brain dead for seventeen hours. Her son had left the hospital to make funeral arrangements. Doctors were preparing to take her organs for donation when the fifty-nine-year-old awakened.

The base of human lineage is a hominid named Lucy by scientists and established by carbon dating to be 3.2 million modern years old. Homo sapiens (modern humans) are currently known to be 195,000 modern years old.

The book of Genesis reveals that God created the universe in an orderly and systematic manner that it is ever kept under God's sovereign control. Details of how everything was accomplished are not provided, only the revelation that the work was completed in six of seven biblical days. No measurement of a biblical day is given. Science establishes by carbon dating planet earth to be 4.54 billion modern years old. The number 4.54 divided by 7 discloses a biblical day to be 648.57 million modern years.

Since 1799, science has displayed without a shadow of doubt, that there is much more to the Bible than can be learned from its strict literal interpretation. Modern science asks and answers the truly great questions—the fathomless wonderment about God, the universe, and humans—and frees the human mind from the age-old constraint of religious doctrine and canonical instruction.

*****

Inspired prophets who wrote the Bible deliberately used parables, allegory, and hyperbole, not intending them to be taken literally or word for word. Such extreme simplification typically leads to human misinterpretation, misconception, and error with interpretation.

Genesis says, "In the beginning God created the heavens and the earth." The Hebrew phrase for "the heavens and the earth" (*hashamayim we ha'erets*) refers to the universe. This means the whole universe (sun, moon, stars, earth, and other planets) were configured from raw material created "in the beginning before the six biblical days of creation." The Hebrew word for the verb *created* (*asah*) refers to an action completed in the past. Thus, the phrase should be worded "In the beginning, God had created the universe."

New Testament Gospels—Mark, Luke, and John—were written anonymously between AD 66 and AD 95 by highly-educated Greek-speaking Christians, 37 to 66 years after Jesus was crucified. Each was written, based on the oral or word-of-mouth tradition of the time.

Mark, the earliest written Gospel, portrays Jesus as a human who is God's Son. In Luke, Jesus is a divine human whose father is not a mortal but God. To begin with, God is neither male nor female, immortal, creates humans, and created the human Jesus; yet Jesus is called "Son of God" in the New Testament. In the Hebrew Bible, an individual or a group of individuals called by God to do God's will are called "Son of God." Sometimes, the entire nation of Israel is called "Son of God."

The writer of John used Mark or Luke as a source and, in John, Jesus is himself "equal" to God but not "identical" to God. These three Gospels were not written as dispassionate, unbiased, and objective histories for impartial readers. Early Christians portrayed Jesus in increasingly exalted terms as time passed.

No fewer than 450 different versions of the first English language Bible (King James) have been reinterpreted and rewritten since AD 1611. Each version has furthered the exaltation of Jesus.

Jesus (4 BC-AD 29) was a faithful Jew working eighteen years (age twelve to thirty) as a carpenter in Nazareth, an inspired prophet for three years with a message of compassion, love and truth, and crucified at age thirty-three. The best attested deeds of Jesus, his baptism at age thirty by John the Baptist, his selection of twelve disciples, his association with outcasts, sinners, and women, and his itinerate preaching ministry in Galilee, altogether indicate that Jesus was an apocalypticist concerned with bringing his message of the imminent arrival of God to the people of Israel before it was too late.

There are religious doctrines of Christendom rooted in scripture, and doctrines added by false traditions. Catholicism is the most egregious promoter of false traditions and objects of worship that are the epitome of anti-Christendom.

The Christian doctrine of Arius (AD 256–336), a priest in Alexandria, Egypt, held that Jesus was the highest of human beings, denying that Jesus was of the same substance or essence as God. As a defense against "Arianism," the Roman Emperor Constantine the Great in AD 325 called the Council of Nicaea, which was held in today's Iznik, Turkey.

Although Jesus's deification was the work of the earliest founders of Christianity, Jesus's deification was formalized centuries later by the statement of doctrine, Nicene Creed, written and adopted by humans for the Christian faith. The creed introduced the doctrine of Trinity, even though the word *trinity* or the idea of "trinity" is nowhere found in the scriptures.

This false religious doctrine of a triune God is the first instance of ecclesiastical corruption. The notion that Jesus is fully divine and fully human at the same time is adversarial to spirituality and to science.

Fewer than a hundred years later, St. Augustine of Hippo (AD 354–430), a native of Annaha, Algeria, was teaching the doctrine of original sin in Rome, Italy. This false religious doctrine, that human infants are born sinners, is the second instance of ecclesiastical corruption.

These two false religious doctrines representing human corruption have been practiced by Christians for more than sixteen-hundred years. Human error and human corruption can be either old or new. Truth is as old as the universe.

*****

Religion and spirituality are not the same. Religion involves changeable interpretations and beliefs based on an unchangeable Bible with contradicting content. Spirituality is unchangeable and law-based starting with the Ten Commandments, Laws of Nature or Transcendent Truths (mathematics, logic, morality) and Laws of Science or Factual Truths (biogenesis, chemistry, physics, thermodynamics, planetary motion).

*****

For the purpose of clarity, my concept of Trinity is diagramed on the following page.

GOD

JESUS

HOLY GHOST or HOLY SPIRIT

Human	Eternal Being	Soul
----------	omnipotent	---------
----------	omniscient	---------
----------	omnipresent	---------
Inspired prophet	Creator	God's image
----------	immortal	immortal
---------	infinite	infinite
---------	eternal	eternal
matter	not matter	not matter
energy	not energy	not energy
male	not male	not male
---------	not female	not female
changeable	unchangeable	unchangeable
in universe	out of universe	in universe; out of universe
in real time	out of real time	in real time; out of real time
teacher of truth	makes truth possible	truth and conscience

The Christian doctrine of Trinity equates **God, Jesus,** and **Holy Ghost** or **Holy Spirit**. These three entities are clearly discrete and related, but neither equal nor identical.

God may be viewed as the Tree of Life with Jesus the only fruit of the highest limb. The soul would flow like tree-sap through all limbs to all the fruits which are humans. Each fruit would ripen individually—one ripens special (Jesus), some ripen evenly, some ripen unevenly, some over-ripen, some never ripen, some are defective, some fall, some rot.

Jesus from the Historical Perspective

January 18, 2019

The source of information for this writing was the Hebrew Union College Library, Jewish Institute of Religion, Cincinnati, Ohio.

The generalized results of my study presented in this writing were derived using an open mind and nonsubjective, non-biased, or preconceived point of view over a period of ten years. As both a scientist and applied scientist, my mind has been trained to examine objectively all sides of a given topic. Stories contained in the Old Testament have been verified and supported by science; not so regarding Jesus and the New Testament.

My approach in this study of Jesus is from the ***historical***, as opposed to the *religious*, point of view. My primary interest is to examine historical **evidence**. It does not mean that I cannot be a believer in Jesus.

Jesus was first known as an obscure Jewish teacher. Later, Jesus became one of the great moral teachers and doer of great deeds of the ages. What is striking and what is little known by Christians today is that there were lots of men in the ancient world who were believed to be divine.

These men were thought to have been miraculously born, empowered from on high to do miracles, to heal the sick, to cast out demons, to deliver spectacular life-transforming teachings, and who were thought to ascended to heaven at the ends of their lives where they live forever. Jesus, born 4 BC, may be the only miracle-working

"Son of God" that we know about in our world, but He was not at all the only one known and talked about in his world.

The mother of Apollonius of Tyana knew that her son would not be a normal child. He became the famous Greek neo-Pythagorean philosopher of the first century AD. She had an angelic visitor come to her prior to her conception, explaining that the one who would be born of her would be divine. His birth was accompanied by miraculous signs and wonders.

As a young child, Apollonius was religiously mature, beyond what the adult religious leaders that he met could have imagined possible. As an adult, he left home to engage in an itinerant preaching mission in Greece, Turkey, and Syria.

He went from village to town teaching his good news that people did not need to be tied to the material things of this world but should live for what is spiritual. Apollonius gathered a number of disciples around him who became convinced that he was no mere mortal.

He did miracles to confirm them in their faith, healing the sick, casting out demons, and even raising the dead. Apollonius taught that sacrifice of animals and prayer were useless and that the only way to converse with God was through intellect. He raised the ire of many of those in power. They brought him on charges before the Roman authorities. Even after he left this world, his followers continued to believe in him.

Like Jesus, the story of Apollonius's life is in question. Some compare Apollonius to Jesus. Others say he was the inspiration for the story of Jesus. Others still say Apollonius was dropped in favor of Jesus when the Christians decided who to believe was the "Son of God."

Apollonius lived the same time as Jesus, although they never knew each other. Their followers, though, knew each other, and they entered into heated debates concerning who was the superior being. His followers claimed that he was a miracle-working "Son of God," born supernaturally, was supernaturally endowed to do miracles, delivered supernatural teachings, and—at the end of his life—ascended to heaven. Jesus, according to the followers of Apollonius, was a magician and a fraud. Jesus's followers argued just the opposite, Jesus was the miracle-working "Son of God," and Apollonius was a fraud.

The Gospels of the New Testament were not written as dispassionate, unbiased, and objective histories for impartial observers. They were not written by eyewitnesses. As two of the authors admit, they inherited the stories from the oral tradition. These Gospels were written anonymously by highly-educated Greek-speaking Christians, not like the lower-class Aramaic-speaking disciples of Jesus.

Jesus's words and actions were passed on by word of mouth by people who were not eyewitnesses to the events and who had never laid eyes on any of the witnesses. The stories about Jesus were changed to fit the new circumstances in which they were told. The Gospel writers also adapted these stories.

The stories in the Gospels were written not less than twenty-seven to sixty-six years after Jesus was crucified. In oral cultures, the natural assumption is that stories are changed depending on the audience and the situation.

The Gospels were ascribed to two of Jesus's disciples, Mathew and John, and two companions of other apostles, Mark and Luke. Jesus was crucified in AD 29 at age 33. Mark was written AD 66–70, Luke AD 80–85, and John AD 90–95.

The writer of Luke used Mark as one of his sources for writing his account ten years later. The writer of John used Mark or Luke as a source. Mark portrays Jesus as a human who is God's Son. In Luke, Jesus is a divine human, whose father is not a mortal but God Himself. Later, in John, Jesus is Himself "equal" with God, but that is not the same as saying "identical" with God. As time went on, Christians began portraying Jesus in increasingly exalted terms.

In the fourth century AD, Christians made the claim that Jesus was "identical" with God and the Holy Ghost/Spirit, which led to such formulations as the Nicene Creed where Jesus was affirmed as being fully divine and fully human at one and the same time.

In the Hebrew Bible, the "Son of God" is an individual or group of individuals called by God to do God's will who mediate God's will here on Earth. Sometimes, the entire nation of Israel is called the "Son of God."

There are stories in the Gospels that did not happen historically as narrated, but that are meant to convey a Christian truth. The Gospels do not contain historical accounts of actual supernatural events. Instead, they recount some natural histories (historical events that were completely natural) that were misinterpreted or misperceived to be miraculous.

The best example of this is the story of George Washington and the cherry tree. As a young boy, George cuts down a cherry tree. His father asks, "Who cut down my cherry tree?" George Washington replies, "I cannot tell a lie. I did it." We know that this story didn't actually happen historically but conveys an important human attribute especially for children—honesty.

Christians in these early years propagated their religion by one person telling another, or two or three people, stories about Jesus in order to convince them that Jesus was the "Son of God," who died for the sins of the world and was raised from the dead. As these stories were told and retold by word of mouth, year after year, by people who had never seen these things happen or who had never known anybody who did, the stories got changed. Some of the changes would have been accidental for sure.

The New Testament Gospels, as valuable as they may be as religious documents of faith, are problematic as historical sources for the life of Jesus. Clearly, the "Infancy Gospel of Thomas" is based on legend and on pious or not-so-pious Christian imagination.

The Gospels are full of discrepancies on almost every point in their accounts of what happened when Jesus was raised from the dead. These accounts were produced by people who believed that Jesus had been raised, who were retelling stories about that event which had been in circulation for several decades among believers who were using the stories, in numerous instances, in order to get people to believe.

Sometime after Jesus's death, whether three days, three months, or three years, some of his followers began to claim that he had been raised from the dead. That much is certain. That claim has transformed our world.

The best attested deeds of Jesus, his baptism by John the Baptist, his selection of twelve disciples, his associations with outcasts, sinners, and women, and his itinerate preaching ministry in Galilee, altogether indicate that Jesus was an apocalypticist concerned with bringing his message of the imminent arrival of God to the people of Israel before it was too late.

Christianity as a religion began not with Jesus's preaching, not with his death, and not with his resurrection, but with the **belief** in Jesus's resurrection.

Jesus preached about the Son of Man, who was soon to come to Earth in judgment against all those aligned against God, whereas the early Christians preached about Jesus who had died and been raised from the dead.

Timeline

1800 BC. Abraham alive
1400 BC. Moses alive
750 BC. Homer alive
650–500 BC. Prophets of Hebrew Bible alive
587 BC. Babylonian conquest of Jerusalem
510 BC. Beginning of Roman Empire
400 BC. Plato alive
333–323 BC. Conquest of Alexander the Great
300–198 BC. Palestine under Egyptian rule
198–142 BC. Palestine under Syrian rule
145 BC. Daniel (final book of Hebrew Bible)
142–37 BC. Maccabean rule
63 BC. Conquest of Palestine by Romans
44 BC. Assassination of Julius Caesar
40–4 BC. Herod, king of the Jews
27 BC–AD 14. Octavian Cesar Augustus as emperor
4 BC. Jesus's birth
4 BC–AD 39. Herod Antipas, ruler of Galilee

AD 14–37. Emperor Tiberius

AD 18–36. Caiaphas, high priest in Jerusalem

AD 26–36. Pilot as governor of Judea

AD 29. Jesus's death

AD 33. Conversion of Paul

AD 27–100. Josephus (Jewish historian)

AD 41–54. Emperor Claudius

AD 54–68. Emperor Nero

AD 66–70. Gospel of Mark written

AD 66–70. Jewish Revolt and destruction of temple

AD 79–81. Emperor Titus

AD 80–85. Gospel of Luke written

AD 90–95. Gospel of John written

AD 110–130. Gospels of Peter, Thomas, and Infancy Thomas written

Bibliography

Allison, Dale. *Jesus of Nazareth: Millenarian Prophet,* Minneapolis: Fortress, 1998.

Brown, Raymond. *The Birth of the Messiah: A Commentary on the Infancy Narratives of Matthew and Luke,* 2nd ed. Garden City, NY: Doubleday, 1993.

Cartlidge, David R., and David L. Dugan, eds. *Documents for the study of the Gospels,* 2nd ed. Philadelphia: Fortress, 1994.

Ehrman, Bart D. *Jesus: Apocalyptic Prophet of the New Millennium.* New York, Oxford University Press, 1999.

Ehrman, Bart D. *The New Testament and Other Early Christian Writings:* A Reader. New York: Oxford, 1998.

Ehrman, Bart D. *The Historical Jesus:* The Great Courses, Chantilly, Virginia, 2000.

Fuller, Reginald. *Interpreting the Miracles.* London: SCM, 1963.

Furnish, Victor Paul. *Jesus According to Paul.* Cambridge: University Press, 1993.

Green, Joel, et al., *Dictionary of Jesus and the Gospels.* Downers Grove, Illinois: Intervarsity Press, 1994.

IRRECONCILABLE RELIGIOUS DIFFERENCES

April 24, 2017

Human nature hasn't changed in the history of humankind, which dates back thousands of years BC, in Ancient Greece.

Religion is important to humans, and it has always been something we're prone to fight about. Their founding of Judaism, Christianity and Islamism took place during a time span of about 2,500 years. Judaism, a transformational and peaceful religion with voluntary conversion, was founded about 1900 BC; Christianity, a transformational and peaceful religion with voluntary conversion, and moral obligation to proselytize, was founded on Jesus's crucifixion and resurrection in AD 29; Islamism, a forced submission religion with political, legal, social, economic, and military components, was founded in AD 610 by Mohammed.

Islamism is built on world conquest and has attacked Jews and Christians in hundred of battles during the past 1,407 years. The two religions worship the same God. The false religion worships Muhammad. Pagan religions have been, and still are, accepting of other beliefs and gods.

It's entirely possible there'll be another outright religious war against Islam, although the politically correct will have to call it something else. The ongoing invasion of Western European countries by Muslims is one aspect of it, although that's not mainly a religious thing *per se*. Muslims are migrating mainly to escape civil war and for economic reasons.

Europe's already a post-Christian society today. Very few Europeans go to church or take Christianity seriously anymore. It's a rather secular society, one in which the state seems to be their new god. Europeans today may be almost ripe for conversion to Islam. That's a serious problem because Islam is incompatible with, and diametrically opposite to, European civilization.

Islam is a threat to Europe because tens of million of migrants have been, and still are being, invited to come and live at the expense of the current residents. Then the migrants treat them with contempt. Europe is likely to collapse from within, as did Rome. As for the European Union, ten percent of Western Europe is already Muslim. In continental Europe, Albania, Kosovo, and Turkey are already Muslim, as are parts of Bulgaria. Ten percent of Western Europe is already Muslim. In southern Russia, there are roughly twenty millions Muslims.

There are always big problems with running an empire, as the Russians, British, French, and Italians have found. London is turning into Karachi, Paris into Kinshasa, and Rome into Lagos. America is discovering extreme Muslim sympathizers are already within our country. America's culture is gradually being destroyed as progressivism, socialism, cultural Marxism, racial hatred, and gender warfare are eating away the foundations of our country. Our college and university liberal professors and the millennial generation (eighteen- to thirty-seven-year-olds) believe in nothing, except that America's capitalism is evil.

Islam, in itself, isn't a real threat. The Koran, which the highly politically correct Americans love to treat with respect, is nothing more than poorly written medieval science fiction. The Koran is living proof that humans are capable of believing absolutely anything.

Muslims are technologically and economically backward. As long as the center of their lives is the Koran—the incontrovertible word of Allah—they'll remain backward. It's tragic because practically everything good on planet Earth has come from the West—freedom, individualism, capitalism, science, technology, literature, to mention only some.

I suspect that most Muslims in Western civilization will fall away from their primitive beliefs by 2070, possibly before, due mostly to scientific and technological advancements. A lot will happen in the meantime.

Humanism

October 24, 2013

John Dewey is known as the father of progressive education and liberalism. He was professor of philosophy at both the University of Chicago and Columbia University, chief designer of the "Humanist Manifesto," and <u>named</u> <u>honorary</u> <u>president</u> <u>of the</u> <u>National</u> <u>Education</u> <u>Association</u> <u>81</u> <u>years</u> <u>ago</u> (<u>1932</u>).

The religious doctrine of humanism has been promoted heavily in America's public schools, colleges, and universities for eighty years since 1933. It has become one of the dominant belief systems of the "new age." Yet most Americans are completely unaware of the actual tenants of this **religion** as was summarized in the 1933 "Humanist Manifesto." Humanism's voluminous manifesto is an atheistic and socialist belief system.

My point-by-point comments hereinafter question humanism's underlying assumptions that have gone largely unchallenged to date. Its preface states in part:

> Today, man's larger understanding of the universe, his scientific achievements, and deeper appreciation of brotherhood, have created a situation which requires a new statement of the means and purposes of religion. Such a vital, fearless, and frank religion *capable of furnishing adequate social goals and personal satisfactions*...must be shaped for the needs of this age. To establish such a religion is a major necessity of the present...We therefore affirm the following.

I understand that the essential purpose of any religion is not merely to serve mundane "social goals" or "personal satisfaction" but to provide the individual human with a conceptual framework for the perception of reality and his/her place within it. The rest is secondary.

> FIRST: Religious humanists regard the universe as *self-existing and not created.*

A "self-existing" universe is equivalent to a universe that's "self-creating," a non-dualistic view in which the creator and the creation are one. The unstated assumption is that the so-called universe is also infinite in all dimensions and that nothing could possibly exist outside of the space-time continuum. Is the current human perception really that complete? At the moment, this viewpoint can only be accepted as a matter or faith, not reason or science.

> SECOND: Humanism believes that man is a part of nature and that he has emerged as a result of a continuous process.

The perception of "nature" in which humans "are a part of" becomes more refined as time passes. For instance, when Darwin and Huxley were promoting their theory of evolution in the nineteenth century, they knew nothing about the complex internal structure of the cell. Science has since shown that it's quite unlikely life somehow "emerged" as a result of a continuous and random process. Darwin's observation that species can adapt to their environment through selective breeding and inheritance is not sufficient to explain their origins. Where are the intermediate forms? How did they survive and reproduce? If the process is continuous, where are the "proto-humans" today?

> THIRD: Holding an organic view of life, humanists find that the traditional dualism of mind and body must be rejected.

Like the oversimplified Darwinian model of biology, the notion that consciousness is simply an artifact of biological processes is increasingly outdated. Given the current knowledge of quantum physics, the view that only the soul/spirit transcends the "mind and body" is not a concept that can simply be "rejected." Is the brain itself the generator of soul/spirit, or is it an electrochemical instrument that receives the subtle impressions of consciousness?

> FOURTH: Humanism recognizes that man's religious culture and civilization, as clearly depicted by anthropology and history, are the products of a gradual development due to his interaction with his natural environment and with his social heritage. The individual born into a culture is largely molded by that culture.

All the symbolic constructs of a culture (language, art, science, technology, religion) certainly develop over time and as human knowledge and communication improve the rate of change accelerates. However, just because cultures and their belief systems are limited in scope doesn't mean that they're incapable of realizing transcendent truths such as the laws of mathematics, laws of logic, and laws of morality. It's rather arrogant for modern humans to assume otherwise.

> FIFTH: Humanism asserts that the nature of the universe depicted by modern science makes unacceptable any supernatural or cosmic guarantees of human values. Obviously, humanism does not deny the possibilities of realities as yet undiscovered, but it does insist that the way to determine the existence and value of any and all realities is by means of intelligent inquiry and by the assessment of their relations to human needs. Religion must formulate its hopes and plans in the light of the scientific spirit and method.

Humanism has *already* denied herein above the "possibility of realities as yet undiscovered." It also has accepted, without proof, the concept of a "self-existing universe" and the origin theory of "random" evolution. It has rejected, without review, the truths embodied in other belief systems and declared them obsolete. Why should the objective process of philosophical and scientific inquiry be constrained by subjective "human needs," whatever they might be?

> SIXTH: We are convinced that the time has passed for theism, design, modernism, and the several varieties of "new thought."

Either a concept is true or it's not regardless of the passage of time. If it's possible that one's perception of the "universe" is finite, it's also possible that there are transcendental aspects of reality, including some of the concepts expressed, however poorly, by past theists and deists. On what basis, other than faith, are humanists "convinced" that these concepts are completely without merit?

> SEVENTH: Religion consists of those actions, purposes, and experiences which are humanly significant. Nothing human is alien to the religious. It includes labor, art, science, philosophy, love, friendship, recreation—all that is in its degree expressive of intelligently satisfying human living. The distinction between the sacred and the secular can no longer be maintained.

As I stated herein previously, the real purpose of religion is not to serve social functions but to provide a conceptual framework for the perception of reality. One could argue that the degree to which a secular religion is centered on mundane social activity is a measure of how conceptually weak it has become.

> EIGHTH: Religious humanism considers the complete realization of human personality to be

the end, *i.e.*, purpose, of man's life and seeks its development and *fulfillment in the here and now*. This is the explanation of the humanist's social passion.

This notion that the "here and now" is all that matters provides license to those whose idea of "complete fulfillment" is to exploit everyone and everything to maximize their own personal pleasure. Why not abandon the laws of morality? Do unto others before they do unto you; he who dies with the most toys wins.

NINTH: In the place of the old attitudes involved in worship and prayer, the humanist finds his religious emotions expressed in a heightened sense of personal life and in a cooperative effort to promote social well-being.

History shows that most people prefer unrestrained self-gratification regardless of "social well-being," whatever that might be. The most voracious and ruthless of these individuals inevitably rise to the top of the societal power structure.

TENTH: It follows that there will be no uniquely religious emotions and attitudes of the kind hitherto associated with belief in the supernatural.

It follows that moral self-restraint will be thrown out the window and that "do as thou wilt" will become the guiding principle!

ELEVENTH: Man will come to face the crises in life in terms of his knowledge of their naturalness and probability. Reasonable and manly attitudes will be fostered by education and supported by custom. We assume that humanism will take the path of social and mental hygiene and discourage sentimental and unreal hopes and wishful thinking.

Speaking of "wishful thinking," in the decades since this manifesto was written, "social and mental hygiene" have drastically declined while "sentimental and unreal hopes" in collectivist programs and self-destructive lifestyles have increased. "Reasonable and manly attitudes" have been suppressed to the point where it's now considered a thought crime to even mention the concept.

> TWELFTH: Believing that religion must work increasingly for joy in living, religious humanists aim to foster the creative in man and to encourage achievements that add to the satisfactions of life.

Self-gratification has proven to be a poor substitute for the self-discipline required to actually achieve the "satisfactions of life."

> THIRTEENTH: Religious humanism maintains that all associations and institutions exist for the fulfillment of human life. The intelligent *evaluation, transformation, control, and direction* of such associations and institutions with the view to the enhancement of human life is the purpose and program of humanism. Certainly, religious institutions, their ritualistic forms, ecclesiastical methods, and communal activities *must be reconstituted* as rapidly as experience allows in order to function effectively in the modern world.

Note that humanists intend to "transform, control, and direct" ALL institutions within the society. Stripping the religious institutions of anything other than superficial social functions has stunted the development of both the individual and the society. When man thinks of himself as nothing more than an animal, he behaves as nothing more than an animal. Some will choose to be sheep; others will be wolves.

> FOURTEENTH: The humanists are firmly convinced that existing acquisitive and profit-motivated society has shown itself to be inadequate and that a radical change in methods, controls, and motives must be instituted. A *socialized and cooperative economic order must be established* to the end that the equitable distribution of the means of life be possible. The goal of humanism is a free and universal society in which people voluntarily and intelligently cooperate for the common good. *Humanists demand a shared life in a shared world.*

Humanists and other collectivists can demand a socialist utopia, but that can't make it happen. Who gets to define the "common good?" How will they force everyone to "voluntarily cooperate?" How is this compatible with a "free society?"

> FIFTEENTH: We assert that humanism will: (a) affirm life rather than deny it; (b) seek to elicit the possibilities of life, not flee from them; and (c) endeavor to establish the conditions of satisfactory life for all, not merely for the few. By this positive moral and intention, humanism will be guided, and from this perspective and alignment, the techniques and efforts will flow.

On the contrary, humanism has allowed the powerful few to exploit the many even more thoroughly than before and to justify their amoral actions at the same time. The road to hell on planet Earth is paved with "positive intentions."

The foregoing precepts began persistently and methodically working their way into America's public schools until finally the hierarchy—textbook writers, editors, printers, publishers, teachers, and buyers—were substantially indoctrinated. American history, civics, values, and such subjects are being deconstructed and rewritten. America's heritage is being systematically censored out of existence in modern public school texts.

Charles Francis Potter (1885–1962), Unitarian minister and theologian, leader and founder of the First Humanist Society of New York, Inc., and another honorary president of the National Education Association, wrote:

> Education is thus a most powerful ally of humanism, and every American public school is a school of humanism. What can the theistic Sunday schools, meeting for an hour once a week, and teaching only a fraction of the children, do to stem the tide of a five-day program of humanistic teaching?

The idea that America's public schools may not promote a religion is yet another myth. Secular humanism, atheism, and now to some extent "new age" are the **religions** taught in America's public (now government) schools. Why aren't the same First Amendment rights and limitations equally applicable to humanism as it is to all religions?

A second Humanist Manifesto was published in 1973. Its Preface reads in part,

> As in 1933, humanists still believe that traditional theism…is an unproved and outmoded faith.

This new Manifesto was divided into subjects on religion, ethics, the individual, democratic society, world community, and humanity as a whole. As to religion, nothing much was changed. As to the subject of ethics,

> We affirm that moral values derive their source from human experience. Ethics are autonomous

and situational, needing no theological or ideological sanction.

Situation ethics now is certainly the basis for the value system taught in America's public (**federal government**) schools.

In the category of democratic society, they added a new item that reads in part,

> It also includes a recognition of an individual's right to die with dignity, euthanasia, and the right to suicide.

The second Manifesto also added the following tenet,

> The separation of church and state and the sepa-ration of ideology and state are imperatives.

Thusly, the ultimate goal of the humanist **religion** is to make the Christian mantra a matter of "political science."

Although the words "separation, church, state" are not to be found in the First Amendment to the Constitution, it is known that Thomas Jefferson used those words to assure the Danbury Baptists that the state would not establish a religion. In those words, he announced that there was a "wall of separation." It's rather clear that the wall was one-way, as opposed to two-way. There was never any intention to say that morality should not be a part of government or of those who govern.

The following article appeared in a 1983 issue of *The Humanist*. Its title is "A Religion for a New Age" by John J Dunphy.

> I am convinced that the battle for humankind's future must be waged and won in the pub-lic school classroom by teachers who correctly perceive their role as the proselytizers of a new faith: a religion of humanity that recognizes and respects the spark of what theologians call divin-

ity in every human being. These teachers must embody the same selfless dedication as the most rabid fundamentalist preachers, for they will be ministers of another sort, utilizing a classroom instead of a pulpit to convey humanist values in whatever subject they teach, regardless of the educational level—preschool day care or large state university. The classroom must and will become an arena of conflict between the old and the new—the rotting corpse of Christianity, together with all its adjacent evils and misery, and the new faith of humanism, resplendent in its promise of a world in which the never-realized Christian ideal of "love thy neighbor" will finally be achieved.

Humanism is a **religion** that rejects the Bible, any supernatural God, and biblical morality. In other tenets, the Manifesto makes an open attack on Christianity, it opposes the free enterprise system, and it advocates socialism.

In *George Washington's Farewell Address*, he said, "And let us with caution indulge the supposition that morality can be maintained without religion."

Thomas Jefferson is frequently presented as a deist or secularist. However, Jefferson said, "My views are very different from that anti-Christian system imputed to me by those who know nothing of my opinions. To the *Corruptions of Christianity*, I am indeed opposed but not to the genuine precepts of Jesus Himself. I am a Christian." He further stated, "The Christian religion is a religion of all the others most friendly to liberty, science, and the freest expressions of the human mind."

Jefferson also is known to have cut all the sayings of Jesus from the Gospels at least four times. They were removed from translations in Greek, Latin, French, and English. He pasted them in a book with his own writings, intending them to be used to explain the teachings to Native Americans. In 1904, the 57th Congress ordered 9,000 copies published, 6,000 for the House of Representatives and 3,000 for the Senate. The title was *The Life and Morals of Jesus Christ of Nazareth* by Thomas Jefferson. The document was accompanied by an introduction written by the librarian of Congress.

In 1947, Supreme Court Justice Black wrote that "The First Amendment requires the state to be a **neutral** in its relations with groups of religious believers and non-believers; it does not require the state to be their adversary. State power is no more to be used so as to handicap religions, than it is to favor them."

In 1962, a pragmatic Kansas Court struck down state-sponsored prayer in a public school, cited no precedent, and stated that exposure of an atheist to other children reciting a prayer could psychologically damage that atheist.

According to J. William Howerton, retired chief judge, Court of Appeals of Kentucky, "Case law and America's Constitution prohibit any governmental activity that sponsors or promotes a particular religion—Christianity, Judaism, Humanism, Atheism, New Ageism—and that there is no basis in law for government to be hostile to a religion."

Humanism, by its own definition and claim, indeed is a **religion**, and it should not be taught in America's public schools any more than is Christianity.

Judge Howerton also says, "One would be hard put to find any of the foregoing historic quotes or similar quotes, from such founders as Adams, Madison, or Mason, in public school textbooks. I'm not aware of any court decision that has directed the removal or censorship of such information from American school children, but the removal has been the desire of some who have worked their way into leadership and can effectively control what books are published and purchased for use in public schools."

Today, it's difficult to find a daily newspaper or news broadcast that doesn't contain some horror story about our society or about the many problems in and with America's schools. In its classrooms, America has gone in a short time from a public school system to a **government** school system, from problems with talking and chewing gum in the classroom to vandalism, beatings, shootings, and killings. We've gone from a daily Bible reading, pledge of allegiance to the

American flag, and prayer to the distribution of condoms, and you name it.

America has been thrust into world leadership, and its ability to fill that role will depend upon the education of its leaders. If American society is confused and out of control and if we don't understand what we are or what we should be, how can we possibly project a desirable image to the rest of the world? How can we project or defend our traditions and beliefs that made America great if we now abandon them and fail to educate our children regarding the foundations of our traditions? We are losing our source of strength.

Americans must reestablish a learning environment with solid values, discipline, and good character traits to succeed in life. Better education and a solid value system will combat crime and cut our social costs due to immorality. Parents again must accept their responsibilities, and educators must again be given more latitude in controlling and disciplining young people at school and in the classroom. Judge Howerton says, "It may well be that some revisions in the Juvenile Code will be required to accomplish any of this."

The greatest cause of concern for a large number of parents is that public school teaching often contradicts, by means of indoctrination, what parents wish to teach their children. Some serious examination must occur in text material, value lessons, teacher education, desired outcome-based objectives, methods of discipline, incentives for learning, and teaching students to think with less indoctrination, to mention a few.

Tough teachers get results. The latest research shows the wisdom of old-fashioned school teaching methods: rote learning, plenty of failure, and stingy praise encourage students to work harder and achieve more. Teachers should give constructive, even painful, feedback. Drill, practice, drill, and memorize. Students who understand that failure is a necessary aspect of learning actually perform better. Strict teachers are better than nice teachers. Creativity can be learned. Grit (passion and perseverance), not talent, is the best predictor of success. Praise makes the student weak, while stress makes the student strong.

Time is of the essence. It's like planting a tree that takes one hundred years to mature. We've no time to waste!

EVOLUTION OF THE CHRISTIAN RELIGION'S CONCEPT OF GOD

December 22, 2009

The third-century BC *Septuagint* is the ancient Greek version of the Hebrew scriptures and regarded as the standard form of the Old Testament in the early Christian Church and still canonical in the Eastern Orthodox Church. The English version of the Bible began with manuscripts written in Old Hebrew, Greek, and—in some cases—Aramaic.

These manuscripts were all copies as none of the original manuscripts, written by the authors themselves, are known to exist. The Dead Sea Scrolls (discovered between 1947 and 1960) date from the last two centuries BC, survive as the earliest substantial Old Hebrew text of the Old Testament.

Darwin has done the Christian religion a favor by making known a significant defect in modern Christian theology. Mankind's scientific and technological brilliance notwithstanding, human understanding of an eternal being today is markedly undeveloped. The constant extinction and appearance of new species unveiled by Darwin is not unlike 2,535-year-old Buddhist meditations on the first noble truth—"existence is suffering"—the prerequisite for transcendent enlightenment called Nirvana and which other religions call God.

Most influential earlier thinkers—Islam's philosopher and scientist, Avicenna (981–1037), Jewish philosopher, Maimonides (1135–1204), Roman Catholic theologian, Aquinas (1225–1274), and German theologian and philosopher, Eckhart (1260–1328)—all understood God as nothing more than a symbolic word that points beyond itself to an indescribable Supreme Being, above and independent of the material universe, whose existence can't be proved except by spiritual intuition and a lifestyle of compassion that enables the cultivation of new capacities of mind and heart. Darwinian evolution supports the early understanding, making it not possible to regard God as simply a divine personality who single-handedly created earth and the universe.

English mathematician and scientist, Sir Isaac Newton (1642–1727), claimed that his cosmic system proved beyond doubt the existence of an intelligent creator with total knowledge and unlimited power. By the end of the 1700s, on the basis of Newton's claim, instead of recognizing the transparency of the symbolic word—*God*—and looking beyond to a Supreme Being, Christians were transforming God into hardened fact. Captivated by such ironclad certainty and reinforced by the "intelligent designer" idea of England's later philosopher and utilitarian William Paley (1743–1805), the clergy started developing a theology that made both Newton's claim and Paley's idea essential to the Christian religion.

This effort to emulate the exacting character of the scientific method has enabled fundamentalist Christians to read scripture with a false literalness that is without parallel in religious history.

The work of Albert Einstein (1874–1955) overthrows Newtonian dogma in the sense that space and time are absolute and fixed entities, proven facts that render Christian fundamentalism irrelevant. Christian fundamentalism, a "born again" form of evangelism, claims infallibility of the Bible and asserts it to be the work of God.

Most members are both socially and politically conservative, living by a strict personal moral code. The theory of evolution indeed has shaken to the core the faith of fundamentalist Christians. Nothing today reflects the validity of this fact better than the Creation Museum, located in Boone County, Kentucky, near Big Bone State Park, where biblical stories are shamelessly dressed-up to look like science. Creationism is a pathetically impoverished concept of trying to explain the infinite immensity of the universe.

To believe that a Supreme Being created the universe for the sole use, benefit, and enjoyment of humans on earth is supremely arrogant and egocentric. Planet Earth is just one of the 766 planets currently known to exist in the universe.

Most modern thinkers believe that the role of religion is to help humans live creatively with realities for which there are no easy solutions and to find an interior haven of peace, not to provide explanations that are wholly within the competence of human reason. Today, however, Christian fundamentalists have opted for unsustainable certainty instead.

Once again, as Avicenna, Maimonides, Aquinas, and Eckhart, Darwin made it not possible to regard God simply as a divine personality who single-handedly created earth and the universe. This concept directs our attention away from "idols of certainty" to a Supreme Being beyond the symbolic word—*God*. Spirituality is not an exact science but a kind of art form that, like classical music, imparts a mode of knowledge that is different from the purely rational and which can't be easily put into words.

Reform Judaism

June 25, 2014

Judaism itself is a law-based religion starting with the Ten Commandments. (Some say that explains why there are so many Jewish lawyers.)

Reform Judaism refers to various beliefs, practices, and organizations associated with the Reform Jewish movement in North America, the United Kingdom, and elsewhere. In general, Reform Judaism maintains that Judaism and Jewish traditions should be modernized and compatible with participation in the surrounding culture. This means that many branches of Reform Judaism hold that Jewish law should undergo a periodic process of critical evaluation and renewal to ensure its ongoing adaptation to a changing world. Consequently, traditional Jewish law is often interpreted as a set of general guidelines rather than as a list of restrictions whose literal observance is required of all Jews.

Reform Judaism arose in Germany in the early 1800s both as a reaction against the perceived rigidity of Orthodox Judaism and as a response to Germany's increasingly liberal political climate. Among the changes made in the 19th Century Reform congregations were a de-emphasis on Jews as a united people, discontinuation of prayers for a return to Palestine, prayers and sermons recited in German instead of Hebrew, the addition of organ music to the synagogue service, and a lack of observance of the dietary laws. Some Reform rabbis advocated abolition of circumcision and the Reform congregation of Berlin shifted the Sabbath to Sundays to be more like their Christian neighbors. Early Reform Judaism retained traditional Jewish monotheism but emphasized ethical behavior almost to the exclusion of ritual. The Talmud (the basis of religious authority in Orthodox Judaism) was mostly rejected, with Reform rabbis preferring the ethical teachings of the prophets (Joshua, Judges, I Samuel, II Samuel, I Kings, II Kings, Isaiah, Jeremiah, Ezekiel, Hosea, Joel, Amos, Obadiah, Jonah, Micah, Nahum, Habakkuk, Zephaniah, Haggai, Zechariah, Malachi).

Modern Reform Judaism, however, has restored some of the aspects of Judaism that their 19th century predecessors abandoned, including the sense of Jewish peoplehood and the practice of religious rituals. Today, Reform Jews affirm the central tenets of Judaism—God, Torah (Genesis, Exodus, Leviticus, Numbers, Deuteronomy), and Israel—while acknowledging a great diversity in Reform Jewish beliefs and practices. Reform Jews are more inclusive than other Jewish movements: women may be rabbis, cantors, and synagogue presidents; interfaith families are accepted; and Reform Jews are "committed to the full participation of gays and lesbians in synagogue life as well as society at large." Reform Judaism is the most liberal expression of modern Judaism. In America, Reform Judaism is organized under the Union for Reformed Judaism (formerly the Union of American Hebrew Congregations) whose mission is "to create and sustain vibrant Jewish congregations wherever Reform Jews live." Approximately 1.5 million Jews in 900 synagogues are members of the Union for Reform Judaism. In 1990, forty-two percent of American Jews regarded themselves as Reform.

Timeline in America

1875. Reform Judaism's Hebrew Union College, in Cincinnati, was founded by Rabbi Isaac Mayer Wise, the architect of American Reform Judaism.

1885. A group of Reform Rabbis adopted the Pittsburgh Platform.

1922. Reform Rabbi Stephen S. Wise established the Jewish Institute of Religion in New York. (It merged with Hebrew Union College in 1950. A third center was opened in Los Angeles in 1954, and a fourth branch was established in Jerusalem in 1963.)

1937. The Central Conference of American Rabbis adopted "The Guiding Principles of Reform Judaism," aka the Columbus Platform.

1976. On the occasion of the centennials of the Union of the American Hebrew Congregations and the Hebrew Union College-Jewish Institute of Religion, the Central Conference of American Rabbis adopted "Reform Judaism Centenary Perspective."

1987. On the occasion of the centenary of the first World Zionist Congress, the Central Conference of American Rabbis adopted the Miami Platform, dedicated to the relationship between Reform Judaism and Zionism.

1993. The Central Conference of American Rabbis formerly stated that a Jewish identity can be passed down through either the mother or the father, thereby making official what had been the state of affairs in many Reform communities since the early twentieth century. Despite its rejection by Conservative Judaism and Orthodox Judaism descent through the mother or the father became the standard for North American Reform and unaffiliated. This led to the disintegration of the interdenominational Synagogue Council of America.

1999. The Central Conference of American Rabbis adopted "A Statement of Principles for Reform Judaism," in Pittsburgh.

Most Reform Jews believe that Jesus was a teacher and activist with a very strong following, preaching for social reform at a time when much political unrest and social upheaval due to the Romans encroaching on their land. Jesus's message of compassion and love fits with the tenets of Judaism in those days and also today. As for Reform Judaism, as it is with any other tenet of Judaism, some believe it, but most don't. Some Jews in first century Roman times, as now, contend that Jesus was a dangerous rabble-rouser; some consider Jesus a faithful Jew whose subsequent deification was the work of the founders of Christianity and, as such, is idolatry. Judaism does not believe in the deification of a human. Orthodox Jews believe in the coming of the Messiah but don't believe that Jesus was the Messiah.

One very important tenet in Reform Judaism is that every religion should be respected. Reform Judaism does not proselytize (try to persuade someone to give up their religious beliefs). If someone chooses to convert to Judaism, that person is welcomed with open arms, as reflected in the book of Ruth.

The concept of land ownership now in Israel is similar to that held by Native Americans. The vast majority, roughly ninety-three percent, of the total land area (excluding occupied areas of the West Bank) are owned by state or quasi-state agencies. Native Americans also held the land in common (more or less tribal)—the land and its wildlife fed, clothed, and sheltered them, and they belonged to the land.

Although there's a total of twenty-five Jewish holidays, only four are defined herein as follows, together with a short glossary of some generally familiar Hebrew words:

Passover. three consecutive days in April commemorating the Exodus from Egypt.

Rosh Hashanah. two consecutive days in September commemorating the Jewish New Year.

Yom Kippur. the day of Atonement.

Hanukkah. eight consecutive days in November or December commemorating the victory of Maccabees over the armies of Syria in 165 BC and subsequent liberation of the Temple in Jerusalem.

Bar/Bat Mitzvah. ceremony celebrating a boy and a girl, at age thirteen, when they become religiously responsible for their acts.

Kibbutz. a collective farm in Israel governed under principles that combine Israeli nationalism with socialism.

Seder. the evening meal and ritual with which Passover begins.

Shalom. peace.

Shofar. the ram's horn sounded during worship on the New Year.

Yiddish. the folk language of Ashkenazic Jews, a mixture mainly of Hebrew and German.

Zohar. a lengthy set of medieval mystical writings.

FAITH AND CONSCIENCE ARE DISAPPEARING IN AMERICA

June 23, 2017

Do leftists have any room left for Christians, Jews, or other believers? This question has been posed countless times, and each time, leftists answer more decisively than before: no. Leftists have triumphed over faith. Now they're targeting our conscience—morals and ethics.

It isn't enough to emancipate transgender people. We must adhere to strict pronoun guidelines and feel in our souls that Chelsea Manning was always a "she." It isn't enough to legalize abortion; we have to like it.

Leftists welcome believers insofar as religion can be used in service of leftist causes. But any expression of theological or moral judgment is met with hostility.

Take for example Vermont Socialist Senator Bernie Sanders' recent tirade against the devout Christian Russell Vought, President Trump's nominee for the Office of Management and Budget. During the confirmation hearing, Sanders grilled Mr. Vought about his belief that Muslims "do not know God because they have rejected Jesus Christ His Son and they stand condemned."

Mr. Vought's statement was a particularly blunt summary of the basic Christian teaching that faith in Jesus Christ is essential to salvation. Plenty of Americans might disagree with the substance, phrasing or both. But Sanders argued that Vought's views were "Islamophobic" and "hateful" and therefore disqualifying.

In spite of that, the leftist senator rode roughshod over the U.S. Constitution, which prohibits religious test for office. What was most depressing about Socialist Sanders' outburst was his gloomy vision of civic life behind it.

Leftist Sanders implied that a devout Christian cannot hold fast to his faith's demanding claim and, at the same time, exercise public authority with decency and honor. In other words, if you disagree with a person's theology, it must mean you hate that person.

America's Republic has stood on the opposite principle: that people can build and share a public square across and even through such differences. That principle is now decaying across much of America, and authoritarian adversaries like Vladimir Putin are no doubt pleased to see our demise accelerate.

But it wasn't Putin who made American politics so inhospitable to the conscience of a large segment of our society.

Religion and America's Young Adults

November 18, 2019

The fastest-growing population on the American religious landscape is people who don't identify with any religion—"**Non-Affiliates**." Recent data from the American Family Survey indicates that their numbers increased from 16 percent in 2007 to 35 percent in 2018. Obama was president eight of those eleven years.

According to the Pew Research Center, during that same period of years, the share of the population who identify as Christians declined from 78 percent of Americans in 2007 to 65 percent in 2018. The rise of non-affiliates is most dramatic among younger people; 44 percent of Americans age 18 to 29 are non-affiliates.

There's no simple answer why this is happening. One part of the answer is the rise of families in which the parents identify with different religions. Children in such families are often raised with exposure to both identities and left to decide themselves which to adopt. In many cases, they eventually chose neither.

Looking at reasons that non-affiliates themselves give for not identifying with any religion, it's clear that they're driven by other forces. Some things about religion, as they perceive it, are actively driving them away. The two most significant reasons they give, according to 2018 Pew Poll, are: 60 percent "question a lot of religious teachings," and 49 percent "don't like the positions churches take on political or social issues."

The specific "religious teachings" and related "positions" they object to most often concern sexuality and science. Many of them question what they perceive as religion's negative views about women's reproductive rights and non-heteronormative activity (same-sex marriage and transgender rights).

However, the non-affiliates aren't simply liberal young adults who are leaving more conservative religions. They're becoming more common across the political spectrum, although more rapidly on the left. Mainline Protestant denominations that tend toward more liberal views of science and sexuality are declining faster than evangelical churches that tend to be more conservative.

What non-affiliates have in common is a tragically narrow understanding of religion as a fixed set of teachings and positions, and that must be submitted to without question. It's presumed that religion is authoritative, univocal, and changeless, and that religious identity is essentially a matter of passive adherence.

Questioning religious teachings and sharing positions has always been an essential part of religion. Reinterpreting inherited scriptures and traditions in light of new meaning is critical to the life of any religion.

Religion's ongoing vitality depends on those who question and challenge inherited teachings and positions. Without such engagement, any religious tradition will die from inside long before it begins to lose adherents.

No doubt, the polls cited above will continue to show a decline in religious affiliation, especially Christian affiliation. But such statistics never tell the whole story, and in this case, the survey questions may be predetermining the results.

What religion needs is sustained conversation in a context that allows and even welcomes different experiences and points of view. Questions such as follow need to be answered. What do you mean when you self-define as religiously non-affiliate? What are the teachings and positions that you question? Did you always question them, or did something in your life lead you to think differently? Were you taught virtue (moral excellence and righteousness) at home by your parents? Concerning religion, non-affiliates are not unimportant.

RELATIVISM AND TRUTH

October 2, 2018

A relativistic culture in which conceptions of truth and moral values are not absolute but are relative to the persons or groups holding them, has taken root in our public education system. Relativism means that our morals have evolved, that they have changed over time, and that they are not absolute.

The culture of relativism believes right and wrong are not absolute and must be determined in society by a combination of factors: observation, social preferences and patterns, experience, emotions, and "rules" that seem to bring the most benefit (including U.S. Supreme Court decisions).

It goes without saying that a society involved in constant moral conflict will not be able to survive for very long. Morality is the glue that holds a society together, and relativism destroys that glue. There must be a consensus of right and wrong for a society to function well.

Universal truths are either <u>transcendent</u> (beyond the ordinary range of perception) or <u>factual</u> (real occurrences known to exist or demonstrated to exist). Transcendent truths are natural laws—mathematics, logic, and morality. Factual truths are laws of science—planetary motion, biogenesis, chemistry, physics, and thermodynamics.

Morality is corroborated through rational thinking and the Ten Commandments—moral absolutes that have yet to be improved upon in many more than two thousand years. Although liars and cheaters may acquire prestige in society, their eventual downfall is assured.

Transcendent truths make rightness mighty, and rightness will eventually prevail as the eternal basis of might.

I'm reminded of today's teachers and professors who show a lack of due concern by wearing a shirt that reads: "Find your truth." This is poor advice that's plastered on the walls of the classroom for the unsuspecting students to absorb.

That belief or opinion pervades our relativistic society. We've all heard something that goes like this: "You have your truth. I have mine." People who embrace this notion insulate themselves from other people, other experiences, and other ideas. Serious conversation is over.

The destructive philosophy of relativism teaches that there is no just and impartial truth. Nothing is objectively good or objectively evil. "Truth" is only personal point of view, fleeting circumstance, and one's own desires. And those views, those experiences, those desires can be understood only by those who live them. Nothing else and no one else matters.

That is the threat that America's campuses face today. Our self-centered culture denies truth because acknowledging it would mean certain feelings or certain ideas could be wrong. But no one wants to be wrong. It's much easier to feel comfortable in saying there is no truth. Nothing can challenge what we want to believe.

I'm also reminded of the first grader who believes 2 + 2 = 22. His teacher said, "You are wrong Sammy, 2 + 2 = 4." Sammy is upset, leaves the room, and goes home. The parents return to the school extremely angry because the teacher had told their son he was wrong. The teacher appears before the school board and is fired.

Abandoning truth creates confusion. Confusion leads to censorship. And censorship inevitably invites chaos on campuses and elsewhere. This isn't simply a matter for academic debate. Parents are watching how educational institutions are resolving these controversies, and most don't like what they see.

The American People's Greatest Inheritance

July 10, 2018

There are two different unchanging universal truths: transcendent (beyond the ordinary range of perception or above and independent of the material universe), and factual (real occurrences known to exist or demonstrated to exist).

We live at a time when many Americans think that (transcendent) **truth** and moral values are not absolute—that moral values and truth are related to the persons or groups holding them. Such thinking contrasts with the vital importance of individual character that is essential to self-government and that right conduct is its own reward. The power of unchanging (transcendent) **truth** can do far more than change lives.

It also seems that we live at a time when too many Americans disregard the wisdom of the past. America is grounded in the teachings and traditions that are inherited by Americans; the same teachings and traditions that are the surest foundation of our boundless future. The United States Constitution is minted in independence and tempered with (transcendent) **truth**.

Human error can be either old or new. **Truth** is as old as the universe.

*****

Today, we indeed live in a growing American economy that is restoring American stature at home and abroad. Businesses large and small, both domestic and foreign, are growing again. Millions of new jobs have been created, unemployment is very low, and there are more job openings in America than ever before in our history.

This is no accident. Under new leadership, America is returning to the principles that have always been the source of our national greatness and strength. Freedom is expanding, taxes are cut, the regulatory state is rolled-back, and authority is returning to the people and to the individual states.

Our Constitution is again being upheld with the God-given liberties enshrined in our Declaration of Independence, including the unalienable right to life. America is again filled with promise, being built anew on a foundation of personal responsibility and individual freedom.

Despite the fact that we live in a time when traditional values and religious convictions are increasingly marginalized by a secular popular culture—a time when it has become acceptable, even fashionable, to malign religious belief—America's faith in religion is growing. Even as some people continue to forecast the decline of religion in American life, the transcendent **truth** is, as our president recently said, "*This is a nation of faith; and faith continues to exert an extraordinary hold on the hearts and minds of our people.*"

Our heritage, as laid out in our Declaration of Independence and our Constitution (both coupled with transcendent **truth**) is the greatest inheritance of the American people. This is because the founders recognized that religious faith is essential to maintaining our republic.

In the words of the nation's first vice president, John Adams: "*Our Constitution was made only for a moral and religious people. It is wholly inadequate to the government of any other.*"

Customs, Traditions, Moral Values

December 18, 2017

My eight-year-old grandson recently asked me if I ever had a girl-friend when I was a teenager. Surprised by his question, I reminded him that it would be five years before he will be a teenager. My response was positive, explaining that, like him, I lived in a rural area more than five miles from school and that my first date was at age sixteen after I had earned my driver's license.

This experience reminded me that an unavoidable problem of youth is the temptation to think that today's behavioral standards are the same as they've always been. Let's take a look at some of the differences between yesteryear and today.

One of those differences is the treatment of girls and women. Generally speaking, there are awesome physical strength differences between males and females. To create and maintain civil relationships between the sexes is to make known to boys, by constant repetition starting at very young ages, that they are not to use violence against a girl or woman for any reason. Special respect is given to girls and women.

Yesteryear, even the lowest of lowdown boy or man would not curse or use foul language to or in the presence of women. To see a boy or man sitting in a crowded bus or streetcar while a woman is standing was unthinkable. It was common decency for a boy or man to give up his seat for a woman or an elderly person.

A boy's use of foul language to a parent, teacher, or other adult would have meant a smack across the face. In the case of the teacher, the boy would also be sent to the principal's office for disciplinary action.

*****

Today, a parent, teacher, or other adult taking corrective action such as described above risks being reported to a local child protective service and even being arrested. Young people today use foul language in front of (and often to) parents, teachers, and other adults, and it's not just foul language.

The modern parental or teacher response to misbehavior is to call for "time-out," which is an open invitation to bad behavior. In other words, miscreants of all ages have been taught that they can impose physical pain on others and not suffer physical pain themselves. Many students today believe it's acceptable to assault teachers. Earlier this year, forty-five public school teachers in Pennsylvania resigned because of student violence.

*****

It has always been considered proper to refrain from sexual intercourse until marriage or at least adulthood. During the 1960s sexual revolution, lessons of abstinence were ridiculed, considered passé, and replaced with school lessons about condoms, birth control pills, and abortion. Out-of-wedlock childbirths are no longer seen as shameful and a disgrace. As a result, the rate of illegitimate births among blacks is over seventy percent, and among whites is over thirty percent.

For more than fifty years, our nation's liberals, the education establishment, pseudo-intellectuals, and the courts have waged war on customs, traditions, and moral values. Many in today's generation have been lead to believe there are no moral absolutes. Instead, what's moral or immoral, right or wrong, is a matter of convenience, personal opinion, or what is or is not criminal.

*****

The first line of defense for America's society is not the law but customs, traditions, and moral values, which are those four important thou-shall-nots: thou shall not murder, thou shall steal, thou shall not lie, and thou shall not cheat. They also include respect for parents, teachers, and others in authority, plus those courtesies contained in Emily Post's book on the rules of etiquette.

These behavior norms are mostly transmitted by example, word of mouth, and religious teachings. They represent a body of wisdom distilled over the ages through experience, trial and error, and looking at what works and what doesn't.

The importance of customs, traditions, and moral values as a means of regulating behavior is that people behave themselves even if nobody's watching. Laws can never replace these restraints on personal conduct in producing a civilized society. There are not enough policemen.

At best, the police and the criminal justice system are the last desperate lines of defense for civilized society. Unfortunately, customs, traditions, and moral values have been discarded without an appreciation for the role they played in creating a civilized society. Today, we're paying the price; that includes the recent revelations regarding the treatment of each other, both women and men.

SAME-SEX MARRIAGE
OR RELATIONSHIPS

March 5, 2019

The Supreme Court of United States, consisting of nine **humans** (six males, three females), ruled (5–4), June 26, 2015, that same-sex marriage is a right according to the U.S. Constitution. This ruling was made, using **2015 social morals** as a basis for judgment, to interpret what the forefathers meant in a document they wrote 217 years ago when social morals were very different. This **unjust** ruling—rendered because God gives the human mind **free will**—has unintended consequences and must be annulled.

Our forefathers walked in the world of 1798 and went to their graves spiritually agonized by the dread of sin and the overpowering fear expected in a day of judgment. Their definition of marriage was not based on human opinions, theologians, sociologists, philosophers, psychologists, or on laws and constitutions—it was based on a **higher moral standard**.

*****

God's definition of marriage is found in Mark 10:6–9: "*But from the beginning of creation, God made them male and female. For this reason a man shall leave his father and mother, and the two shall become one flesh; so they are no longer two, but one flesh. What therefore God has joined together let no man separate.*" There is no clearer definition of marriage in the New Testament than in 1 Corinthians chapter 7.

"*Be fruitful and increase in number, fill the earth*" (Genesis 1:8). Biology shows it impossible for same-sex marriage partners to give birth to children. A pastor has to be "*a husband of one wife*" (1 Timothy 3:2). This is repeated in Titus 1:6 and elsewhere.

Paul was familiar with homosexuality in the culture where he lived since he wrote two corrective letters to the Corinthians about it. Furthermore, Paul's writings on the subject are no different from that taught in the Old Testament. Paul wrote in 1 Corinthians 6:9–10, "*Or do you not know that the unrighteous will not inherit the kingdom of God? Do not be deceived; neither fornicators, nor idolaters, nor adulterers, nor effeminate, nor homosexuals, nor thieves, nor the covetous, nor drunkards, nor revilers, nor swindlers, will inherit the kingdom of God.*" He continued in the book of Romans 1:26–27 writing, "*For this reason God gave them over to degrading passions; for their women exchanged their natural function for that which is unnatural, and in the same way also the men abandoned the natural function of the woman and burned in their desire toward one another, men with men committing indecent acts and receiving in their own persons the due penalty of their error.*"

God will not compromise on same-sex marriage and the **sin of homosexuality** (Titus 1:2) Additional biblical verses relative to the subject of this writing are: Genesis 1:27, Leviticus 18:22 and 20:13, 1 Timothy 1:9–10, and Revelation 21:8.

Religious Truth and Spiritual Truth

Religious truth, spiritual truth, and biblical truth are not the same.

Theology is the study of Jesus, God, and religion, which is a collection of systematized, changeable opinions or **beliefs** based on static or fixed **biblical truth**. This is nurtured in a seminary or theological school to train or indoctrinate, as opposed to educating, ministers, priests, and rabbis. As opinions or beliefs change, so changes **religious truth**.

Spirituality is an art and a science and a discipline in a university curriculum of the liberal arts and sciences (except medicine, law, and theology). It is a system of values, by which a person lives, that involves critical analysis of assumptions and beliefs leading to the pursuit of wisdom by:

- intellectual means and moral self-discipline,
- investigation of the nature, causes, or principles of reality, knowledge, or values, based on logical reasoning,
- ethics,
- observation and experiment,
- metaphysics (the nature of reality, the relationship between mind and matter, substance or inherent characteristic, fact and value), and
- the nature of knowledge.

The depth-of-understanding **spiritual truth** increases, as opposed to changes, slowly with time and throws the whole relation of humans to God and God's universe into perspective.

THE MOST ANCIENT
HATRED STILL EXISTS

November 1, 2018

The October 24 Tree of Life Synagogue massacre in Pittsburgh represents the most ancient and malignant mental disease in all human society. Anti-Semitism isn't aimed at Jewish behavior or support for Jewish immigration or support for Israel, it's just plain hatred.

Such irrational hatred manifests itself in murder almost daily in the Middle East. Jews are killed simply because they're Jews, as they have been throughout history. This is why millions have sought refuge in the religious protections embedded in the Constitution of the United States and also in the Jewish state of Israel.

The outpouring of support and grief for the victims of the Pittsburgh synagogue massacre is a reminder of America's unique role as a refuge for the world's religions. Muslim states often persecute non-Muslims as well as Muslims who don't share their brand of Islam. Communist China persecutes people of all religions. America protects them.

There are fewer anti-Semitic acts in America than in most of the rest of the world and the sources of anti-Semitism range across the political spectrum. This includes some on the right like the Pittsburgh murderer and some from the pro-Palestinian left, especially on many of America's campuses of higher education.

The most firm and resolute supporters of Israel and the Jewish people are evangelical Christians and orthodox Catholics. Perhaps, this is because as people of faith themselves they know what it's like to be mocked and shunned in a popular culture that's increasingly secular.

American patriots would do well to ignore the political blame artists that are distracting attention from the real sickness—an enduring hatred that goes back thousands of years. That is the disease to banish from American life, even if it can't be purged from the minds of some people.

ADVICE FOR WASHINGTON, DC

June 6, 2019

With my apologies to Psalm 2 New International Version, I submit the following advice.

> Some of America's leaders rise up
> and band together against God;
> to destroy civilization.
> Why do liberals in Congress conspire
> and plot against God in vain?
>
> The souls of leaders need awakening,
> and mental shackles thrown off.
> They will be rebuked in God's anger
> and terrified in God's wrath.
>
> Therefore, you leaders, be wise;
> be warned, liberals in Congress.
> Serve the American people with fear,
> your current ways will lead
> to your destruction.

The Future of the United Methodist Church

March 13, 2019

The United Methodist Church, America's third largest religious protestant denomination has 6.8 million members and nearly 6 million members in foreign countries. At their February 23–26 General Conference in St. Louis, the delegates voted in favor of retaining their ban on same-sex marriage. Of the 864 delegates present at the conference 363 were from foreign countries, mainly Africa where United Methodism is strongly traditional.

United Methodism in America has lost an average of nearly one hundred thousand members each year since 1969. Yet the denomination gains more than one hundred thousand adherents in Africa each year. The Democratic Republic of Congo alone has three million members. More Methodists are in church there on a typical Sunday than in the United States.

Kenshasa, capital city of the Dominican Republic of the Congo, had a 2017 population of 11,855,000. Brazzavile, capital city of the smaller Republic of the Congo, had a 2016 population of 5,125,821. The two huge capitals are adjacent, separated by a river, and each is amazingly modern with impressive architectural buildings and engineering structures. If this surprises you, get on the internet and see for yourself.

United Methodism's increasingly global composition underlines the collapse of once-dominant mainline Protestantism in America. In the 1960s, seventeen percent of Americans belonged to a mainline church. Today, it's five percent. Thanks to its foreign membership, United Methodism is the only growing mainline church. The face of the denomination has changed in less than four full years since 2015.

Africa's surge in growth has perplexed America's liberal United Methodist bishops and clergy. They have long assumed their denomination would follow Lutherans, Episcopalians, Presbyterians, Congregationalists, and others in liberalizing on the subject of sexuality. But at each general conference, held every four years, since 1972, their ban on same-sex marriage has been affirmed.

Most American United Methodist Bishops praised energetically the "One Church Plan," which would have allowed local churches to choose their own policies on same-sex marriage. The delegates in St. Louis defeated this measure by a vote of 475 to 389.

In its place, conservative American delegates joined the foreign delegates to pass the "traditional plan" by a vote of 458 to 406. It enhances enforcement of current teaching and allows liberal congregations to leave with their buildings if unwilling to abide.

But it is not that simple: the United Methodist denomination owns its congregations' buildings. Some conservative delegates had threatened dividing the church into factions if the liberalizing plan passed. Liberal Methodists are now carefully considering their exit options, especially as the church is leaving them behind.

The 2024 General Conference will be held in Manila, the first ever outside America. In 2028, it will be in Zimbabwe with African delegates in the driver's seat. When the general conference returns to the United States in 2032, Americans will be a minority in what was once called "America's Church."

Some liberal United Methodists unrealistically ignore these demographic and politically influenced obstacles to the same-sex marriage ban and promise to fight indefinitely. They imagine that United Methodism is still a mainline Protestant body that can be urged with gentle and repeated appeals through progressive protest.

Others are more realistic. Some of the liberal clergy predict protest, disobedience, and departures. A meeting with "bishops and other key leaders" is scheduled for some time after Easter Sunday 2019 to discuss the denomination's future.

Nobody knows the number of Methodists that would become members of a new liberal denomination. Only about 800 or three percent of America's more than 30,000 church congregations have affiliated with the unofficial minority LGBTQ caucus. A recent church poll found forty-four percent of American laypeople identify as conservative, twenty percent as liberal, with most of the remaining thirty-six percent somewhere in between.

The founder of Methodism, John Wesley, boasted that the world was his parish. This pompous speech is being fulfilled 281 years later, with unexpected consequences for America and the world due to the United States Supreme Court's unjust ruling in late June 2015.

Yesteryear Wasn't Like Today

February 6, 2019

An unavoidable weakness of youth is the temptation to believe that what is seen today has always been. This was particularly noticeable in the Parkland, Florida, high school murders almost a year ago.

One of the responses to those murders were calls to raise the age to purchase a gun and to have more-thorough background checks; to make gun purchases more difficult. That perception sees easy gun availability as the problem; the solution of which is to reduce the availability.

The vision that sees "easy" availability as the problem ignores the fact of U.S. history that guns were far more available yesteryear. With truly easy gun availability, there was nowhere near the gun mayhem and murder that's seen today.

My temptation is to ask those who believe that guns are today's problem whether they believe that guns were nicer yesteryear. What about the calls for bans on the AR-15 assault rifle? According to FBI statistics, rifles accounted for only 2.1 percent (368) of the 17,250 homicides in the United States in 2016.

That means restriction on the purchase of rifles would do little or nothing for the homicide rate. Leaders of the gun control movement know this. Their calls for more restrictive gun laws obviously are part of a larger strategy to outlaw gun ownership altogether.

Gun ownership is not the problem. The problem is a widespread decline in moral values, which has nothing to do with guns. That decline includes disrespect for those in authority, little accountability for antisocial behavior, disrespect for oneself, and—most importantly—disregard of spiritual teachings that reinforce moral values.

Let's take a look at some fundamentals of this decline. If any of our ancestors who passed away before 1970 were to return today, they wouldn't believe the kind of personal behavior that's all too common: that students could get away with cursing and assaulting teachers, that school districts employ school police officers, that school districts arm teachers

There are other forms of behavior today that would have been deemed grossly immoral yesteryear. For example, there are businesses that advertise they'll help you avoid paying all the money you owe.

Although you and a seller agreed to terms of a sale, if you fail to live-up to your part of the agreement, these businesses will assist you in ripping-off the seller. My thinking is that's immoral, but it's so common today that many folks give it no thought.

There's another moral failing that, in my mind's eye, is devastating to the future of our nation. That failing, which seems to have wide acceptance by the American people, is the notion that Congress has authority to forcibly use the resources of one American to serve the purposes of another American.

That is nothing less than legalized theft and accounts for roughly three-quarters of federal spending. When God gave Moses the commandment "Thou shall not steal," God didn't mean thou shall not steal unless you get a majority vote in the U.S. Congress.

A Three-Step Approach
to Success in Life

April 2, 2018

The vast majority of young adults in India, Japan, Korea, and China believe the path to success clearly runs through the sequence of education, work, and marriage in that order. This message isn't much discussed in America. When it is discussed, it's controversial. Liberals dismiss it as a right-wing conservative idea. They should not. Clearly, this three-step sequence is associated with a much lower chance of being poor and much better odds of realizing the American Dream.

A large group of America's millennial generation has been tracked by a national sociological survey regarding how well the success sequence worked. For ages 28 to 34, 53 percent who had failed to complete all three steps were poor. The poverty rate dropped to 31 percent among those who completed high school, 16 percent among those who had a high school diploma and a full-time job, and 3 percent for those who also put marriage before having a baby.

Models were used to predict the odds of being in poverty, after considering such factors as intelligence, childhood family income, race, and ethnicity. Those young adults who grew-up in low-income families and followed the three steps had a poverty rate of only 6 percent, compared with 35 percent for their peers who missed one or more steps. Eighty percent (80 percent) of those with lower-income backgrounds made it into the middle- or upper-income brackets when they followed all three steps, versus 44 percent for those who missed one or more steps.

Young adults from more-privileged backgrounds generally get the message from parents, teachers, and peers that they need to get an education, work, and marry before having children, and most of them act accordingly. However, this message doesn't filter down to young adults from poor and working-class families, among whom unmarried parenthood is more than twice as common as in the upper-middle class.

It's time we start sharing this three-step sequence to success with those who need it the most. There are some ways of entering adulthood that are more prudent than others. As we have done with teen pregnancy, we need to teach the sequence to success in our schools, incorporate it into MTV shows, and launch media campaigns targeting young adults from poor and working-class communities. By taking such intelligent action, we can spread in America these words of wisdom from Asia.

President Trump Stands-Up for Religious Freedom

September 25, 2019

Last year, after the United States pulled-out from the United Nations Human Rights Council, some wondered if the United States would withdraw from the UN altogether. President Trump has now made clear that he intends to engage the UN where it has potential to make a positive impact on those suffering human rights abuses, particularly abuses of the right to freedom of religion.

On September 23, President Trump became the first American president to convene a meeting on religious freedom at the United Nations. He began the UN general assembly's annual session with a "Global Call to Protect Religious Freedom."

Our president declared, "No right is more fundamental to a peaceful, prosperous, flourishing society than religious freedom, yet it is rare around the world. As we speak, many people of faith are being jailed, murdered, often at the hands of their own government." According to Pew Research, as of 2009, more than eighty percent (80 percent) of the world's population lived in nations that restrict religious freedom.

President Trump is also scheduled to hold bilateral meetings with several world leaders, including Pakistan's prime minister and Egypt's president. He will speak to them about violations of human rights of religious minorities, including Christians. Topics addressed will likely be Pakistan's blasphemy laws and Egypt's Islamic extremist groups.

Last July, the second annual ministerial to advance religious freedom was held in Washington, DC. Officials from more than a hundred countries and more than a thousand civil-society leaders gathered to discuss the subject. President Trump played a pivotal role in several religious-freedom victories, including the acquittal of Asia Bibi, a Pakistani Christian accused of blasphemy, and the freeing of Pastor Andrew Brunson after two years in Turkish captivity.

At the UN, our president announced that the United States is committing twenty-five million dollars to religious freedom efforts and launching a coalition of businesses for religious freedom. A few weeks ago, the Trump Administration launched International Religious Freedom Alliance, the first body devoted to advancing religious freedom. The alliance is intended to build on efforts to date and bring like-minded countries together to confront challenges of international religious freedom. It's an issue of moral duty.

Chapter 2
Serenity in a Private Nature Preserve

June 12, 2007

Whatever events that disgust people living in urban areas and infuses them with the passion for rural life and its pleasures render a service to mankind. It's easy in this world to live in the world like the rest of the world; it's easy in solitude to live your own way; the eminent person is one who—in an urban setting, in a rural environment or in the midst of a crowd—keeps with perfect pleasure the independence of solitude.

City and suburban life is about how people fit-in with other people. Rural life is about how people fit-into nature and about how nature shapes us. Privilege and responsibility are two sides of the same coin. We have the privilege to own land, and we have the responsibility to repair environmental wrongs of predecessors. Land isn't inherited from our parents; it's borrowed from our children. The way we act reflects who we are.

I hung-up my garb for the last time December 31, 1998, as a licensed professional geologist and licensed professional engineer consultant headquartered in suburban Cincinnati, Ohio. My wife Valeska and I chose to relocate and live secluded in our rural preserve to be inspired by nature and its effect, to face the essence of life, and to learn what it has to teach; not to discover after our minds-and-bodies die that we had not lived fully. We wanted the relaxing effect of being solitary and thoughtful but not lonely.

It's difficult for me to waste something as precious and inspirational as time spent in our Classified Forest and Wildlife Habitat located in southeast, Dearborn County, Indiana. Our unpolluted lake and rustic western red cedar home are situated in the middle of the preserve.

Nature has healing powers. Being in nature allows the mind to rest and recover, like an overused muscle. I'm fully alive, greet each day with anticipation, welcome every opportunity, enjoy the happiness and treasures the beauty of life offers, will never outgrow my sense of wonder, and continually view the world and my part in it with interest and enthusiasm.

I'm free to be creative, think my own thoughts, value the power of imagination, discover new paths to reach my dreams, believe in the value of work and strength of love and friendship, put my best into every challenge, able to benefit from every challenge, find the means to improve the world in some small way, set my own course, live by my own standards, strive to be the best that I can be, and create my own destiny.

Since the thoughtless age of youth, I have not wantonly killed a wild animal that holds its life by the same tenure that I hold my own. Seeing the artistic wonders of the natural world through my own eyes as I walk in our preserve, and through the eyes of my dogs as they run excitedly, effects a positive change in my spirit and in the spirit of each canine. I'm reminded every day that I should strive to be as good a person as my dogs believe that I am.

Fewer than five percent of my hours are spent outside the preserve, where oxygen is effortlessly and deeply inhaled as the tree leaves filter pollen and other airborne pollutants. Upon entering our preserve, you will enter a new world and see with new eyes. Almost immediately, you'll be faced with the trivial and fleeting character of your own existence.

Colored by nature, our preserve is a picture gallery of notable kind; it contains no mediocrities. From boundary to boundary, the Creator has hung it with masterpieces to captivate your heart and spirit and clear your mind—wildflowers, trees, and wildlife to charm the eye and music of birds to charm the ear. It's where passion comes to play.

Everywhere, the forest is so still, so fragrant. The remote silence is broken frequently April through October by a wonderfully soothing symphony of cicadas, a chorus of numerous seasonal and transient birds of the forest including the piccolo calls of wood thrush and hermit thrush and the ventriloquism of mocking birds. Though both kinds of the thrushes are shy, arriving on April 30 each year, the female rarely abandons her nest on account of intrusion. The same nest is often occupied for a series of years, her annual repairs consisting either of a new plastering and lining or a new lining only. Her eggs are a beautiful shade of blue. Humming birds abound, beginning in early May.

Notable also is the winter silence broken often by the wren's trill, the song of chickadees, and the noise of a pileated woodpecker drilling the typically square hole in a standing dead tree. On summer nights, hoot owls are heard hunting along an intermittent creek bed bordering on the west.

Beautifully colored transient, hermit-like wood ducks can be secretly watched during early spring, occasionally swimming or entering the four isolated (water-bound) wood-nesting boxes. Also in early spring, and late fall, transient Canada geese honk loudly, especially while I'm angling from my boat.

The lateral line along sides of the bass and trout function as a sixth sense, enabling them to pick up minute changes in water pressure and quickly locate moving objects. I'm challenged because I use only two of my five senses while the fish are using all their six senses.

Neither mosquitoes nor no-see-ums are bothersome during daytime or nighttime in the preserve; a bat population flying at night over the lake maintains total control of them. The bats find shelter in the bark of the numerous huge shagbark hickory trees.

A windbreak of twenty-eight- to thirty-eight-inch diameter white pines, along two boundaries of the forest, give way to an expansive interior of more than thirty species of deciduous hardwoods with little or no undergrowth.

Bark from white ash trees can be boiled to leave a residue of salt substitute. White pine trees start new growth during Lent each year, and by the time Easter day arrives, most of the longest stems will have branched to form a cross.

Trunks and stems of the old-growth deciduous trees are trim and straight, and the ground surface is hidden under a thick cushion of dead leaves, humus, and scattered mosses of vivid green colors. When dew is on the grass early in the morning on the crest of our earth dam, it will not rain during that day; when it's not there just after darkness, it'll rain before morning. When the sugar maple leaves turn over to show their underside, thunder and lightning will soon come. When birds fly low and silently, a storm is coming.

In April, blooming wild myrtle thickly carpets a couple of acres alongside the west arm of the lake, and pinkish-white spring beauties almost hide the remaining acres of forest floor. Morel mushrooms flourish best on south-facing slopes. Many dogwood and redbud trees grow along much of the lake's shoreline.

Taking over later on are jack in the pulpit, violets, dutchmen's breeches, dwarf larkspur, ginger, wood poppy, blood root, hepatica, trillium, wild orchids, bellflower, squirrel corn, ginseng flowers, and jewel weed (nature's cure for poison ivy). Autumn is a second spring; every leaf is a flower.

It's a remote environment of rural setting where peace and tranquility come naturally and life is in harmony with the rhythms of nature. The forest floor holds bones of hardwoods so old no living person has seen them when those trees were merely saplings ten to twenty feet or so tall. Annual growth rings on some fallen or harvested trees number more than 290 in our oak and hickory climax forest.

In winter months, the acorns, hickory nuts, black walnuts, and beechnuts not already buried or consumed by wildlife scatter over a deeply leaf-laden forest floor. A lush carpet of white pine needles or decayed leaves is more welcoming than the most luxurious Persian rug.

Great shafts of spring and summer sun will split the lofty canopy as litter-fall of the climax forest come floating down—twigs, seeds, strips of shagbark hickory and other tree bark. Straight rows—colonnades—of trees grow from the seedbed of hardwoods that had fallen many years before and rotted to become earth itself. The forest floor is a map of fallen trees that lived countless years before collapsing; a rise here, a dip there, a mound or moldering hillock. Green-hued antlers of deer have been found decaying under a fallen red oak.

Deep among the trees it's enjoyable just to lay on the soft floor of the forest and gaze up at tall branchless tree trunks to uppermost limbs that form the lofty canopy. Early spring and late summer winds blow the treetops around, sometimes inducing a momentary vertigo. It's easy to wonder while looking at the shagbark hickory's complicated bark, following its grooves to the canopy of branches sixty feet or more above.

Often, I'll just wander the forest and smell the fresh air, especially if I tire of reading or my mind gets stuck on something I'm writing. Most of the time, I'm sunk in thought, but at some point, on most such walks, there comes a moment when I look up and notice, with clarity of mind and a kind of first time astonishment, the amazing complex delicacy of a tree.

The casual ease with which elements come together to form a composition of nature, whatever the season or wherever I focus my gaze, that is absolutely perfect. Not just fine or splendid but perfect; cannot be improved. No human manages their affairs as well as does a tree.

For all its mass, a deciduous tree is remarkably delicate. All of its internal life exists within three rather thin layers of tissue just beneath its outer bark—inner bark, cambium, and sapwood—that together form a moist sleeve around dead heartwood. These three layers perform all the intricate science and engineering needed to keep a tree alive and the efficiency with which they do it is a wonder of life.

Quietly, without any noise, a tree lifts substantial volumes of water, even hundreds of gallons in the case of a large tree on a hot day, from its roots to its leaves where it's returned to the atmosphere.

Inner bark, the pipeline through which food is passed to the rest of the tree, lives for only a short time then dies, turns into cork, and becomes a distinct part of the protective outer bark.

Cambium, the growing part of the trunk, annually produces new live inner bark and new wood in response to hormones, produced by leaf buds each spring, that are passed down through the inner bark together with food from the leaves.

Sapwood, the pipeline that moves water up to the leaves, is new wood that dies and turns into heartwood.

Heartwood is the central pillar supporting the tree. Although dead, it will not decay or lose strength while the outer layers are intact. It's a composite of hollow, needlelike cellulose fibers cemented together by lignite and, in many ways, is as strong as steel. A 12-inch long piece of 2" x 2" heartwood set vertically will support a weight of twenty tons.

The bottom of steel railroad rails will wear too thin, requiring the installation of new rails, before the supporting wood ties need replacement.

The three layers of living tissue also manufacture lignum and cellulose. They regulate the storage of tannin, sap, gum, oils, and resins; distribute minerals and nutrients, and convert starches into sugar (maple syrup, for example) for future growth. Because all this is happening, a tree becomes terribly vulnerable to invasive organisms. The reason a rubber tree, for example, seeps latex when cut is its way of saying to insects and other organisms, "Not tasty. Not for you. Go away."

Living in our mainly deciduous forest is like living in a large city with many different communities (tree species) and lots of families with moms and dads (mature trees) and numerous children (immature trees) of all ages. A community of mature female and male trees is powerful. Trees in a forest environment create an ecosystem that moderates extremes of heat, cold, and potentially damaging winds, stores a huge amount of water, and generates humidity.

Deciduous tree roots extend more than twice the spread of their crowns, creating a complex web of life underground where as much as half of the biomass of the forest is hidden. Trees are very social and the shapes of their crowns enable them to physically help each other.

Trees communicate with others of the same species by means of a sense of smell (blossoms) and through electrical signals from root systems. This connection among trees in a forest helps them exchange news about insects, droughts, and other dangers.

Mature trees can deter destructive creatures like caterpillars by flooding their leaves with tannin, making the leaves less tasty and so incline the caterpillars to look elsewhere. If infestations are particularly severe, trees of the same species communicate the fact. Oak trees, for example, release a chemical that tells other oaks in the vicinity that an attack is underway.

In response, the neighboring oaks increase their tannin production to better withstand the coming onslaught. Oak trees are not mature and don't produce acorns until they're fifty years old or older. Severe drought causes trees to "scream" at acoustic frequencies above the range audible to the human ear.

Yellow poplar and aspen are the fastest growing trees in our forest. Mature oak trees and beech trees blossom only every three to five years, and acorns, hickory nuts, black walnuts, and beechnuts fall only under the (female) mother tree. Beech trees are capable of friendship and go so far as to feed each other. It takes beech trees eighty to 150 years to reach maturity and produce nuts.

Slow growth when beech trees are young enables them to live three hundred to five hundred years. Mature beech trees can send more than 130 gallons of water a day through its branches and leaves into the atmosphere.

Trees are sanctuaries. Whoever knows how to speak to them and how to listen to them can learn the truth, undeterred by particulars, and the ancient law of life.

A rich cathedral gloom pervades pillared aisles; stray flecks of warm summer sunlight that strike a trunk here and a branch yonder are strongly accented, and when they strike the moist humus, they fairly seem to burn. The most enchanting effect is that produced by the diffused light of afternoon sun. No single ray is able to pierce its way in at that time of day, but the diffused light takes color from the foliage and pervades the place like a faint, green-tinted mist, the theatrical fire of a fairyland.

The suggestion of mystery and the supernatural that haunts this forest at all times is intensified by its unearthly glow. There's something about being alone with my thoughts and nature that's really deeply energizing and deeply calming.

I'm unable to adequately describe our majestic forest or the feeling that it inspires. One feature of the feeling is a deep sense of contentment. Another feature is a buoyant, boyish gladness. A very conspicuous feature is the sense of remoteness of the workday world and complete emancipation from it and its affairs.

While feeling these things, I also grope without knowing it toward an understanding of what the spell is that's found in our forest—a strange, deep, nameless influence, which, once felt, cannot be forgotten. It leaves always behind it a restless longing to feel it again; a longing like homesickness; a grieving, haunting, yearning that will plead, implore, and prosecute 'til it has its will.

Many people, imaginative and unimaginative, cultivated and uncultivated, have come to roam our preserve. Some say they find perfect rest and peace when they're troubled; all frets and worries sink to sleep in the presence of the beneficial solitude our preserve provides.

I've gained a profound feeling for the forest and nature in general and am attracted by the gentle power of the forest. It's a spiritual necessity, an antidote to the pressure of modern life. I now understand the colossal scale of the world. I've found patience and fortitude I didn't know I had. I've discovered a part of nature that hundreds of millions of people scarcely know exists.

I've made a friend. I've come home. My life is fulfilled. I know the value of companionship and solitude. I have peace within and in the world around me. The outside world is incomprehensibly intricate, and yet our preserve makes a simple sense in my heart that I feel nowhere else.

The tonic of wilderness is crucial to my health and happiness. I belong here. In wilderness is the preservation of mankind's world. Sorry, but I wouldn't have written so much about myself if there were anyone else I knew as well.

A MARVEL OF NATURE

July 24, 2019

The study of honey bee biology goes back to Aristotle (384–322 BC), making it one of the oldest subjects of scientific inquiry. Honey bees provide us with a natural sweetener and wax for making candles and other products.

Honey remains one of nature's best and most versatile examples of a naturally produced product used in cooking, beverages, cosmetics, and medicines. In 2016, America consumed 450 million pounds of honey. One spoonful each morning of honey produced in the general area where you live really does help to control allergies.

While honey is an important product, the greatest value of bees is in the pollination of nuts, fruits, and vegetables. Tens of thousands of beehives are transported to pollinate almonds in California; blueberries in Maine, Georgia, and Florida; cherries in Michigan; apples in Washington and New York; melons in Indiana; cranberries in Wisconsin; and sunflowers in North Dakota.

Some plants are self-pollinated (tomatoes, peppers, peas, peanuts, and citrus); and other plants are wind-pollinated (corn, soybeans, walnuts, and pecans).

Acting as One
Honey bees are social insects that live together in large numbers known as a colony, which is the biological living unit of a queen bee (the fertile mother) and tens of thousands of workers (sterile females) and drones (fertile males). The hive is a structure (either natural or human-made) in which honey bees live. A comb is the sheet of hex-

agonal cells made by honey bees to store honey, pollen, and brood (eggs, larvae, and pupae).

It's the workers (sisters and daughters of the queen) who perform the majority of tasks inside and outside of the hive.

Honey bees can't survive long on their own outside of the colony. Worker bees perform specific jobs based on their age. Young adult workers perform in-hive tasks like feeding the larvae and queen, building wax combs, processing nectar into honey, keeping the hive cleaned, and guarding the colony.

As those adult workers age, their flight muscles develop to allow them to do out-of-hive tasks such as removing dead, dying, and diseased bees away from the colony, and—most importantly—foraging for pollen, nectar, water, and propolis. Propolis is resin from plants (including poplar trees) that honey bees use as a "bee glue" in the hive and as an antimicrobial medicine for the colony.

The oldest workers in the colony generally perform the most energetically demanding and dangerous work of foraging for pollen, scouting for forage areas, and finding new colony locations. Ultimately, these are the final jobs of female honey bees.

This division of labor among the adult workers is a model of efficiency, like a factory assembly line in which each worker has a defined and indispensable role. When a forager bee comes back with nectar, she doesn't deposit the nectar directly into a honey cell. Her priority is to get back to foraging. Instead, she passes the nectar to a receiver bee that will then pass it along to other receivers until it is placed in a cell.

If the forager bee cannot find a receiver, she will buzz and recruit bees to become receivers. Once the forager bee has transferred the nectar to the receiver, she can immediately return to her duties of finding more nectar and pollen.

It Smells Like Home

Like other insects, honey bees sense odors (smell) with their antennae. Every colony has its unique chemical "signature" smell that allows the guard bees to recognize that the incoming forager bees belong to that colony and are not foreign bees seeking to rob honey.

Within a hive, the bee's bodies secrete a hydrocarbon blend onto the bee's surface. The hydrocarbon also picks-up particular floral, wax, and propolis scents that set them apart from other bees in the area—even those bees that may be from an adjacent colony just a few feet away in a large apiary that contains hundreds of hives.

An Information Processing Center

With a workforce of more than forty thousand, it's imperative that a hive is able to clearly and rapidly communicate the needs of the group—the same is true for smaller colonies of a few thousand honey bees. Given that the inside of a hive is dark, the only true way of communicating is by smell and vibrations.

There are certain chemicals that honey bees release and can detect with their antennae. The bees then react to the specific messages these chemicals convey. The chemicals can communicate the presence of the queen, the queen's health, what and when to feed developing larvae, and when an attacker is threatening the hive.

Dancing for Direction

Like humans, honey bees have a symbolic language. Bees use their famous "waggle dance" as a language. These dances allow a returning forager to communicate with her hive mates about the direction and distance of pollen and nectar.

Scientists have identified two different dance languages: the round dance and the waggle dance, for which Karl von Frisch won a Nobel Prize in 1973. The round dance happens when nectar and pollen resources are close to the hive (within about one hundred feet).

The forager bee will turn in circles alternating to the left and the right. While this conveys the message that flowers are near, the round dance does not provide information about direction. While dancing in a circle, the forager passes off small amounts of nectar to several different foragers.

Not only can the newly recruited foragers taste the nectar, but also they can pick-up the smell of the flowers from the forager's body. Taste and smell are valuable forms of information that become a signature of what the foragers are searching for around the hive.

Incidentally, this is the primary reason flowers smell the way they do. While not all flowers are pleasing to humans, their various odors include a range of chemicals that attract a diverse group of potential pollinators.

As the distance to the food source gets farther away from the hive, the round dance coalesces into the waggle dance. The waggle dance communicates information about both the distance and direction if the flowers.

Inside the darkness of the hive on the top of the comb, the returning forager bee who has information to convey will dance in a pattern close to a figure eight. On the near-vertical comb, the bees interpret the direction of the sun to be always at the top of the hive.

So if the source of the nectar is ninety degrees to the left of the sun, the forager performing a waggle dance will orient her head in that direction with respect to straight up. Honey bees can tell which way is up using gravity, and they can follow the dancer by feeling the wind of her buzzing wings.

The foragers responding to this information will leave the hive at an angle of ninety degrees to the left of the sun and travel in the general direction of the food source. If the flowers are two miles from the colony, the bee will orient to the direction and vigorously shake and vibrate.

If the food source is one mile away, she will shake and vibrate faster for a shorter duration of time than if it is two miles away. The length of time that the forager waggles conveys to the other workers how far away they will have to search.

The dance does not pin point exactly where the plant patch is, but it provides the general location of where to slow down and search. Once in the general vicinity, worker bees will rely on visual and smell cues to locate the flowers. The overall vigor and intensity of the dance is also a cue; it excites other bees when a forager is more animated and will influence the numbers of foragers recruited.

Honey Bees Remember

Amazingly, a forager remembers where she has been. She has a mental map in her brain that allows her to return to the same place that she fed the day before and that allows her to find her home when she's done.

The compound eyes of a honey bee don't see with as much resolution as human eyes. Researchers believe that what a bee sees is akin to a very crude enlarged image. But that doesn't mean visual cues are unimportant. Bees can and do see, learn, and recall a variety of landmarks and cues, including floral smells, shapes, patterns, and colors.

They're also very good at perceiving movement. As a bee gets closer to a flower patch, visual cues take over. Color (specifically ultraviolet light) is another very important cue. Her eyesight is good enough that when she is flying she can discriminate familiar but general shapes and patterns.

The Bee Factory Produces Bee Bread and Honey

Most organisms need a diverse diet consisting of minerals, carbohydrates (sugars), fats, and amino acids (proteins) to survive and reproduce. Honey bees get these essential nutrients from flowers. Nectar (produced by the glands of flowers to attract pollinators) is rich in sugar and becomes the bee's main energy source. Flower pollen is the main source of amino acids that make-up proteins (and some fats) that provide the bee bread for the bee's body.

Honey bees are willing to eat fresh nectar (which has far more water and less sugar than honey) and pollen as it comes into the hive. However, altering nectar and pollen gives them flexibility in storing these products for those inevitable times when pollen and nectar become scarce in early spring and late fall.

Carbohydrates and Nectar

Honey is not just a repository of concentrated nectar. It is a manufactured product that uses nectar as the primary ingredient. The process of converting nectar into honey begins with the foragers.

Foraging bees lap-up minute amounts of nectar from flower glands located at the base of the female portion of the flower or from extrafloral nectaries (depending on plant species). That foraging bee will digest some of that nectar for its own energy needs.

But most of the nectar will remain in the bee's honey stomach, an organ that is adapted for transporting nectar and bringing it back to the colony for eventual storage. The foraging bee visits flowers until she fills her honey stomach, and then either continues foraging until she has a full load of pollen or simply returns to the hive.

While the nectar is in the honey stomach, the enzyme called invertase begins to break the more complex sugars (such as sucrose) into glucose and fructose, which are easier for honeybees to digest (as well as for humans and other animals). Upon returning to the hive, the forager opens her mandibles and allows a receiver bee to suck out the regurgitated nectar.

The forager usually transfers the nectar to two or more receivers who then place a drop of nectar into a cell. The process of exchanging food like this is called trophallaxis. During the process of transferring nectar from one receiver to another, the bees add other enzymes to help break down the original nectar and stabilize it against degradation.

Nectar is sixty to eighty percent water, depending on the plant species. Conversely, honey is eighteen percent water, illustrating another way bees refine nectar. Honey's lower water content helps preserve it. Worker bees remove the water by fanning their wings in the hive to evaporate as much water as possible, effectively acting as tiny dehydrators. Bees don't fan their wings at each and every cell, but the passing of air throughout the hive helps evaporate the water.

Reducing the water content also increases honey's sugar content, so it provides greater energy per unit volume than the more dilute nectar. Given that honey is the "high octane" fuel for the extremely active bees, the more concentrated the product, the more energy the bees obtain.

Removing the water from the nectar isn't the only way honey bees preserve nectar. They also add preservatives to prevent honey from spoiling. Like humans, bees must constantly battle ubiquitous bacterial and fungal organisms that cause food to spoil.

Honey bees add an enzyme called glucose oxidase to make honey mildly antiseptic and sterile. Glucose oxidase works at the honey's surface where it combines with oxygen to turn glucose into gluconic acid and hydrogen peroxide.

Nectar to Honey: A Sweet Job

Honey also has such a high concentration of sugar and such low water content that it draws moisture from any microorganism that lands in it. These features, combined with the fact that honey is acidic, makes it highly unlikely that microorganisms can survive in this hostile environment.

Once bees fill a cell in their comb with honey, the bees build a wax cap over it. Over time, the cap turns darker as the air escapes. At this point, the cell is considered sealed, and the honey inside may remain edible and unspoiled for a very long time.

Proteins and Pollen

Pollen from the anther (male part of the flower) is a colony's protein source. As bees fly, they become electrostatically-charged. As a result, when bees land on a flower, pollen literally "jumps" off the anther and attaches to the hairs on the bee's body. These hairs are also branched, which helps hold pollen.

This adaptation makes the business of collecting pollen easier. However, bees must considerably manipulate the plant structure to get enough pollen for a full load. As the bees work the flowers and collect the pollen on their bodies, they will brush pollen into a pollen basket found on the outside of her hind legs. Once a bee fills the baskets with pollen, she returns to the hive.

Instead of passing pollen to other bees like they do with nectar, a foraging bee that returns to the hive with loaded pollen baskets will deposit her load somewhere near where young larvae are being raised. Young nurse bees are the principle consumers of stored pollen called bee bread, which they feed to the larvae.

Bees also enzymatically process and age the bread. Other bees will pack the pollen into a cell. After the pollen forager has completed her task, she may consume some honey for energy and then return to the foraging site to retrieve more pollen.

Pollen Processing: A Versatile Foodstuff

Honey bees can eat pollen like they eat nectar, but pollen's outer coating can be difficult to break down and digest. Young adult honey bees (nurse bees) turn pollen into a more digestible product called bee bread.

Nurses digest bee bread into their guts, and then glands in their head use the digested protein to produce royal jelly or brood jelly. Older worker larvae are fed a mixture of chewed-up pollen and diluted honey in addition to brood jelly; however, the queen is fed royal jelly throughout her life.

Saving for a Rainy or Cold Day

Honey bees store honey and pollen so the colony has food when flowers are in short supply, on rainy days when foraging is limited, or through the winter when the bees are clustered in the hive for months on end. For an organism with a colonial lifestyle and enormous energy needs, the ability to store food resources is essential. Without it, honey bees would periodically run out of food and starve to death.

During the spring and fall, flowers don't bloom on the same date each year. In fact, when flowers bloom can vary by weeks from year to year. This is why a hive needs thousands of foragers to take advantage of flowers when they are blooming. The next flush of flowers and weather are both unpredictable in timing and abundance, so gathering the products from flowers is critical when they are available.

The fall nectar is particularly variable from year to year. Honey bees depend heavily on the late-season rush of golden rod, asters, and other plants in the fall. This last flush of flowers is critical to provide the colony with enough stored honey to help them survive the winter.

Drinking at the Mud Hole

Honey bees gather minerals and a variety of salts from shallow and often stagnant water puddles. It sounds counterintuitive, but the pristine and clear waters of a babbling brook are less appealing to honey bees. Bees prefer brackish and mucky waters because they contain a range of micronutrients not easily found during their visits to plants.

A Room with Six Walls

Each honey bee has glands on the lower side of its abdomen that secretes a clear liquid wax. After a few minutes, this material solidifies but remains pliable by chewing. Chewing the wax in their mouths, workers build the comb walls tilted slightly upward to keep the honey from flowing out of the cell.

Hexagonal cells are characteristic of a honey bee comb. A hexagonal cell with its six walls has been shown to be the most efficient way of using all the space available. The six-sided cell also maximizes strength while minimizing the amount of wax needed for building the walls.

When a frame in a man-made hive is completely full of honey or pollen, it can weigh several pounds, and yet the hexagonal design doesn't sag or stretch. Bees must expend a lot of energy to produce wax. It takes eight ounces of honey combined with secretions from the bees themselves to make just a single ounce of wax.

An Air-Conditioned Hive

Honey bees require very specific temperatures in the hive to protect their brood and food reserves. If the hive temperature gets too hot, foragers will collect water and bring the water back to the hive in their stomachs.

Foragers bringing water back to the colony transfer it to receivers who put small droplets into empty cells, or close to individual brood cells, but do not touch the larvae or eggs. Workers at the entrance will fan their wings to create air currents inside the hive that transfers the heat into the water, which is an evaporative cooling process.

A Call to Arms

A honey bee colony represents an incredibly rich and uncommon food source. Pounds of honey and thousands of vulnerable and protein-rich larvae inside the hive make a tempting target for any animal brave enough to tear into it. Honey bees will aggressively defend the resources they have worked so hard to acquire, process, and store because their future depends on them. In fact, the venom in their sting is a potent deterrent to many mammals, although it is sometimes insufficient to completely keep them at bay.

Workers known as guard bees defend the entrance against marauding insects and mammals that try to gain access to the hive's contents. Marauders can include honey bees from other colonies (robber bees), many species of yellow jackets, as well as mice, skunks, raccoons, and bears. Honey bees must be particularly vigilant when foragers from other colonies attempt to rob honey after the last fall flowers have bloomed.

Guard bees defend the hive against insects such as wasps by biting and stinging them. Against larger invaders such as mice, honey bees rely on an accumulation of workers to sting the animal. An adult worker has a serrated stinger, which is intended to lodge in its target. When a honey bee stings, unlike wasps and many ants, it loses its stinger and the venom gland from inside its abdomen and dies shortly afterward.

The embedded stinger continues to pump venom, appearing like a very tiny beating heart. But more important, it smears the area with an alarm pheromone that alerts other bees of immediate and impending danger, and it marks the spot for others to sting. That's why one sting often leads to more in short order.

Bees may have poor eyesight, but they have excellent odor perception, so they can track invaders even as they run away. The alarm pheromone recruits more members of the hive to come to the site of the "battle" and offer their assistance.

Airlifting the Dead, Deformed, Diseased, and Dying

It's common for dead, deformed, diseased, dead, and dying bees to be found in or near a hive by other colony residents. A group of bees quickly identifies and drags these bees out of the colony, sometimes close to the entrance, but often farther away.

The bees that do this job are called undertaker bees. Sometimes, undertaker bees actually pick-up their dead sisters and fly away with them. They remove them from the hive for hygienic purposes to get them away from the colony where healthy bees will not come in contact with them. When dead bees are deposited at the entrance, they are often consumed by ants, yellow jackets, and other scavengers.

Biology of the Honey Bee

The sterile worker bees go through the egg, larvae, and pupa stages in twenty-one days; the fertile drone bees require twenty-four days; the fertile queen bees take sixteen days.

The Queen

Regardless of the colony's size, there generally is only one egg-producing queen in the hive at any one time. The colony periodically rears new queens as a means to disperse and develop new colonies and to replace aging and failing queens.

It's primarily the type of brood cell that tells workers whether to feed the larvae food that is appropriate for a worker or a queen. Queen cells start from wax cups that point down, and the bees elongate the cell as the queen grows to a shape that resembles a peanut.

A productive queen lives two to four years. She is distinguished from the workers by her large size. In particular, a queen has an enlarged abdomen that extends well beyond the wings and a wider thorax. The queen starts laying eggs in late winter or early spring. Nurse bees start eating pollen that was stored in the fall, which is an essential ingredient for making protein and lipid-rich royal jelly.

Feeding the queen royal jelly stimulates her to lay eggs.

When fresh pollen is available in the spring from plants (such as maple trees), the brood rearing rate increases greatly. This begins a spring colony buildup during which the queen can lay 1,500 eggs per day.

The Drones

There are usually six hundred to one thousand drone bees in larger colonies. Colonies produce an abundance of drones each spring. These male reproductive bees are rather unique in that they hatch from an unfertilized egg laid by the queen.

Drones have no father, and their genetic makeup comes only from the queen. When the queen mates with many drones during a mating flight, she stores her sperm in a round organ in her abdomen. The queen can control whether an egg that is about to be laid is fertilized. She measures the cell prior to laying an egg in it. If it is a larger, drone-sized cell, she does not open the valve to allow sperm to enter the egg. The egg will then hatch as drone larvae.

Drones are not individuals in the colony workforce. Their sole purpose is to congregate outside the hive, in drone congregation areas, and mate with newly emerged virgin queens from nearby colonies. Drones use their keen eyesight to find females in flight. A drone is easily identified by the large eyes that cover much of its head and meet at the top (unlike females that have a space between the eyes).

Drones cannot sting, forage, or help in any colony tasks. They are a drain on colony resources and are useful only during mating, which occurs while the weather is fair.

The Workers

The colony's success depends on sterile female workers that perform virtually all the work. While foragers are seen gathering nectar, pollen, water, and propolis, they only represent about twenty to thirty-five percent of a colony's total workers. The remainder of the colony performs key tasks within the hive.

A worker bee's life span varies with the time of year. During most of the year, when the brood nest is expanding and foragers are bringing nectar and pollen back to the hive, a worker bee may live six weeks. During the winter (when activity is much slower), a worker bee can live for five or six months.

When rearing the brood, workers maintain a hive temperature of about 93 degrees F. Young workers clean cells, feed the queen, remove debris, and add wax to cells. Whether it is feeding larvae, keeping the hive clean, or doing the multitude of small tasks involved in colony maintenance, these younger bees reliably transition from one job to the next.

But there is also flexibility in these task schedules. For example, if an off-target pesticide application kills a large number of foragers, young adult bees may become precocious foragers. If all the nurse bees are removed from a colony, certain glands of older bees will become active, and the bees will revert to nursing duty.

At about three week old, a worker bee that has spent her entire life within the colony is ready to take on her final and most difficult task; that of a forager working outside of the hive. New foragers begin by performing orientation flights in late afternoon around the hive.

Hundreds of these soon-to-be foragers fly close to the hive, memorizing everything around them in a mental map of where the hive is located. Within a few days following the onset of these orientation flights, the foragers start scouting for pollen, water, nectar, and propolis.

For the next couple of weeks, the forager will travel back and forth to the hive covering many miles. Individual foragers will specialize in collecting pollen, nectar, propolis, or water. However, foragers can switch duties; collecting pollen one day, then water the next, depending on the information she receives from the colony.

If a returning forager is inundated with receiver bees, she not only gets unloaded quickly, but also she receives positive reinforcement that induces her to continue foraging for whatever she brought in to the hive. Additionally, she might perform a bee dance to recruit more foragers. This is how the colony communicates whether their provisions are in short supply, or relatively abundant, and foragers change their foraging patterns accordingly.

Most honey bees have a typical round-trip flying distance of two to four miles and travel at a speed of about fifteen miles per hour. Bees can use the nectar in their honey stomachs much like a gasoline tank. If a nectar forager needs energy as she is traveling, she will refuel in flight by opening a valve in the honey stomach that releases nectar into the midgut.

Foraging is physically demanding and carries a tremendous physiological cost for the honey bee. After a few weeks of foraging, a honey bee forager has worked herself to death.

Information for the above writing: "The Complex Life of the Honey Bee," 2017, Purdue University.

NATURAL LAWS AND
LAWS OF SCIENCE

August 11, 2017

Natural laws are uniform and interdependent, eternally fixed, do not change, and apply throughout the whole universe. They apply in the future just as they have applied in the past. If the laws of nature suddenly and arbitrarily changed tomorrow, then past experimental results would tell nothing about the future. Mankind can depend on the laws of nature to apply consistently throughout time.

The universe obeys certain laws of science to which all things must adhere. These laws are precise, and many of them are mathematical in character. If the universe were merely an accidental by-product of the "big bang" theory, why should it obey any natural law or scientific principal, such as "cause and effect?" Everything in the universe, every living plant and animal, and every particle of matter or light wave is bound by laws that it has no choice but to obey. Nothing in the universe is haphazard or arbitrary.

Birth, growth, death, and decay are inevitable for all living organisms, states of mind, and societies. New forms arise out of the old; each determined by that which preceded it. This process of change is not chaotic but is regulated by the principle of "cause and effect," which is unchanging, impersonal, and impartial.

All that is born must die except the human soul, which is not born and not compounded; it is neither matter nor energy, unchanging, immortal, and infinite. It is known only through direct experience beyond sense perception, is completely unrelated to anything with which humans are familiar, and cannot be described, conceptualized, or fully understood by the human mind.

Nature and natural laws exist in perfect harmony. Natural laws and laws of science are universal truths that are either <u>transcendent</u> (beyond the ordinary range of perception) or <u>factual</u> (real occurrences known to exist or demonstrated to exist).

Natural Laws (Transcendent Truths)

Laws of mathematics, unlike the laws of physics, are not "attached" to any part of the universe. Like the laws of physics, some laws and properties of mathematics can be derived from other mathematical principles.

Laws of logic, on which all natural laws depend, allow rational thinking regarding the relationship between elements and between an element and the whole in a set of principles, events, objects, or individuals.

Rational humans instinctively know many of the guiding principles in the laws of logic. The law of noncontradiction, for example, states simply that "A" and "not A" cannot exist at the same time and in the same relationship. Logic can involve deductive reasoning (inference from a general principle) or inductive reasoning (deriving general principles from particular facts or instances).

Laws of morality, on which the qualities of good individual character and right ethical behavior depend, are corroborated through rational thinking and substantiated biblically. The reality of the laws of morality is perceived in the power for positive change from bad individual character and unethical behavior.

The law of personal and interpersonal behavior is self-enforcing and states that a person is required to think, say, and do what is right in order to get a right result. Humans in general have free will to shape their individual lives, human societies, and the fate of those societies.

Rational thinking exclusively from natural laws causes awareness of a higher power that communicates through the principle of "cause and effect" to establish order in human lives, affairs, and society.

"Failure to conform with natural laws imposes penalty." For example, you cannot swim, and the three-person fishing boat you're sitting in sinks into deep water, and you're not wearing an appropriate lifesaving jacket. Another example would be you racing on foot without proper body protection through a large patch of tall briars.

To obey the laws of morality is unconditional. "Right human behavior is logical and moral, and it succeeds; contradictory behavior is illogical and immoral, and it fails." "Conformity to the laws of morality is mandatory; nonconformity accounts for the chaotic and deadly affairs of individual humans and human societies."

Laws of Science (Factual Truths)

The **law of biogenesis** states simply that living organisms reproduce only from other living organisms of their own kind. It also can be expressed using only three words, two of which are scientific terms—ontogeny (origin and development of an individual living organism from embryo to adult) recapitulates (repeats in concise form) phylogeny (evolutionary development of a living organism).

All living organisms follow specific **laws of chemistry**, one of which creates a nucleic acid carrying genetic information known as DNA. These laws give different properties to the various chemical elements, each composed of one particular type of atom and chemical compounds.

When given sufficient activation energy, for example, the lightest element (hydrogen) will react with oxygen to form water. Water has the ability to hold a large amount of heat energy. When frozen, water forms snowflake crystals with six-sided hexagonal symmetry. Salt (sodium chloride) crystals have a cubical symmetry. It's the six-fold symmetry of water ice that produces "holes" in its crystals, making it less dense than water. That's why ice floats on water, whereas essentially all other frozen compounds sink in their own liquid.

Properties of chemical elements and chemical compounds are not arbitrary. The elements are logically organized in a tabular arrangement (periodic table of chemical elements) according to their atomic numbers so that elements with similar physical properties are in the same horizontal column. Elements in the same vertical column have the same outer electron structure. These outer electrons determine the physical atomic characteristics. Atoms and molecules have various properties because of their outer electrons being bound by the laws of quantum physics. In other words, chemistry is based on physics.

Laws of physics describe the behavior of the universe at its most fundamental level. There are many different laws of physics, and they describe the way the universe operates. Some of these laws describe how light propagates, how energy is transported, how gravity operates, how mass moves through space, and many other phenomena. These laws are characterized mathematically.

The second law of thermodynamics asserts the irreversibility of natural processes, the impossibility for something to arise out of nothing, the impossibility that everything already existed in the universe, a power outside of the universe created the universe and everything in it, the flow of energy maintains order and life, entropy occurs when living organisms cease to take in energy and die, everything over time tends toward disorder, randomness, and disorganization.

Laws of planetary motion are three in number. Planets orbit in ellipses with the sun at one focus of the ellipse; thus, planets are closer to the sun than at other times. They speed-up as they get closer to the sun within their orbit. Those with orbits farther from the sun take much longer to orbit than planets that are closer. These laws also apply to the moons of planets.

Conclusions

It must be first acknowledged, in order for the laws of morality to be transcendent truths, that humans (homo sapiens) are special multicellular organisms of the animal kingdom and that they have dominion (a caretaker role) over only a very tiny speck of the universe—the planet Earth.

No questions of nature are unanswerable. Whatever the perfect order of nature awakens in human minds, the perfect order of nature can answer. Nature is an endless combination of repetition of very few laws. Our consideration of what takes place around us every day shows that a higher power than our will regulates events.

Nothing is solid and secure on planet Earth; everything tilts and moves. Anything that could stand without tilting and moving would be crushed by the turbulence of natural forces it resisted. We cannot build our structures as we will but as we must.

Our personal lives could be easier and simpler than we make them, and the world could be a happier place; there is no need for struggle, convulsion, despair, wringing of the hands, or the gnashing of the teeth, we each create our own ruin. We interfere with natural law.

Although liars and cheaters may quickly acquire prestige in human society, their eventual downfall is assured. Natural laws make rightness mighty, and rightness will eventually prevail as the eternal basis of might.

Every effort of science to understand the secrets of nature reveals that behind the discernible laws there remains a subtle, intangible, and inexplicable force demanding profound respect and reverence beyond anything the human mind can comprehend. Science is inspired with the aspiration for truth and understanding; seeking to uncover the unchangeable laws that govern reality. In so doing, science rejects the notion that the Creator interferes in the events of creation, a role that would violate creation's vast principle of "cause and effect."

The source of inspiration for science is in the sphere of spirituality. To be spiritual is to sense that underlying anything experienced there is a sublime force touching you indirectly; something the human mind cannot grasp. Science without spirituality is weak and ineffectual. Spirituality without science is sightless and without direction.

The realm of science is to ascertain the truth. The province of spirituality is to evaluate human thoughts and actions in light of what should be the truth. The Creator's unlimited power, total knowledge, and simultaneous presence everywhere is beyond human comprehension. To even suspect that the Eternal Being responds directly to human prayer that concerns only oneself is incomprehensible. Human prayer for another human may be answered.

Even though atheists can't account for laws of logic, they must accept the fact that such laws indeed do exist in order for rational thinking to occur. Could the cliché "stupid is as stupid does" apply to the atheist intellect?

Learning a New Trick from My Old Dog Freedom

March 19, 2019

My best buddy Freedom turned eleven (seventy-seven in dog years) the same year I turned eighty-eight. Though I'm eleven years older, we're basically at the same stage of life, namely, getting old. We're handling it about the same, we both have a heart problem—his is a malfunctioning heart valve, and mine is atrial fibrillation.

I'm not complaining. I am still having a wonderfully good life, and I'm content with my pacemaker. But Freedom is more than content. He's happy, often exuberantly happy, constantly finding excitement and joy in everyday events.

It has occurred to me that maybe I could learn some life lessons from Freedom by paying him more attention. Perhaps, I could find even more happiness in my own life by doing some things Freedom does, except of course drinking water from the toilet.

One thing Freedom does is love people. He is extremely friendly. Even though, when he was age four, his previous owner died and he was placed in SPCA Cincinnati. He shows no fear of strangers, human, or canine. He is determined to shower smiles and love upon everybody he gets anywhere near. And he is always making new friends.

Everybody loves Freedom, a coonhound/Australian cattle dog mix with orange merle coat. It's hard not to. He greets all visitors, whether or not he's ever met them before, by running to them, a big smile on his face, tail wagging, and expressing his love for them with every inch of his quivering-with-happiness body.

He is ecstatic when, for example, the Terminix man comes to check the termite bait stations around the house exterior. Anyone who lives in the middle of a forest preserve sprays monthly to rid the house of tree roaches and mice the size of mature squirrels.

The Terminix man is just one of Freedom's best friends. He follows him from room to room, ready and eager to assist in the event he needs to be licked. He's like this with all visitors; every one of them is his best friend. He is fifty-five pounds of pure, unstoppable affection, with a paw scrape of love.

I'm much, much less social than Freedom. Whatever the reason, when confronted with people I don't know, my assumption is that I may not like them. And the older I get, the more reluctant I am to meet new people. When I'm alone in a social setting, which is the usual case, I never strike-up conversations. I'm shy.

The result is that at my age, I know a ton of people, but I have few close friends, mostly people I first met long ago. And the truth is, most of them are no longer around—they're dead. I think this is true with many guys my age; we don't view talking about our personal lives as an acceptable activity.

Imagine two people who are acquaintances and who have both just been diagnosed with serious, possible fatal, diseases. Now imagine that they run into each other at a car wash and, while waiting for their cars, they spend a few minutes talking. If these people are women, they will quickly discover their common plight, and they will be in tears and hugging and possibly go to the nearest bakery for commiserative doughnuts.

But if these two people are men, it's entirely possible that neither will even mention his medical situation. It's probable that their entire conversation will involve discussing a recent decision by an NFL quarterback, whom neither of them knows personally or will ever meet, to throw a pass to a running back on third and twelve when the deep receiver is wide open. ON THIRD AND TWELVE! Sometimes, I think the main purpose of professional sports is to give guys something to talk about that does not involve them personally.

My point is that women tend to be better at making and keeping friends. My deceased wife, Valeska, who was a lady, had dozens, maybe hundreds of friends and made new ones regularly. Whenever she saw or heard from any of these friends, they had a conversation, usually involving their personal lives that could easily last longer than medical school. She was closer to all her friends than I am to any of mine.

I am, through death and distance, losing and drifting apart from my friends. And what bothers me about this is when I stop to think about it, that it really doesn't bother me. The older I get, the more accustomed I am to solitude. I can spend the entire week alone and be perfectly content.

That's me, content. No complaints. But I'm thinking I shouldn't settle for being content. I think that even at eighty-eight, I should still be aiming to be happy, like Freedom. So one big lesson from Freedom is make new friends and keep the ones you have.

Making friends, at this point, will not be easy for me, but I intend to try. When I meet new people, I'm going to make a conscious effort not to hide behind my writing barrier nor use my age as an excuse to be a recluse. I'm going to think about Freedom; about the trustful, open, unreservedly joyful way he approaches everybody. I'm going to look these new people straight in the eye, and with a positive, welcoming attitude, I'm going to shake their hand again.

And I'm going to get in touch with longtime friends I haven't seen in a while, assuming they're still alive. We'll catch-up on our lives, and we'll share our feelings about things that are important to us. Such as the idiocy of throwing a short pass on third and long.

HUMANS AND NATURAL LAW

November 16, 2012

There is no evidence that human affairs have established peace, stopped criminal activity, avoided ultimate death, or eliminated any other consequence of human life on planet Earth. Despite all human effort to produce an entirely peaceful and productive society, human society remains adversarial and afflicted.

Human society is comprised of do-gooders at one end of the spectrum and terrorists at the other, each group reacting to the realities of life with irrational judgments that contradict natural law. Humans also form personal plans consisting of likes and dislikes, wants and don't—wants that contradict natural law and cause seemingly endless trouble. The power to change human behavior is in perceiving the reality of natural law.

The Creator communicates through natural law to establish order in human lives, affairs, and society. For example, humans learn from tumbles and other hurtful happenings at a very early age to reason and obey the law of gravity.

Human activity in accordance with the reality of natural law assures conformity with the Creator's plan. And when they reason exclusively from natural law, humans become aware of a higher purpose in life.

A fundamental principal of natural law is the reality that *for every action in nature, there is an equal and opposite reaction.* This principal can be expressed as follows: *Failure to conform to natural law imposes penalty.*

Restated in terms of human behavior the principle becomes: *Right behavior is logical and moral, and it succeeds; contradictory behav-*

ior is illogical and immoral, and it fails. Elevated to a higher level, it becomes nature's *law of absolute right,* plainly pointing-out that morality is a human duty.

Conformity to nature's law of absolute right is mandatory; nonconformity accounts for the chaotic and deadly affairs of humans and human society. The Creator awaits human adjustment to nature's *law of absolute right,* knowing that the welfare of humans and human society depends on taking the right action in every moment of every situation.

With knowledge of individual human needs and the needs of human society from the very beginning, the Creator has arranged nature to meet those needs. Nature was set into motion by a Creator who constantly watches over it, guiding everything in it from birth through life to death and infinite time.

Natural law expresses the Creator's plan for a peacefully vibrant and productive human society. Humans are a part of nature, and they communicate with the Creator every minute of every day, yet no human knows the number of planets, solar systems, or galaxies in the universe.

Science knows that every newly developed telescope enables sight farther into the universe, causing realization of the meager extent of human knowledge and that humans are not the only intelligent species in the vastness of the universe.

THE DOORMAN

December 20, 2018

A friend of mine and his family lived in a plush apartment building located on the edge of downtown Atlanta, Georgia. The man who worked the door to the building had done that for more than thirty years. Everyone who knew him loved him.

His name was Carlos Nino, and he came to the United States, at age eighteen, from the outskirts of Bogota, Columbia. He had little money and education. Carlos married an American girl, kept two jobs to support his family, and put both his sons—Kenneth and Jason—through college.

My friend knew him for about forty years. Carlos started as a porter and had graduated to doorman. He greeted tenants and visitors alike with a smile and a warm hello. Carlos stooped low to talk to babies in carriages and little children. He ran outside to help the elderly carry bags of groceries.

My friend said Carlos became family. They talked about their children. He once told my friend his son Kenneth, just out of law school, was already earning twice as much as he. You could see the pride radiating from his face.

My friend told me Carlos had told him a few years ago his wife was suffering from breast cancer. He planned to retire soon to help care for her. The week before Carlos left, my friend stationed himself in the lobby with an oversize greeting card and asked residents passing by for signatures and messages.

Within hours, the card was full, and my friend had to go buy another. The same happened to a second card and then to a third.

After three days, more than a hundred well-wishers had bid Carlos goodbye.

On his last day at the door, my friend handed Carlos the cards. Carlos touched his hand to his heard. Carlos had no idea what to say, and so he said nothing and everything.

My friend and Carlos stayed in touch, and he learned that Carlos's wife's cancer was in remission. But Carlos himself became sick. His kidneys were failing. It was as if he had relieved his wife's suffering by taking it on himself.

My friend never saw Carlos again. The last time they spoke by phone, Carlos assured him his health was improving. As proof, Carlos pointed out he had managed to walk around the block that afternoon. Word of his death at age sixty-four came to my friend through a fellow doorman.

Carlos was not only a dear man but also a great doorman, a classic case of how your job is what you decide to make of it. He felt privileged to be a doorman and put his heart into his job every day. His is the story of an immigrant come true.

Carlos wanted to earn his keep and be of service. Some people are put on planet earth to show the rest of us how to be. He taught all who knew him an important lesson: try to do some good, and do it while you still can.

An Unusual Act of Courtesy

October 23, 2018

It's 6:15 p.m. on a July Saturday, and I'm on the sidewalk along-side a huge parking lot and twelve-story office building complex that occupies a square block in downtown Cincinnati. I'm walking to pass some time 'til my 7:00-p.m. reservation at one of my favorite fine-dining restaurants about six blocks from Symphony Hall.

The lot with mainly yellow-lined parking spaces is deserted. It's a Monday-through-Friday kind of place. There's no one around today. A car pulls in. At the nearest corner of the building, the lights are on at a medical facility of some sort, and it seems to be open. That's where the car is heading.

The parking spaces, none of them marked as reserved, are set-off by white lines. The driver, a man who appears to be in his late seventies or early eighties, parks. He slowly gets out using a cane, and his wife exits on the passenger side. Theirs is the only car in the lot.

Maybe a doctor has made special arrangements to meet them here. Thirty to perhaps fifty of those white-lined parking spaces are unoccupied. The people working at the medical facility must have private parking spaces elsewhere because their cars aren't visible.

The couple begins walking toward the building, and the wife asks, "Are we parked too far over?" He turns and looks at the car he'd just parked. His tires on the driver's side are extending over the painted line next to it but just barely. "You're right," he says. "We're in someone else's space."

He walks slowly with his cane back to the car, unlocks it, and slowly gets in. He starts the ignition, backs-up, and pulls into the space again, so his tires are between the lines. It's clear this is not some obsessive-compulsive habit. It's a gesture of courtesy for someone he will never meet—someone who almost certainly will never show-up.

"Better?" he calls to her from the window. "It's good now," she calls back. He slowly reemerges. No one would have known, not in this empty lot. No one would have minded that his tires were over the line. He wasn't inconveniencing other motorists because there were none on this Saturday evening.

Here were a man and woman who I know play by the rules all the time. The idea of not reparking that car would never have occurred to them. Maybe it's a generational thing; maybe not. All my eighty-eight-year old mind knew, as I saw them together slowly walking toward the building, was that they had just made my day happier.

It was one of those split-second decisions to do something the right way, even when it's so small, even when it doesn't matter. They entered the building, and I wished I knew them.

Mind Your Manners

August 26, 2019

Born at the beginning of the great depression, I was a teenager during the last three years of the seven-year-long World War II, 1939–1945. Courteous behavior and politeness prevailed in a highly-civilized American society and culture showing moral and intellectual advancement marked by refinement and sophistication. Great nations run in part on manners—the lubricant that allows the machine to hum. The America we have known in the past must continue in this way.

My generation grew-up at a time when a young person's response to parents, teachers, and older people habitually showed respect for position in society—"Yes, ma'am; no, ma'am" or "Yes, sir; no, sir." Excepting active military personnel and veterans, when did you last hear those words spoken by a young person?

Some people may think I'm just a grouchy old man, but I don't see today's society and culture conforming to those conventional standards of behavior or morality and self-respect. We have become very rude, not from ignorance, but from indifference surrounded by affluence.

In our daily dealings, we've grown negligent and careless in dress and appearance. Let me explain using the following example. Many people today, especially adults, show disrespect at formal events including Symphony Orchestra Concerts or Sunday Church Service by wearing T-shirts, sportswear, shorts, and other casual attire.

It's discourteous to walk on a busy sidewalk with your eyes trained on an iPhone with disregard for others who must make way for you so as not to harm you. It would be better if you would at least make brief eye contact and nod as if you are a fellow human being.

Many folks have apparently forgotten that the phrase "Excuse me" is a request, not a command. "Excuse me" is an abbreviated question expressed in a soft voice: "Would you excuse me, please? Thank you." It's not a command to be barked as you push your way through a crowded aisle.

There is the matter of "No problem." You perform a small courtesy, and I thank you. You reply "No problem" instead of "You're welcome." Your response implies: "If it were at all challenging, you would never be courteous."

Today's first name culture is fully established. It's vulgar and inhuman when done by a stranger. It shows disrespect for person and privacy, and the experience is assaultive. A first name is what you're called by intimates and friends and belongs not in a stranger's mouth.

You may grant permission, that's your right. But a stranger can't seize permission, that's not their right.

I receive written and telephone solicitations from people I've never met, "Dear Jim" and "Good morning, Jim." I honestly wonder, *Do I know you?* And then I realize that's what they want me to wonder because if I think I might know them, I'm more likely to respond. It's called marketing.

Everyone in America suffers—literally suffers—from the erosion of the essential public courtesies that allow us to move forward in the world, happily and with some hope. If a person campaigning for political office whose slate also included "America, reclaim your manners," that person would win in a landslide.

I'm merely suggesting a less selfish and vulgar way of being. Surely, all Americans can consider that. Thank you. I'm grateful to have you as a reader.

TODAY IS THE TOMORROW
WE NEEDED TO THINK
ABOUT YESTERDAY

April 14, 2004

As demonstrated by their way of life and actions during the tenth through early twentieth centuries AD, Native Americans recognized that the land and its wildlife are a precious resource not made for them to tinker with and to plunder. They were aware that mountains, hills, valleys, canyons, plains, lakes, rivers, streams, forests, vegetation, and the atmosphere are marvels of nature to be treasured. And they believed that land comes from the "Great Spirit" and belongs to no man.

They possessed a positive genius for knowing how to deal with the earth, natural terrain, and wildlife. In the states of Ohio and Illinois, earth workings of the tenth through fourteenth century mound builders fit harmoniously into the environment and do not disturb nature's equilibrium. This culture's many earth structures show an amazing depth and scope of understanding of the natural environment as it relates to their life and the solar system.

Native Americans knew how to conserve the productive power of the land and wildlife for their progeny's use. Conservation and environmental compatibility obviously were a priority in their minds and actions.

They realized that nature has her own rhythms, characterized by the regular occurrence of strong and weak elements. Nature provided for them physically, socially, spiritually, and emotionally. They were tied to the land and wildlife, without which they would lose their cultural identity and ultimately, themselves.

From 1625 to 1910, Native Americans tried, as would any human, to defend their way of life and to protect themselves and their families against aggressive intruders. Intruding "civilized" non-indigenous Anglo-Saxons looked upon the Native Americans as barbaric and savage.

To justify mistreatment of Native Americans, the aggressive intruders in 1869 fabricated *"Manifest Destiny,"* a document that in their minds lifted land greed to a lofty plane. *The rich and beautiful valleys…are destined for the occupancy and sustenance of the Anglo-Saxon race. The wealth that for untold ages has lain hidden beneath the snow-capped summits of our mountains has been placed there by Providence to reward the brave spirits whose lot it is to compose the advance guard of civilization. The Indians must stand aside or be overwhelmed by the ever advancing and ever increasing tide of immigration. The destiny of the aborigines is written in characters not to be mistaken. The same inscrutable Arbiter that decreed the downfall of Rome has pronounced the doom of extinction upon the red men of America.*

A wrong was done the Native American—an injustice due to greed, fueled by ignorance, irresponsibility, and a careless sort of kindness unaccompanied by wisdom. Not much has changed in the minds and actions of nonindigenous Americans. Our shameful greed continues unrelentingly today.

Excessive groundwater withdrawal to irrigate the arid southwest and southern California has virtually depleted the Ogallala aquifer, North America's largest underground water resource, because the natural recharge is incapable of keeping pace. Simplistic consideration now is being given to move water from the Northern Rockies of Canada, and even from Lake Superior, to desert lands in the southwest and southern California.

Nonindigenous Americans today make deserts bloom and natural lakes die and clear-cut forests to develop the land. We make flat land by excavating hills to fill valleys. To destroy the natural environment seems to be our strongest instinct. We conquer nature, bend it to our will, and use it wastefully until it is virtually destroyed.

We move on, leaving the waste behind while looking for more wonders of nature to conquer and ultimately destroy. The cause of our hunger is greed and what we eat is the natural environment.

It's unsettling that nature no longer is considered sacred. Every place in America is fast becoming like any other—homogenized and prepackaged. No ridge or slope is too steep, no mountaintop too high, no valley too pristine for development.

Huge residential subdivisions, seas of concrete and asphalt, and more commercial strip malls are built, and many are unoccupied. Pristine natural lakes, the azure blue Lake Tahoe in California, for example, are now polluted by reckless shoreline overdevelopment.

Too many Americans are unwilling to acknowledge that once destroyed, natural terrain and lakes cannot be restored. This outrageous rape of America's rugged beauty we readily misidentify as progress.

Majestic forests are disappearing at an alarming rate and ozone alerts are at a record high. The oldest living things on this earth—trees—are a good measure of the health and quality of the environment. Living trees are multitask performers and provide social, ecologic, emotional, spiritual, and economic benefits.

Their beauty inspires and awes, their leaves provide oxygen and clean the air humans and wildlife inhale and exhale. Their roots control runoff and seepage entering streams and lakes and help stabilize soils on steep slopes.

City, county, state, and federal governments too long have placed a low-to-no priority on effective control of land development. Our citizenry has been blinded too long by applicable regulations that are too weak, too late, and/or not enforced due often to governmental corruption or ambivalence.

For too long, America has turned a deaf ear to land, water, air, and noise pollution, and the plunderers of our natural world must be identified and effectively controlled, today and in the future, for the benefit of future generations.

Earthquakes East of Mississippi River and in Missouri

April 30, 2008

Earthquake awareness and preparedness is generally lacking in the eastern United States where, by popular conception, it is thought to be earthquake-free. People living in the Ohio-Kentucky-Indiana-Illinois region perhaps should reconsider this matter.

Earthquake severity and frequency (hazard) and likelihood of harm (risk) vary, depending on the geology. Since no earthquake of significant magnitude (6.5 or greater) has occurred in the Ohio-Kentucky-Indiana-Illinois region, assessing earthquake hazard in that region is handicapped by the lack of appropriate data.

Ground motion causes most damage during an earthquake. The larger the magnitude, the stronger the ground motion it generates. The closer a site is to the epicenter, the stronger the ground motion. Ground motion from a large earthquake in New Madrid, Missouri, for example, would be larger along the Ohio and Mississippi River valleys in Western Kentucky and Southern Illinois than in the more distant central interior part of these two states.

Soft soils overlaying hard bedrock tend to amplify ground motions, causing damage even at sites 65–70 miles from the epicenter. Many Ohio-Kentucky-Indiana-Illinois communities along the Mississippi and Ohio River valleys are set on soft soils prone to ground rolling in waves.

The damage in Maysville, Kentucky, during the July 27, 1980, earthquake at Sharpsburg, Kentucky, was caused by amplified ground motion. Strong ground motion can cause soft sandy soils to liquefy or behave like fluid, resulting in foundation failure of architectural and engineering structures, and also can trigger landslides on some steep slopes.

The oldest written records of earthquakes in the eastern United States date back to the middle 1500s. Since then, hundreds of quakes have been recorded. A magnitude 6.5 must be reached before a quake is considered significant. Ten of the more important Eastern U.S. quakes, occurring between 1755 and 1954, are listed as follows:

> **1755, Cape Ann, MA.** Magnitude 6.0, felt from Chesapeake Bay to Nova Scotia. Walls, chimneys and stone fences fell in Boston. Waves, like in the ocean, were reported on the earth surface.

> **1811–1812, New Madrid, MO.** A series of quakes with magnitudes 8.6, 8.4, and 8.8 are the largest in recorded history. The earth surface rolled in waves several feet high. Great waves overwhelmed many boats on the Mississippi River and washed many thousands of trees into the river. Church bells rang in Boston, 1,100 miles away.

> **1884, New York, NY.** Magnitude 5.0, felt from southern New Jersey to Vermont.

> Greater damage was in Jamaica and Amityville, NY, where large cracks appeared in walls, glass windows were broken, and chimneys toppled.

> **1886, Charleston, SC.** Magnitude 7.7, earth strongly shaken for 100 miles, felt for a radius

of 800 miles. Widespread and extensive damage to buildings, railroad, and communication lines.

1895, Charleston, MO. Magnitude 6.2, felt in 23 states, extensive damage to buildings in Charleston and in Cairo, IL.

1897, Giles County, VA. Magnitude 5.8, felt from Georgia to Pennsylvania. Old brick buildings cracked and bricks were thrown from chimney tops.

1925, St. Lawrence River. Magnitude 7.0, felt from Virginia to eastern Canada and west to the Mississippi River. Damage and loss of life was minimal due to sparse population in the area of the epicenter.

1929, Attica, NY. Magnitude 5.8, felt from Ohio to Ontario, New York, Pennsylvania, Connecticut, Maine, and Vermont. Two hundred fifty chimneys were toppled, and walls cracked as far away as Sayre, PA.

1944, Massena, NY. Magnitude 5.6, felt from Maine to Michigan to Pennsylvania and Maryland. Damage estimated at $2,000,000 (1944 value) in the area of the epicenter.

1954, Wilkes-Barre, PA. Magnitude 5.0, damaged hundreds of buildings, cracked streets and sidewalks, snapped buried water and gas lines. Damage estimated in excess of a million dollars.

Following is a list of six important earthquakes, occurring between 1980 and 1988, with epicenter in the Ohio-Kentucky-Indiana-Illinois region.

7/27/1980, Sharpsburg, KY. Magnitude 5.1, felt in parts of five states. Broke glass windows and toppled chimneys in Maysville, KY. Damage estimated at one million dollars.

1/31/1986, Lake Erie, OH. Magnitude 5.0, felt from Ontario to Virginia. Epicenter 30 miles northeast of Cleveland, OH.

7/12/1986, St. Marys, OH. Magnitude 4.5, felt through parts of Ohio, Kentucky, Indiana, and Michigan.

6/10/1987, Lawrenceville, IL. Magnitude 5.0, shook parts of 16 states—Missouri to South Carolina to Canada. No serious injuries or damage.

9/6/1988, Sharpsburg, KY. Magnitude 4.5, no damages.

10/4/1988, Lawrenceville, IL. Magnitude 3.5, shook Southeastern Illinois and Southwestern Indiana.

Earthquakes with epicenter in Ohio, magnitude 2.0 or greater, 1980–2007, are grouped as follows:

1980–1989. 27 quakes, magnitude 2.0 to 5.0

1990–1999. 31 quakes, magnitude 2.0 to 3.6

2000–2007. 54 quakes, magnitude 2.0 to 4.5

January 1, 2008. a magnitude 3.1 quake occurred, epicenter at Lakeline, Ohio

Earthquakes with epicenter in Illinois, magnitude 2.4 or greater, 1962–1988, are grouped as follows:

1962–1969. 16 quakes, magnitude 2.7 to 5.5

1970–1978. 11 quakes, magnitude 2.4 to 4.4

1980–1988. 17 quakes, magnitude 3.0 to 5.1

April 18–25, 2008. 16 earthquakes (magnitude 2.1 to 5.2) occurred in Southeastern Illinois. Epicenters were at Bellmont, 12 quakes with magnitude 2.1 to 3.7; Mt. Carmel, 3 quakes with magnitude 2.1 to 5.2; and one quake with magnitude 5.2 at West Salem.

January 1, 2008. a magnitude 2.5 quake occurred. Its epicenter was Blandville, Kentucky.

A Different Kind of Earthquake Rearranged Mid-America
The three major shocks in the New Madrid, Missouri, series of earthquakes are the largest, most severe shocks anywhere on record. Suddenly, without any warning at 2:15 a.m., December 16, 1811, the first shock occurred (magnitude 8.6); at 9:00 a.m., January 23, 1812, the second shock (magnitude 8.4); and at 3:45 a.m., February 7, 1812, the third shock (magnitude 8.8).

As usual in major earthquakes, there were many intervening shocks that were less severe but only when looked at in light of the three major shocks. These earthquakes were gigantic disturbances that caused major topographic changes over an area of fifty thousand square miles (the size of New York State) and strongly shook an area of more than one million square miles.

Shocks were felt over two-thirds of North America. Shaking was recorded in New Orleans, Boston, New York, Colorado, Montana, and northern Canada. Repeated strong shocks rocked Louisville, Kentucky, two hundred miles away. In Cincinnati, Ohio, four hundred miles distant, the shocks toppled chimneys.

In Washington, DC, eight hundred miles away, the shocks awakened sleepers, rattled dishes and windows, stressed walls until they emitted cracking sounds, and rocked buggies and wagons in the streets. A whole region sank three to nine feet in the area of greatest destruction, extending from Cairo, Illinois, 150 miles south to Memphis, Tennessee, and from Chickasaw Bluffs in Tennessee 40 miles west to Crowley Ridge in Arkansas. Mississippi River water rushed into the great depression.

The Earth Looked Like Ocean Waves

The ground rose and fell as earth waves, like swells of the ocean, passed across the ground surface, tilting huge old-growth trees, interlocking branches, and opening up the soil in deep cracks. Landslides swept down the steeper slopes. Along the Mississippi River the shocks crumbled banks at numerous places, and what the tremors did not dislodge, the large waves sweeping the river did. The great waves on the river swamped many boats and washed others ashore. Whole islands disappeared, and new islands appeared where none existed before.

Severe Shocks for a Year and a Half

For forty-eight hours, December 16 and December 17, 1811, the shocks continued at rather short intervals, gradually diminishing in intensity. They occurred sporadically until January 23, 1812, when there was a second severe shock almost as intense as the first.

On February 7, after two weeks of virtually no shocks, there were several tremendous upheavals greater than the initial shock of December 16. For several days, the earth was in constant tremor, and for a full year, smaller shocks occurred at intervals then gradually died out.

Record keeping at that time was so unsystematic that the total number of shocks was not counted and recorded. One observer in Louisville, Kentucky, actually counted and recorded more than 250 shocks before giving up.

An exhaustive study of the available eyewitness reports and written records was made in the 1970s and 1980s by a University of Kentucky geology professor. He estimates 1,900 shocks were strong enough to be felt 200 miles away in Louisville, eight of them violent shocks.

Fissuring and Flooding

The most spectacular physical changes were local depressions 20–30 miles long by 4–5 miles wide, some of them flooded. Two of these are large—Reelfoot Lake in Tennessee and St. Francis Lake in Arkansas—and popular with fishermen today. The flexing and waving of the earth surface broke the earth open in great fissures, and some of these also filled with water.

Rumbling, Whistling, Eerie Noises

There was rumbling due to shifting of the soil and the deeply buried bedrock layers. As water and sand gushed up through cracks and holes in the ground, they pushed out air and other gas that whistled and made eerie noises. Along the Mississippi River and its tributaries, as cracks opened in the earth they quickly flooded, and as they closed again, the water spewed like a geyser high into the air with large volumes of sand, mud, and gas.

A witness on horseback observing the sand blows and geysers reported: "*There was a blowing up of the earth with loud explosions. It rushed out in all quarters bringing with it an enormous quantity of carbonized wood, reduced mostly to dust which was ejected to a height of from 10 to 15 ft., and fell in a black shower mixed with the sand which its rapid motion had forced along.*"

Pollution and Changed Land Features

Another observer wrote: "*The sulphurated gasses that were discharged during the shock tainted the air with their noxious effluvia and so strongly impregnated the water of the river to a distance of 150 miles below that it could hardly be used for any purpose for a number of days. Many hundreds if not thousands of acres of land were made useless by deposits of sand spewed out that flowed over the land, thus destroying the trees and covering the fertile topsoil. These are referred to as sand scatters. The sand is in some places up to five feet in thickness but generally only one or two feet.*"

Not only did the earth cave in, but also it heaved up in domed areas. These domes, some fifteen miles wide and twenty feet high, formed islands or uplifted land, formerly in the flood plains, to new high and dry levels.

Human Lives Lost?

The total number of lives lost is not known. The population in the area was small and widely dispersed. Records show at least half a dozen known dead, but the figure very well could have been one hundred or more, especially since many Indians lived in the area. Many deaths could have gone unnoticed because of the catastrophic nature of the shocks.

Undoubtedly, there would have been more fatalities if the buildings had been built with stone, brick, and plaster. Fortunately, the buildings were largely log and wood frame and more or less rolled with the shocks, rather than crumbling around their inhabitants and crushing them.

What Caused the New Madrid Earthquakes?

The truth is: nobody knows the answer for certain. Some experts claim they were caused by volcanic activity. Others maintain they were caused by imbalance of earth forces due to sand and gravel deposits from the last ice age.

It is most probable that some combination of several complex factors was the cause. During the four and a half months from December 2, 1811, to April 26, 1812, New Madrid was the epicenter for thirty-six shocks that took place sixteen thousand to fifty thousand feet below ground.

Firsthand Account of a Voyage Down the Mississippi River

April 1, 1812
Mississippi River

Dear Aunt:

About the first of March last I received a letter from you, and omitted answering it until now, which was, not occasioned, or owing to negligence, but because I thought the intelligence I would have to give, if I wrote truly, would occasion you some little uneasiness, as at that time I was engaged in making preparations to make a voyage to New Orleans and am now so far on my way. Last winter I entered into a copartnership with Joseph Hough, of Hamilton (Ohio) with the intention of carrying on the business of merchandizing; we purchased a quality of flour and whisky in the Miami country and located two flat boats on the Miami river which we have brought out of that stream and are thus far on our voyage. When we go to New Orleans, we shall sell our cargo, go round by sea to Philadelphia, and purchase goods and return them to Hamilton (Ohio).

As you no doubt heard very alarming accounts about the earthquake and other dangers of descending the Mississippi River, I suppose you would have looked upon me as going to certain destruction. Thank kind Providence, I think we have now passed those dangers, and if some untoward accident does not overtake us shall pass safely to New Orleans and if flour bears the price, which I understand it does, we shall make something very handsome. Our cargoes consists of seven hundred barrels of flour and some whisky and pork which we purchased in the Miami country on very reasonable terms, as the reports prevailing of the angers to be encountered from the Indians and the Earthquakes had so much frightened the people that none would venture to encounter them. These stories I consider improbable but have since found too much reality to exist in them, particularly those relating to the earthquakes.

I shall give you some little account of what I saw and experienced, although it must be a very cursory account, as I was only on shore at certain points, and then but a short distance from the river. The following is extracted from the journal which I kept.

Soon after entering the Mississippi River, we began to discover the effects of the earthquake—the region of which we were now approaching. Above New Madrid (Missouri) on the west side of the river is a grove of cotton wood and willow trees two or three miles long, these were all bent up stream and stripped of their leaves and branches in a singular manner, it is said that at the time of the violent shock the river at this place for some time ran up stream with great velocity, and from the appearance I have no doubt of the fact, as I know of nothing else that could have produced the appearance here exhibited—we were now experiencing considerable shocks every few hours.

We passed New Madrid in the afternoon, intending to land before night. Mr. Hough had command of one boat and myself of the other, we each steered our own boat and had only two other hands on each boat to row. Mr. Hough, who was rowing to shore to land on the west side of the river, discovering that the landing place would be a crit-

ical situation, by signs motioned me to keep out. I immediately turned my boat and rowed for the middle of the river again; I made every effort to land on the other shore but was unable; at dark I made a willow-island in the river and fastened to the willows, where we remained all night in a very exposed situation. The island was all overflowed but barely sufficient where we lay to float our boat which drew somewhat over three feet of water. The river was falling and myself and hands were obliged frequently during the night to jump overboard into the water, cold as it was, to push off the boat and prevent her getting fast aground. As soon as day dawned, we put off from our dangerous harbor, in a dull rainy morning and at ten o'clock landed at the Little Prairie (now Hayti, Missouri) about thirty miles below New Madrid. Here had been a small village of some twenty houses and a settlement extending back six or eight miles from the river, principally French and Spaniards. On landing, we soon discovered that the place where we moored had been part of the town, now the bed of the Mississippi River. A considerable portion, several acres, on which part of the town had stood, had sunk down with the buildings and the river flowed over the place. The place where we made fast our boat was a burying ground, part had sunk into the river, and coffins were exposed along the bank. The tenants had been Roman Catholics, as the cross was erect at the head of each grave. A large cross made of strong cypress wood placed, no doubt, at the grave of some pious Christian, was broken and prostrated to the earth. Although it rained considerably, after securing our boat, I wrapped myself in my great coat and went on shore to see what discoveries I could make. Of about a dozen houses and cabins which I saw, not one was standing, all was either entirely prostrated or nearly overturned and wrecked in a miserable manner; the surface of the ground cracked and fractured in every direction. At the back part of the village, I found three Frenchmen who were sheltering themselves in a temporary booth of boards taken from some of the desolate houses. They informed me in broken English that the beautiful village and settlement was now wholly destroyed. The inhabitants had fled with what property they could take with them. They and only they were left to tell the passing stranger of the melancholy fate of the place. I continued my excursion about two miles back from the river, although it was with considerably difficulty, and at every step witnessed some new phenomenon of the desolating effects of the Earthquake.

The surface of the ground was cracked in almost every direction and stood like yawning gulphs, so wide that I could scarcely leap over them, at other places I came to spaces of ground several poles in width, sunk down two or three feet below the common level of the ground. But what particularly attracted my attention were circular holes in the earth from five or six to thirty feet in diameter, the depth corresponding with the diameter so as to be about half as deep as wide, and surrounded by a circle of sand two or three feet deep, and a black substance like stone coal but lighter, probably carbonized wood, I took some pieces of this to the boat, and putting them on the fire I found they would burn, at the same time producing a strong and disagreeable sulphurous smell. The holes I presume must have been produced by a strong current of air issuing from the bowels of the earth, throwing up sand and water and this black substance which was perhaps wood, long imbedded in the earth prostrating the trees and everything else where they happened and producing the most horrible disorder. I observed in several instances where small explosions had occurred under large trees, that the trunk of the tree was split up ten or twelve feet and separated two or three feet at the ground and thus remained standing. The day was dark and gloomy with little light; I heard and felt from time to time the rumbling noise of these explosions; all nature around me had the most melancholy appearance. A sudden dread came over me all at once and I returned to the boat. I lay at Little Prairie until the afternoon of the next day during which time we experienced eight or ten shocks, some of them so severe as to shake from their places loose articles on the boat. Each shock continued about two minutes and was preceded by a rumbling noise like thunder or the discharge of a cannon at a great distance. We experienced slight shocks at intervals for the distance of one hundred miles above and below Little Prairie. The shores of the river in this region presented the most melancholy spectacle, the banks cracked and fractured, trees broken off and fractured, and in many places acres of ground sunk down so that the tops of the trees just appeared above the surface of the water. All nature appeared in ruins and seemed to mourn in solitude over her melancholy fate.

In the afternoon the next day, Mr. Hough, with the other boat, made his appearance. The place where we had to land was in the head of an outlet so far down that he was unable to put out and gain the channel of the river again from that place, but the next day with great labor and the aid of some friendly Indians, who came along, they towed the boat some twenty or thirty rods up stream, from whence they were able to regain the channel.

I am now lying at shore on the bank of the Mississippi River, I suppose about 100 miles above Natchez (Mississippi). *Yesterday, a violent storm compelled us to land here, it continued all night so violent as to require us to be up to prevent waves from washing our boats on shore. The high wind still continues today and the river so rough that we cannot pursue our voyage. I therefore devote the day to writing you this letter intending to put it in the Post-Office when I arrive at Natchez. You may suppose that I am not in a very comfortable situation for writing, nor do I feel in a mood for writing after the fatigue I have undergone. I have brought a boat loaded with 350 barrels of flour from the Miami to this place with only two hands; labor, watching, and anxiety have at times reduced me to almost exhaustion. Dear Aunt, your affectionate Nephew*

James McBride

Trees Are Important for Nature's Pollinators

February 10, 2016

You may be asking yourself, "Who or what are pollinators, and why should I care?" Many species of insects and even some vertebrates are pollinators. Insects include—but aren't limited to—honey bees, native bumble bees, bee flies, pollen wasps, ants, butterflies, moths, and beetles. Vertebrates are mainly bats and birds but aren't limited to these only. However, honeybees are the number 1 pollinators in the United States.

Important pollinators such as honey bees, bumble bees, and monarch butterflies have gained much attention in recent years due to concerns about declining populations. Pollinators are currently facing many threats, such as lack of nectar and pollen, pests, disease causing bacteria or fungi, pesticides, invasive plants, climate change, and lack of suitable nesting sites.

Pollination is the movement of pollen from the male part (stamen) of one flower to the female part (pistil) of another flower. Without pollination, most plants can't make seeds and fruits. Many plants are wind-pollinated, including most grains such as corn and wheat, but other plants rely on animals to carry pollen from flower to flower.

Animal pollinators are essential to the food we eat. It's estimated that one in three bites of food we take can be traced back to the role of animal pollinators. A 2012 study by Cornell University estimates that bees and other insect pollinators contribute twenty billion dollars annually to U.S. farm income by pollinating fifty-eight crops, including almonds, apples, oranges, walnuts, berries, and squash.

In addition to their role on farms and in gardens, pollinators are essential to the survival of native plants. Approximately seventy-five percent of all plants depend on animal pollinators to move pollen from plant to plant.

Without the work of pollinators, many native plants couldn't produce seeds to insure the plant's next generation. These seeds and the fruit that often accompany them also provide important food sources for about twenty-five percent of birds and many mammal species.

Many people today are concerned about the health and survival of bees, including honey bees, native bumble bees, and the hundreds of lesser-known native and wild bees that call the U.S. home. Bees are considered the most important group of pollinators because they are uniquely adapted to gather and transport pollen. Bees' fuzzy bodies and branched hairs help female bees collect pollen into special structures, such as pollen baskets on the hind legs or long hairs on legs of the abdomen. Bees rely on flowers to feed their young, so they actively seek out and visit flowers. Flowering plants provide nectar and pollen for a bee's diet.

Pollen is an essential source of protein for developing bee larvae, and nectar provides a carbohydrate source. Honey bees convert nectar into honey by adding an enzyme that breaks down the complex sugars into simple sugars. Bees, in turn, transport pollen from flower to flower as they gather food, allowing for plant fertilization and the production of seeds and fruit.

Flowers also provide shelter and gathering places for pollinating insects. Flowers depend on repeat visits by pollinators, so they may offer small rewards repeated at regular intervals to encourage return trips. To attract visitors, flowers use a variety of strategies, including petal color, scent, ultraviolet light patterns, and nectar guides (lines and marks on petals to direct pollinators to a reward). Bees in particular use floral qualities such as polarized light patterns, petal texture, temperature, humidity, and static charge to help them locate flowers.

Bees typically visit one or only a few flowering species during each feeding trip, even when other flowers are available, a behavior called flower fidelity. Bees also feed close to their nesting sites, less than one-half mile, a practice called central place feeding. These practices make bees especially reliable couriers to move pollen to receptive flowers.

While trees provide many well-known ecological benefits, the importance of trees as a source of food for bees often is overlooked. When in bloom, a large tree can provide hundreds of thousands of nectar- and pollen-filled flowers. Because a tree's flowers are often high up in the canopy out of view, the thousands of insects visiting these flowers are rarely noticed.

Early-blooming trees such as maples, willows, redbuds, and dogwoods provide food at an especially critical time. In March and April, queen bumble bees are establishing new colonies at a time when few other flowers are in bloom.

Feeding honey bees take advantage of tree flowers in early spring to bring food back to the growing hive, which may be short on stored food after a long winter. Later in the spring, black locust and tulip trees provide a rich source of nectar, just as the hive's demand for food increases. For honey bees, honey stored during this period of "honey flow" is crucial to build the hive and ensure the health of the colony through the following winter.

Besides providing an essential source of food for pollinators, trees also provide important nesting and overwintering habitat. Bees that nest in cavities make their nests in the pith of twigs of elderberry and sumac trees or in abandoned beetle borrows in dead trees.

Brush piles, dead standing trees, and fallen wood provide important nesting and overwintering habitat for bees and butterflies. Bare soil can provide habitat for ground-nesting solitary bees such as mining bees or sweat bees commonly on south-facing slopes.

Key trees for bees are listed below. Even though some of the listed trees are wind pollinated, they still provide important pollen resources for bees. Maple, Boxelder, Honey Locust, Buckeye, Horse chestnut, Tulip Poplar, Alder, Magnolia, Serviceberry, Crab apple, Catalpa, Black gum, Hackberry, Sourwood, Red Bud, Wild Cherry, Dogwood, Hop tree, Yellow Wood, Oak, Hazelnut, Black locust, Hawthorn, Willow, Persimmon, Sassafras, Ash, Basswood, Linden, and Elm.

Just the Birds, the
Fish, and Me

August 28, 1983

Little Abitibi Lake, Northeast Ontario, Canada

This remote place is a 455-mile drive north from Toronto, partly on Kings Highway and partly on TransCanada Highway, through Barrie, Orillia, Huntsville, North Bay, Temagami, Kenogami Lake, and Porquis Junction to Cochrane, Ontario. The Canadian National railroad extends west from Quebec through Cochran, then another 130 miles through Kapukasing to Hearst.

Cochrane is 185 miles south from Moosonee and Moose Factory, which is located at the mouth of Moose River in James Bay, and which is accessed from the south only by railroad, the Polar Bear Express, north out of Cochrane. Valeska and I took this all-day trip. Located in Cochrane is an amazingly wonderful Chinese restaurant, the Mandarin, with top-notch servings. When driving anywhere in Canada, even in the most remote smallest village, there will always be a Chinese restaurant serving absolutely delicious food.

Drive about twenty miles east from Cochrane on Provincial Road 652, five miles short of its very end, the end of pavement, then north through wilderness roughly twenty-five miles on an (unnamed), really winding, gravel and dirt road to the (unmarked) Abitibi River. Canoe downstream (generally southward) a mile or so through thick, dense vegetation hanging over the very narrow river, to the northern tip of Little Abitibi Lake, which is located twenty miles (straight-line distance) west from the Ontario/Quebec borderline.

*****

A rare and beautiful sight greets me on the lake this morning, August 18, and the sun's shining in a clear blue sky. It's still a chilly 58 degrees at 8:00 a.m., as it has been every day, but the sunlight alone is enough to make a little multicolored forest of mushrooms near our campsite shrivel in horror.

This part of North America, my world, has seen nothing but rain for most of July and all August until today. It has rained every day, including today beginning about 9:30 a.m., sometimes without ceasing all day and then all the next day and the next since our arrival four days ago. When large mushrooms begin erupting overnight through a carpet of weeds, you know you've had rain.

This bad weather is superb for those who fish: loons, bald eagles, gulls, mallards, otters, minks, and me, a lone creature bundled in fleece and foul-weather gear holding a rod-and-reel. When I choose to endure the raw conditions and get out on the water, I catch some ravenous smallmouth bass, walleye and northern pike, each four to eight pounds or more. Nevertheless, I'm clearly outclassed by those other animals fishing with wings.

On these cold, dismal days when a gloomy and dark mass of clouds oozes rain onto a flat lake that's as still as death, the beautiful swimmers—glistening, red-eyed loons—own the water. Above them, bald eagles circle, ready to dive at full speed to the water surface for fish; gulls cruise above or floating on the lake's surface, waiting for action to come their way; mallards paddle in flocks of ten to fifteen, dipping or diving near shore for vegetation and insects.

There are no fishermen other than me, no other shoreline camps, human sounds or nonnatural sounds. With our campsite barely visible in the mist, I'm alone in a place of my choice. Nothing from my position two hundred yards from shore would've appeared different anytime during the past hundred years, only the modern Old Town Canoe in which I'm perched.

By closely watching the fishing birds, I locate a lake-bottom bedrock outcropping that should produce a smallmouth bass. Five adult loons and two youngsters are close. I always avoid casting when loons are nearby.

Loons dive very deep and travel underwater amazing distances, aided by their strong legs and webbed feet situated near the rear of their bodies, and have the remarkable ability to stay underwater for as long as two minutes. A loon that disappears from view on one side of my canoe can pop-up a hundred feet or more on the other side.

During this strange summer that has been shipped-in from someplace still farther north, the normally shy loons have been extraordinarily bold. On this day, I am treated to the thrill of a gorgeous, hefty, yard-long unfamiliar kind of bird surfacing only a few yards away. Its large, round red eyes seemed to regard me critically—*"I fish to live. You fish to what?"*

Chatter from above interrupted my imaginary conversation with that huge bird as two bald eagles that rarely fish in matrimonial pairs were communicating (chip, chip, chip, yewk, yewk) while circling above and staring down at the water. One drifted lower and lower then abruptly dived straight for the water, wings folded back, turning upward at the last second. It hit the water feet first with a huge splash that resounded in the stillness, rising with a fish clasped in its talons.

When other bald eagles that nest near Little Abitibi Lake joined together in an avian fishing tournament, I decided it was time to mosey, easing through rocky narrows to another spot that even on sunny days has about it an air of loneliness and mystery. Thick stands of huge pines, oaks, and other tree species are everywhere along the shore. In today's misty gloom, this small part of the lake seems especially eerie.

Yet another collection of loons is nearby but not so close as to be endangered by the hook on my lure. I cast into a feeding cover typical for smallmouth bass, using a five-inch purple rubber worm with emerald flake.

One of the adult loons raised its head, opened its black, dagger-like beak and emitted its famous aaaWHAAhaooo, its voice catching at the beginning of each distinct note; the ghostly cry echoing in the brooding depths of the surrounding forest. I felt like a visitor in primeval surroundings. The frightened loons then began their characteristic cackling over-and-over, again-and-again, which causes uncontrollable human laughter. Valeska also heard them over at our campsite and said she too couldn't stop laughing.

An urgent tap-tap-tap and pull on my line rudely summoned me from my amusing reverie. What's this? A fish! Quickly, I jerked the rod over my right shoulder to set the hook on a huge smallmouth that leaped twice above the water surface as I reeled it in then swam in circles with tremendous pull. It dashed for the front of the canoe, dived under the canoe, wrapped my line around something, I'll never know what, and won the battle. I cut the line and headed for camp.

As I paddled back through the rocky narrows toward camp where Valeska was busy writing letters and reading, I longed for the sun now setting somewhere behind the dark, gloomy clouds. I'm wet, cold, hungry, exhausted, and fishless, but I don't care. It's remote Ontario, and I love it.

We broke camp and quit eating only freeze dry food and fish, returned to the van, and drove back to the tent campground in Cochran. After putting-up a wet tent, for the second time on this trip, we went to Mandarin Restaurant for another delicious Chinese dinner. Valeska and I ordered our meals, started a conversation with another couple sitting at the next table, and in a short time, they joined us at our table.

We told them of our fantastic experience on Little Abitibi Lake and learned that the gentleman was a bush pilot who flew a plane with pontoons. He told us that Little Abitibi Lake is a fly-in destination and that he flies fishermen to a small four-bunk wood shack with barrel stove located on the southern tip, 1-1/2 miles south from where Val and I were camped. He said he'd never seen anyone but his customers on the lake and was amazed that we, being non-natives unfamiliar with the area, had driven to and actually found Abitibi River.

I showed him the small-scale (twenty kilometers to the inch) topographic/road map we'd gotten at the local boat, motor, and canoe rental place. Also I told him there was an old model car already parked alongside the road, which I assumed was another fisherman's car, so we guessed this was the place we wanted to go. He immediately confirmed that we indeed had found Abitibi River and Little Abitibi Lake.

The pilot said the old model car had been parked at that spot for more than a year and that he'd flown over and seen it parked there many times. He suspected it probably was left there by the Indian family, natives of the Canada bush, living several miles to the east.

This one-time experience of being secluded in the northern Canada bush, although we learned later was very risky—lots of bears—is one that Val and I shall never, ever forget.

How to Prevent
Forest Wildfires

January 22, 2019

Owning a forest since 1970, having it certified as a private forest and wildlife preserve by the state of Indiana in the early 1980s, and living in the middle of it since 1999, I have become an active participant in scientific forest management and preservation. Politicians say that the rising incidence of catastrophic wildfires in California is "the new normal." Wrong!

The experience in 2018 is neither new nor abnormal. It is, in fact, the old normal. The devastation that unfolded is how nature manages forests. Like an untended garden, an abandoned forest will grow until it chokes itself to death. Nature deals with such overcrowding through fatal epidemic diseases, drought, and ultimately catastrophic wildfire.

Geologists studying charcoal deposits in California estimate that prehistoric wildfires destroyed between 4.5 million and 11.9 million acres a year. When Juan Cabrillo dropped anchor in San Pedro Bay in October 1542 (the height of the Santa Ana fire season), he named it the "Bay of Smoke."

Our modern sensibilities were staggered at the devastation of the Camp Fire, which incinerated 153,000 acres, wiped-out the entire town of Paradise, and claimed at least 86 lives. Yet in 1910, the "Big Bum" in Idaho and Montana consumed three million acres, wiped-out seven towns, and killed 87 people in a significantly smaller and sparser population.

The U.S. Forest Service had formed only five years earlier, in 1905, driven by scientific breakthroughs in the understanding of forest ecology. The first wave of American conservationists didn't watch helplessly as the cycle of catastrophic overpopulation followed by catastrophic wildfire wiped-out entire forests. Instead, they believed management could keep forests healthy and resilient for generations.

Excess timber comes out of a forest in two ways: it gets carried-out or burned-out. For much of the twentieth century, harvesting excess timber produced thriving forests by matching tree density to the ability of the land to support it. On federal lands, foresters designated surplus trees, and loggers bid at auction for the right to remove them, with the proceeds going to the U.S. Treasury. These revenues were then put back into forest management and shared with local communities.

In the 1970s, Congress passed a series of laws subjecting federal land management to time-consuming and cost-prohibitive environmental regulations. Instead of generating revenues, forest management today costs the government money. As a result, timber harvested from federal lands has declined eighty percent while acreage destroyed by fire has increased eighty percent.

A half-century of environmental regulation hasn't helped the forests thrive. A typical acre in the Sierra can support roughly eighty mature trees, but the current density is more than three hundred trees. A single fully grown tree can draw a hundred gallons of water from the soil on a hot day. Drought kills overcrowded forests quickly.

The environmental Leftists blame climate change. Yet this doesn't explain the dramatic difference between federal land and private forests that practice scientific forest management. The boundary lines can often be seen from the air because of the condition of the forests. It's interesting that the climate decimates only the lands hamstrung by these environmental laws.

Decaying forests or wildfires make a mockery of laws aimed at reducing carbon emissions. Wildfires in the United States pump an estimated 290 tons of carbon dioxide into the air every year. Healthy, growing forests absorb it. Milling surplus trees sequesters their carbon indefinitely and renews the forests ability to store still more.

Today's environmental laws have restored the old normal, making epidemic diseases, drought, and fire a constant source of widespread devastation of our forests. A healthy forest that is maintained and preserved for the enjoyment of future generations is an above normal condition produced by modern forest management. Ironically, in the name of improving the environment, we have surrendered our forests to a policy of neglect, which, as it turns-out, is not favorable.

UPPER PENINSULA MICHIGAN

July 2, 2018

From the summit of 1,327-foot Marquette Mountain, the view is a pleasing mix of natural beauty and industrial power. Dense pine and fir and hemlock forests descend to the red sandstone churches and office buildings of Marquette, the largest town (population 21,355) in the UP.

In Marquette's Upper Harbor of Lake Superior, the massive elevated Presque Isle Ore Dock has 200 pockets, each accommodating 250 tons of iron ore (taconite) pellets that are discharged into the hold of 1,000-foot long cargo ships. Closer to my lofty perch, a bald eagle is plunging toward unseen prey in Lake Superior's cold blue waters.

Marquette offers a remarkable inventory of historic architecture. The Marquette County Courthouse, built in 1904, is where scenes were filmed in the 1959 movie, *Anatomy of a Murder*. Starring Jimmy Stewart, Lee Remick, and Ben Gazarra, the movie was adapted from the 1958 novel of the same title written by the defense attorney in the case on which the book is based.

UP residents call themselves "Yoopers." Those living in Marquette experienced a record 319 inches of snow in 1989. Even in July and August, when daylight stretches past 10:00 p.m., Lake Superior breezes average below eighty degrees with humidity readings usually thirty to seventy percent. The big sky sunsets are special.

Restaurants are packed with patrons enjoying Lake Superior whitefish, lake trout, and Coho salmon.

Pasties (pronounced pass-tees) make great picnic lunches eaten lakeside on Presque Isle. They are delicious Finnish turnovers stuffed with beef, potato, onions, rutabaga, and brown gravy poured over the top. Jean Kay's Pasties, Marquette, are the absolute best. The best ice cream, by far, anywhere in America, is found at Jilbert's Dairy in Marquette.

The UP, a picturesque region of wonderful unspoiled forests and wilderness, has been the summer playground for many Midwesterners for more than a century. This began in the very early 1900s and included Henry Ford, Thomas Edison, Louis Graveraet Kaufman, and other famous leaders of industry and commerce.

They each owned huge acreages and created lavish lakeside "cabins," in the northernmost Marquette County area of the Huron Mountains, which rivaled the Adirondack "camps" of the Eastern Seaboard elite. By the mid-twenty-first century heyday of the American automobile, Detroit assembly-line workers as well were flocking to the UP.

With Lake Superior to the north, Lake Michigan to the south, and Lake Huron to the east, the UP covers 16,542 square miles (29 percent of Michigan's total landmass). The UP land area is larger than Massachusetts, Connecticut, Rhode Island, and Delaware combined.

Since 1957, the upper and lower peninsulas have been connected by the five-mile long Mackinac suspension bridge. Almost half of the UP's southern border is shared with Wisconsin. The north abutment of the bridge is in the UP in St. Ignace, from which a passenger boat departs every half hour for magnificent Mackinac Island where the only form of transportation is by horse-drawn carriages or bikes.

Only 302,037 people (0.03 percent of Michigan's 9.99-million residents) live amid the UP's woodlands, waterfalls, and trout streams. Ernest Hemingway, who trout fished in the UP as a boy and young man, paid reverence to the region in a 1925 Nick Adams short story: "Big Two-Hearted River." "He stepped into the stream," Hemingway wrote. "His trousers clung tight to his legs, his shoes felt the gravel. The water was a rising cold shock."

Particularly enjoyable is the scenic stretch along Lake Superior, between the ship locks (operated by gravitational forces only) in Sault Ste. Marie on the east, westward 265 miles to the lonely crescent beaches of the Keweenaw Peninsula. Looming on the horizon is Lake Superior, an inland sea, despite its fresh water; so huge it holds more water than the other Great Lakes combined and is 1,600 feet at its deepest.

Tahquamenon Falls is the site of two cascades that disgorge fifty thousand gallons of water per second, putting them behind only Niagara in volume among waterfalls east of the Mississippi River. The Upper Falls, surrounded by one of the UP's last remaining old-growth forests, features a fifty-foot drop.

The Native American Ojibwa tribe called Lake Superior "Gitchigami" (meaning "big water"). It was memorialized in Henry Wadsworth Longfellow's epic poem, "The Song of Hiawatha." The first of ten verses follows *By the shores of Gitchie Gumee, by the shining Big-Sea-Water, Stood the wigwam of Nokomis, daughter of the Moon, Nakomis. Dark behind it rose the forest, rose the black and gloomy pine-trees, Rose the firs with cones upon them; bright before it beat the water, Beat the clear and sunny water, beat the shinning Big-Sea-Water.* Longfellow's inspiration for the poem is the scenic Pictured Rocks National Lakeshore that stretches for fifty miles east from the town of Munising to Grand Marias.

Movement of continental glaciers shaped Lake Superior ten thousand years ago, and wind and water continue to mold its shore-line. Some cliffs are shaped like ship hulls jutting into the lake, and crashing waves have carved caverns into others.

The Pictured Rocks are like giant freshly painted abstract works of art. There are a few cliff formations elsewhere along the shoreline but nothing as big or with as many colors. Hundreds of large and small waterfalls and springs splash down the cliffs, reacting with minerals in the sandstone to create a palette of colors—browns and reds from iron, blues and greens from copper, and black from manganese.

Michigan's northernmost point is at Copper Harbor, situated on the northern tip of the Keweenaw Peninsula. The 1,328-foot Brockway Mountain offers a breathtaking view of both Copper Harbor and Lake Superior. It's a four-hour voyage via the Isle Royale Queen IV from Copper Harbor to Isle Royale National Park near the United States/Canada boundary.

The UP's sprawling wilderness has remained intact over the many years. Visitors are awed by its untrammeled beauty. Sand and pebbles and driftwood cover the lakeshores, mayflies rise and drift like thistledown, and forests are filled with the hum of bees and the pink of milkweed flower clusters.

Many tourists are reluctant even to glance at their map while driving for fear of missing a sight, whether small or spectacular. Everywhere tourists feel far away from cities and twenty-first century civilization.

Confessions of a Laid-Back Piscatorial Addict

December 2005

A quarter of the way into 1999, I woke-up to find myself retired and relocated to my southeast Indiana "Heaven;" an old forest of mature hardwoods with a very high and dense canopy, essentially no undergrowth, and lake in the center. I had torn-off my engineer and geologist mask of professional accomplishment and satisfaction, closed the Louisville branch, and fled my Cincinnati office to my own Forest Preserve and Wildlife Habitat in southeast Indiana.

My physical condition of poopitude—the price of overripe maturity and departure from the twenty-four-carat fast lane professional quality life—had vanished. I was enjoying a sense of peace and tranquility and taking in some of the purest oxygen I've ever had, with the sweet aroma of spring wildflowers, in a forest that few will ever experience to the fullest.

Never again would I have to waste another day by having to dress-up in the morning and go to the office, instead of being in my forest or practicing the piscatorial arts fishing in my lake. I was overcome by a sudden sense of remoteness and solitude where humankind and wildlife mingle with the uneasy feeling that we, two- and four-footed alike, are but fleeting pauses in the immeasurable unraveling of time.

Since fleeing the baying hounds of success, I've become reclusive while resuming reading and writing in a place of solitude without loneliness. I now live my life with purpose and meaning beyond that when consumed by my profession.

To spend my remaining life in my own way is the only true measure of success. Thoreau was right when he said, "The tonic of wildness is crucial to our health and happiness." Any man is fulfilled who knows the value of companionship and solitude and who is at peace with himself and the world around him.

I've learned not to be bound by limits I place upon myself. It's only when I reach beyond what I think I can do that I almost surely do far more than I thought I could. I have also learned that numbers are like people; torture them enough, and they'll tell you anything.

Most inspiration for my thoughts comes when I'm alone with my two Australian shepherds walking and yodeling in the forest, four miles each day, or in the boat fishing. It's like an intimate relationship. If another person is with us, it's a distraction. Dogs are the only living beings that have found and recognize an unquestionable, tangible, absolute, and definite god—the human.

Dogs know to whom they must devote the best of themselves. They have no need to seek a more perfect, superior, or infinite power. My dogs are my protection against life's insults, a defense against the world and the somewhat vain conviction of being truly loved and less alone.

As a geologist at age twenty-three, I ceded the town of my birth to the U.S. Geological Survey office, and as an engineer at age twenty-eight, to Eddie Hannan and to Hunter Martin, both of whom had taken it over anyway and later to Bobby Florence when he came of age. They each ruled it well, and I have no complaints.

During my professional career, I staked out a claim in several other places, and I'm glad that they have been jumped. My best claim is the tristate area of southwest Ohio, northern Kentucky, and southeast Indiana.

Many Americans are serious anglers, constantly casting ahead the lure-of-expectation, hoping to hook a piece of the future, and something unimaginable takes the lure. I became a serious piscator in a moment of midlife irresponsibility about three years after my lake had filled to the principal spillway level and was stocked with fish in early 1972.

I fish now because I suspect that I'm going this way for the last time and don't want to waste the trip as the innumerable trees around my lakeshore take special delight in parting me with my favorite flies and lures. 'Tis better to have lured and lost than never to have lured at all.

I sit in silence and take in everything going on around me, the lapping of waves against the boat, rustling of leaves on the shore, a breeze that blunts the bite of a sun that would thaw the heart of an IRS auditor, my two canine buddies asleep and snoring—Rascal on the front bench seat and Samantha in the bottom of the boat. To paraphrase another patriot, I regret that I have but one life to give to fishing.

The more I prowl the forest and fish with my four-leg companions, the more I realize how little we humans really know about the planet we vainly believe was made for us to tinker with and to plunder. Humans are complex beings: we make deserts bloom and lakes die. To destroy seems to be the strongest instinct of many non-native Americans.

Many Americans seek to conquer nature, to bend her to their will, and to use her wastefully until she is virtually destroyed, then they simply move on, leaving the waste behind them, looking for new places to conquer. They're like monsters, always hungry, and what they eat is land.

The fact is, most human forms possess a positive genius for not knowing what in heaven's name they're doing when dealing with the earth and natural terrain. Their actions, to improperly develop or rape natural terrain, ruin it for all those who knew the terrain before it was spoiled.

The result is an imbalance of natural forces, left for future generations to rebalance as much as possible. "Environmental compatibility" considerations today are a low-to-no priority in peoples' minds and actions.

Humans must remember that nature possesses her own rhythms—the kind of movement characterized by regular recurrence of strong and weak elements—and we must follow those rhythms, not try to dominate them. Earth is a plastic solid and the product of complicated geologic, hydrologic, climatic, and other ongoing natural processes.

This fundamental and dynamic character of nature must always be taken into account so that the works of mankind fit as harmoniously as possible into the environment and do not disturb nature's equilibrium any more than necessary. To conserve the productive power of a land area or lake, urban or rural, for the use of future generations is an essential requirement, and one that must guide all human workings.

We don't inherit the earth from our parents. We borrow it from our children. Nature to be commanded must be obeyed. In order to be obeyed, nature must first be understood. Our country is poised on a pinnacle of wealth and power, yet we live in a land of vanishing beauty, increasing ugliness and shrinking open space where the overall environment is diminished daily by pollution, blight, and noise.

It seems this is a brief description of our present conservation crisis. It's odd that modern civilization seems to have given up believing in the devil when modern civilization itself is the only explanation for it. As a member and compatriot in the Sons of the American Revolution, the past is my inspiration, the present is my duty, and the future is my hope. Aristocracy is of the soul, not the cloth.

Occasionally, I'll think of my forest as a wilderness and pretend to be lost within it—a temporary state that was permanent to my hardy paternal ancestors from 1650 to the mid-twentieth century. The forest canopy closed over my head makes me feel the presence of a force beyond myself, an intuition shared by everyone who has walked in my forest.

I've learned that when dew is on grass of the crest of my earth dam in the morning, it'll not rain during that day; when it's not there just after darkness, it'll rain before morning. When birds fly low and silently, a storm is coming. When sugar maple leaves turn over to show their underside, thunder and lightning soon will come.

If children and their barking playmates live in the forest, there's no need to worry about them and where they are. Our children's today is all our tomorrows. Discipline is good for their soul, but their heart wants freedom.

Those persons are free who think their own thoughts and set their own course, live by their own standards, and create their own destiny. I give thanks for my many valuable experiences with nature; fleeting glimpses of what life still might be everywhere if it weren't for many American's helpless lust for "progress."

The silent majority in American it seems failed to speak-out while many college campuses were becoming places for alcohol and drug abuse and sexual experimentation, much of which today is known to start even in middle schools and high schools. We pollute the air with profanity and pornography and call it freedom of expression, covet our neighbor's possessions and call it ambition, abuse power and call it politics, don't discipline our children and call it building self-esteem, reward laziness and call it welfare, ridicule the time-honored values of our forefathers and call it enlightenment, exploit the poor and call it the lottery.

Too many colleges today are only **training** students how to work or perform within one or more thematically connected fields of endeavor, the simplistic goal being to obtain a job, instead of **educating** by the intellectual process of seeking truth and knowledge from fact and logic. It's high time our clergy speak loud and clear about moral truths, commitment in marriage, responsibility in parenthood, civility in behavior, refinement in language and pride in appearance, instead of only the love of God.

Many people today, including some congressmen, believe the United States Constitution expressly provides for separation of church and state. Wrong! Read it! It says, "Congress shall make no law respecting an establishment of religion, or prohibiting the free exercise thereof." Where is the word *separate*? Where is the word *church* or *state*?

We humans are not descended from apes. Charles Darwin never claimed we are. This British naturalist's writings have been misconstrued and lampooned since 1859 when his *On the Origin of Species* was published. Read it! Where are the terms "theory" and "evolution?" What Darwin actually said was that the myriad species inhabiting Earth are a result of repeated branching from common ancestors, a process that came to be called "evolution."

The mechanism of evolution, natural selection, determines how plants and animals come to look and behave as they do. "Theory" and "evolution" are two terms misunderstood by the world's general population. Some of the confusion stems from the phrase "theory of evolution," but much of it comes from the words of Clarence Darrow, an American criminal lawyer and social reformer.

When scientists say "theory," they mean a statement based on observation or experimentation that explains facets of the observable world so well that it becomes accepted as fact. They don't mean an idea created out of thin air nor do they mean an unsubstantiated belief. It's interesting to note that John T. Scopes, the schoolteacher convicted in the 1925 Tennessee "Monkey Trial," is buried near the Oak Grove Cemetery entrance, Paducah, Kentucky.

Humans are but one of the many varieties of animals on planet Earth, all which are subject to the same basic laws of science in their struggle for existence and survival of the fittest. In the competition for survival, some humans succeed and some fail because no two are equally endowed by nature and by environment in body, character, and mind.

The constant obscure savagery of nature lurks below the apparent placid surface of things. Lice under the common loon's wings battle each other. Obviously, fish swimming below dwell in a submerged turmoil of cannibalism.

How can mankind hope for peace when combat and strife, not peace and calm, are the norms of nature? Is peace an unnatural state and all the elaborate plans of mankind to achieve it in plain perversion of nature?

Could it be that peaceful humans are unnatural? Such is a rather bleak prospect in these days of terrorism and nuclear proliferation. It seems humans never do evil so completely and cheerfully as when they do it from some religious conviction. There's no place in a fanatic's head where reason can enter.

Fishing, what most people think is a harmless predilection, is an incurable progressive disease, and I'm mired in its terminal stages.

Apparently, I fell on my head when a baby, but it seems to me that any person who would admit a dislike for angling probably would denounce both mother-love and moonlight.

I can understand that a person may not care for golf. But the individual who doesn't like to simultaneously experience nature and outwit fish, in my eyes, is hardly normal. He's supercivilized, and I for one don't know how to deal with him. Nevertheless, since the Lord takes not away from man those hours spent in fishing, I'll live at least 30 more years to be 105.

Piscators scheme, the truth is not always in them, they toss in their sleep, dream of great dripping fish shapely and elusive as mermaids, arise cranky and haggard from their fantasies, complain of a need for fresh unpolluted air, sunshine and relaxation, occasionally have blank expressions, can hear a fish sneeze a half-mile away, occasionally are deaf to the wife, and have little taste for work. Some of them awake in the mornings throbbing of pulse, with tongue transformed into a twice-baked potato, and grope their way to the water faucet for another drink.

Piscators are both cultured and worldly. Their broad and diversified interests make them delightful, even absorbing companions, and they'll talk about anything under the sky so long as it concerns fishing. Spots, speckles, and stripes dance before their very eyes due to their intentness and detachment during seizures.

Not only does their majestic itch goad them on when pursuing their passion but also endlessly spurs them when their time on the water is over, and they're once again back home with feet under the dinner table. The truth is, fishing's as self-indulgent and addictive as would be taking dope. What good then can one say for fishing? Simply this: it's got work beat by miles and is indelicately great fun.

Fishing is essentially a one-on-one pursuit best enjoyed in solitude, one's sense of isolation from the scurrying human-swarm being a large part of the enjoyment. And since I practice the art of piscatorial pursuit most days from mid-March through October while other anglers have to work, I find myself fishing with my two canine buddies.

Scarcely a day passes when I fail to behold a piciform's bucket-size swirl of a rise, *kerplonk*, and seldom a week when I'm not left blinking by being cleaned out, *ping*, absolutely one of the most exciting sounds in all fishing. Keeping my lure in the water is advantageous in this era when flying fish are so scarce, except in some of the more imaginative outdoor magazines—no mistakes, no experience; no experience, no wisdom.

Like most piscators, I'm optimistic and tend to forget my bad days when the fish have lockjaw.

Fishing is the world's only sport that's fun even when you fail. It isn't the quality of the fish that counts, it's the quality of the means used in catching them. The only thing possibly wrong with fishing, as it is when doing nothing, is that you never know when you've finished.

By fishermen, I mean only artificial fly or lure piscators, in case the rumor has gotten around that there are other ways to deceive game fish. Non-fly and non-lure bait-flingers I regard as nothing more that meat-hunting barbarians. By the word *fishermen* I include the ladies, bless their hearts, while clinging to the politically incorrect term not out of chauvinism, honestly, but rather because I tend to throw-up when calling any fisherman a fisherwoman or fisherperson.

I also confine my explanation only to true piscators, excluding alleged fishermen, chronic duffers and beginners, not so much out of compassion but simply to narrow the field. Just what makes one a true fisherman? Freud might have had some theories that would make some folks blush, but since he's unavailable for collaboration, I'll give it a whirl.

I suppose a true fisherman should be able to cast a lure or present a fly without producing a tsunami. Then on the other hand, all of us know habitual tidal wavers who, like fools, test the depth of new water with both feet when wading, will listen not to one spurt of piscatorial wisdom, and who sometimes manage to top the field while hurling old shaving brushes and feathered shoehorns.

It's probable that the fish they catch would have as avidly hit an anvil. The true piscator can only widen his eyes and shrug and raise outstretched arms in the international sign language of defeat.

No two fisherman playing fields ever are alike; even the same water constantly shifts and changes before their eyes.

Fishing is unlike any other sport in the world, indoors or out, all which indeed is an excellent measure of its mystique and charm. Pursuing fish, when done for pleasure and what other reason is there, isn't even remotely related to sports involving athletes or their games.

On those days when I'm skunked, my wife consolingly says the fish all fled together in terror when they recognized my canine pals and me together in the same boat—they know good piscatorial-pursuing partners when they see them. Valeska knows that giving me her advice after suffering such injury to my piscatorial ego would be like giving me medicine after death.

I've owned several expensive so-called name fly rods and spinning rods that turned out to be magnificent buggy whips and tent poles. While most good graphite rods are expensive, without love and care, you can easily wind up owning merely an ornate broomstick.

Ed, a fellow Lions Clubs friend, an alleged fisherman with occasional disposition of a bilious buffalo, uses gear that was around when Stonehenge was still under warranty, a steel casting rod held together by adhesive tape at the joint, a winch for a reel, and an eighty-pound test line tied to a coiled piece of bedspring for a leader, which in turn is attached to a hook big enough to fasten a screen door. He heaves out his harpoons, flails away like a man beating a rug, and sputters "it's c-c-cold!" as he flounders to his feet and falls again in shallow water, threshing and blowing like a beached whale. And above all, in the voice of a Sunday morning TV preacher unveiling his zip code road to salvation, Ed intones he's an avid trout fisherman!

When Ed decided to take up fishing, he and his wife Joanne rented a boat and poles, bought some bait, and went out on a southeast Indiana piscary. After a few minutes, they were in an isolated cove where some small bluegills were biting. They had more than enough fish aboard in an hour and decided to head home.

As he pulled up the anchor, Ed said, "We really should mark this spot so we can come back." Joanne agreed and started to chalk a big X on the bow of the boat. Ed watched in amazement and shouted, "You idiot, how can we be sure we'll get the same boat next time?"

If the bull bluegills in my piscary grew to several pounds, these dripping eruptions of nature would be the ultimate trophy fish. They also would drag me out of the boat and beat the snot out of me. They seem to have a grudge and look at me as if I'd just insulted their mother and sister in the same breath.

For a period of about two weeks in early May each year, really big bluegill nest in six-inch to twelve-inch deep water on the sand beach of my lake. These fish have an attitude, are 8–10" long, 1–2" between the eyes, and turn into 8-pound bass for about 20 seconds when I use wispy fly tackle tipped with a tiny popping bug.

There's a thumping strike that runs up the leader and line into my 9-foot graphite fly-rod, and the fight is slab-sided and tenacious. Their fierce run makes the fly line hiss through much deeper water, leaving behind a tiny wake like a deadly torpedo.

Their fillets are the approximate size of Delaware and a fantastic meal along with hush puppies. A hush puppy, you know, is cornmeal brought to heavenly status. There's as much skill in making good hush puppies as anything ever dreamed up by Julia Childs. Please consult with Valeska on this matter. Bluegill-eating is like finishing off a chocolate sundae by crunching the maraschino cherry. Sorry, but I'm salivating all over the keyboard and the electronics are shorting out and sparking.

On occasions, the huge, shy bottom-dwelling blue channel catfish in my lake are known to take a fly while swimming near the surface for a bit of daylight tanning. The tip of my rod will go down suddenly like a bulldozer is hooked to it, heading straight for the nearest submerged brush pile.

Either I turn that catfish, which is like turning a wild mustang with a lasso made of dental floss, or it dives into the brush and wraps the line around something immovable—another *ping*. Oh, well! Several catfish in my lake are probably still festooned with a fly hook, like underwater punk rockers, bearing a faint white lip scar and a dim memory of an unpleasant time and plotting revenge.

There are some people who equate the hunter and piscator, and I intend to set these folks straight. Since the dawn of mankind, the hunter has gone forth with his slings, bows and arrows, stalked and spied his quarry and then, muttering a prayer to tribal gods, hurled at it a projectile of some sort—a rock, boomerang, poison dart, spear, or steel-nosed bullet. All hunters, ancient and modern, share one thing in common. Once the projectile is released, the hunter controls it not. He either makes a hit or misses it; if the former he's a hero, otherwise a bum.

The quarry the piscator stalks is almost always hidden and unseen. Except for the rising fish he can only hope for, he always pursues the will-o-the-wisp. When he's lucky and gets a strike, he becomes directly and personally engaged with his quarry by a pulsing extension of his arm—hand to rod to line to leader to fly or lure.

Unlike the hunter, the piscator is successful not when he smites a discernable victim that usually is fleeing in terror both the hunter and projectile but infinitely more subtle and deceptive when his unsuspecting quarry eagerly seeks-out and impales itself upon a tasteless fly or lure. The piscator's art is excitement, the hunter's annihilation. If all the hunters in the world were laid end-to-end, some piscators say it probably would be a good thing.

From mid-June through September each year, Valeska and I live in the log home we built in 1990 on the waterfront of an inland lake in the subarctic Lake Superior wilderness of Upper Peninsula, Michigan; home of the Ojibwa and Chippewa Native American tribes. A wrong has been done all Native Americans—a wrong due to white man's greed for land, fueled by ignorance, irresponsibility, and a careless sort of kindness unaccompanied by wisdom.

The UP covers more land area than the states of Massachusetts, Connecticut, Rhode Island, and Delaware combined. Some highway signs read: **End of Earth 2, Marquette County 4**. Many modest cities in the United States have larger populations than the whole UP. This is where prowling young monsters astride 1,000-horse power jet skis "politely" dash in on the crest of their own tidal wave to inquire "How's the fishing?" "Great, 'til you got here, Buster," I plan to respond someday when much older, more frail, wearing glasses, and obviously more unable to defend myself.

Too plentiful also are those assorted outdoor itinerants and tourists who respect not applicable laws of fishing or of watercraft, show no courtesy toward piscators, and thoughtlessly use the pristine cold-water streams and natural lakes as their personal garbage pails and gasoline receptacles. As it is with cobwebs, some such laws snag small flies but allow wasps and hornets to breakthrough.

It's true that few piciform ever were slain by flying beer or cold drink cans and plastic or broken glass bottles, but their gleaming presence in such fishing waters surely spoils the enjoyment and precious illusion of space and solitude and simple pine- and cedar-laden cleanliness. It seems we Americans often willingly forget that privilege and responsibility are two sides of the same coin. Sometimes, methinks some of us descend from hogs.

Simply put, the UP is one of the best hunting and fishing areas anywhere in the United States—a wilderness paradise where, when quietly alone, you're as likely to see a bear or bald eagle as a human. It possesses in great abundance three of nature's noblest creations: brook trout, ruffed grouse, and white-tailed deer; along with three of nature's tastiest creations: coho salmon, lake trout, and walleye.

There are sharp-tailed grouse, rabbits, deer, and black bears galore, as well as excellent brook, rainbow and brown trout fishing, not to mention tourist animals such as moose, gray wolf and beavers, and whitefish, small-mouth bass, muskellunge and assorted stuff like that. These facts, thank heaven, are not yet widely known, although Ernest Hemingway tried with his story *Big Two-Hearted River*.

It would be ironic, and certainly a devastating thought to contemplate, if this writing would help bring about discovery of "Yoopers" and their beloved UP. Yet comfort is taken when I reflect that the people who might find and deflower this beautiful wilderness rarely hold still long enough to read anything such as this epistle.

And I ruefully might add that due to TV, they appear to have developed a particular resistance to reading for pleasure, similar to the manner in which the Michigan state bird, mosquitoes the size of jet fighters, learned to thrive on DDT. Apparently, all these people willingly read are AAA roadmaps and trip tiks, speedometers, odometers, billboards, and signs proclaiming "Kozy Kabins with Lake View 1500 Feet Ahead."

They obediently whiz through all summer long, sightlessly racing along labeled channels of asphalt, focusing only upon traveling five hundred miles per day, an achievement that somehow seems to ease the peculiar nature of their pain. They know not the existence of the true UP. They've never really been there.

And then there's the special art of trout fishing which often involves standing ankle deep to knee deep in rapids of an ice cold stream and the casting of a level line or a weight-forward line with fly at its tip while not impaling your own ear. Part of the charm is that trout, unlike other fish, will respond only to quietude, humility, and endless patience.

Their lateral line detects low frequency vibrations, and their ears are covered by skin, rendering them invisible to the naked human eye. Their eyes are the primary sense for finding food and detecting danger both in and out of water.

Taste and texture are detected in their mouths and objects sensed as nonedible are quickly ejected. A trout's nostrils can detect scents diluted by water to a few parts per million. One thing trout abhor is any piscator who tries to show off and glorify himself at their expense.

This sort of thing they will sense almost instantly by some mysterious telepathy running up through the rod and down the line and leader to the fly. Once this message is flashed, the trout conspire to bring the poor wayward piscator back to humility; either that or to the brink of a nervous breakdown. Ah, the nose-thumbing trout!

My lure casting for Coho and Chinook salmon, bless their pugilistic hearts, takes place while standing on large slick rocks waist deep in the ice-cold tributary or shore waters of Lake Superior. Due partly to the difficulty in maintaining my balance on such treacherous footing, it's probably as close to being a contact sport as there is in fresh water fishing.

Many of the heavyweight Kings (Chinooks) are females full of spawn. The punishing force of their strike takes care of setting the hook and the jolt from their hit, which always is below the belt, almost tears the rod from my hands and puts me on the ropes gasping for breath. While trying to keep the rod tip up as high as possible, the bottom half can be held vertical with much difficulty, but the upper half will be pointing directly at the old girl.

My reel buzzes as she takes off fifty to seventy-five yards of line almost as quickly as it takes to snap a finger, making it a long distance battle while swimming left and right in front of me. Fighting a thirty-pound Chinook salmon, never resting nor letting the fish rest, is comparable to a three-round fight in its requirements for good physical condition, balance, and footwork.

It's in a class with steer bulldogging and other ungentle sports. Salmon respect not the drag of any good reel and, like the pirates of old, probably celebrate with boisterous partying and wild splashing after cleaning my plow and parting me with some of the more valuable instruments used in my particular practice of the piscatorial arts.

On most evenings before retiring, I go out back of our log home in the north woods to my wonderful cedar-lined sauna (pronounced "sow-na") for a much-needed sweat. The Finnish sauna is a testimony to the continuing influence of the UP's early white settlers.

And however much the Finns may have lost over the years of their original culture, they haven't lost the tradition of baking-and-steaming themselves. Neither have they nor I lost faith in that tradition's healing component.

A half-hour in my authentic Finnish sauna will cure any indisposition, including ridding myself of a frustrated ego on those occasional mornings or early evenings when the fish win. I fire up the wood stove to 180 degrees Fahrenheit, put on my birthday suit, sit on the highest wooden bench, douse myself and the hot rocks with water, and await the arrival of some real heat.

It arrives very quickly and then keeps on arriving until the sauna reaches two hundred degrees. Periodically, I'll cool off under my fifty-six-degree well-water shower. Some say it's too hot. I say it's not and will douse the hot rocks with more water for more steam.

A curious thing then happens. I seem to enter a wholly different physical state, one where I find myself totally relaxed and possessed by a sense of well-being so complete that it makes the heat-and-steam inconsequential. I feel like a new person, no aches, no pains. In that state, I'll make a firm resolve. A perfect sweat helps clarify one's thoughts, to get another good cool night of sleep, then get on the water again at 9:30 the next morning, after the regular daily 2.6-mile wilderness walk south to another huge inland lake, with my two canine buddies before breakfast.

A word of caution: once you've experienced a Finnish sauna, you're hooked. The four principal rules of the authentic Finnish sauna are:

1. Yuu sit on top pench at yuu own rdisk.
2. If tuu muts team kets yuu reel tissy, yuu dumbel down ant prake yuu pones at own rdisk.
3. If svet kets in yuu eyes, chust pi ink a coppla dimes.
4. If yuu ket tuu hot, ko chump in ta lake!

After spending our first month of 3.5 in the UP each summer, my two canine pals develop a seemingly "Swedish" accent in their bark—it's "Voof," instead of "Woof." When we arrive back home in Indiana each year, they seem to lose their accent by the end of October.

This rapid loss of accent is helped along by their hobby of occasionally visiting the former dairy farm across the county road where they enjoy a good roll in twenty-year-old manure piles, followed by a few of my imprecations. Even after several baths, there's a distinct and unsubtle fragrance about them that lasts a few days. It's not as bad, though, as their fragrance after making the acquaintance of a UP skunk during our early morning walk in the dark, about an hour before departing for the eleven-hour drive to our southeast Indiana home.

Photos appearing in fishing magazines today show too many smirking fisherman heroes holding aloft almost equally burly fish, many three feet between the eyes, they have derricked up, or when a block-and-tackle was handy, even vaster specimens of inert piciform. The gaping specimens being held by fishermen at risk of rupturing themselves often can be distinguished from the victims only by their grins.

It seems some fishermen are as obsessed with size as the judges of our so-called beauty contests. They're not beauty but booby contests. It strikes me sad beyond words that anglers themselves would permit probably the world's oldest and finest contemplative pastime to evolve into a competitive rat-race, such as we've allowed the game of basketball to degenerate into sort of a commercialized, professional Bohemian dance performed mostly by bored pituitary freaks. The whole repetitious big-fish gallery is nothing more than a dreamy and dull parade of champion winchers and weightlifters using lines strong enough to tow barges.

Thank God my daddy allowed me before age twelve to learn what Ivory soap tastes like for using bad words, learn honesty by being cheated, learn pain by burning my hand on a hot skillet and sticking my tongue on frozen metal, learn what a black eye is like when fighting for something I believed in, learn humility by being humiliated, learn to make my flipper and slingshot instead of wishing for a store-bought one, learn sorrow by holding my little dog Fritzie in my arms as she died, and the joys of companionship and fishing.

Even though Daddy made me sit still and be quiet and talk in a whisper, words weren't really necessary, just fishing side-by-side was enough; barefoot with wet mud squishing between my toes in Kentucky's McCracken County; digging red worms and grubs in Mom's flower garden during the '30s and in our Victory garden during WWII; cutting fishing poles in the Madison Woods canebrakes; anxiously awaiting Dad's arrival home from work at the ICRR Round House, an hour earlier on Saturday afternoons, to go fishing; holding a sixteen-foot-long cane pole waiting and watching for the cork to move while drowning red worms or grubs and wildly slapping mosquitoes; sitting in the shade of huge sycamores on the banks of Clark's River near the U.S. Route 68 bridge or Cold Springs Creek; cypress knees rising above water level in the Mississippi River backwaters of Barlow Bottoms in Ballard County; sitting in a leaky flat-bottom wood boat in the middle of Metropolis Lake; under a scorching sun while sitting on searing hot limestone rip-rap along the Tennessee River bank below brand new Kentucky Dam; jug-fishing in the Ohio and Tennessee Rivers with friends as a teenager.

The only time Daddy would chew tobacco was while fishing. Every time before putting our lines in the water, he would spit tobacco juice on the baits for good luck. Never was he fortunate enough to sport fish using artificial flies or lures or to again live in a rural forest as he did when a boy and early teen years.

There are no superlatives in describing my two "heavens" where nature's finest hours will last forever. In whatever form of nature comes my happiness, I hug it to my heart unquestioned. There are occasions when I best not seek to see too clearly, for the surface of things is enchantment enough.

Like a child, I'm satisfied with the little things. In the simple joys of the heart, I forget my intolerable destiny. From the cheerfulness of Indiana and UP songbirds, the rich tenderness of spring wildflowers, and the vigorous waves of the Lake Superior shore, I gain a deep desire to live radiantly.

I respect the forest, fishing, and the wilderness—they're not just a legacy, they're my natural heritage, places where the quality of life is there to be lived, and that's where I belong. If only Daddy could be with me now during just the month of June to share the joys of two weeks each in my Indiana and UP "heavens."

It's not what I have but what I do that is my kingdom. When my soul is taken as my body and mind die, it will be known that I used everything God gave me. The English poet Gerard Manley Hopkins may have said it best in his poem: *What would the world be, once bereft of wet and of wildness? Let them be left, oh let them be left, wildness and wet, long live the weeds and the wilderness yet.*

Silent Language of a True Leader

October 7, 2016

Public speakers can send nonverbal messages that will shape the opinions that each of us have about them. A **true leader**, for example, will achieve just the right balance of power and authority with warmth and empathy.

When a speaker's body language conveys too many power signals, that person appears aloof. When a speaker's body language conveys too much warmth, that person will not set himself/herself apart from others and command attention.

Following are some of the more important nonverbal messages.

- True leaders hold their head straight and avoid tilting or cocking it to either side. The head will be tilted back, but not too much; otherwise, the speaker comes across as arrogant.
- True leaders smile sparingly because too much smiling makes them seem weak. The most effective smile starts small and grows as the speaker walks across the stage.
- True leaders know that making too little eye contact with the audience will make them seem deceptive, and that too much eye contact can turn into a "stalker stare."
- True leaders, when making a point, will use their whole hand rather than just their index finger. Pointing with just an index finger makes a speaker seem overly aggressive.

- True leaders avoid gestures (touching the neck, pulling on their shirt collar or lifting their hair) because they convey anxiety rather than a calm and controlled temperament.
- True leaders, whether sitting or standing, convey confidence by "steepling" with their fingers pressed together toward the sky in an almost church-like steeple or in a prayer position.
- True leaders don't hide behind a lectern but rather move around on the stage to convey energy and engage the audience. Walking, pausing, and then walking again works best.
- True leaders speak slowly and pause. Talking fast makes the speaker appear less authoritative.

ESSENTIALS OF PROPER GOVERNMENT

October 22, 2019

Government must understand the nature of God, the laws of nature, the laws of science, the nature of history, and the nature of humankind. People of virtue are the conscience of society; but when humans get piled upon one another as in large urban areas, virtue and conscience will become corrupt.

The government that gives to those who are not willing to work that for which those who are willing to work cannot exist for long. It is every generation's obligation to pay its own debts. Future happiness of the governed is assured if they can prevent government from wasting the treasury, under the pretense of taking care of the governed.

History proves too much government results in bad government and that liberty must be renewed periodically with the lives of patriots as well as the lives of tyrants. It is tyrannical if the government even attempts to compel the governed to subsidize the propagation of generally disbelieved or abhorred ideas.

Finding Good Leaders

November 5, 2018

People who indeed are leaders mean what they say, and you can tell it. They sincerely hold the views they support, and advancing them is their only project and purpose. The ideas they stand for aren't merely policy points on issues, they're held together by a central overarching intention that springs from a general but discernible philosophy.

Great leaders are capable of arguing for the things they believe in. They make their case by making you think along with them, logically, from point A to point B, and beyond. Their words aren't emotional, as do politicians nowadays because they think persuasion by powerful discourse means removal from reality.

When leaders rely on logic and fact, voters do feel something—gratitude at the implied respect and warmth in a community of thought and belief. Eloquence in leaders is desirable but not necessary. It's good if they can make their case in a way that's memorable.

President Franklin D. Roosevelt and President Ronald Reagan were great and eloquent speakers. General Dwight Eisenhower led American forces through World War II, managed the early days of the Cold War, developed the concept of an interstate highway system and started the construction. It was his actions that were eloquent.

Good leaders live in the real world and don't insist on grand ideologies they can squeeze together and push down on our heads. They know the facts and work within them. They respect reality.

Leaders are aware of being the object of many eyes. This puts a responsibility on them to act with respect for their own dignity and ours. Even if they're not in the mood, they must uphold standards of presentation. Children are watching and taking cues. That means the future is watching.

Good leaders are survivors. That's part of how they show loyalty to what they stand for, by being there to stand for it. They survive by shifting strategies and tactics but not principles. They admit when they're wrong, in part because it's refreshing, but politicians rarely do it.

Serious leaders bother to have command of the facts. Leadership isn't all lofty impulses; they know local and national facts because they've studied and absorbed them. Good leaders know the difference between stubbornness and perseverance. When they're afraid to look like they backed down, to themselves or to others, that's stubbornness. When they're willing to pay a price for where they stand, every day, that's perseverance.

Anyone who would do political good must come to it from a higher ground. Beware of any intellectual who inspires divisiveness and overpowering fear among the people. That person thereby confesses to be a coward. Then all things on planet Earth are at risk.

THE CHALLENGE TO MERITOCRACY IN AMERICA TODAY

April 11, 2018

America's competitiveness and scientific achievement will be lost as a consequence of today's drive for the functional equivalence of sexual identity. It's profoundly irresponsible for the source of identity politics—academia—to use the poison of identity politics to prioritize diversity over talent.

Throughout music history, the greatest composers have been male. Where is the female counterpart to Bach, Mozart, Beethoven, Schubert, Chopin, Brahms, Strauss, or Debussy? Madam Marie Curie didn't need a female role model to investigate radioactivity. She was motivated by a passion to search for knowledge and to understand the world.

The nonequivalent distribution of high-end math skills belongs to males: they outnumber females on both the bottom rung of math cluelessness and the top rung of math insight. In the United States, there are 2.5 males on the top 0.01 percent of math ability for every female in that category.

This is not a matter of gender bias and cultural conditioning; gender differences in math aptitude show up as early as kindergarten. The persistent claim of gender bias is a war on merit; in other words, it's ideological, not derived from observation or experiment.

Such information is undoubtedly good news for China, as that country furiously pushes ahead with its unapologetically meritocratic system of science training and research.

America Needs to Upgrade
Its Electrical System

June 14, 2018

Most Americans are aware that our electrical system is inefficient and vulnerable to natural threats such as severe weather, windstorms or ice storms, but many are unaware of human-created threats such as cyber and electromagnetic attacks. To be competitive in the twenty-first century, we need to upgrade our electric grid of mostly above ground transmission wires.

Periods of high demand, such as during a prolonged heat wave, often triggers regional imbalances in electrical supply and demand, leaving consumers to contend with sudden price increases and brownouts or blackouts. During periods of low demand, insufficient transmission capacity also means that surplus electricity is wasted rather that sold to other regions.

America's electric grid relies on alternating-current (AC) technology that dates back to its creation in the last half of the 1800s. Thanks to technological breakthroughs, direct-current (DC) technology can now transmit electric power over longer distances with far less power loss than our existing AC networks.

America's greatest danger is the potential for nationwide blackout due to solar storm, cyberattack, or especially an electromagnetic (EMP) bomb. If any of these three events were to occur, America could be put back into the mid-1800s, and a large percentage of our population would not survive.

The Climate Institute has proposed constructing a new overlay network that balances the generation and consumption of electrical power. This concept of a North America Super-grid would be a multimodal, high-voltage DC transmission network extending across the lower-48 states, possibly linking with Canada, Alaska, and Mexico.

The new grid would: work as a resilient backbone to America's existing electrical grid, be built largely underground alongside highway or railway rights-of-way, and be less vulnerable to attack.

Because transmission distance would no longer be a constraint, the new grid would provide easy transfer and trade of electrical power from renewable and traditional sources between power-abundant and power-hungry regions. The increased transmission capacity would turn America's enormous size into a distinct advantage.

It would permit, for example, the transmission of inexpensive energy, produced by Mojave Desert solar farms or Great Plains wind farms, to east coast urban centers, supplementing more expensive power derived from the use of fossil fuels. China is aggressively building nationwide high-voltage DC lines. The European Union is planning seventeen new super-grid projects on the continent.

The North American Super-grid could transform America much like the Interstate Highway system did when it was started in 1955 during the Eisenhower administration. In contrast to the localized economic payoffs received from new highways and bridges, it would benefit the entire American economy while producing significant environmental and security improvements.

It would be fitting if our real-estate developer president propels America into the super-grid era by expanding his infrastructure permitting, by executive order, to cut still more red tape.

Some Thanksgiving
Observations

November 28, 2019

Born into and raised by a loving and patriotic family of Christian faith, I attained my training and educational goals and reached success in the professional world. I was blissfully married fifty-two years, and our adopted and attentive oldest son is nearby with loving and thoughtful wife and two well-mannered young sons.

Living retired twenty years—eleven alone—in my own private rural forest and wildlife preserve, I am not lonely but inspired and take joy walking, reading, researching, and writing.

Train and educate children to be happy, not to be rich. Chances are they will grow-up with greater character and virtue and know the value of things, not the price. True inner happiness does not come from material things. When lost, most such things can be found or replaced.

Family and friends are to be treasured. Treat yourself well, and cherish others. There is a difference in a human being and being a human. The eleven best doctors available are sunlight, rest, diet, physical and mental exercise, self-respect and self-confidence, unpolluted air to breathe and water to drink, family, and friends. Maintain them all, and enjoy a healthy life.

THE PRIZE

November 19, 2017

Imagine that you had won the PRIZE described below. Each morning, your bank would deposit $86,400 in your private account for you to use. This prize has a set of rules. 1. Every penny that you do not spend during each day will be taken away from you. 2. You cannot simply transfer your unspent money into some other account. 3. You can only spend the money. 4. Each morning upon awakening, your bank opens your account with another $86,400 for that day. 5. Your bank can end the prize without warning, at any time, and can close your account, and you will not receive a new one.

What would you personally do? You would buy anything and everything you wanted not only for yourself but for all the people you love and care about, even for people you don't know, because you couldn't possibly spend it all on yourself.

You would try to spend every penny and use it all because you knew it wouldn't be replenished the next morning.

To be real, you're already a winner of this PRIZE. The PRIZE is TIME—86,400 seconds every day. Spend each of them wisely.

A MESSAGE FOR MY
GRANDSONS TO REMEMBER

April 23, 2016

I am very fortunate and proud to have two grandsons, boys today, who will grow into fine, respected, and successful young men. Jamie and Alex, your daily prayer always should be: "Lord, give me the determination and tenacity of a weed."

An oak tree is fifty years old or older before dropping its first acorns. In your life, you will be judged by what you finish, not by what you start. If you do not see results right away, don't worry about it. All great achievements require time and tenacity. **A great oak tree is only a little accord that held its ground.**

If you are tempted to stop, just think of the famous music composer Johannes Brahms, who took seven long years to finish his famous lullaby. **It takes the hammer of your persistence to drive the nail of success.**

Any diamond was transformed under heat and pressure and made good only because it stuck to its job. You will find that the meaning of the word *succeed* is simply to persevere—**remain constant to your purpose, idea, or task in the face of obstacles or discouragement.**

Be persevering because the last key on the ring may be the one that opens the door for you. Hanging on a while longer than your competition makes you a winner. **Become noted for finishing important, difficult tasks.**

The road to success runs uphill, so you must not expect to break any speed records. Impatience can be costly. Your greatest mistakes will happen because of impatience. **The power to hold on in spite of everything, to endure—this is the winner's trait.**

Two important qualities for you to have in life are **patience and wisdom**, both of which will happen naturally as you grow older.

THERE'S NO LUXURY IN
A FAMILY CAR RIDE

July 25, 2018

As a young boy, our family car trips were in a dingy black A-Model Ford, with three boys in a back seat with very little padding over coil springs, designed to seat only two adults. In those days, the 1930s, cars didn't ride smoothly, and roads were mostly not paved, black-topped, or tarred, only gravel and awfully dusty. It was on these four-hour, fifty-mile, rough-riding trips to my paternal grandparents that we brothers bonded; reading Burma Shave signs, trading baseball cards and comic books, and seldom black eyes.

During the 1940s, family trips were made in a shiny blue 1940 Plymouth sedan on mainly paved, blacktopped, or tarred, occasion-ally graveled roads. On December 7, 1941, our family trips changed. Both older brothers joined the military. The oldest served in North Africa and Italy, and the middle brother bombed Germany from Italy. With both brothers away from home and before obtaining my driver license in 1946, the quite comfortable back seat was mine.

The oldest brother married in 1946, moved to Memphis, Tennessee, entered the business world with an uncle, and began raising a family. The middle brother was discharged from the mil-itary with combat fatigue, lived at home and suffered many related problems for a couple of years, then entered college on the GI bill. In 1950, Dad purchased a new eight-cylinder Packard sedan, with flashing turn signals that weren't yet legalized. Gee-whiz, that was the heaviest, biggest, sleekest car I'd ever driven.

My wife and I bought a luxurious new 1959 Pontiac sedan as a "family car." If you've ever driven one, you know what I mean. Family excursions in this fancy car with two little people were neither relaxing nor luxurious. They're wars, each of them, with little people resistant to negotiation and hell-bent on noise, destruction, and spilling thousands of Cheerios into the seat crevices and on the floor.

That's just the start of it. These little people were good boys, mostly, but all it took to get the youngest to upchuck in the car was the mention of the word *car*. This, in turn, almost always set-off a regurgitation chain reaction with the older brother, who sees his little brother's expulsion and begins to dramatically expel himself. You really have to see it, and smell it, to believe it. Within minutes of leaving home, the back seat resembled a shabby diner surrounded by a bacterial outbreak.

Sometimes, we'd get lucky. The boys would hang onto their stomachs. Instead, they simply brawled. Pinches, punches, kicks, bites, eye-gouges—we refereed it all. We should've installed chicken wire and padding and held five-round title-matches. Just the fact that these little guys could tangle in such close quarters was impressive.

Our boys, it's clear, had short arms and legs.

We tried to feed them. Usually, it started with some thoughtfully considered healthy snacks: celery sticks, apple slices, organic juice boxes. But there's only so much healthy snacking a youngster will stand. By the end of a long trip, we were tossing them chocolate chip cookies, like they're sea lions at the aquarium.

I know what you're thinking: Why not give them iPads? Such devices have removed a lot of torment from the family car trip. But there were no iPads in those days. It makes me feel guilty, though. I wanted them to join me in marveling at the countryside, hunting for Alaska license plates and loudly singing, "Take me home." After all, family car trips were how I saw only a small part of only three states as a youngster.

The Phrase "Over the Hill" Is Outdated

March 7, 2018

Prime Minister Winston Leonard Spencer Churchill, at sixty-six to seventy-one years of age, led Great Britain through World War II (1939–1945). One fact often missed is that Churchill's defining moment arrived at age seventy-seven when voters gave him a second act (1951–1955). Churchill's words and actions in the summer of 1940 were the product of a long life checkered by soaring triumphs and catastrophic failures. Each prepared him for that critical time.

Too often, employers in America don't believe in second acts. Because of discrimination based on age in today's workplace, people over age fifty seldom ever get a second act. Age should never be the sole basis for deciding whether a person is hired or fired, promoted or demoted. The law requires as much. Yet most employers have mastered methods to make discrimination difficult to prove in courts.

Unfortunately in America, age discrimination is based on perception rather than performance. Workers over fifty are burdened by an outdated definition of "old." Despite evidence to the contrary, they are unfairly judged to be costly, less productive, and unable to learn.

Despite this, there are literally numerous examples of adults much older than fifty who have accomplished extraordinary things.

Ray Kroc was age fifty-two when he switched careers to turn McDonald's into the world's largest fast food chain. At eighty-seven, thirty days younger than me, Warren Buffett remains one of the world's savviest investors. Grandma Moses started painting seriously at age seventy-eight. Diana Nyad was sixty-four when she became the first person to swim from Cuba to Florida without a protective shark cage.

Advances in health are making accomplishments that require mental acuity and physical endurance commonplace among older people. Whatever declines they may experience with age can be offset by their accumulated knowledge, wisdom, perspective, and attitude.

While some of those people facing discrimination often turn to government, the record shows that business corporations can shatter cultural barriers more quickly. Many companies have contributed to the advancement of women and people of color. Nevertheless, older workers are rarely represented in corporate inclusion initiatives.

What might business advocacy for workers over age fifty look like? First, companies should avoid stereotypes in campaigns aimed at older consumers. Second, they should evaluate employees on performance, without any stigma on age. Finally, they should realize that the tone at the top matters.

Executives should recognize the contributions of older workers and engage them in planning and product development. Silicon Valley can shift its youth-obsessed culture. The qualities older workers have acquired during their lives are just as important to business success.

Refire (Not Retire) the Mind, Body, Heart, and Soul

February 28, 2016

Retired life is special. Don't miss it. Every day, there's new opportunity for adventure and learning. Focus on health and vitality, continued learning, rewarding relationships, meaningful involvement, and develop a personal sense of spirituality.

Get away from a tedious or fixed way of doing things, take advantage of the opportunity to live a fuller, more exciting life. Change attitude, play, laugh, and love more, be spontaneous and take new low risks.

Get away from comfort zones. For example, enroll in a class on an unfamiliar subject at a local college or university. This will create a new setting with different people. Take a new route to an old destination. If at first it's slightly uncomfortable, that's good! Another comfort zone has been created.

Form an "Impromptu Group," an informal group of five couples or ten widow or widower friends with a wide range of cultural interests. The group agrees that if a member invites another member to do something, the member invited will say yes, unless previously committed to something else.

Fairly recent epidemiological research shows that a strong purpose in life helps older people sleep better, have a lower risk of heart attack and stroke, keep chromosomes intact, and be far less likely to develop Alzheimer's disease. I understand the National Institutes of Health (NIH) has given no attention to these important findings.

What would happen if a new drug were discovered with the same effects, a drug without three pages of tiny print listing side effects, but costs nothing? It would be put in our drinking water.

Researchers also have discovered that older people who place importance in close relationships, community involvement, and personal growth (and achieve these goals) have a sense of well-being. And on the other hand, older people who aspire to money, fame, and appearance (and achieve these goals) often have a sense of ill-being.

Why Not Rediscover Drop-Ins?

January 10, 2019

When did it become uncommon to stop by the house of a friend or close relative for an unannounced visit? Today, we plan everything ahead of time, even things that shouldn't need planning. Some of us are surprised to even get a phone call without first receiving a text message.

My parents' friends, brothers, sisters, and cousins never made plans ahead of time to visit each other—they just dropped-in. This was a common happening between my maternal and paternal aunts, uncles, and cousins living in my Kentucky hometown, other places in western Kentucky, southwest Indiana, northwestern Tennessee, southeast Missouri, and eastern Oklahoma.

It was inspired by the generation of my paternal grandparents. They and their friends dropped-in on each other constantly. One neighbor couple who lived down the gravel road from them would show-up at any time or any day at their front door with an empty egg carton.

My paternal grandparents were chicken farmers, and Grandma always had homemade grape wine on hand. They would pull-up chairs for conversation, pour wine, and send them home with a full egg carton.

Sure, my grandparents didn't work away from home and were confined by their chicken farm, so it was easier for them to be hosts-on-the-quick than it is for most couples today. But their generation also placed more of a premium on people being together. It used to be part of everyday life. Nowadays, it's a ticket event.

When we finally do host others, we're not very good at it. The last time I invited a cousin for a visit, I discovered that I had nothing to offer her to eat but Keebler's Fudge Stripe Cookies. Grandma always kept her small kitchen stocked with above-average snacks that could be laid-out in minutes. I'll never forget her Ritz Cracker box full of fresh-and-crisp crackers sitting at the left edge of the metal shelf above her kitchen wood cook stove, kept fresh by the stove itself.

Grandma and Grandpa were always ready to host. And if nobody showed-up, they were not disappointed to spend an evening listening to news on the table radio or playing music records on the Victrola.

Give it a try this year. Rather than making plans with friends and relatives, just drop-in. And be ready for them to do the same. You'll hit some snags along the way. Occasionally, your friends or relatives won't be home. But you'll still have a bottle of Welsh's Sparkling nonalcoholic white grape juice cocktail and a box of doughnuts.

CHAPTER 3
The American's Creed

September 18, 2017

I believe in the United States of America as a government of the people, by the people, for the people; whose just powers are derived from the consent of the governed; a democracy in a republic; a sovereign nation of many sovereign states; a perfect union, one and inseparable; established upon those principles of freedom, equality, justice, and humanity for which American patriots sacrificed their lives and fortunes. I therefore believe it is my duty to my country to love it, to support its Constitution, to obey its laws, to respect its flag, and to defend it against all enemies.

William Tyler Page (1868–1942)

The American's Creed is a summary, in one hundred words, of the fundamental principles of American political faith as set forth in its greatest documents, its worthiest traditions, and by its greatest leaders. It is not an expression of individual opinion on the obligations and duties of American citizenship or its rights and privileges.

I firmly believe that each member of Congress should be required to memorize the American's Creed before taking office. Thereafter, each and every member of Congress should be required to repeat it in-unison at the opening of each and every session of Congress.

THE FEDERALIST PAPERS

June 25, 2015

There's no better aid for understanding the principles of limited government underlying the Constitution than the words of the Founders themselves. *The Federalist Papers* defended the merits of the proposed *Constitution* as a necessary and good replacement for the 1781 Articles of Confederation, which had proven defective as a means of governance. Written following the *Constitutional Convention of 1787, The Federalist Papers* is the foremost American contribution to political thinking. Thomas Jefferson (1743–1826) described *The Federalist Papers* as "the best commentary on the principles of government, which ever was written."

The Federalist Papers is a collection of eighty-five essays written under the penname of *Publius* by Alexander Hamilton (1755?–1804), James Madison (1751–1836), and John Jay (1745–1829). Hamilton wrote fifty of the papers, Madison thirty, and Jay five. Seventy-seven were published serially in *The Independent Journal* and *The New York Packet* newspapers between October 1787 and August 1788. All eighty-five were compiled and published later in 1788 by A. and J. McLean. *The Federalist Papers* explain the merits of the Constitution while confronting objections that were raised by its opponents, and the purpose of the papers was to influence the vote in favor of ratifying the Constitution.

Federalist No. 1 (by Hamilton) laid-out the debate using broad political terms: "It has been frequently remarked, that it seems to have been reserved to the people of this country, by their conduct and example, to decide the important question, whether societies of men are really capable or not, of establishing good government from reflection and choice, or whether they are forever destined to depend, for their political constitutions, on accident and force."

Federalist No. 10 (by Madison) discusses the means of preventing rule by majority faction and advocates a large commercial Republic and is generally regarded as the most important of the eighty-five papers from a philosophical perspective.

The foregoing paper is complimented by *Federalist No. 14*, in which Madison takes measure of America, declaring it appropriate for an extended Republic, and concluding with a memorable defense of the constitutional and political creativity of the Federal Convention.

In *Federalist No. 84*, Hamilton makes the case that there is no need to amend the Constitution by adding a Bill of Rights, insisting that the various provisions in the proposed Constitution protecting liberty amount to a "bill of rights."

Federalist No. 78 (by Hamilton) lays the groundwork for the doctrine of judicial review by federal courts of federal legislation or executive acts.

Federalist No. 70 presents Hamilton's case for a one-man chief executive.

In *Federalist No. 39*, Madison presents the clearest exposition of what has come to be called "federalism."

In *Federalist No. 51*, Madison distills arguments for checks and balances in an essay often quoted for its justification of government as "the greatest of all reflections on human nature."

In *Federalist No. 10*, *Publius* confronts one of the most important anti-*Federalist* arguments against ratification—republican government is impossible in a territory as large as America. In fact, such an undertaking had never been successful. In response, *Publius* proposes that the principle remedy for the political disease of majority faction (a disease most incident to republican government) is the large or extended sphere or territory. *Publius* writes, "Democracies have ever been spectacles of turbulence and contention; have ever been found incompatible with personal security and the rights of property; and have in general been as short in their lives as they have been violent in their deaths."

In the summer of 1787, the Framers labored to set-up a political regime that would not only secure liberty and republicanism but also bring energy and stability to the national government. Because of the failures of government under the Articles of Confederation, American political institutions were at risk. In order to secure these institutions, the Framers constructed a republican form of government that, among many other important features, instituted a new form of federalism.

In constituting a new government, the Framers knew that written rules (what *Publius* calls "parchment barriers") would not be enough by themselves to protect liberty and prevent tyranny. Instead, *Publius* looks to the "interior structure" as the best means for keeping the branches of government properly and effectively separated. Separation of powers, the most important of the Constitution's "auxiliary precautions," works to prevent tyranny, and by keeping each branch within its proper sphere of authority allows each branch to do its job well.

The Framers understood that the legislative branch is by nature the most powerful in a republican government. Experience of government under the Articles of Confederation, which state legislatures routinely encroached on executive and judicial powers, confirmed this. Thus, the Framers divided the legislative branch into two parts: the House of Representatives and the Senate. In addition, they differentiated them as much as possible, consistent with the principles of republican government, with the goal of preventing tyranny and encouraging good government.

Following their experience under the Articles of Confederation and armed with the improved science of politics, the Framers instituted a unitary executive in the office of the president. Unlike the executive office in any other republic, it was designed so as to ensure energy and responsibility in the executive, which are absolutely essential for good execution of the laws, and therefore for good government.

In the Declaration of Independence, one charge leveled against King George III was that he had "made Judges dependent on his Will alone." In framing a republican government, the Founders believed that an independent judiciary was indispensable. *Publius* argues that the term of life tenure during good behavior and a protected salary ensure this independence.

In *Federalist No. 84, Publius* writes, "The truth is, after all the declamation we have heard, that the Constitution is itself, in every rational sense, and to every useful purpose, a Bill of Rights." In other words, the structure of the Constitution protects the rights of the people. In addition, the American people retain all powers not granted to the Federal and State governments.

In conclusion, the Constitutional Republic relies on structure, representation, and limitations on the functions of the Federal government.

American government today is much different from the Constitutional Republic outlined in *The Federalist Papers*. Administrative regulations and entitlements are two distinguishing features of the modern American government. These new features require a kind of government that is unlimited, disregards separation of powers, and violates the supreme law under which it claims to operate.

Nowhere does the word *democracy* appear in the Constitution. The word *democracy* does appear in *Federalist No. 10*, in which a democracy is defined and clearly feared by the Founders. Today, nonetheless, *democracy* is the one word used by Americans in describing the Federal government.

At roughly the same time in 1787 that the proposed Constitution was being written, a University of Edinburgh history professor, Alexander Tyler, wrote that the Roman Empire was a Republic and that Athens was trying to be a Democracy some two thousand years before.

"A democracy is always temporary in nature; it simply cannot exist as a permanent form of government. A democracy will continue to exist up until the time that voters discover they can vote themselves generous gifts from the public treasury. From that moment on, the majority always votes for the candidates who promise the most benefits from the public treasury, with the result that every democracy will collapse due to loose fiscal policy, which is always followed by a dictatorship. "The average age of the world's greatest civilizations from the beginning of history has been about 200 years. During those years, these nations always progressed through the following sequence:

- from bondage to spiritual faith;
- from spiritual faith to great courage;
- from courage to liberty;
- from liberty to abundance;
- from abundance to complacency;
- from complacency to apathy;
- from apathy to dependence;
- from dependence back to bondage."

According to Professor Joseph Olsen, Hamline University School of Law, St. Paul, Minnesota, official records show that in the 2002 presidential election, citizens voting Republican were mostly tax-paying land or property owners, whereas those voting Democrat were mostly living in government-owned tenements, living off welfare.

EQUALITY ENGENDERS HUMILITY IN AMERICA

October 20, 2018

Two competing forces—precedence and equality—have battled for foremost importance since the founding of the United States of America. In May, four months before the September 1789 signing of the Constitution, there was a debate over how the leader of the United States should be addressed.

John Adams advocated a "first among equals" mentality, campaigning for the American president to be "His Highness, the president of the United States, and protector of the rights of the same."

Such a lofty title, Adams argued, was necessary to confer appropriate respect for the chief executive of the emerging country's federal government. He believed it to be especially important since not all the thirteen states, at that particular time, had adopted the Constitution.

"His Excellency," "His Elective Highness," and "His Majesty George" also were proffered. George Washington was satisfied with the unassuming "Mr. President."

Thomas Jefferson, author of the country's "all men are created equal" system of belief, disagreed with Adam's title campaign as "superlatively ridiculous." In an 1803 memorandum to his cabinet, President Jefferson outlined new procedures that required his guests to check their status at the door. He wrote, "When brought together in society, all are perfectly equal, whether foreign or domestic, titled or untitled, in or out of office. No titles being admitted here, those of foreigners give no precedence." Congressmen, judges, lords, foreign diplomats—all were equal in the Jefferson White House.

The Adams-Jefferson debate was revived by Senator Barbara Boxer (D-CA) in 2009, when like a modern Adams she corrected a brigadier general: "You know, do me a favor, could you say 'Senator' instead of 'ma'am'? I worked so hard to get that title, so I'd appreciate it."

Fortunately, Americans still emulate Jefferson's skepticism of inordinate difference. Such demands for difference are contrary to the American standard of democracy. Yet the longing for priority over others will never be entirely eradicated. This created complications in Jefferson's time and continues today.

Jefferson once snubbed the British ambassador to the United States and his wife during a state dinner in 1803; the president didn't prepare a planned seating arrangement. Rather, he hosted the dinner at a round table. Unlike a rectangular table, no one could be distinguished as a guest of honor.

Many visitors to America today are often confused and suspicious of our informality, especially in the South and Midwest. Language is partly a contributor to this cultural casualness. Numerous languages offer two forms of the pronoun "you," which are used for formal and informal settings.

One form is meant for close friends and family; the other shows social distance and respect for peers and superiors. Americans today are informal unless formality is explicitly needed or commanded as in Senator Boxer's case.

Finding a balance gets to the heart of American equality. The self-evident truths in America's founding documents refer to equal treatment under the law. These laws don't mean that all people are equal in their abilities, interests, or life outcomes.

The American belief recognizes that each human life is valued equally and that everyone is owed and owes to others a level of respect by virtue of being a part of the human community. The democratic view of respect is well-represented in America where people of every income level wear blue-jeans and demonstrate an equal measure of courtesy to all.

Surrendering professional narcissism is easier said than done. But a person's competing desire for precedence and equality can be eased by drawing distinctions in settings—private and public, informal and professional.

Showing respect that highlights persons that have authority is important in professional settings. A clear chain of command is critical in places like courtrooms and battlefields; deferring to title and rank in those settings makes sense.

When professional titles are referred to in private and social settings, they distract from the equal value in all persons. Imagine if Senator Boxer demanded her family and friends refer to her as such in private settings.

Before the subject of presidential titles was brought-up for debate, George Washington had already offered his thoughts on this topic. In 1788, he wrote to Alexander Hamilton, "I hope I shall always possess firmness and virtue enough to maintain (what I consider the most enviable of all titles) the character of *an honest man*."

From America's beginning, the first president voluntarily surrendered rank-related pretense to avoid exalting himself as Adams liked or offending others as Jefferson did later.

George Washington's aim was to better value and respect fellow Americans. Why can't each of us endeavor to do the same when it comes to America's political situation today?

President Lincoln's Lessons of Reconciliation

November 12, 2018

As people are troubled over America's political division into more hostile units, many also note that it's worse than ever before. The 2016 election might have brought-out the worst in many, but it's nothing compared with the Civil War. This well-known narrative has been often told as a secular story. Less appreciated is how spirituality helped bring Americans together after deadly conflict.

April 1865 was mostly a time of optimism. The Civil War was all but over. The Confederate Capital, Richmond, Virginia, fell on April 3. President Abraham Lincoln even walked through the defeated city.

A few days later, General Robert E. Lee surrendered his Army of Northern Virginia to General Ulysses S. Grant at Appomattox Court House. General Lee sent his troops home, averting a guerrilla conflict. All that was left was mopping-up small pockets of resistance and preparing for the postwar settlement.

Good Friday that year came on April 14, the beginning of the Christian calendar's three most important days. Across the country, North and South, Christians gathered in their churches to remember the crucifixion of Christ and express sorrow and unhappiness over their sins, which made such a sacrifice necessary.

Desiring some emotional release after four years of war, President Lincoln declined to attend any worship service that day. He did decide, however, that he and Mrs. Lincoln would that evening attend a comedy at Ford's Theatre.

That play was overshadowed by another performance, by the actor turned assassin John Wilkes Booth. In killing President Lincoln, Booth believed he carried on the spirit of the Confederacy. He announced from the stage that he would avenge the Confederacy's loss. "*Sic semper tyrannis*," he shouted—"thus always to tyrants."

As American's grieved, one of the most common means of mourning was to identify Lincoln's sacrifice with Christ's. Both died on Good Friday after giving their lives for others. This sacralizing of President Lincoln's death continued as his body was carried across the country to be laid to rest in Springfield, Illinois.

The path of reconstruction might have been less rocky if Americans had heeded some of his final words instead of deifying Lincoln or demanding retribution. Lincoln's second inaugural address, delivered a month before his death, drew heavily on biblical themes.

President Lincoln spoke to both sides without shying away from making distinctions or abandoning his own commitments. He blamed the South for pushing the nation to war, especially over slavery.

"It may seem strange that any men should dare to ask a just God's assistance in wringing their bread from the sweat of other men's faces." But in that Critique, President Lincoln urged humility. "Let us judge not, that we be not judged."

Balancing his criticism, he argued that the horrible bloodshed of the war was a judgment on the North too. President Lincoln closed by calling all to steady service. "*With malice toward none, with charity for all, with firmness in the right as God gives us to see the right, let us strive on to finish the work we are in.*" The most important of these tasks was "*to bind-up the nation's wound, to care for him who shall have borne the battle and for his widow and orphan.*"

President Lincoln concluded that this humanitarian vision could cross borders and ethnic divisions, providing an example to the world.

A desire to "bind-up" must be a precondition for resetting some of the fractures our nation is experiencing today. Americans should look to President Lincoln's words as an enduring call to reconciliation.

Rediscover the Wisdom in Reading American History

October 5, 2019

A Latin proverb *Vox audita perit littera scripta manet* can be translated, "The heard voice perishes, but the written letter remains." My father's eighth-grade education did not include the study of Latin, and neither did I study Latin in school.

Nonetheless, following graduation from high school, my father told me, "Son, believe nothing you hear and half of what you read." I didn't realize at the time, but that statement was Dad's common sense translation of that Latin proverb.

My main habit since retiring twenty-one years ago is reading—documented history is my favorite. Reading American history gives me a sense of the future as a time I know will come because at age eighty-nine, I remember that many other tomorrows have come and gone.

As we are experiencing today, a culture without memory will necessarily be barbarous and easily tyrannized, even if it is technologically advanced. The incessant waves of daily events occupy too much of our attention and defeat our efforts to connect the past, present, and future.

This will divert us from understanding the human things that unfold in time, including the path of our own lives. When a day passes, it's no longer there. Only a story remains. If stories weren't written, humans would live like beasts for the day only. All human life is one long story.

In times like today, when old institutions are being replaced by institutions not necessarily in accord with most people's preconceived hopes, our political thought needs to look backward as well as forward. It's hard today to get young people interested in the past because they are already firmly convinced that we're living in a time that's unprecedented—enjoying transformative pocket-sized technologies—that there's no point in looking at what took place during the eighteenth, nineteenth, and twentieth centuries. To them, America's past has been superseded, just as our present world is forever in the process of being superseded.

An important lesson in history is that acts of statesmanship often require courage and imagination, even daring, especially when the outcome seems doubtful. So accustomed are we to thinking about Abraham Lincoln in heroic terms that we forget the depth and breadth of his unpopularity during his entire time in office.

Except for Donald Trump today, few, if any, of our great leaders have been more comprehensively disdained, loathed, and underestimated while in office. A low Southern view of Lincoln, of course, was to be expected, but it was widely shared in the North as well.

According to his biographer, "Lincoln's own associates thought him a Simple Susan, a baboon, an aimless punster, a smutty joker." An abolitionist called him "a huckster in politics, a first-rate, second-rate man." His opponent in the 1864 presidential campaign openly disdained him as a "well-meaning baboon."

The foregoing is a perfect example of the wisdom that the study of American history can provide. It's my hope that such wisdom be an impelling force for each of us to rediscover as a humane and generous example for Americans today.

Leftists Are Rewriting American History

June 20, 2017

The most effective way to destroy a country and its people is to deny and obliterate the peoples' own understanding of their country's history. The former Union of Soviet Socialists Republics (USSR) was established in 1922 and collapsed in 1991. Censorship, rewriting of history, and eliminating undesirable people became a part of Soviet's effort to ensure that the correct ideological and political spin was put on Russian history. Deviation from that official propaganda was punished by confinement in Siberian labor camps and execution.

In America today, there are numerous leftist efforts to rewrite our country's history, and there's no punishment. The New Orleans, Louisiana, mayor had a Confederate Monument of General Robert E. Lee removed recently. In St. Louis, Missouri, a thirty-eight-foot-tall granite monument to the Confederacy is currently being removed. In Richmond, Virginia, there have been calls for the removal on Monument Avenue of Confederate President Jefferson Davis and Generals Robert E. Lee, Stonewall Jackson, and J.E.B. Stuart statues. A Memphis, Tennessee, mayor wanted the Confederate General Nathan Bedford Forrest, as well as the graves of Forrest and his wife, removed from a city park.

Not only have Confederate statues come under attack. The name of J.E.B. Stuart High School in Falls Church, Virginia, brings calls for a name change. These leftist rewriters of history have had almost total success in getting the Confederate flag removed from state capital grounds and other public places.

Removing statues of Confederates and renaming buildings are just a small part of the true agenda of America's leftists. America's costly Civil War (1861–1865) is an undeniable fact of our nation's history and will not go away by means of cultural cleansing.

> Tariffs and excise taxes were the only source of Federal revenue from 1789 until Federal Income Tax began after 1913. During the 1850s, tariffs comprised ninety percent of the federal revenue. In 1859, for example, southern ports paid seventy-five percent of those tariffs.
>
> The South believed their agricultural interests were being used by Congress to protect the manufacturing interest in the North. John C. Calhoun, SC (U.S. Rep. 1811–1817, Sec. of War 1817–1825, V. President 1825–1832, Se. of State 1844–45, U.S. Sen. 1845–1850) strongly believed that "a tariff for purposes of protection, and not for purposes of revenue only, is unconstitutional."
>
> Eleven southern states considered the tariffs tantamount to the Navigation Acts of King George III, which had driven Colonial America to Revolutionary War against England (1775–1783).
>
> When Abraham Lincoln wrote the Emancipation Proclamation in September 1862, the war was going badly for the Union. As a politician, Lincoln wrote, "I view the Proclamation as a practical war measure, to be decided upon according to the advantages and disadvantages it may offer to the suppression of the rebellion." Both London and Paris at that time were consid-

ering recognizing the Confederacy and assisting its war effort.

In response to this Lincoln wrote, "I will also concede that Emancipation would help us in Europe, and convince them that we are incited by something more than ambition." Contrary to what many U.S. history books state or imply, Lincoln's several uncensored writings and speeches do not prove that he was against slavery.

Thomas Jefferson owned slaves, and there's a monument in Washington, DC that bears his name. George Washington also owned slaves, and there's a monument to him as well in Washington, DC.

Will leftist rewriters who call for removal of statues in New Orleans and Richmond call for the removal of monuments honoring slaveholders Jefferson and Washington? Will leftist rewriters demanding a change in the name of J.E.B. Stuart High School demand the name of our nation's capital be changed? Will leftist rewriters call for name changes for James Madison University and for George Mason University? Madison ("father of our Constitution") owned slaves, and Mason (author of a part of our Constitution's Bill of Rights) also owned slaves.

Rewriting American history will be a huge challenge. Imagine the task of purifying just our nation's currency. Slave owner George Washington's picture is on the one-dollar bill; slave owner Thomas Jefferson's on the two-dollar bill; slave owner Andrew Jackson's on the twenty-dollar bill; slave owning Union General Ulysses S. Grant's on the fifty-dollar bill.

The challenges of rewriting American history are endless. At least half of the fifty-six signers of the Declaration of Independence were slave owners. Also consider that roughly half of the fifty-five delegates to the 1787 Constitutional Convention in Philadelphia were slave owners. Do these facts invalidate the U.S. Constitution, and would the leftist rewriters of history want to convene a new convention to purge and purify our Constitution?

The work of Obama tyrants and busybodies is not finished. When they accomplish one goal, they move their agenda to something else. If we Americans give an inch, they'll take a yard. I'm not alone in emphatically saying don't give them the inch to start with! The hate-America leftists will use every tool at their disposal to achieve their agenda of discrediting and demeaning our history. Our history of slavery quite simply is the most convenient tool to further their cause.

Socialists Don't Know History

August 9, 2019

"History repeats itself, first as tragedy, then as farce." I can't help but mumble this famous sentence whenever I read or hear about the new Democratic Socialist Party—distinctly not the 1937–1953 Democrat Party. Socialism caused the death of more than one hundred million people under Lenin, Stalin, and Mao, but progressives who don't know history want to give it another go.

Not all the democratic socialists are young like Alexandria Ocasio-Cortez who will not be thirty until October 13. What are Bernie Sanders' and Joe Biden's excuses? Bernie, seventy-eight years old September 8, proudly calls himself a democratic socialist, and Joe will be seventy-seven on November 20.

The phrase "democratic socialist," like the phrase "military justice," is an oxymoron. Under socialism, the state always takes priority over the people. No self-identified socialist regime in the world—all which have been installed by professional revolutionists—has ever been the least bit democratic.

In his earnest self-righteousness and inflexibly-held positions, Bernie reminds me of Stalin. Whenever he hammers home his points in his staccato speech, using his hands for italics, I'm reminded of Stalin. Bernie isn't a Stalinist, but judging by his temperament and rigidity, in Stalin's day, he might have been.

After its twenty-year run early in the 1900s with Eugene Debs and others, socialism was last resorted to in a serious way in the United

States during the Great Depression 1929–1939. It was thought a cure-all for the busted economy, a reshuffling of the cards that would result in everyone being dealt a winning hand. Socialism gave them lots to theorize about until WWII came about December 7, 1941.

Michael Harrington's 1962 book, *The Other America*, set the War on Poverty in motion. Harrington himself was an avowed socialist. Other intellectuals (like many K-12 teachers and college professors today) feel that electoral politics is beneath them and find only the clearing of the decks of capitalism through socialism worthy of their interest.

Many of these intellectuals feel it a betrayal to abandon the idealistic politics of their youth and college days and have not departed from their advocacy of socialism. A magazine called Jacobin, with a 2017 circulation of thirty thousand, offers its own description, "socialist perspectives on politics, economics, and culture."

Many say that these excesses of progressivism have brought on the election of President Trump and that his abrasive personality apparently has stimulated the interest in socialism. The pendulum continues to swing, as so often in our country, from extreme to extreme, never resting for long at stability and good sense.

Some of the Democrats who are looking to socialism aren't old enough to remember the sixty-nine-year-long socialist horror called the Union of Soviet Socialist Republics. Like many of the young today, they learned their catechism from Howard Zinn's "A People's History of the United States"—the popular and widely taught textbook describing America as a country of unrelieved misery, pervasive injustice, and general wretchedness. After reading Zinn, himself a lifelong radical, socialism might seem to these young Democrats an obvious, an inescapable, conclusion.

Throughout its history under various regimes, in its pursuit of an untrustworthy utopian equality, socialism has produced no great thinkers or enduring science. It has been death to entrepreneurship. Yet it is an idea—or more accurately, the ideal—that refuses to die.

The socialism currently advocated by the Democratic Socialist Party brings to mind another sentence, "Those who cannot remember the past are condemned to repeat it." Contemplating the return of socialism, this time in an American setting, I can only say, God prevent!

America Has Always Been an Exceptional Nation

January 25, 2019

We Americans like to believe that we are an exceptional nation of exceptional people. We're people who love our country and compassionate treatment more than ourselves. The condition of America being exceptional or unique, a topic of debate between Obama and Romney in 2012, serves as a litmus test of patriotism.

At the founding of our constitutional republic, America seemed not only exceptional but almost peculiar. From the beginning of time, human societies had organized as hierarchies; pyramids with kings at the top, nobles in the middle, and commoners on the bottom.

Starting in the 1680s with Sir Isaac Newton and other naturalists, enlightenment overthrew hierarchy. They dismantled the "Great Chain of Being," which described creation as a hierarchical system, and came to understand nature as a rational order.

By the mid-eighteenth century, enlightened thinkers transferred the overthrow of hierarchy to the political realm. They argued in the same vein that no human being was born with inherent qualities that entitled them to rule or be ruled.

In 1776 when the American colonists rebelled against King George III, their replacement was to be not another hierarchy. Rather, it was a constitutional republic with no orders, ranks, or prelates, religious liberty for all, and an equal entitlement for everyone to "life, liberty, and the pursuit of happiness." This was simply without precedence. The birthday of a new world was at hand.

Europeans were less enthusiastic. In 1870, Otto von Bismarck said, "One cannot lead or bring to prosperity a great nation without the principle of authority—the Monarchy." But Americans compensated for the vacuum created by monarchs and nobles by inventing an abundance of private, voluntary associations.

According to Alexis de Tocqueville, the extraordinary fragmentation of administrative power in 1832 America was offset by the proliferation of religious, moral, and cultural associations which substituted themselves for the lords and bureaucrats that choked European societies. In the absence of hierarchy, any American could make what he would of the American landscape. Americans had stopped doing what others told them they must do. Americans had escaped from Europe's involuntary idleness, slave-like dependence, poverty, and useless labor to toils of a very different nature, rewarded by ample subsistence.

Abraham Lincoln expressed this perfectly when he said that Americans "stand at once the wonder and admiration of the whole world." And why? Because "every man can make himself." "The prudent, penniless beginner labors for wages awhile, saves a surplus with which to buy tools or land for himself, then labors on his own account another while, and at length hires another new beginner, which is the just and generous, and prosperous system, that opens the way for all."

Not quite for all, though, especially not for the nearly four million blacks who were held in slavery before the 1861–1865 Civil War. But the war itself became an instance of exceptionalism since it was fought to eliminate slavery and redeem the American republic's claim to have been "conceived in liberty and dedicated to the proposition that all men are created equal." The Civil War may be the most exceptional time in all American history, for there is no record of any other conflict quite like the war Americans waged among themselves to "die to make men free."

The stupendous success of America's politics and economics inevitably triggered the urge to export them to an "unenlightened" world, which is when exceptionalism began to wobble. Until the twentieth century, Americans generally understood their political and economic freedoms as examples to be followed, not commodities to be transferred.

World War I and World War II placed Americans, willingly and unwillingly, into the role of democracy-exporters. And we've learned that other nations don't welcome such exports or don't offer fertile ground for their growth.

Americans have been handed-back examples of our own shortcomings, along with demands that we conform to standards of international institutions. And from that has risen the feeling of fear and apprehension that our exceptionalism is at best simply odd and, at worst, simply arrogant.

After the horrors of the twentieth century, it may be that no nation-state, no matter how perfect the founding principles, can seem sufficiently free of errors to warrant the label "exceptional." Americans certainly have become less economically mobile, less likely to participate in voluntary associations, and more likely to look to a European-style administrative state for solutions.

But to reject exceptionalism is also to reject the fundamental philosophical principles on which the American republic was founded. To do so would be the same as relegating the guarantee of "life, liberty, and the pursuit of happiness" to the level of myth. We don't need to claim perfection to reclaim exceptionalism. After all, the exceptional principles that guided America's founding may turn-out to be the last best hope on earth.

U.S. History Most
Americans Do Not Know

March 12, 2013

Much documented American history has been twisted, warped, or omitted in many, if not most, public school U.S. history books. It's been said that "American history is longer, larger, more various, more beautiful, and more terrible than anything any one has said about it." Americans share a common history that both divides us and unites us. If we can't face history honestly, how can we learn from the past? Voltaire, pen name of French philosopher Francois Marie Arouet (1694–1778), wrote, "If we believe absurdities, we shall commit atrocities." American James A. Baldwin (1924–1987) wrote, "Every historical moment teaches not only something about the event or person but also something about the time of its (writing)."

Undoubtedly, the declared rationale for *political correctness*, which is to prevent people from being offended, plays a role in the reluctance of historians to deal with all related facts. *Political correctness* is best defined as over-concern for broad political, social, and educational change, often to the exclusion of more important matters. A nation declines when the majority of its citizens come under the influence of *political correctness*, which dismantles all restraints on self-indulgence established by tradition, beliefs, manners, customs, and law.

IMPORTANT HAPPENINGS LEADING TO THE CIVIL WAR

Tariffs and excise taxes were the only source of Federal revenue from 1790 until Federal Income Tax began after 1913. During the 1850s, tariffs comprised ninety percent of the federal revenue. In 1859, southern ports paid seventy-five percent of those tariffs. This was a significant source of discomfort in the South—they believed their agricultural interests were being used by Congress to **protect** the manufacturing interests in the North. South Carolina's John C. Calhoun (U.S. Rep. 1811–17, Sec. of War 1817–25, V.P. 1825–32, Sec. of State 1844–45, U.S. Senator 1845–50,) strongly believed that "*a tariff for purposes of **protection**. and not for purposes of revenue only, is unconstitutional.*" Southerners considered the tariffs as similar to the Navigation Acts of King George III, which had driven Colonial America to Revolutionary War with Britain (1775–83).

THE CIVIL WAR ITSELF

In 1860, before the Civil War (1861–65) actually began, thirty-five states comprised the United States of America. The Union began with nineteen states, becoming twenty in 1863 when West Virginia was admitted after seceding from Virginia in 1861. Eleven states made up the Confederacy. Four border-states (Missouri, Kentucky, Maryland, and Delaware) were "neutral" as they contained both Union and Confederate loyalists. Both slaves and free blacks were among those who fought and died for Confederate causes. Stonewall Jackson had three thousand fully equipped black troops scattered throughout his corps September 17, 1862, at Antietam, the war's bloodiest battle. Black Confederate soldiers no more fought to preserve slavery than did their successors fight in World War II to preserve Jim Crow Laws (1877–1965) and segregation. They fought because their homeland was attacked and fought in the hope that their future would be better. Records show that slaves serving the Confederacy in some capacity numbered between 60,000 and 93,000. Nearly 180,000 free blacks and runaway slaves served the twenty Union states.

In an 1858 letter, Abraham Lincoln (1809–1865) wrote, "*I have declared a thousand times, and now repeat that, in my opinion neither the general government, nor any other power outside the United States, can constitutionally or rightfully interfere with slaves or slavery **where it already exists**.*"

In a Springfield, Illinois, speech, Lincoln explained, "*My declarations upon this subject of Negro slavery may be misrepresented, but cannot be misunderstood. I have said that I do not understand the Declaration (of Independence) to mean that all men were created equal **in all respects**.*"

Debating with Illinois Senator Stephen Douglas (1813–1861), Lincoln said, "*I am not, nor ever have been, in favor of making voters or jurors of Negroes nor of qualifying them to hold office nor to intermarry with white people, and I will say in addition to this that there is a physical difference between the white and black races, which I believe will forever forbid the two races living together on terms of **social and political equality**.*" (As for "physical difference," does the huge predominance of Negro participation in today's high school, college, and professional sports support Lincoln's statement?)

U.S. history books state or imply that Lincoln's Emancipation Proclamation freed the slaves and that the proclamation proves Lincoln was against slavery. Lincoln, as a **politician**, wrote, "*I view it (the Emancipation Proclamation) as a **practical war measure**, to be decided upon according to the advantages or disadvantages it may offer to the suppression of the rebellion.*" At the time (September 22, 1862) Lincoln wrote the proclamation, the war was going badly for the Union. Both London and Paris were considering recognizing the Confederacy and assisting in its war effort. In his response to this, Lincoln wrote, "*I will also concede that emancipation would **help us in Europe**, and convince them that we are incited by something more than ambition.*"

The Emancipation Proclamation was not a universal declaration. It **detailed** where slaves were freed—only in the United (Confederate) "States and parts of States in rebellion against the United (Union)

States." The proclamation excepted twelve parishes in Louisiana and the city of New Orleans, all forty-eight counties of West Virginia, and seven counties in Virginia plus the cities of Norfolk and Portsmouth, "which are for the present, left precisely as if this proclamation were not issued." And furthermore, slaves remained slaves in those ("neutral") states **not in rebellion**—Missouri, Kentucky, Maryland, and Delaware. My great, great-grandfather, Judge Harrison Hough (1811–1865), the first circuit judge in southeast Missouri, represented Missouri at the 1861 Peace Conference in Washington, DC. Twenty-nine well-cared for slaves, living in nine individual houses, worked his two thousand acres of cotton in Mississippi County, Missouri, at the time of his death.)

The **hypocrisy** of the proclamation was heavily criticized. William Seward, Lincoln's own secretary of state, said, "*We show our sympathy for slavery by emancipating slaves where we cannot reach them and holding them in bondage where we can set them free.*" Years earlier, in 1848, Lincoln articulated his view of secession in a speech to the U.S. House of Representatives regarding Texas and the war with Mexico. His view would have been welcomed seventy-three years earlier in 1775. "*Any people anywhere, being inclined and having the power, have the right to rise up and shake off the existing government and form a new one that suits them better, nor is this right confined to cases in which the whole people of an existing government may choose to exercise it. Any portion of such people that can may revolutionize and make their own of so much of the territory as they inhabit.*" Why didn't Lincoln feel the same about Texas's secession with the Confederacy twelve years later? Undoubtedly, it was the substantial preponderance of federal revenue generated by agriculture in the South. No "responsible" **politician** would let go of that much revenue.

EXAMPLES OF MISCONSTRUED U.S. HISTORY

Americans have been taught since childhood that the Pilgrims came to America on the Mayflower, landing at Plymouth Rock in 1620, "for religious freedom." **This is questionable**. Netherlands for many years before 1620 had been a haven for persecuted minorities of Europe: the Jews, the Belgian Walloons, the French Huguenots, and the English Separatists. The English Separatists returned to England for a short time to escape poverty and being assimilated into Dutch society. These Separatists then came to America on the Mayflower to escape further persecution in England. Upon arrival, the Pilgrims immediately set up a theocratic society and either imprisoned or expelled their own believers who spoke against ministers. In 1658, Plymouth passed a law against "Quaker ranters." The Puritans to the north of Plymouth were even worse. Decades passed before Massachusetts granted Jews and Roman Catholics the same freedom to worship as in other colonies. Representing the Pilgrims as pioneers of religious **tolerance** is preposterous.

Amherst, Massachusetts, and the college located there were named for Jeffrey Amherst, commander of British forces during the final battles of the French and Indian War. His victories against the French helped England acquire Canada. Even after France had been defeated, Native Americans and England fought on in what is known as Pontiac's Rebellion. In the summer of 1763, Native Americans had besieged Fort Pitt. British forces under Amherst "*bought time by sending smallpox-infected blankets and handkerchiefs to the Indians surrounding the fort, which started an epidemic among them.*" Amherst informed his field commanders that he viewed the Indians as "*the vilest race of beings that ever infested the earth, and whose riddance from it must be esteemed a meritorious act for the good of mankind. You will therefore take no prisoners, but put to death all that fall into your hands.*" It's outrageous for America to honor Jeffrey Amherst, whose most important connection with American history was an **act of genocide**. He employed the world's first known **use of germ warfare** in his attempt to extirpate Native Americans.

The cover of the brochure issued at Valley Forge National Historic Park is a reproduction of General Washington's letter to the Continental Congress saying, "*Naked and starving as they are we cannot enough admire the incomparable patience of the soldiery.*" That letter, dated February 16, 1776, was written twenty-two months before the army arrived at Valley Forge in December 1777. Inside the brochure is printed, "*Valley Forge is the story of an army's epic struggle to survive against terrible odds, against hunger, disease, and the unrelenting forces of nature.*" This statement falsely implies that the soldiers experienced extraordinary suffering due to unusual cold weather as they were encamped here in the winter of 1777–1778. In the introductory film—*Valley Forge, A Winter Encampment*—the narrator states that "*The troops were generally ill-equipped to deal with the harsh winter before them.*" Less than a minute later, he admits that "*the Valley Forge winter was generally moderate*" and then goes on to say that the log huts the soldiers built were nice and warm and supplies were available, although the food was often monotonous.

Two years later, Washington and his troops spent the 1779–1790 winter at Morristown, New Jersey. At the **Morristown** National Historic Park, the National Park Service correctly points out that it was the **worst winter in a hundred years**. The Morristown Park draws far fewer visitors simply because "everyone already knows about the 'terrible' winter the troops endured at Valley Forge."

SLAVERY

July 25, 2017

Slavery was common among ancient people such as the Egyptians, Babylonians, Greeks, Persians, Armenians, and many others. Large numbers of Christians were enslaved during the Ottoman wars in Europe. White slaves were common in Europe from the Dark Ages to the Middle Ages.

Europeans joined with Arabs and Africans after AD 1600 and started the Atlantic slave trade. Brutal black-on-black slavery was common in Africa for thousands of years. Most slaves brought to America from Africa were purchased from black slave owners. Native Americans owned thousands of black slaves.

At the beginning of the 1800s, an estimated three-quarters of all people alive were entrapped in bondage against their will either in some form of slavery or serfdom. In 1830, there were 3,775 free black people in America who owned 12,740 black slaves. Many black slaves in America were allowed to hold jobs, own businesses, and own real estate.

The first black slave owner in American history was a black tobacco farmer named Anthony Johnson. North Carolina's largest slave owner in 1860 was a black plantation owner named William Ellison.

The most unique aspect of slavery in the Western world was the moral outrage against it, which began to emerge in the 1700s and led to massive elimination efforts. It was Britain's military sea power that put an end to the slave trade. And America fought a costly war in 1861–1865 that brought an end to slavery.

Unfortunately, these facts about slavery are not in the lessons taught in our public schools and colleges. Instead, there is a gross misrepresentation and suggestion that slavery was a uniquely American practice.

While slavery is one of the grosses encroachments on human liberty, it is not unique or restricted to America, as many liberal academics would have us believe. Much of the indoctrination of young people paints our nation's founders as racist adherents to slavery, but the story is not so simple.

At the time of the 1787 Constitutional Convention in Philadelphia, slaves were about forty percent of the population of the Southern colonies whose primary activity was agriculture. Apportionment in the House of Representatives and the number of electoral votes each state would have in presidential elections would be based on population.

Southern delegates to the convention wanted each slave to be counted as one person, and Northern delegates wanted only free persons of each state to be counted. The compromise reached was that each slave would be counted as only three-fifths of a person.

Many criticize this compromise as proof of racism. My question is, would these grossly misinformed critics have found it more preferable for slaves to be counted as whole persons? Slaves counted as whole persons would have given slaveholding Southern states much more political power.

Or would the critics of the founders prefer that the Northern delegates not compromise and not allow slaves to be counted at all? If they did, it's likely that the Constitution would not have been ratified.

Would blacks be better off if Northern states had gone their way and Southern states having gone theirs, resulting in no U.S. Constitution and no Union? Black abolitionist Frederick Douglas understood the compromise, saying that the three-fifths clause was "a downright disability laid upon the slaveholding states" that deprived them of "two-fifths of their natural basis of representation."

Patrick Henry shared Douglas's vision. In expressing the reality of the three-fifths compromise, he said, "As much as I deplore slavery,

I see that prudence forbids its abolition." With this Union, Congress at least had the power to abolish slavery by 1808. Many of the founders abhorred slavery. James Wilson believed the anti-slave trade cause laid "the foundation for banishing slavery out of this country."

America's 150-Year Experiment

July 13, 2015

Abraham Lincoln issued a presidential proclamation September 22, 1862, which became an executive order effective January 1, 1863. Otherwise known as the Emancipation Proclamation, it was issued as a war measure during the Civil War 1861–65.

The order proclaimed the freedom of black slaves in the ten (Confederate) states that were still in rebellion. It applied to more than three million of the four million black slaves, which was 14.4 percent if the total population.

The order did not apply to the four slave states that were not in rebellion (Kentucky, Maryland, Delaware, and Missouri, which were unnamed) nor to Tennessee (unnamed but occupied by Union troops since 1862) and lower Louisiana (also under occupation). Specifically excluded also were the forty-eight counties in Virginia used to form the state of West Virginia in 1861.

The proclamation and order were based on the president's constitutional authority as commander in chief of the armed (Union) forces; it was not a law passed by Congress. In addition to the war goal of reuniting the Union of States, it made the eradication of slavery an explicit second goal of the war. The proclamation didn't compensate slave owners, didn't outlaw slavery, and didn't grant citizenship to the ex-slaves.

The Experiment

The government has tried for the past 150 years to determine its capability to do something previously untried in world history. And that is to integrate black and white races. Today, the black minority is 14.1 percent of the total population, and the white majority is still huge.

Cultural Differences

Black people taken from African tribes with no written language and no intellectual achievements, initially were brought to America by European slave traders, and sold into slavery. The white citizen majority, on the other hand, descended from Europeans who created a century's old advanced state of cultural, intellectual, and material development.

Government Action

Acting on a policy unfair to both racial groups, the government released a newly freed mostly uncivilized black slave culture into a civilized white culture.

The government has concocted program after program, insisting all the while that the experiment would work if they could find the right formula. A Freedmen's Bureau existed 1865–72, the Great Society was initiated in 1964–65, a war on poverty was declared, civil rights laws were passed, public housing projects built, preferences ordered, etc., etc., etc. Congress passed new laws and forced them into the lives of citizens in ways that would otherwise have been unthinkable. National Guard troops were called in and ordered to enforce public school integration. Freedom of association was outlawed. Black children were bussed to white schools and white children bussed to black schools. Endless efforts to close the academic achievement gap were tried with special programs, relaxed academic standards, and much money. Public and private statements on race such as "Say No to Racism" were published to keep the backlash of white people in check. Public banners on social justice were displayed commanding white citizens to celebrate diversity. Anything that might salvage the government's experiment was declared useful.

The Result

Through all the years, roughly ninety percent of black citizens have shown an inability to function in a white culture that's unsuited to them. South Chicago is a war zone. Detroit is bankrupt. Most predominantly black cities are beset by degeneracy and violence. These 40.5 million black people accept no responsibility for their own failures. Instead, they attack civil authority with anger and resentment.

In Detroit, Oakland, Watts, Los Angeles, Newark, Philadelphia, Milwaukee, Cleveland, Cincinnati, Buffalo, St. Louis, Ferguson, El Paso, Atlanta, Memphis, Birmingham, and Baltimore, rioting and looting is rampant, and all have populations 24.2 to 32.5 percent below poverty level. The most common characteristic of these predominantly black cities is that, for decades, all them have been run by Democrat administrations. What's more is that most of these cities have black mayors, chiefs of police, school superintendents, and principals and have black-dominated city councils. Newark hasn't had a Republican mayor since 1907, Milwaukee since 1908, St. Louis since 1949, and Cleveland since 1989. Einstein once said, "The definition of insanity is doing the same thing over and over again and expecting different results."

The black mayor of Memphis has proposed to exhume the bodies of Confederate General Nathan Bedford Forest and his wife and remove them from a city park. He must think marshaling resources to do that is more important than dealing with the city's 145 murders, 320 rapes, 6,900 aggravated assault calls, and 3,000 robberies. Records show that Memphis's black homicide victims all were murdered by other black citizens.

Some people promote the false narrative, in the wake of the Charleston murders, that it's white racists who are the interracial murderers. That's nonsense! FBI crime victimization statistics show that blacks commit eighty percent of all interracial violent crime.

What does banning from a public place the Confederate flag, which is alleged to be a symbol of slavery, have to do with the problems of black citizens today? As far as that goes, in the madness of political correctness, the case could also be made for banning the American flag because some slave ships sailed under the American flag.

Why not ban the use of the "racist" term "thug" in reference to black criminals looting businesses? Why not have more mayors, as the NYC Mayor Bill de Blasio does, teach that what black people and mulattos need to fear most are policemen, especially those who are white?

Viciously punching of random white citizens on public thoroughfares "for the thrill of it" or random beating to death of white citizens "out of hate" have nothing to do with poverty. Meanwhile, government propaganda insinuates the experiment hasn't failed—they need more money, more time, more understanding, more programs, and more opportunities.

Nothing changes no matter how much money is spent, how many laws are passed, how many black people are in Hollywood or portrayed on TV, or who (even a mulatto) is president. Most black citizens argue it's the black culture that creates their behavior. They simply don't understand it is black citizens that create their own culture. Others blame white privilege.

Conclusions Drawn

Roughly ten percent (4.5 million) of black Americans indeed have become entrepreneurs, lawyers, scientists, medical doctors, and law-abiding good and respected citizens. Social stability can't be achieved unless the black elite convinces most of the other 40.5 million black citizens to shape-up and fill today's void of (nonacademic) trade school craftsmen.

Immigrants from Asia and India who aren't white and not rich have quietly succeeded since 1965 when this nation opened its doors to the third world. While children of these people excel in academics, win spelling bees, are National Merit Scholars, and earn top SAT scores, black youth are committing more than half of the violent crimes.

Our government's experiment has failed not because of white culture, white privilege, or white racism. It's failed because the black culture is a crime-dominated, unfixable mess. Most black citizens don't want to change their culture but expect others to tolerate their violence and amoral behavior. They have become incompatible with other races by their own design, not because of the racism of others, but by their own hatred of nonblacks.

If all white citizens were to become angels tomorrow, it would do nothing for the problems plaguing the ninety percent segment of the black community. Illegitimacy, family breakdown, crime, and fraudulent education indeed are devastating problems, but they aren't civil rights problems. Those black youths awarded high school diplomas can write or compute no better than a white seventh or eighth grader. There's little or nothing that government or white citizens can do to solve these problems. The solution lies with black citizens.

Most government leaders refuse to acknowledge that white citizens are becoming exhausted with black social pathologies—the violence, the blind black racial solidarity, the bottomless pit of grievances, and the active hatred of nonblacks. Minorities—black, gay, atheist, Muslim, and illegal citizens—rule in government today. White majority frustration could likely reach the point of crisis if government doesn't prioritize positive changes by the second quarter of 2017.

No free nation can exist when freedom of choice is legislated away from a racial majority while at the same time that freedom of choice is legislated to a racial minority. Neither national wealth nor individual wealth can be multiplied by dividing it.

The Genius of Benjamin Franklin 244 Years Ago

February 27, 2019

From his witty sayings to his numerous inventions; from his studies of electricity and his discovery of the "Gulf Stream" to his role in drafting the Declaration of Independence; from his work in securing French support for the American Revolution to his service in the Constitutional Convention, the breadth and depth of Benjamin Franklin's contributions have shaped America and the world as a whole for more than two centuries and will continue to do so for untold millennia.

Sometime about 1775 during the French and Indian War, Benjamin Franklin was given a commission by Pennsylvania's governor, Robert Morris, to take charge of the northwestern frontier. It was during this time that Franklin's insights into behavioral psychology first became apparent.

"We had for our chaplain a zealous Presbyterian minister, Mr. Beatty, who complained to me that the men did not generally attend his prayers and exhortations. "When they enlisted, they were promised, besides pay and provisions, a gill (1/4 pint) of rum a day, which was punctually served out to them, half in the morning, and the other half in the evening.

"I observ'd they were punctual in attending to receive it, upon which I said to Mr. Beatty: 'It is perhaps below the dignity of your profession to act as steward of the rum, but if you were to deal it out and only just after prayers, you would have them all about you.'

"He liked the tho't, undertook the office, and, with the help of a few hands to measure out the liquor, executed it to satisfaction. Never were prayers more generally and more punctually attended. "I thought this method preferable to the punishment inflicted by some military laws for non-attendance on divine services." Franklin had once again demonstrated that he was a man ahead of his times and is justly credited with his contributions to the field of behavioral psychology.

History of Labor
Versus Machine

October 31, 2019

There still seems to be a growing fear even today that automation is going to take away jobs, and that something has to be done to stop it. Many politicians believe that "something" involves raising the price of automation, perhaps by taxing each robot or by demanding that companies find jobs elsewhere for displaced workers.

History tells us that policies aimed at restricting or slowing automation comes with a steep price tag. It's important to remember that the acceleration in economic growth that followed the Industrial Revolution, which first began in England around 1750, was caused by the steady adoption of automation technologies that allowed the production of more with fewer people.

Before 1750, per capita income in the world doubled every six thousand years. Thereafter, it has doubled every fifty years. One explanation for why economic growth was stagnant for millennia is that the world was caught in a technology trap, in which labor-replacing technology was consistently and vigorously resisted for fear of its destabilizing force.

For most of history, the politics of progress were such that the ruling classes had little to gain and much to lose from the introduction of labor-replacing technology. They rightly feared that angry workers might rebel against the government.

Opposition to labor-saving technology has a long history. Following are some of the more notable incidents of technology-related labor unrest from the Roman Empire to last year.

> **69–79**. Roman Emperor Vespasian refused a labor-saving device for transporting stone columns to Rome's Capitoline Hill saying, "How will it be possible for me to feed the populace."

> **1412**. Due to resistance by the Silk Spinners Guild to a **silk-twisting mill**, the City of Cologne declared that "many persons who earn their bread in the guild in this town would fall into poverty, for which the town council agreed that neither this mill nor in general any similar mill shall be made or erected, either now or in the future."

> **1470s**. **Guttenberg's printing press** drew protests from Italian professional writers in Genoa in 1472, German card makers in 1473 Augsburg, and French stationers in 1477 Lyons.

> **1551**. **The gig mill**, which is estimated to have allowed one man and two boys to do the work of eighteen men and six boys, was prohibited in Britain.

> **1589**. **England's Queen Elizabeth** refused to grant William Lee a patent for the landmark labor-replacing stocking-frame knitting machine, saying, "Thou aimest high, Master Lee. Consider thou what the invention could do to my poor subjects. It would assuredly bring to them ruin by depriving them of employment, thus making them beggars."

1632. King Charles I of England banned the casting of buckets, it might ruin the livelihoods of the craftsmen who were still making buckets the traditional way.

1768. The first steam-powered sawmill in Limehouse, for which its founder had been awarded the gold medal of the British Society of Arts, was burned to the ground by five hundred sawyers who claimed that it had deprived them of employment. Parliament passed and Act in 1769 that made the destruction of machines a felony punishable by death, but the law didn't prevent similar disturbances.

1789. Angry woolen workers destroyed machines in the Paris manufacturing suburb of Saint-Sever. A long series of similar incidents followed, casting a long shadow over France.

1802. Kaiser Francis I blocked the construction of new factories in Vienna and banned the importation and adoption of new machinery until 1811. When plans were put before him for the construction of a steam railroad, he responded: "No, no, I will have nothing to do with it, lest the revolution might come into the country."

1811. A stockinger's apprentice responded to his master's reprimand by taking a hammer to a Stocking-frame, which started the destruction of machines in the lace and hosiery trades. Over the next few years, only the machines considered innovations or threatened employment were destroyed. The British government took an increasingly stern view of any attempt to halt the force of technology and deployed troops against the rioters known as Luddites.

1830. **The Captain Swing riots** that broke-out in this year included more than two thousand riots across Britain that targeted agricultural machines. Again, the British government took a harsh line, ordering the Army as well as local militias to take action against any rioters; 252 death sentences were passed, though some sentenced to death were deported to Australia or New Zealand.

1870s. **Elias Grove's wheat-threshing machine** was destroyed in a fire in Baltimore. Ten days later a letter arrived: "Mr. Grove, you will stop your other machine or next it will be your life. We intend to stop your steam threshing. We do not get enough work through the winter and summer." A number of U.S. farmers had received similar threatening letters in the 1870s.

1895. The introduction of machines in the **La Ferme cigaterre factory** in Saint Petersburg, Russia, led to a riot. The employees, who feared unemployment, smashed the machines and threw the fragments out the windows.

1930s. **President Franklin D. Roosevelt's** administration tried to slow the pace of mechanization. Of the 280 regulations issued by the National Recovery Administration, 36 included restrictions on the installation of new machines.

2018. **Members in the Culinary Union in Las Vegas** voted to authorize a strike if contract negotiations with casino operators failed to address concerns including job security and retraining regarding automation. "We support innovations that improve jobs, but we oppose automation when it only destroys jobs." A strike of fifty thousand workers was averted with agreements that set goals regarding technology and automation for worker retention, job training, and advance notice of implementation and severance packages.

The Truth about Robert E. Lee

November 8, 2017

Robert E. Lee, who has recently been outlandishly characterized as a traitor, embodied in countless ways the deeply moving tragedy of the Civil War. Lee was an honorable man living at a time when men and women of good faith, on both sides, made their stand where there conscience had made them stand. It would be a glaringly obvious misfortune if the current political debate destroys his story.

Lee's lineage was impeccable. His father, "Light-Horse Harry" Lee III, was a celebrated Revolutionary War general and close friend of George Washington. Lee himself descended from two signers of the Declaration of Independence. His wife, Mary Custis, who later became a devoted Confederate, was a great-granddaughter of Martha Washington and, through adoption, of George Washington himself.

As war seemed imminent in 1861, President Abraham Lincoln offered Lee command of the Union Army, a position he, being a top graduate of West Point, had always wished for. He was fifty-five years old at the time. Lee agonized over whether to fight for the Confederacy. Despite being an avowed Federalist with heartfelt desire for compromise to save the Union, he gave-in to the permanency of birth and blood.

Lee wrote to a friend, "I cannot raise my hand against my birthplace, my home, my children, save in the defense of my native state." He became the commanding general of the Confederate armies while predicting that the country would pass "through a terrible ordeal."

Like Lincoln, more often than not Lee referred to the other side as "those people" rather than "the enemy." Still he was never much of a hater. With words that could have been said by Lincoln, he talked of the cruelty of war, how it "filled our hearts with hatred instead of love for our neighbors."

Nor was Lee fond of slavery once describing it as "a moral and political evil." True, he did benefit from slavery. But the next day after the Emancipation Proclamation took effect in 1863, General Lee went a step further than did Thomas Jefferson and freed his family slaves, fulfilling the wishes of his father-in-law, George Washington Parke Custis.

As the Confederacy faced destruction in 1865, General Lee supported a dramatic measure to put slaves in uniform and train them to fight, which would have effectively emancipated them. At the end of the war, Lee gave an interview to the New York Herald in which he strongly condemned Lincoln's assassination, saying that "the best men of the south" had long wanted to see slavery end. Later, he declared, "I am rejoiced that slavery is abolished."

Probably, Lee's most powerful statement about race relations came at the end of the war in St. Paul's Church, the congregation of the Richmond, Virginia, elite. To the intense dislike of the congregants, a well-dressed black man advanced to take communion and knelt down at the altar rail. The minister froze, unsure what to do. Lee knelt down next to the black man to partake of communion with him.

Finally, Lee's greatest legacy was not in war but in peace. He took great pains to heal the bitterness that divided the country after Appomattox. When Lee surrendered to Ulysses S. Grant in one of the most moving scenes in American history, the military situation remained quite dangerous. The war was still going on.

Jefferson Davis, the Confederate president, was on the run, calling on Southerners to take-to-the-hills and wage guerilla warfare. There were still three Confederate armies, and hatreds between North and South were at their peak.

Five days after the surrender, Lincoln was assassinated. Had the South undertaken guerilla warfare, it's more than likely the United States would have broken-up into two countries.

At Appomattox, President Lincoln and General Grant gave generous terms to the South, paving the way to reconciliation. They found a willing partner in Lee. Being neither a citizen of the Union Lee once loved nor of the Confederacy that ceased to exist, he publically rejected the idea of a guerilla struggle.

Most important, by April 1865, Lee no longer spoke of "we" or "our country." He now spoke as a United States citizen, thereby leading the way to a reunited country. This is the reason when there were calls to try Lee for treason, Grant vigorously opposed them.

From 1865 until death in 1870, Lee served as president of Washington College in Lexington, Virginia. Today, the name of the school is Washington and Lee University. What would Robert E. Lee have thought of the recent events of today? He might have supported the moving of his own statues. In 1869, Lee was invited to participate in a ceremonial meeting of officers at Gettysburg, Pennsylvania, to commemorate the battle there six years earlier. He declined, writing: "I think it wiser not to keep open the sores or war but to follow the example of those nations who endeavored to obliterate the marks of civil strife, to commit to oblivion the feelings engendered."

The debate will surely continue over whether to move the Confederate monuments out of public view, as it will over whether to rechristen spaces bearing the names of Jefferson, Andrew Jackson, Woodrow Wilson, and even Washington. Where will it end?

Robert E. Lee's story should serve as a reminder that the past is more complex and difficult to understand than the political debate of today suggests. It's important to take public sentiment into account but not at the expense of ignoring or causing the American public to turn away from history.

Events Leading to World War II and Some Events of World War II

April 7, 2017

July 29, 1921	Adolph Hitler becomes Fuhrer (leader) of the National Socialist German Workers (Nazi) Party.
October 29, 1922	Fascist leader Benito Mussolini is appointed the premier of Italy.
January 30, 1933	Adolph Hitler is appointed the chancellor of Germany.
June 14, 1933	The Nazis make all other political parties in Germany illegal.
October 25, 1936	Hitler and Mussolini announce a Rome-Berlin alliance—the Axis.
March 12, 1938	Germany invades Austria and annexes it the next day.
September 29, 1938	German, Britain, France, and Italy sign the Munich Pact allowing Germany to invade Sudeten territories of Czechoslovakia.
March 15, 1939	German troops enter Prague and complete the invasion of Czechoslovakia, ignoring the Munich Pact.

March 31, 1939	Britain declares that it will support Poland in the event of an attack.
August 19, 1939	Allies form nonaggression pacts with Turkey, Greece, Romania, and Poland.
August 23, 1939	Germany and USSR sign a secret non-aggression pact dividing-up Poland.
September 1, 1939	**Germany invades Poland— World War II begins.**
September 3, 1939	Britain, France, Australia, and New Zealand declare war on Germany after German forces penetrate deeper into Poland.
September 10, 1939	Canada declares war on Germany.
September 17, 1939	The USSR invades Eastern Poland.
September 27, 1939	Poland surrenders to Germany.
November 30, 1939	The Russo-Finish War begins when the USSR invades Finland.
December 18, 1939	The first Canadian troops arrive in Britain.
March 12, 1940	Finland surrenders to the USSR, ending the brief Russo-Finish War that began when the USSR invaded Finland November 30, 1939.
April 9, 1940	Denmark surrenders to Germany. Germany invades Norway.
May 10, 1940	Winston Churchill becomes the new prime minister of Britain, replacing Chamberlain. Germany invades the Netherlands (Holland); Netherlands surrenders four days later. Germany invades Belgium.
May 26, 1940	Operation Dynamo begins, the evacuation of the British Expeditionary from Dunkirk on the Belgian coast.

May 28, 1940	Belgium surrenders to Germany.
June 10, 1940	Norway surrenders to Germany. Italy declares war on Britain and France.
June 14, 1940	German troops enter Paris.
June 18, 1940	The USSR invades the Baltic States.
June 22, 1940	France surrenders to Germany.
June 30, 1940	Germany invades the Channel Islands. This will be the only part of Britain to be occupied by the Germans.
July 3, 1940	The British sink the French fleet at Oran.
July 10, 1940	The Battle of Britain begins. Germany bombs Britain, and the British defend themselves from the air in what Winston Churchill would call their "finest hour."
August 3, 1940	Italy invades British Somaliland, marking the beginning of World War II in Africa.
August 14, 1940	The U.S. and Britain sign the Atlantic Charter declaring their joint opposition to fascism, despite the United States being nominally neutral.
September 27, 1940	Germany, Italy, and Japan sign the Tripartite Pact, making Japan part of the Axis.
October 7, 1940	Germany invades Romania.
October 28, 1940	Italy invades Greece but fails to conquer it.
October 31, 1940	The Battle of Britain ends. The powerful German Luftwaffe fails to crush British morale.
November 23, 1940	Hungary and Romania sign the Tripartite Pact, becoming part of the Axis.
December 3, 1940	Greece invades Italian-held Albania.
March 1, 1941	Bulgaria signs the Tripartite Pact, becoming part of the Axis.

March 11, 1941	The U.S. Congress passes the Lend-Lease Act giving President Roosevelt the authority to sell, transfer, or lease war goods to any government of any Allied country, thereby effectively ending U.S. neutrality.
March 25, 1941	Yugoslavia signs the Tripartite Pact, briefly becoming part of the Axis, but the pro-German government is toppled two days later.
March 30, 1941	The German Afrika Korps begins its offensive in North Africa.
April 6, 1941	Germany invades Yugoslavia and Greece.
April 10, 1941	The United States occupies Greenland.
April 13, 1941	The USSR and Japan sign a neutrality pact.
May 27, 1941	Bismarck, German battleship, sunk by British warships while she was on her maiden voyage.
May 31, 1941	German airborne troops defeat the British in Crete.
June 4, 1941	Britain invades Iraq and overthrows its pro-German government.
June 22, 1941	Germany invades Russia, thereby beginning Operation Barbarossa; Italy and Romania declare war on the USSR.
June 23, 1941	Hungary and Slovakia declare war on the USSR.
June 26, 1941	Finland declares war on the USSR.
July 7, 1941	The United States occupies Iceland.
September 15, 1941	Germany begins the Siege of Leningrad. It would not end until January 27, 1944.
October 1, 1941	The United States begins supplying the USSR under the Lend-Lease Act.
October 2, 1941	Germany begins the drive toward Moscow.

November 22, 1941	Britain gives Finland an ultimatum: halt all offensive operations against the USSR or face a war with Allies.
December 5, 1941	Germany abandons attack on Moscow; the USSR counterattacks.
December 7, 1941	**Japan attacks the U.S. Naval Base at Pearl Harbor, Hawaii.**
December 8, 1941	The Allies, except USSR, declare war on Japan.
December 8, 1941	Japan invades Siam and Malaya.
December 11, 1941	Germany and Italy declare war on the United States.
December 22, 1941	The Arcadia Conference between the United States and Britain begins in Washington, DC.
December 25, 1941	Japan invades Hong Kong.
January 1, 1942	The Declaration of the United Nations is signed by the leaders of twenty-six nations.
January 2, 1942	Japan captures Manila in the Philippines.
January 12, 1942	Japan invades Burma.
January 14, 1942	Arcadia Conference concludes, at which Roosevelt and Churchill agree on "Germany First" policy.
January 20, 1942	Germany holds the Wannsee Conference in Berlin to find a "Final Solution" for the Jews.
January 26, 1942	The first U.S. troops arrive in Britain.
February 15, 1942	Japan invades Singapore.
April 9, 1942	U.S. troops on Bataan in the Philippines surrender to the Japanese, and the Bataan Death March begins.
April 18, 1942	Doolittle's raiders bomb Tokyo.

May 4, 1942	U.S. Navy repels the Japanese at the Battle of the Corral Sea. This helps save Australia and blocks of the Japanese juggernaut in the Pacific.
May 6, 1942	The remaining U.S. troops on Corregidor in the Philippines surrender to the Japanese.
June 4, 1942	The United States defeats the Japanese at the Battle of Midway. Together with the Battle of the Coral Sea, this marks the turning point in the war in the Pacific.
June 18, 1942	The U.S. Army Corps of Engineers initiates the Manhattan Project to develop the atomic bomb.
July 3, 1942	Japanese troops take Guadalcanal.
July 22, 1942	Germany begins deporting hundreds of thousands of Jews from the Warsaw Ghetto to the Treblinka concentration camp.
August 7, 1942	U.S. troops land on Guadalcanal.
August 22, 1042	Brazil declares war on Germany and Italy.
October 23, 1942	The battle between German and British troops at El Alamein in North Africa begins.
November 8, 1942	Allies invade North Africa, beginning Operation Torch.
November 10, 1942	Vichy French forces stop fighting the Allies. Allied forces begin moving into Tunisia.
November 13, 1942	British troops recapture Tobruk, Libya.
January 1, 1943	The Declaration of the United Nations is signed by the leaders of twenty-six nations.
January 2, 1943	Australian and U.S. Army forces under General McArthur fight back the Japanese at Gona in New Guinea.

January 31, 1943	Over ninety thousand German troops at Stalingrad surrender to the USSR. It is a significant turning point in the war against Germany.
February 8, 1943	U.S. troops complete the capture of Guadalcanal from the Japanese.
April 19, 1943	The Warsaw Ghetto Uprising begins after German troops attempt to deport the ghetto's last surviving Jews. About 750 Jews fought back the Germans for about a month.
May 11, 1943	The Trident Conference between the United States and Britain begins. Roosevelt and Churchill decide to delay the Allied invasion of France and in its place plan the Allied invasion of Italy. In Alaska, U.S. troops land on Atu in the Aleutian Islands to retake it from the Japanese.
May 12, 1943	Axis forces in North Africa surrender.
May 16, 1943	German troops crush the last resistance of the Warsaw Ghetto Uprising and kill thousands of Jews. The rest are sent to the Treblinka concentration camp to die.
July 10, 1943	Over 160,000 Allied troops land in Sicily, beginning Operation Husky.
July 24, 1943	The Allies begin bombing Hamburg.
July 25, 1943	Benito Mussolini's fascist government is overthrown in Italy. The new Italian government begins peace talks.
August 15, 1943	Allies land in the South of France, beginning Operation Anvil.
August 17, 1943	Operation Husky, the Allied invasion of Sicily, is successfully concluded when U.S. troops take Messina.

August 11, 1943	The Quebec Conference between the United States and Britain begins.
August 15, 1943	U.S. troops retake Kiska Island in the Aleutians.
September 3, 1943	British troops land on mainland Italy, beginning the Allied campaign in Italy. U.S. troops land six days later.
September 10, 1943	German troops occupy Rome. Mussolini soon declares himself the head of a new fascist Italian government in German-occupied Northern Italy.
October 13, 1943	Italy declares war on Germany.
November 1, 1943	U.S. Marines land on Bougainville in the Solomon Islands.
November 8, 1943	The Tehran Conference begins. Roosevelt, Churchill, and Stalin meet together for the first time.
November 20, 1943	U.S. Army troops land on Makin Island in the Gilberts. Marines land on Tarawa. Within four days, both islands were secured but at the cost of thousands of casualties.
December 1, 1943	The Tehran Conference between the United States, Britain, and the USSR is successfully concluded. Roosevelt, Churchill, and Stalin agree that the Western Allies would invade France in June 1944 and that the USSR would launch a new offensive from the east.
December 2, 1943	Australian and U.S. Army forces under General McArthur fight back the Japanese at Buna in New Guinea.
December 14, 1943	Casablanca Conference begins. Allies agree that Germany must surrender unconditionally. Allies begin planning invasion of Sicily.

December 24, 1943	General Dwight Eisenhower is named Supreme Commander of the Allied Expeditionary Forces.
January 22, 1944	The Allies land in Anzio, Italy.
January 27, 1944	The German siege of Leningrad that began September 15, 1941, finally ends.
February 20, 1944	The Allies begin a massive bombing campaign of Germany.
February 22, 1944	The USSR bombs Stockholm, Sweden. Four days later, the USSR bombs Helsinki, Finland.
March 19, 1944	German troops occupy Hungary.
May 12, 1944	German troops in the Crimea surrender.
June 4, 1944	The Allies capture Rome.
June 6, 1944	D-Day. Operation Overlord—the Allied invasion of German-occupied Western Europe—begins on the beaches of Normandy, France.
June 8, 1944	Britain invades Syria and overthrows its Vichy French government.
June 13, 1944	German launches its first V-1 flying-bomb on Britain.
June 15, 1944	U.S. troops make an amphibious assault on the Japanese-held Island of Saipan in the Marianas.
June 19, 1944	The United States defeats the Japanese in a massive air battle known as the Battle of the Philippine Sea. The Japanese lost more than four hundred planes and three carriers. This victory paved the way for eventual success in the Mariana Islands invasion.
June 27, 1944	The Allies liberate Cherbourg, France.
July 7, 1944	Japanese troops on Saipan surrender.

July 9, 1944	Allies liberate Caen, France.
July 20, 1944	German military leaders attempt but fail to kill Adolf Hitler in the Rastenburg Assassination Plot. Hitler then kills about two hundred suspected plotters. U.S. troops make an amphibious assault on the Japanese-held Guam in the Mariana Islands.
July 23, 1944	U.S. troops make an amphibious assault on the Japanese-held Tinian in the Mariana Islands.
August 10, 1944	U.S. troops complete the recapture of Guam.
August 15, 1944	The Allies land in the south of France, beginning Operation Anvil.
August 20, 1944	The USSR invades German-occupied Romania.
August 23, 1944	Romania surrenders.
August 25, 1944	The Allies liberate Paris, France.
September 8, 1944	The USSR invades Bulgaria. Germany launches the first V-2 flying-bomb on Britain.
September 9, 1944	Bulgaria makes peace with the USSR then declares war on Germany.
September 11, 1944	Allies enter Germany.
September 17, 1944	The amphibious Allied airborne assault in Arnhem, Holland—Operation Market-Garden—fails to shorten the war against Germany.
September 26, 1944	The USSR occupies Estonia. Over six thousand Allied survivors of Operation Market-Garden in Arnhem, Holland, are taken prisoners by the Germans.
October 1, 1944	USSR troops enter Yugoslavia.

October 4, 1944	The Allies enter Greece, following the withdrawal of German troops.
October 14, 1944	The Allies liberate Athens, Greece.
October 20, 1944	The Allies capture Belgrade, Yugoslavia.
October 21, 1944	The Allies capture Aachen, the first city to be taken in Germany.
October 23, 1944	USSR troops enter East Prussia.
October 26, 1944	The U.S. Navy defeats the Japanese in the Battle of Leyte Gulf. The Japanese Navy is now virtually powerless.
November 4, 1944	Axis forces in Greece surrender.
November 24, 1944	U.S. B-29 bombers begin the massive bombing campaign against mainland Japan. In Europe, the Allies capture Strasbourg.
November 29, 1944	Allies capture Albania.
December 16, 1944	Germany begins its last-ditch Offensive in the Ardennes, beginning the Battle of the Bulge.
December 26, 1944	U.S. troops hold Bastogne, stalling the German offensive in the Ardennes.
January 9, 1945	U.S. Army troops land on Luzon in the Philippines.
January 26, 1945	Japanese troops retreat to the coast of China.
January 27, 1945	USSR troops liberate Auschwitz and Birknau extermination camps, uncovering evidence of the murder of approximately one million people.
January 28, 1945	In Western Europe, the Battle of the Bulge ends. The Germans cannot recover their military losses. Few people besides Hitler believe Germany can win the war.

February 4, 1945	The Yalta Conference begins. Roosevelt, Churchill, and Stalin discuss plans for Europe after the war, and Stalin agrees to declare war on Japan. In the Pacific, the Allies finally retake Manila.
February 13, 1945	The Allies begin firebombing Dresden, Germany, killing at least twenty-five thousand.
February 19, 1945	U.S. Marines land on Iwo Jima.
February 20, 1945	Allies capture Saarbrucken.
February 23, 1945	U.S. Marines take Mt. Suribachi on the Island of Iwo Jima. The photograph of the Stars and Stripes being raised upon the summit becomes the most legendary of the war.
March 3, 1945	Finland declares war on Germany.
March 7, 1945	The Allies capture two significant targets in Germany—the Remagen Bridge over the Rhine River, and the city of Cologne.
March 9, 1945	U.S. firebombing Tokyo kills about eighty-five thousand Japanese.
March 20, 1945	Allies capture Mandalay, Burma.
March 26, 1945	U.S. troops complete the capture of Iwo Jima from the Japanese, at the cost of twenty-five thousand U.S. casualties.
March 30, 1945	USSR troops capture Danzig.
April 1, 1945	U.S. troops invade Okinawa, the first Japanese home island to be reached. In Europe, the Allies surround over three hundred thousand German troops in the Ruhr Valley, and the final Allied offensive in Northern Italy begins.

April 11, 1945	U.S. troops reach the Buchenwald concentration camp and discover that the prisoners liberated themselves from a forced evacuation. A few days later, the British troops liberate the Bergen-Belsen concentration camp for women.
April 12, 1945	President Franklin D. Roosevelt dies of a cerebral hemorrhage at age sixty-three. Harry S. Truman becomes president of the United States.
April 13, 1945	USSR troops capture Vienna, Austria.
April 18, 1945	The last of the German troops trapped on the Ruhr River surrender.
April 23, 1945	USSR troops reach Berlin.
April 25, 1945	U.S. and USSR troops meet at the Elbe River in Germany.
April 28, 1945	Benito Mussolini is captured by anti-fascists and executed.
April 29, 1945	U.S. troops liberate Dachau concentration camp where they discovered evidence of gruesome medical experiments.
April 30, 1945	Adolf Hitler and Eva Braun commit suicide in a Berlin bunker as USSR troops advance through the city. Nazi propaganda minister Joseph Goebbels is scheduled to become the new German Chancellor, but he also kills himself (after having his wife and six children killed). Karl Doenitz is named as Hitler's successor.
May 2, 1945	USSR troops complete the capture of Berlin. The remaining German troops in Northern Italy surrender.
May 7, 1945	Germany surrenders unconditionally.
May 8, 1945	VE Day is declared—Victory in Europe.

May 9, 1845	USSR troops occupy Prague and the Allies liberate the Channel Islands.
June 21, 1945	U.S. troops complete the capture of Okinawa, providing a secure base for the final assault on Japan.
July 16, 1945	The world's first atomic bomb is successfully tested in New Mexico—The Trinity Test. The parts of the bombs to be dropped on Japan are already on their way. In Germany, the Potsdam Conference between the United States, Britain, and the USSR begins. Disagreements on the future of Europe plant more seeds for the upcoming Cold War.
July 26, 1945	The United States, Britain, and China issue the Potsdam Declaration which gives an ultimatum to Japan: unconditionally surrender immediately, or face "prompt and utter destruction." In Britain, Clement Atlee replaces Winston Churchill as Prime Minister.
July 30, 1945 only	The USS Indianapolis is sunk on its way to Leyte Gulf. Of 1,196 aboard, only 316 remained alive when they were rescued from the water almost five days later. It marked the worst naval disaster of World War II.
August 6, 1945	A U.S. B-29 named Enola Gay drops the "Little Boy" atomic bomb over Hiroshima, Japan.
August 8, 1945	The USSR declares war on Japan. USSR troops invade Japanese-held Manchuria.
August 9, 1945	The U.S. B-29 named Box Car drops the "Fat Man" atomic bomb on Nagasaki, Japan.

August 14, 1945   Japan agrees to unconditionally surrender.

August 15, 1945   V-J Day is declared—Victory over Japan.

September 1, 1945   Four telegrams were sent between
                    General McArthur and President
                    Harry Truman as follows:

1. McArthur to Truman: "Tomorrow, we (he and Nimitz) meet with those yellow-bellied bastards and sign the surrender documents, any last-minute instructions!"
2. Truman to McArthur: "Congratulations, job well done, but you must tone down your obvious dislike of the Japanese when discussing the terms of the surrender with the press because some of your remarks are fundamentally not politically correct!"
3. McArthur to Truman: "Will comply, sir, but both Chester and I are somewhat confused, exactly what does the term politically correct mean?"
4. Truman to McArthur: "Political correctness is a doctrine, recently fostered by a delusional, illogical minority and promoted by a sick mainstream media, which holds forth the proposition that it is entirely possible to pick-up a turd by the clean end."

September 2, 1945   Japan signs the formal surrender agreement aboard the USS Missouri in Tokyo Bay. World War II, the most devastating war in human history, is over.

GREAT BATTLES DESCRIBED

JAPANESE ATTACK PEARL HARBOR, December 7, 1941

Admiral Husband Kimmel was commander-in-chief of the U.S. Pacific fleet, when Japanese forces brazenly attacked Pearl Harbor. Kimmel stared in horror as many Japanese planes piloted by kamikazes attacked his fleet. Following the attack, Kimmel was relieved of his command of the Pacific Fleet and demoted to Rear Admiral. However, the United States was ill-prepared for the sneak attack, and the fault does not rest on Kimmel alone.

U.S.—3.682 killed or wounded. Japan—65 Kamikaze pilots and other pilots killed.

DOOLITTLE RAIDERS BOMB TOKYO, April 18, 1942

General Jimmy Doolittle is known for leading his daring and historic raid over Tokyo four months after the Japanese attacked Pearl Harbor. For his leadership in that raid, he was awarded the Medal of Honor and promoted two grades. But few people know that General Doolittle also played a key role in defeating Nazi Germany. As commander of the Eighth Air Force, he changed the policy requiring escorting fighter planes to remain with the bombers at all times. With this change in tactic, escorting P-51 Mustangs began strafing German airfields and transport facilities while returning to base. Thus resulted in devastating blows to Germany's infrastructure and secured air supremacy for Allied Air Forces over Europe.

CORAL SEA AND MIDWAY, May 4–7, 1942, and June 7, 1942

Ten days after the Japanese attack on Pearl Harbor, Fleet Admiral Chester Nimitz was named commander-in-chief of the U.S. Pacific Fleet. The fate of the war in the Pacific Theater rested on his shoulders. In the years that followed, Admiral Nimitz proved himself to be one of the best naval warfare tacticians in history. Nimitz dealt the Japanese forces the most stunning and decisive blow in the history of naval warfare at the Battle of Midway. Three years after this battle, Admiral Nimitz (with General McArthur) accepted the unconditional surrender of the Japanese on behalf of the United States aboard the USS Missouri.

United States losses—658 killed (Coral Sea). United States losses—307 killed (Midway).

GUADALCANAL, August 7, 1942–February 9, 1943

Fleet Admiral William F. Halsey, an aggressive and effective commander who was never content with playing defense, took command of the South Pacific Fleet at a time when victory was far from certain. Admiral Halsey proved his skill as he led his fleet in the decisive Naval Battle of Guadalcanal, which forced the Japanese to finally abandon the island.

United States losses—7,104 killed or wounded.

OPERATION TORCH/NORTH AFRICA, November 8, 1942– May 7, 1943

Following early defeats in North Africa, General George S. Patton was made commander of U.S. II Corps, a decision that would pay huge dividends. General Patten was hard on his men but instilled incredible discipline. His supreme confidence was infectious, causing his men to fight harder. Following success in North Africa, General Patton commanded the 7th Army in Sicily, taking Palermo and Messina. His greatest fame was commanding the 3rd Army in its race across France toward Germany and the relief of the beleaguered 101st Airborne Division at Bastogne.

United States losses—1,199 killed or wounded.

OPERATION MARKET GARDEN, September 7–25, 1944

Lieutenant General James "Jumpin' Joe" Gavin was the youngest commander to ever lead a division and was respected greatly by his men of the 82nd Airborne. He earned the nickname because he would engage in combat drops with the paratroopers he commanded. The plan was to invade Germany through the Netherlands, thus circumventing the northern end of the Siegfried Line. The strategy did not work, but General Gavin broke his back in two places during his combat drop, yet that injury could not stop him from fighting side-by-side with his men.

United States losses—17,200 killed, wounded, captured.

CHINA, BURMA, INDIA THEATER, February 1942–August 1945

George Marshal once said that he gave "one of the most difficult assignments" of any theater commander to General Joseph Stillwell. General Stillwell led U.S. and Chinese forces against Imperial Japan in the C-B-I Theater. Japan's military depended heavily on the rich natural resources found in China and Southeast Asia. General Stillwell's job was to roll back the tide of Japanese occupation and disrupt the flow of these resources. His no-nonsense leadership style made him an effective commander for the task which also involved Louis Mountbatten, Claire Chennault, and Chiang Kai Chek.

SICILY AND ITALY, July 10, 1943–August 17, 1943/September 3, 1943–May 2, 1945

General Omar Bradley proved his leadership skills in the invasion and liberation of Sicily, which resulted in the collapse of Mussolini's fascist regime. He played a crucial role in defeating the Axis powers of Europe. From the Normandy landing through the end of the war, General Bradley had command of all ground forces invading Germany from the west. At one point, he had nearly 1.3-million men under his command—the largest force ever to serve under one field commander in U.S. history.

Allies losses—24,850 killed, wounded, captured.

D-DAY NORMANDY, June 6, 1944

Prior to the outbreak of World War II, General Dwight D. Eisenhower had never held an active, command, and was not considered a contender to head major military operations. That concept changed when General Eisenhower's outstanding administrative and organizational abilities were noticed by the Army Chief of Staff George Marshall. Eisenhower's leadership was put to the test as supreme commander for the allied invasions of North Africa, Sicily, and Italy. It was in his role as supreme allied commander of the Allied

Expeditionary Force during the invasion of Normandy, France, that General Eisenhower would see his greatest triumph. He would go on to become U.S. president and one of the most admired Americans in history.

Allies losses—10,000 killed, wounded, captured.

BATTLE OF THE BULGE, December 16, 1944–January 25, 1945

Three years after Pearl Harbor, victory in Europe was in sight for the Allies. Then on December 16, 1944, the Germans pierced the Allied front in an offensive to become known as the Battle of the Bulge. The 101st Airborne Division (Ft. Campbell, Kentucky), surrounded and under siege in the town of Bastogne, was presented with a surrender demand from the Germans. To this, the acting commander of the 101st, Brigadier General Anthony McAuliffe, had a one-word response: "NUTS!" He and the 101st would continue the fight and hold on to Bastogne.

IWO JIMA, February 19, 1945–March 26, 1945

General Howard "Howlin' Mad" Smith is known as the father of modern amphibious warfare. In the months leading up to World War II, General Smith led the Army, Navy, and Marines in extensive amphibious assault training. This training played a crucial role in Allied victories in both the Pacific and the Atlantic theaters. General Smith is best known for leading the Marines of Task Force 56 to victory in the Battle of Iwo Jima.

United States losses—26,038 killed or wounded.

OKINAWA, JAPAN, April 1, 1945–June 23,1945

As the United States pushed deeper into Japanese-occupied territory, it became necessary to plan for the possible invasion of Japan. The staging point for that invasion was to be Okinawa, a heavily fortified Japan island. Tasked with seizing Okinawa was the strict and tough General Simon B. Buckner, Jr. He led the largest and longest amphibious assault in the Pacific Theater, and he successfully led his men to victory during the bloody eighty-two-day battle. In the final days of the battle, General Butler was killed in combat, making him the highest-ranking officer to be killed by enemy fire during World War II.

United States losses—82,600 killed or wounded.

OPERATION DOWNFALL, November 1, 1945–March 1946

General Douglas McArthur proclaimed "I shall return" when he left the Philippines in the face of the Japanese onslaught in 1942. He would keep that promise, when after more than 2.5 years of fighting, he stepped ashore Leyte Island on October 20, 1944. He oversaw plans for Operation Downfall—the invasion of Japan itself—which was made moot by the deployment of the atomic bombs on Hiroshima and Nagasaki. Estimates varied, but nearly all studies agreed that the invasion would have resulted in the deaths, at minimum, of hundreds of thousands of Americans and Japanese. On September 2, 1945, General McArthur (with Admiral Nimitz) accepted the formal Japanese surrender aboard the USS Missouri, ending World War II.

Much of this writing is adapted from information provided by World War II Veterans Committee, a Division of the American Veterans Center.

The World War II Operation Magic Carpet

July 18, 2019

Although a form of the United States Selective Service System registration remains a requirement for male citizens at age eighteen, mandatory military service (the draft) ended in 1973. This makes the registrants eligible for mandatory military service, should the draft need to be reinstated.

We now have two generations who may never serve in our military and who do not understand how fortunate they are to live in a free country. We don't speak German, Japanese, North Korean, or Vietnamese instead of the English language because of the sacrifices made by draftees and volunteers in military service.

I say this to my sons and grandsons who have no idea how patriotic we old timers really are and will never forget. This is one e-mail with proof of United States history that never appeared in our children's and grandchildren's schoolbooks.

Remember what General Dwight D. Eisenhower said about the Jewish Holocaust at the end of World War II with Germany? "Get all of it on record now, get the films, get the witnesses, because somewhere down the road of history some bastard will get up and say that this never happened."

How true that statement has become in the United States!

A veteran—whether on active duty, retired, or national guard, or reserve—is a person who at one point in their life wrote a blank check made payable to "The United States of America" for an amount of "up to and including their life." That, my friend, is honor. There are too many people in this country today who no longer understand honor.

*****

In 1939, there were 334 thousand U.S. military servicemen, not counting the coast guard. In 1945, there were more than twelve million U.S. military servicemen-and-women, including the coast guard. At the end of World War II, over eight million of these military men and women were scattered throughout Europe, the Pacific, and Asia.

During the war, 148 thousand troops were shipped from the U.S. mainland each month to Europe, the Pacific, and Asia. The rush to get them home ramped-up the number to 435,000 each month for fourteen consecutive months. Bringing them home was a massive logistical headache.

Army Chief of Staff General George C. Marshall anticipated this and had already established in 1943 Operation *Magic Carpet*. Germany surrendered in May 1945. The job of transporting three million troops home became an army and merchant marine problem; they converted three hundred *Victory and Liberty* cargo ships into troop transports.

The Japanese surrender in August 1945 came none too soon, but it put an extra burden of five million troops on Operation *Magic Carpet*. The war in Asia had been expected to go well into 1946, and the Navy and War Shipping Administration were hard-pressed to bring home all the soldiers earlier than anticipated. The transports carrying them also had to collect the numerous POWs from recently liberated Japanese camps, many of whom suffered from malnutrition and illness.

With the war over in Asia in October 1945, the U.S. Navy began converting all available vessels to transport duty. On smaller ships like destroyers capable of carrying three hundred troops, soldiers and marines were told to hang their hammocks in whatever nook or cranny they could find.

Aircraft carriers were particularly useful as their large open hangar decks could house three thousand or more troops in relative comfort, with bunks sometimes in stacks of five welded or bolted in-place. The navy's cruisers, battleships, hospital ships, even LSTs (landing ship, tanks) were packed full of troops yearning for home.

The *USS Sarratoga* transported home a total of 29,204 servicemen during Operation *Magic Carpet*. There were twenty-nine ships dedicated to transporting war brides; women married to American soldiers during the war.

Two British ocean liners under American control, *Queen Elizabeth* and *RMS Queen Mary*, had already served as troop transports before and continued to do so. Each was capable of carrying up to 15,000 people, though their normal capacity in peacetime was less than 2,200.

The amount of time required to get home depended a lot on circumstances. Troops going home from Australia or India would sometimes spend months on slow vessels. *USS Lake Champlain*, a new Essex-class aircraft carrier that arrived too late for the war, could cross the Atlantic and take 3,300 troops home in under four days and eight hours.

Enormous pressure was on the operation to bring home as many troops as possible by Christmas 1945. A secondary operation, Operation *Santa Claus*, was dedicated to that purpose. Due to storms at sea and an overabundance of servicemen and women eligible for return home, only a fraction were home by Christmas day, but many were at least on American soil.

America's mainland transportation network was overloaded. Trains heading west from the East Coast were on average six hours behind schedule, and trains heading east from the West Coast were twelve hours late. Lots of freshly discharged troops found themselves stuck in separation centers but faced an outpouring of love and friendliness from the local citizens. Many townsfolk took-in freshly arrived troops and invited them to Christmas dinner in their homes.

Other townsfolk gave their train tickets to soldiers and still others organized Christmas parties at local train stations for soldiers on layover. A Los Angeles taxi driver took six soldiers to Chicago.

Another taxi driver took a carload of servicemen to Pittsburgh, Buffalo, Manhattan, the Bronx, Long Island, and New Hampshire. Neither of the drivers accepted a fare beyond the cost of gasoline.

All-in-all, though, the Christmas deadline proved untenable. The last twenty-nine troop transports, carrying some two hundred thousand men from the China-India-Burma theater-of-operations, landed on American soil in April 1946. That brought Operation *Magic Carpet* to an end. An additional 127,000 soldiers didn't arrive home and lay-down the burden of war until September 1946.

*****

PHOTO 1:   Soldiers returning home on the *USS General Harry Taylor*, August 1945.

PHOTO 2:   Hammocks crammed into available spaces aboard the *USS Intrepid*.

PHOTO 3:   Bunks aboard the Army transport *SS Pennant*.

PHOTO 4:   Troops performing lifeboat drill aboard the *Queen Mary*, December 1944, before *Operation Magic Carpet*.

PHOTO 5:   U.S. soldiers recently liberated from Japanese POW camps.

PHOTO 6:   Crowded deck of the *USS Saratoga*.

PHOTO 7:   Overjoyed troops returning home on the battleship *USS Texas*.

PHOTO 8:   Troops crowded on an LST.

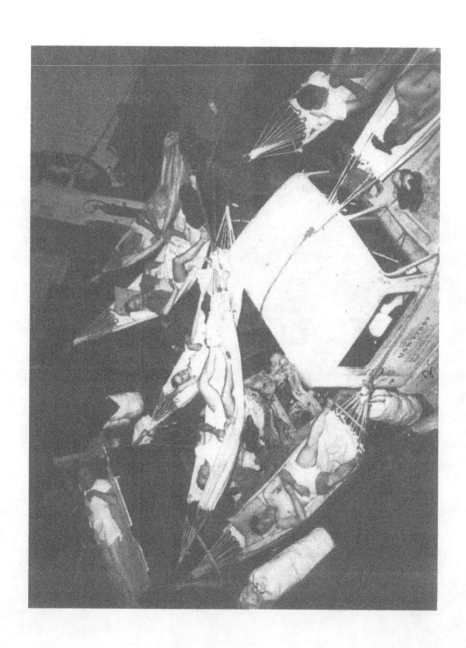

America's Fundamental Problem

February 29, 2018

The normal behavior listed below define a concept of adult responsibility that was a major contributor to America's productivity, educational gains, and social coherence between the end of World War II in 1946 and the mid-1960s. Be a patriot ready to serve your country, get married before you have children and strive to stay married for their sake, get the education you need for gainful employment, work hard, and avoid idleness, go the extra mile for your employer or client, be neighborly, civic-minded, and charitable, avoid coarse language in public, be respectful of authority and stay clear of substance abuse and crime.

Today, too few Americans are qualified for the jobs available. The male working age labor-force participation is at 1928–1930 Depression era lows. Opioid abuse is widespread. Homicidal violence plagues inner cities. Almost half of children are born out of wedlock, and even more are raised by single mothers. Many college students lack basic skills, and high school graduates rank below those from two dozen other countries.

That the middle-class culture embodied by these norms has broken down since the 1960s largely explains today's departure from a normal social culture. Re-embracing that culture would go a long way toward addressing this seriously destructive problem.

AMERICA'S FORGOTTEN
STATESMAN

May 4, 2016

America's first president, George Washington (1732–1799), is probably our greatest and most decent statesman, and we celebrate his birthday each February. March 16 is the birthday of probably the second-most important and decent statesman, James Madison (1751–1836).

Although Madison became America's fourth president, which is marked by the War of 1812, his presidency is not the main source of his greatness. There would have been an entirely different America without Madison's enormous input and foresight at the contentious 1787 Constitutional Convention in Philadelphia.

There were fifty-five delegates to the convention. Like Madison, some had a formal college education while others did not. From Madison's notes about the quality of the debates and discourse, a reader cannot tell who was college-educated and who was not. The delegates ranged in age between twenty-six (Jonathan Dayton) and eighty-one (Benjamin Franklin), the average being forty-two.

Alexander Hamilton was a key figure at this convention. He called for a president for life with total veto power over the legislature. **Most of the delegates**, led by Madison along with John Adams, **wanted a republic. None wanted a democracy**.

Madison, who would become known as the "Father of the Constitution," argued that in a pure democracy, "there is nothing to check the inducement to sacrifice the weaker party or an obnoxious individual." Delegate Edmund Randolph agreed, saying, "In tracing these evils to their origin, every man had found it in the turbulence and follies of democracy." Adams added, "**Remember, democracy never lasts long. It soon wastes, exhausts, and murders itself. There never was a democracy yet that did not commit suicide.**"

Eleven years earlier, Madison had helped develop the Virginia Constitution, and it was his Virginia Plan that served as the basis for debate in the development of the U.S. Constitution. Madison, along with Hamilton, argued for a **strong but limited central government** that could unify the country.

During the Constitutional Convention, a proposal was made that would have allowed the federal government to suppress a seceding state. Madison rejected it, saying, "A union of the states containing such an ingredient would provide for its own destruction. The use of force against a state would look more like a declaration of war than an infliction of punishment and would probably be considered by the party attacked as a dissolution of all previous compacts by which it might be bound."

This vision of a state's independence and right to secede was expressed at Virginia's ratification convention, which held, "The powers granted under the constitution being derived from the people of the United States may be resumed by them whensoever the same shall be perverted to their injury or oppression." Ratification documents of New York and Rhode Island made similar statements. In fact, Rhode Island's anti-federalist resistance against the Constitution was so strong that civil war almost broke-out July 4, 1788.

Madison's political genius is mostly seen in his contribution to the Federalist Papers, which were co-authored with Alexander Hamilton and John Jay. The papers were written to persuade the citizens of New York (and secondarily other states) to ratify the Constitution. Ratification was no easy task.

The 1783 Treaty of Paris, which ended the Revolutionary War against Great Britain, held that **each state was a sovereign nation.**

As such, each state feared giving up its rights to a powerful central government. Anti-federalists wanted some sort of guarantee that states would remain sovereign, the power of the federal government would be limited, and it would be recognized as a creation of, an agent of, and a servant of the states. They said their votes to ratify could only be obtained if the Constitution contained a **Bill of Rights** guaranteeing the rights of the people and their states. The most notable and influential anti-federalists were Patrick Henry, Samuel Adams, George Mason, and Richard Henry Lee.

These words do little justice to James Madison's greatness as one of America's Founding Fathers. A day honoring his birth would help us learn more about his contribution and, as well, learn how much America, which identifies itself today as a democracy, has betrayed Madison's vision of a republic and what constitutes a free people. All Americans, including its leaders, should memorize the three short sentences John Adams made about democracy.

THE PREAMBLE TO OUR CONSTITUTION

November 9, 2019

In these divisive political times, one well-worn text that merits re-examining is the Preamble to The Constitution of the United States of America. Do you remember when you had to memorize it? I sure do. The year was 1942, Miss Grace Hargrove's sixth grade class, Andrew Jackson Grade School, Paducah, Kentucky. That made Miss Clara Winston's eighth-grade civics class easier at Washington Junior High when we also had to memorize the first part of the Declaration of Independence.

> *We the People of the United States, in Order to form a more perfect Union, establish Justice, insure domestic Tranquility, provide for the common defence, promote the general Welfare, and secure the Blessings of Liberty to ourselves and our Posterity, do ordain and establish this Constitution for the United States of America.*

Regrettably, I have not devoted the time necessary to carefully examine the meaning of the Preamble until now, seventy-seven years later. Today's many departures from constitutional principles and practices by Progressivism's modern-day heir—the Democrat Party—have triggered this writing.

I've developed an appreciation of the Founder's understanding of human nature, the rule of law, the separation of powers, federalism, justice, and property rights. I've learned to distinguish liberty from license, legitimate government from tyrannical government, and to recognize the connection between rights and duties.

In summary, I've learned the conditions of liberty, the extent to which those conditions have been undermined and how they might be recovered and preserved. The Preamble does much more than add rhetorical flourish to our governing Constitution. It concisely declares America's answers to the most fundamental questions of political life—every one of which is contested today.

Consider its opening and closing: "We the People do ordain and establish this Constitution for the United States of America." Every political community has to decide who is ultimately sovereign. Our commitment to popular rule stems from a belief in the inherent equality of all human beings.

As equals, the only rule is self-rule. In so committing, America was one of the first countries to reject the rule of the few elites, building on an English commitment to freedom. But unlike Britain's customary constitution, "We the People" would record the structures and conditions of our rule, setting them in stone as a standard for liberty.

The Preamble's middle portion articulates the ends that popular rule serves. Again, there are many possible answers. Ancient Sparta pursued glory through war, and in its later years, Rome sought empire. Many governments since have chased the same thing.

The Founders chose another route, a summary of the just ends of political society. These ends were grounded in human virtue, not greed or vainglory. Moreover, unlike the Progressive thought of men like Woodrow Wilson, they sought justice in the eternal principles of human nature, not an evolving "right side of history."

By writing that they would "establish justice," the Founders recognized that politics does not define what is right. They sought to follow, secure, and preserve justice as declared by the laws of nature and God.

For another, they declared their intent to "insure domestic Tranquility" and to "provide for the common defence." The Founders recognized the dangers inherent to life. Thus, America would seek to protect the lives, liberties, and property of its people from all threats, internal and external.

They would also commit to "promote the general Welfare," recognizing that, while we have our own particular needs and desires, we also have many things in common. Culture, safety, and communal pursuits are a part of living full lives. These common possessions need to be protected and cultivated as much as individual goods.

This commitment connects to the further purpose of securing "the Blessings of Liberty to ourselves and our Posterity." Liberty bestows an indefinite number of blessings, allowing us to fulfill our purposes as human beings, to seek the good, virtue, and the worship of our Creator.

We must secure these not only for us but for our children and children's children.

Finally, the Founders sought in the Constitution "to form a more perfect Union." The rule of the people and their commitment to certain purposes came in the form of a common bond. They were united by more than geography, forming a partnership to rule in the pursuit of justice and the common good.

The Preamble's commitments articulate the basis of our Union. But every one of them is contested today, even the most fundamental—self-rule. A battle spreads forcefully over whether "We the People" or some learned subset of the populace should rule. Both sides use the same language of liberty and general welfare but mean different things by them. Our common bond seems strained to the point of tearing.

These concerted efforts against the Preamble are expected to continue until the 2020 election, possibly longer depending on the election results. The following restatement of Romans 3:12–17 (NIV) may best describe today's Democrat politicians.

They have turned away from America, there is no
good in them, they have become worthless. The way

of cooperation and peace they do not seek, ruined lives and misery mark their ways. Their lips are covered with the poison of vipers, tongues are addicted to lying, mouths full of bitterness and hate. Their throats are open graves.

It's sad but true that the huge stage on which the Democrat candidates stand during their debates has not one American flag on it. That fact says a lot about today's Democrat Party.

Let us seek to learn anew from the Preamble. Such education should renew our bonds. We should work so that our "more perfect Union" will strengthen itself, forged together again in and by the Founders' vision.

The Value of Knowing American History and Civics

May 31, 2017

Americans are losing the facts of America's history and civics. It has become a crisis, a disastrous change. Our public schools have trained (as opposed to educated) two consecutive generations, and almost finished with a third, of young Americans who are by and large historically illiterate. These people are today's parents, grandparents, teachers, and professors. Can graduates of our parochial schools and we (older) patriots muster the influence necessary to save this country?

A well-known historian described a college student who thanked him for his lecture and said, "Before today, I didn't know the original thirteen colonies were all on the East Coast." Another college student once asked him, "Aside from Harry Truman and John Adams, how many other presidents have you known?"

What explains this dumbness? Some blame boring public school textbooks put together by committee and are scrubbed clean of the politically incorrect. Many argue that so much strange, culturally fashionable garbage is jammed into public school curricula that essentials have been forced out. The political leftists/socialists/progressives/communists all point to a certain negativity, a focus on our national sins that has crowded out our achievements. This is counterproductive.

A sophisticated presentation of our triumphs and tragedies makes our national sins more deeply moving and powerful. Historical balance leaves young minds not cynical but inspired—we can right the wrongs, we've done it before, and we can do it again. The story of America is our strength, our greatest national resource. To preserve it is to save America.

History is a story. What's the past to us was the present in the 1700s for America's founders, their present. George Washington, John Adams, and Thomas Jefferson were acting in real time and didn't know how things would turn out. They were never certain of success. Had a poll been taken in Philadelphia in 1776, the founders would have scrapped the idea of independence—a third of the people were against it, a third for it, and the remaining third was waiting to see who came out on top. Nothing had to happen the way it happened. America has come far by means of trial-and-error. History neutralizes excessive pride in the present.

Knowing America's history and civics will make you a better person, a patriot, and help save the country that our older patriots have known.

Presidential Elections
of 1824 and 1828

March 5, 2016

The election year of 1824 in America was in a relatively settled period. The War of 1812 was fading into the past. The Missouri Compromise in 1821 had put the contentious issue of slavery aside, where it would remain until the 1850s.

A pattern of two-term presidents had developed in the early 1800s: Thomas Jefferson, elected in 1800 and 1804; James Madison, elected in 1808 and 1812; James Monroe, elected in 1816 and 1820. As Monroe's second term reached its final year, four major candidates were intent on running for president in the **1824 election**.

John Quincey Adams (1767–1848), Republican of Massachusetts, son of the second president John Adams, had served since 1817 as secretary of state in Monroe's administration. By his own admission, he didn't have an exciting personality, but his Harvard education and extraordinarily long career in public service made him well qualified for the job of president. And secretary of state was considered the obvious path to the presidency; Jefferson, Madison and Monroe had all held the position.

General Andrew Jackson (1767–1845) became a larger than life hero, known best as "Old Hickory," following his victory over the British at the Battle of New Orleans in 1815. He was elected a Democrat Senator from Tennessee in 1824 and immediately began positioning himself to run for president in the next (1828) election. The main concerns voters had about Jackson were that he was self-educated, had a fiery temperament, killed men in duels, and had been wounded by gunfire in various confrontations.

Henry Clay (1777–1852) of Kentucky was speaker of the House of Representatives and a dominating political figure of the day. He was known as the "Great Compromiser" and had pushed the Missouri Compromise through Congress. Clay had a potential advantage if three or more candidates ran, and none of them received a majority of the Electoral College votes. If that happened, the election would be decided in the House of Representatives where Clay wielded great power. It had already happened in the 1800 election that was won by Thomas Jefferson.

William H. Crawford of Georgia was a powerful political figure, having served as a senator, and secretary of the Treasury under James Madison. He was considered a strong candidate for president but, in 1823, suffered a stroke that left him partially paralyzed and unable to speak. However, some politicians still supported him.

In these early days of campaigns, the candidates themselves did not do the campaigning. The actual campaigning was left to managers and surrogates. When the votes were tallied from across the country, Andrew Jackson had won a plurality of the popular as well as the electoral vote. In the Electoral College tabulations, Adams came in second, Crawford third, and Henry Clay finished fourth.

While Jackson won the popular vote that was counted, some of the twenty-four states picked electors in the state legislature; thusly, these states did not tally a vote for president.

The U.S. Constitution dictates that a presidential candidate needs to win a majority in the Electoral College and no one met that standard. So the election had to be decided by the House of Representatives.

In an odd twist, the one man who would have a huge advantage in such a situation, the Speaker of the House Henry Clay, was automatically eliminated because the Constitution says only the top three candidates could be considered.

In early January 1824, Adams invited Henry Clay to visit him at his residence, and they spoke for several hours. It's unknown whether they reached some sort of deal, but suspicions were widespread.

On February 9, 1825, the House of Representatives held its election, in which each state delegation would get one vote. Henry Clay had made it known that he was supporting Adams, and thanks to Clay's influence, Adams won the vote and was thus elected president.

Andrew Jackson was furious. And when President John Quincy Adams named Henry Clay to be his secretary of state, Jackson denounced the election as "the corrupt bargain." Many assumed Clay sold his influence to Adams so he could be secretary of state, thereby increasing his own chance of being president someday.

Andrew Jackson was so wildly angry about what he considered manipulations in Washington that he resigned his senate seat. Jackson returned to Tennessee and began planning his **1828 campaign** that would make him president.

Jackson's marriage on the frontier nearly forty years earlier, when he was twenty years old, became a major issue in the campaign.

Jackson was accused of adultery and vilified for running off with another man's wife. And his second wife Rachel was accused of bigamy and being fat. Rachel had been married to another man before Jackson, and a question arose about when her first husband had divorced her and when she began living with Jackson. Jackson and Rachel believed she had been divorced when they married, but there was (and still is) some legitimate doubt about the timing.

Jackson's military glory was turned against him when a Philadelphia printer published a "coffin handbill" showing six black coffins of militiamen Jackson had ordered executed. General Jackson indeed had ordered the execution of six militia members accused of desertion in 1815.

The supporters of Jackson began spreading a rumor that Adams while secretary (when a teenager) to the American envoy to Russia had procured an American girl for the sexual services of the Russian Czar. The attack was no doubt baseless, but supporters of Jackson delighted in it, even calling Adams a "pimp" and claiming procuring women explained his great success as a diplomat.

Those opposed to Adams mocked him as an elitist, and his refinement and intelligence were turned against him. He was even derided as a "Yankee" at a time when that connoted shopkeepers reputed to take advantage of consumers.

Adams was also attacked for having a pool table in the White House and allegedly charging the government for it. It was true that Adams had a pool table in the White House, but he paid for the table with his own funds.

As these scurrilous charges appeared in the pages of partisan newspapers, Adams reacted by refusing to get involved with the campaign tactics. He was so offended by what was happening that he even refused to write in the pages of his diary from August 1828 until after the November election.

Jackson, on the other hand, was so furious about the attacks on himself and his wife that he got more involved. He wrote to newspaper editors giving then guidelines on how attacks should be countered and how their own attacks should proceed.

Jackson's appeal to the "common folk" served him well, and he handily won the 1828 popular vote and the Electoral College vote. It came at a price, however. His wife Rachel suffered a heart attack and died before the inauguration, and Jackson always blamed his "political enemies" for her death.

When Jackson arrived in Washington for his inauguration as president, he refused to pay the customary courtesy call on the outgoing president. And John Quincy Adams reciprocated by refusing to attend the inauguration of Jackson. The bitterness of the election of 1828 resonated for many years.

The rotten campaigning of 2016 is not a repeat of the dirty 1828 campaign; it's a creation of the "great divider" Obama, his Muslim administration, and his extreme progressivism.

HAPPY CONSTITUTION DAY, THREE DAYS LATE

September 20, 2018

At Independence Hall in Philadelphia 231 years ago, our nation was floundering. The United States were anything but united. America's first governing document, the Articles of Confederation, had created a "league of friendship" among the thirteen colonies, but they hadn't coalesced into a country.

For four months, delegates to the Continental Convention huddled behind closed doors. Those outside were wary of those inside. On the final day, Benjamin Franklin delivered the last great speech of his life, urging delegates to adopt the Constitution "with all its faults." It worked. No more royal absolutism.

The Framers were not tinkerers. They upended things. The Constitution inaugurated a revolutionary device. James Madison's design was infused with the genius of Isaac Newton; three separate coequal branches locked together by competing interests.

The truly extraordinary element was that these three rival branches derived their power from three unrivaled words: "We the People." In an era of kings and sultans, nothing was more radical than the idea that ultimate sovereignty resides not in the government but in the governed.

In 1789, Thomas Jefferson wrote: "Whenever the people are well informed, they can be trusted with their own government." This statement underscored what the Constitution presupposes: an enlightened citizenry is indispensable to American self-government.

Today, more than two centuries later, We the People's civic illiteracy is absolutely staggering. Seventy-one percent of Americans can't identify the Constitution as the law of the land, according to a 2015 study by Cincinnati's Xavier University.

Ten percent of U.S. college graduates think Judith Scheindlin (TV's "Judge Judy") sits on the Supreme Court, according to a 2015 American Council of Trustees and Alumni poll. Only thirty-two percent can name all three branches of government and thirty-three percent can't name a single one, according to the 2018 Annenberg Constitution Day Civics Survey.

I'm upset that the generation of Americans with access to the most information is also the least uninformed. James Madison warned of this especially: "A popular government without popular information is but a prologue to a farce or a tragedy, or perhaps both."

Even a well-informed populace doesn't guarantee good governance, but an engaged citizenry with its sleeves rolled-up will. Citizenship isn't a spectator sport. Our Constitution is an exquisite charter of freedom, but freedom requires patriots; it demands fierce defenders, not feeble bystanders.

President Calvin Coolidge (1923–1929) understood the genius of what happened 231 years ago: "To live under the American Constitution is the greatest political privilege that was ever accorded the human race." That privilege must never be taken for granted. We the People are, and will remain, the world's oldest Constitutional Republic.

AMERICA'S SILENT GENERATION

January 7, 2019

Those of us born between 1930 and 1940 are among the smallest number of Americans born during any ten-year period since the early 1900s. We're called the "Silent Generation," born between the birth of the "Greatest Generation" and the birth of the "Baby Boomers."

We're the last generation that climbed out of the Great Depression. We remember World War II, which unnerved the structure of our daily lives. We're the last to see gold stars in the front windows of grieving neighbors whose sons were killed in the war.

We're the last to experience ration books for everything from sugar to strawberries to shoes to stoves to kerosene to gasoline. We bought war stamps at school, saved tinfoil, and poured grease into tin cans during the war. We saw cars sitting upon blocks because tires weren't available.

We returned milk bottles and soda bottles to the store where they were sent back to the plant to be washed and sterilized, refilled, and used over-and-over. Groceries were bagged in brown paper bags that were reused as schoolbook covers to protect public property (books provided by the school) from being defaced by our scribbling.

When thirsty, we drank water from a fountain or drinking glass. Plastic cups, plastic straws, and plastic water bottles didn't exist. We refilled writing pens with liquid ink. Ball-point pens didn't exist. We replaced the razor blade when it got dull, instead of throwing away the whole razor device.

We either walked or rode our bikes to school. We washed cloth baby diapers and reused them because throwaway diapers didn't exist. We put washed clothes through a wringer by hand and dried them outdoors on a line. We wore hand-me-down clothes from older brothers and sisters.

In the kitchen, we mixed, blended, and stirred by hand. We had one radio in the house, not one in every room. When packaging fragile items to send in the mail, we used wadded-up old newspapers to cushion it because styrofoam or plastic bubble wrap didn't exist. We used a push lawnmower that exercised us physically. Fitness clubs and treadmills didn't exist. We cultivated land using horses, mules, or tractors with steel wheels and cleats.

We walked up-and-down stairways in every store and office building because there was no such thing as an escalator. We walked six blocks pulling an empty wagon to and loaded wagon from the grocery store. We pierced the nose of only pigs and hogs and tattooed an ear or a rump of only cattle.

Telephones hung on the wall usually in the hallway, one to a house, a two- or three-party line, and you talked to a human operator. Our only real understanding of what the world was like came from reading the National Geographic in the school library.

Computers were called calculators. They only added and were hand-cranked. Typewriters were driven by finger pounding, throwing the carriage left-handed, and changing the ribbon. Internet and GOOGLE were words that didn't exist.

We remember milk being delivered early in the morning, placed on the front porch, and the cream on top freezing and raising the circular cardboard top above the bottle. We well remember the popular song "Milkman, Keep Those Bottles Quiet," as we waited anxiously for fathers and brothers to be discharged from the WWII military and come home.

Newspapers and magazines were written for adults and the evening news was broadcast on the radio by Gabriel Heatter. We were the last generation who had to find-out for ourselves. Depression poverty was deep-rooted. Malaria, tuberculosis, and poliomyelitis were still cripplers. As we grew-up, America was exploding with growth.

The G.I. bill gave returning veterans the means to gain a higher education and spurred the growth of colleges and universities. Veteran Administration loans fanned a housing boom. Pent-up demand coupled with new installment payment plans put factories to work. New paved highways brought jobs and mobility.

Veterans joined civic clubs and became active in politics. The radio network expanded from just a few hundred to thousands of stations. We were suddenly free from confines of the great depression and World War II, and we threw ourselves into exploring opportunities we had never imagined.

We weren't neglected, but we weren't focused like today's all-consuming family. Our parents were glad that we played outdoors until the street lights came on and the lightening bugs came out. We were busy discovering the post-war world. We entered a world of overflowing plenty and opportunity. We felt secure in our future.

After forty-six years, the Union of the Soviet Socialist Republic "Iron Curtain" and "Cold War" ended in 1991, and China had become Red China in the meantime. Some of us experienced military service during the Korean War, which still remains today a dark presage of the future.

President Eisenhower sent the first "advisers" to Vietnam then planned and began construction of America's Interstate Highway System. Castro set-up camp in Cuba and Kruschev came into power in the USSR.

We are the last generation to experience an interlude when there were no threats to our homeland. We came of age in the 1940s and 1950s. World War II was over and concern about terrorism, global climate change, and perpetual economic insecurity didn't haunt our lives.

We grew-up at the best possible time, a time when the world was getting better, not worse. We're America's Silent Generation. More than ninety-nine percent of us are either retired or deceased, yet those who remain feel privileged to have lived in the best of times.

HYPHENATED AMERICANS

November 25, 2017

My paternal ancestors descend from Dirck Hoff, born 1599, Luttenborg, Netherlands. His son and wife arrived in New Amsterdam (now New York City) December 1650. They were white **indentured slaves** of David Pietersen de Vries, then owner of what today is known as Staten Island.

More than 664,000 white men were killed to end **black slavery** in America during four years of Civil War, ending 152 years ago (1865).

Southern United States white-dominated legislatures enacted state and local "separate but equal" segregation laws in 1896. These Jim Crow laws were enforced for a period of sixty-nine years until fifty-two years ago (1965).

Although no white person alive today in America has legally owned a black slave, about ninety percent of black America is locked in economic hardship and inner city gang violence. Why? It's because of their culture (the totality of socially transmitted behavior patterns, arts, beliefs, institutions, and all other products of black human thought), and their adoption of Democrat Party government dependence.

Black people taken from African tribes, with no written language and no intellectual achievements, initially were brought to America by European slave traders and sold into slavery. The white citizen majority in America, on the other hand, descended from Europeans who created a centuries-old advanced state of cultural, intellectual, and material development.

Acting on a policy unfair to both racial groups, the American government released a newly freed mostly uncivilized black culture into a civilized white culture. Citizenship was not granted to the freed black people until the 14th Amendment to the Constitution was ratified July 9, 1868.

Through these 149 years, ninety percent of black citizens have shown an inability to function in a white culture that is unsuited to them. These 36,450,000 blacks accept no responsibility for their own failures. Instead, they attack civil authority with anger and resentment.

This is the fault of black America. No one can solve this problem but black America itself. No one can throw enough money at it. America has tried that. Black America needs to look in the mirror and stop blaming others, especially white people.

In Detroit, Chicago, Oakland, Los Angeles, Newark, Philadelphia, Milwaukee, Cleveland, Cincinnati, Buffalo, St. Louis, El Paso, Atlanta, Memphis, and Baltimore, rioting and looting is rampant, and all have black populations twenty-four percent to more than thirty-two percent below poverty level. The most common characteristic of these fifteen cities is that, for decades, all of them have been run by Democrat administrations.

A substantial percentage of black America is very successful in this dominant white society, but it's not enough. Too many black youth are being left behind.

The American government has tried for 154 years to determine its capability to do something previously untried in world history. That is to integrate black and white races. Today, there are 40,500,000 black Americans (14.1 percent of the total population).

America had eight years of the first black president, ending November 7, 2016. Black athletes and entertainers routinely earn multimillion-dollar incomes. I'm fed-up with black athletes disrespecting the National Anthem and the American flag and displaying their non-gratitude for the innumerable freedoms we all have in America.

Those black athlete millionaires who disrespect the American flag have never been handed a folded flag or served in the military.

Do black lives matter? This is a special kind of stupidity. If the ninety percent of black Americans locked in poverty and gang violence suddenly left America:

- citizens in poverty would drop 36 percent;
- prison population would drop 39 percent;
- welfare recipients would drop 45 percent;
- gang members would drop 56 percent;
- chlamydia cases would drop 57 percent;
- homelessness would drop 60 percent;
- syphilis cases would drop 61 percent;
- AIDS and HIV cases would drop 69 percent;
- gonorrhea cases would drop 73 percent;
- average ACT scores would go up 5.8 points;
- average SAT scores would go up 106 points;
- average IQ would go up 7.9 points;
- placing America third in the world (tied with Japan);
- average American income would go up over $21,200 per year;
- Democrats would lose 81 percent of their voting base;
- many criminal defense attorneys would have to find other work. Yes, black lives do matter.

Obviously, I'm white, conservative, a disabled veteran serving my country at a time when our military was color blind, and I know that I'll be called racist by some. I can also say I don't care what color your skin is, but I do care about your actions. Blacks have opportunity in America. All they have to do is be and act like respectable citizens.

They should try to find the same opportunity anyplace else in the world. By being born in America, they've already won the economic lottery and should take advantage of it. One of the major problems with the past couple of generations of American young people is that they've been taught cultural socialism instead of American history. They've been taught to be a victim.

We have a real problem due to Leftist dispersion of America's formerly homogeneous culture. The Leftist agenda is that multiculturalism is perfect and should be adopted. This agenda encourages citizens to be less American by identifying their ethnicity using hyphenated names such as African-American or Mexican-American.

I'm proud of my tenth generation Netherlands paternal heritage, but I don't want to be less American by identifying myself as Holland-American or Dutch-American. My deceased wife was proud of her fourth generation German paternal and maternal heritage, but she didn't want to be less American by identifying herself as German-American.

BLACKS ARE BLINDED BY THEIR REAL PROBLEMS

June 25, 2018

White Liberals and the Progressive Socialist Democrat (preferably Demonrat) Party are major beneficiaries of keeping most black voters feeling angry, victimized, and resentful. It's extremely important to both their political success and their avowed efforts to change the United States of America.

Racial harmony would be a disaster for Leftists, be they politicians, academic Liberals, or mainstream news media (Liberats). As for black politicians and black civil rights hustlers, Booker T. Washington (1856–1915), a black educator born into slavery, explained their agenda, when he wrote the following: *"There is another class of coloured people who make a business of keeping the troubles, the wrongs, and the hardships of the Negro race before the public. Having learned that they are able to make a living out of their troubles, they have grown into the settled habit of advertizing their wrongs; partly because they want sympathy and partly because it pays. Some of these people do not want the Negro to lose his grievances, because they do not want to lose their jobs."*

Instead of admitting that racism has declined over the years, blacks argue all the harder that racism is still alive and more treacherous than ever.

Blacks hold-up race as a shield to keep them from seeing what they don't want to see in themselves.

Thought patterns including victimization, separatism, and anti-intellectualism impede black advancement much more than racism because they underlie the black community's response to all race-related issues. Dysfunctional inner-cities, black underachievement, and corporate glass ceilings will continue to exist until such patterns of thought disappear.

Although still flawed in its race relations, America is the least racist white-majority society in the world. America has a better record of legal protection of minorities than any other society, white or black.

Furthermore, America offers more opportunities to a greater number of black persons than any other society. It's rather distressing to observe how the anti-Americanism that started in the 1960s has become prevalent in the black community today.

The anti-Americanism that dominates the black identity has been so ruinous to black America that they are worse off today by almost every social or economic measure than they were under segregation.

In 1950, female-headed households were only eighteen percent of the black population. Today, seventy percent of black children are raised in single-parent households. In the late 1800s, there were only slight differences between the black family structure and those of other ethnic groups.

In the 1925 New York City, eighty-five percent of kin-related black households were two-parent households. In 1938, eleven percent of black children were born to unwed mothers. Today, about seventy-five percent of black children are born to unwed mothers.

In 1900, the duration of black unemployment was fifteen percent shorter than that of whites; today, it's about thirty percent longer.

Is there anyone else who will suggest that there was less racial discrimination during earlier time periods?

SELF-RELIANCE IS
NOT OBSOLETE

May 16, 2019

Ralph Waldo Emerson's essay—"Self-Reliance"—is a statement of American values in 1841. "Whoso would be a man must be a non-conformist." "God will not have his work made manifest by cowards." "Society everywhere is in conspiracy against the manhood of every one of its members." "The sinew and heart of every man seem to be drawn out, and we are become timorous, desponding whimperers." "We are afraid of truth, afraid of fortune, afraid of death, and afraid of each other."

Today's members of the American Psychological Association regard these values as obsolete and a disease manifested by behavior that is habitual, maladaptive, and compulsive. They say that "Western culture defines specific characteristics to fit the patriarchal ideal masculine model." "The socialization of masculine ideals starts at a young age and defines ideal masculinity as related to toughness, indifference to pleasure or pain, heterosexism, self-sufficient attitudes, and lack of emotional sensitivity and of connectedness."

Things sure have changed! When Emerson (1803–1882) was writing, Americans like Henry David Thoreau (1817–1862), Margaret Fuller (1810–1850), and Lucretia Mott (1793–1880) were skeptical of authority and valued dissent and independence of thought. They understood that dependence makes you vulnerable, even though we all do depend on one another in various ways, and if you rely on government for food, clothing, and shelter, you are at its mercy.

And as Thoreau argued in "Civil Disobedience," if you depend on the government, you are disabled from resisting it. Recognizing that relationship between freedom and self-reliance, many feminists since Abigail Adams (1744–1818) have taught that women must become less dependent on men.

Emerson's essay is about self-development and self-realization, values that Americans in their right mind praise; it's about the importance, for each of us and for society, of independent thought. "A boy is in the parlour what the pit is in the playhouse; independent, irresponsible, looking out from his corner on such people and facts as pass by, he tries and sentences them on their merits, in the swift summary way of boys, as good, bad, interesting, silly, eloquent, troublesome. He cumbers himself never about consequences, about interests: he gives an independent, genuine verdict. You must court him: he does not court you."

Even more than in Emerson's time, we today tend to think in groups or as groups. Many of us vociferously express opinions we do not actually hold; we came to hold them through a process of self-deception. It has turned us into tribes of warring, slavish conformists. Perhaps, without realizing it, psychologists today are articulating a set of moral norms. That is also what Emerson was up to in his essay, though he was unaware of it.

These two systems of values are incompatible; an additional sign that America, for better and worse, has become something like the opposite of what it was 178 years ago.

America's Political Disorder and Confusion Parallels China's Cultural Revolution

September 4, 2017

American patriots are forced to live through much unpleasant emotional disorder and confusion as we see our country so divided with some people bitterly angry at each other. All the shouting, violence, and destruction of historical monuments have brought to the minds of our older patriots the recollection of having seen this before. We are clearly experiencing a Cultural Revolution in America that's inspiring a lot of fear and uneasiness.

America's movement is similar to the (1966–1969) China Cultural Revolution, in which Mao Zedong was a leading figure. Karl Marx may have been right after all when he declared that history repeats itself, first as tragedy, second as a farce (foolishly empty show or mockery). **Both of these movements started on college campuses and spread from there.**

*****

At Beijing University, the most elitist college in China, a group of students triggered China's Cultural Revolution. The group called themselves the Red Guard, and they feverishly worshiped China's dictator, Mao Zedong, and his socialist/communist ideology. In their manifesto, the Red Guard: questioned the usefulness of knowledge and condemned their professors and university administrators for harboring "intellectual elitism and bourgeois tendencies" and for stalling China's progress towards a communist utopia.

Mao Zedong used these overzealous and ignorant teenagers as a political tool to purge his enemies and shape China's society to his own liking. His appearance at a massive Red Guard rally at Tiananmen Square in mid-August 1966 elevated the Red Guard status. This event allowed the Red Guard political legitimacy and officially kicked off China's Cultural Revolution fifty-one years ago. The Red Guard's ideas quickly spread from colleges to high schools.

Nobody on school campuses dared challenge the Red Guard, and they were encouraged when the school authorities capitulated. They led students to strike, refusing to take classes from people who they considered to be less than ideologically pure.

Professors, teachers, and school administrators were paraded and forced to make many public self-criticisms about "transgressions" against government sanctioned orthodoxy. College entrance exams were soon suspended, and many universities and high schools were closed. The entire educational system was paralyzed.

Without schools to attend, the Red Guards traveled all over China spreading their ideas and tactics. Other people, such as factory workers unhappy with the shortages, organized their own groups to challenge the leadership of their own work-units.

Since nobody was working, businesses, factories, and many government agencies were shut-down. The entirety of China fell into lawlessness and chaos.

*****

America became divided during eight years of the Leftist administration of the Great Divider, President Barack Hussein Obama. During the 2016 presidential campaign, many millions of millennials (Generation Y) supported the Leftist Democrat party socialist candidate Bernie Sanders.

Like Mao Zedong's Red Guards, some of America's college students and their supporters have been shouting-down anyone who disagrees with them. America's overzealous and ignorant teenagers and millennials—modern-day "Red Guards"—demand: that college campuses be an inclusive and safe place, but are bent on making sure the campus is an unwelcoming and unsafe place for anyone who doesn't show unconditional support for student-sanctioned orthodoxy.

From Yale University to Middlebury College, professors and administrators have caved to the preposterous demands of these student mobs. That kind of zealous demand for thought conformity has now expanded from college campuses to the business world.

When Google engineer employee, James Damore, raised questions in a memo about Google's diversity training, he was fired. Nothing could be more dystopian than for your thoughts to be controlled by the world's largest information-communication-documentation hub, and punish you for wrong thinking.

The Red Guard firmly believed that in order to build a new China, they had to wipe out the old one.

They traveled around China, eradicating anything representing China's feudalistic past: old customs, old cultures, old habits, and old ideas. Temples, shrines, museums, heritage sites, and even Confucius's tomb were defaced, ransacked, or totally destroyed.

The Red Guards dug-up the Ming Dynasty (1368–1644) tombs, denounced their oppression against Chinese people, and burned the remains. In the meantime, many cities and towns renamed their streets with new revolutionary names. Mao Zedong pictures and statues were everywhere.

The intensity and enthusiastic devotion of the Red Guard to cleanse the past is being repeated in America. Since the events in Charlottesville, calls to remove or destroy Confederate statues have gotten louder.

Some places, such as the city of Baltimore and Duke University, have already taken actions to remove Confederate statues. During a recent weekend, more and more historical monuments were vandalized, some having nothing to do with the Confederacy, and streets were renamed.

Every civilization, every country, and every generation of people has its own good, bad, and ugly. In order for America to define our future, we must know our past. The most effective way to destroy America is to deny and obliterate the people's own understanding of their history.

Any country that tears-down its statues is toppling more than brass and marble, it's toppling itself. When statues are torn-down, avenues of communication between generations also are torn-down.

Both of these movements justify violence on the basis of their perceived moral authority.

Some Chinese cities were engulfed in violence to such extent order was restored through military takeover. If you think that level of violence and lawlessness cannot occur in America, you must watch the videos of violent protests at Yale University, UC at Berkley, and Middlebury College. Fringe groups such as Antifa insist that violence is justified against anyone they deem to be haters, racists, or fascists. After honing their vicious tactics on college campuses and facing little or no push-back, these groups have taken their tactics elsewhere.

During the 2016 presidential rally in San Jose, anti-Trump demonstrators attacked Trump supporters and local police. Since the election of President Trump, such belief in "righteous beating" has received support from left-leaning mainstream media, and from some politicians currently in office.

This so-called legitimate violence from the radical-left fueled the violent response from far-right groups, which led to Charlottesville. America has fallen into a vicious cycle: violence from one side induces a violent response from the other side, which becomes an excuse to justify more violence.

True Americans should be alarmed by the similarities between our Cultural Revolution and China's Cultural Revolution. To preserve our country, we have to find the energy of a common national sentiment and reaffirm the uniformity of principles that once united us as Americans.

America's Cultural Revolution is endangering the republic we hold dear.

BREAKING CONSTITUTIONAL LAW IN OUR PUBLIC SCHOOLS

August 4, 2015

The National Education Association (NEA) has promoted the religious doctrine of humanism in America's public schools, colleges, and universities for eighty-two years (since 1933). Yet most educators are unaware of the actual tenants of this atheist and socialist belief system. Humanism is a religion that regards the "universe as *self-existing and not created.*"

As the researcher and writer of this document, I assert my firm belief that a "self-existing" universe is equivalent to a "self-creating" universe in which the creation and creator are one—an omnipotent, omniscient, and omnipresent Eternal Being who is neither male nor female and exists outside of nature, of the universe, and of time.

The precepts of humanism have persistently and methodically worked their way into America's public schools until finally the educational hierarchy—textbook writers, editors, printers, publishers, teachers, buyers—were substantially indoctrinated. American history, civics, moral values, ethical values, and sociology on all levels—personal, societal, global—have been deconstructed and rewritten. America's heritage has been systematically censored out of existence in modern public school texts.

The leader and founder of the First Humanist Society of New York, Inc. wrote: "Education is thus a most powerful ally of humanism, and every American public school is a school of humanism. What can the theistic Sunday schools, meeting for an hour once a week, and teaching only a fraction of the children, do to stem the tide of a five-day program of humanistic teaching?"

Regarding the subject of ethics, humanism affirmed in 1973 "that moral values derive their source from human experience. Ethics are autonomous and situational, needing no theological or ideological sanction." Concerning the subject of Democratic Society, humanism added a new tenant in 1973 that reads in part, "It also includes a recognition of an individual's right to die with dignity, euthanasia, and the right to suicide."

Situation ethics is the basis of the value system taught today in America's public school system, and the ultimate goal of the humanist religion is to make the Christian mantra a matter of political science. In other tenants not presented in this writing, humanism makes an open attack on Christianity, opposes the free enterprise system, advocates socialism, and rejects the Bible, biblical history, and biblical morality.

The following article titled "A Religion for a New Age" appeared in a 1983 issue of *The Humanist*. "I am convinced that the battle for humankind's future must be waged and won in the public school classroom by teachers who correctly perceive their role as the proselytizers of a new faith; a religion of humanity that recognizes and respects the spark of what theologians call divinity in every human being. These teachers must embody the same selfless dedication as the most rabid fundamentalist preachers, for they will be ministers of another sort, utilizing the classroom instead of a pulpit to convey humanist values in whatever subject they teach, regardless of the educational level—preschool day care or large state university. The classroom must and will become an arena of conflict between the old and the new—the rotting corpse of Christianity, together with all its adjacent evils and misery, and the new faith of humanism, resplendent in its promise of a world in which the never-realized Christian Ideal of 'love thy neighbor' will finally be achieved."

U.S. Supreme Court Justice Black wrote in 1947 that "The First Amendment requires the state to be a neutral in its relations with groups of religious believers and nonbelievers; it does not require the state to be their adversary. State power is no more to be used so as to handicap religions, than it is to favor them."

According to its own definition and claim, humanism indeed is a religion, and it should not be taught in America's public schools any more than any other religion, be it Christianity, Judaism, humanism, Atheism, Islamism, Hinduism, Buddhism, etc. **How can the National Education Association get away with this? First Amendment rights and limitations are equally applicable to the religion of humanism as they are to all other religions?**

America's public schools have gone from problems with talking and chewing gum in the classroom to vandalism, shootings, and killings. We've gone from a daily pledge of allegiance to the American flag to the distribution of condoms. No longer are student minds allowed to wander freely and imaginations roam.

Educators today teach that the powerful insights of history and sociology all are here and now matters to be grouped together in social studies. National curriculum standards for social studies, first published in 1994, are presented in the following ten themes:

> Culture
> Time, Continuity, and Change
> People, Places, and Environments
> Individual Development and Identity
> Individuals, Groups, and Institutions
> Power, Authority, and Governance
> Production, Distribution, and Consumption
> Science, Technology, and Society
> Global Connections
> Civic Ideals and Practices

If America's society is confused and out of control, if we don't understand who we are and what we should be, how can we possibly project a desirable image to the rest of the world? How can we defend the traditions and beliefs that made America great if we abandon them and fail to educate our children regarding the foundations of our traditions?

America's public schools must reestablish a learning environment with solid values and discipline that enable young people to develop good character traits and succeed in life. Parents again must accept their responsibilities, and educators must again be given more latitude in controlling and disciplining young people at school and in the classroom.

The greatest cause of concern for a large number of parents is that public school teaching often contradicts by means of indoctrination, what parents wish to teach their children. There's a need for serious examination of text material, value lessons, teacher education, desired outcome-based objectives, methods of discipline, incentives for learning, teaching students to think with less indoctrination, etc., etc., etc.

Latest research shows the wisdom of old-fashioned school teaching methods: rote learning, plenty of failure, and stingy praise encourage students to work harder and achieve more. Tough teachers get results. Teachers should give constructive, even painful, feedback. Drill, practice, drill, and memorize. Strict teachers are better than nice teachers. Students who understand that failure is a necessary aspect of learning perform better. Stress makes the student strong while praise makes the student weak. Creativity can be learned. Student grit (passion and perseverance), not talent, is the best predictor of future success.

Time is of the essence. It's like planting the oak tree that takes fifty years to mature and bear acorns. We have no time to waste!

Sad but True Reality

March 12, 2019

Years ago, university and college presidents and librarians protected American history; that enormous storehouse of past attitudes and behaviors that define our common heritage. Many university and college presidents and librarians are acting together secretly to fraudulently, illegally, and deceitfully expunge this inheritance.

Some people might ask, "Who cares what abusive power a superrich institution of privilege and unaccountability like Yale perpetuates on its legacy." All true American patriots, I'm certain, are deeply troubled by what has taken place and is continuing, and they care very much!

Yale, Harvard, and Stanford are the main leaders of Progressive hatred of free expression and other politically correct attitudes. They have elusively inserted the virus of political correctness into the bloodstream of public life, instead of helping to preserve our common inheritance they work to completely destroy it.

The idea of respecting the beliefs or practices of others—"I disapprove of what you say, but I will defend to my death your right to say it."—is instilled in the lives of patriots. This solemn pledge has been replaced by, "I disapprove of what you say, therefore you cannot say it."

This Marxist-tinted ideology in our institutions of higher learning has had a number of decades to saturate the minds of those who now benefit from our free-market society. This toxic ideology has marinated their minds, disguised as moral duties in many of our universities and colleges.

Today, graduates of these institutions are using positional advantages to manipulate the fundamentals of political and corporate power in America. I'm reminded of the battle between fervent supporters of freedom and those intoxicated with power who said freedom is negotiable—freedom then roused itself and fought back.

At risk is nothing less than survival of our common history.

Eighth Grade
Schooling in 1895

February 9, 2018

My father, born 1893, Wolf Island, Missouri, the son of a farmer, had an eighth-grade education and worked forty-three years at the Illinois Central Rail Road facility, Paducah, Kentucky. He was the boiler inspector for forty years, had the only office in the huge Round House, and maintained all records for the boiler on each of the many steam locomotives assigned to him. In a large photo taken in 1958 (the year he retired), today in the Paducah Rail Road Museum, my dad is shown standing alone beside the boiler of one of the most powerful steam locomotives the ICRR had ever built; other Round House workers stand on the ground beside it.

While studying solid geometry and trigonometry in the twelfth grade, I was amazed that Dad could solve some of the basic problems using what I assumed was practical thinking and wisdom. Although Dad grew-up on the farm, his eighth education enabled him to succeed in the major industrial transportation mode of the time.

The 1895 Salina, Kansas, eighth-grade final examination, which lasted five hours, follows. This basic curriculum was modified as required to fit the major agricultural crops, corn for example, in other states.

Students in those days attended school only seven months because they had to help plant and harvest crops. When I was in school, we attended eight and a half months. Today in Indiana, students attend school ten months.

Grammar (Time, one hour)

1. Give nine rules for the use of capital letters.
2. Name the parts of speech and define those that have no modifications.
3. Define verse, stanza, and paragraph.
4. What are the principle parts of a verb? Give principle parts of "lie," "play," and "run."
5. Define case; illustrate each case.
6. What is punctuation? Give rules for principle marks of punctuation.
7–10. Write a composition of about 150 words showing how therein that you understand the practical use of the rules of grammar.

Arithmetic (Time, 1 hour, 15 minutes)

1. Name and define the Fundamental Rules of Arithmetic.
2. A wagon box is 2 ft. deep, 10ft. long, and 3 ft. wide. How many bushels of wheat will it hold?
3. If a load of wheat weighs 3,942 lbs., what is it worth at 50 cts./bushel, deducting 1,050 lbs. for tare?
4. District No. 33 has a valuation of $35,000. What is the necessary levy to carry on a school seven months at $50 per month and have $104 for incidentals?
5. Find the cost of 6,720 lbs. of Coal at $6.00 per ton.
6. Find the interest of $512.60 for 8 months and 18 days at 7 percent per annum.
7. What is the cost of 40 boards 12 inches wide and 10 ft. long at $20 per metre?
8. Find bank discount on $300 for 90 days (no grace) at 10 percent.
9. What is the cost of a square farm at $10 per acre, the distance of which is 640 rods?
10. Write a Bank Check, a Promissory Note, and a Receipt.

U.S. History (Time, 45 minutes)

1. Give the epochs into which U.S. history is divided.
2. Give an account of the discovery of America by Columbus.
3. Relate the causes and results of the Revolutionary War.
4. Show the territorial growth of the United States.
5. Tell what you can of the history of Kansas.
6. Describe three of the most prominent battles of the Rebellion.
7. Who were the following: Morse, Whitney, Fulton, Bell, Lincoln, Penn, and Howe?
8. Name events connected with the following dates: 1607, 1620, 1800, 1849, 1865.

Orthography (Time, one hour)

1. What is meant by the following: alphabet, phonetic, orthography, etymology, syllabication?
2. What are elementary sounds? How classified?
3. What are the following, and give examples of each: trigraph, subvocals, diphthong, cognate letters, linguals?
4. Give four substitutes for the "u" caret.
5. Give two rules for spelling words with final "e." Name two exceptions under each rule.
6. Give two uses of silent letters in spelling. Illustrate each.
7. Define the following prefixes and use in connection with a word: bi, dis, pre, semi, post, non, inter, mono, sup.
8. Mark diacritically and divide into syllables the following, and indicate the sign that indicates the sound: card, ball, mercy, sir, odd, cell, rise, blood, fare, last.
9. Use the following correctly in sentences: cite, site, sight, fane, feign, vane, vain, vein, raze, raise, rays.
10. Write 10 words frequently mispronounced, and indicate punctuation by use of diacritical marks and syllabication.

Geography (Time, one hour)

1. What is climate? Upon what does climate depend?
2. How do you account for the extremes of climate in Kansas?
3. Of what use are rivers? Of what use is the ocean?
4. Describe the mountains of North America?
5. Name and describe the following: Monrovia, Odessa, Manitoba, Hecla, Yukon, St. Helena, Juan Fernandez, Aspinwall, and Orinoco.
6. Name and locate the principal trade centers of the United States. Name all the republics of Europe and give the capitol of each.
7. Why is the U.S. Atlantic Coast colder than the Pacific Coast in the same latitude?
8. Describe the process by which the water of the ocean returns to the sources of rivers.
9. Describe the movement of the Earth. Give the inclination of the Earth.

This final examination gives a whole new perspective to the statement, "My parents, grandparents, or great-grandparents only had an eighth-grade education." It also helps demonstrate how the U.S. educational system has kept in-step with the transition from what was in 1895 mostly a farming economy, to a widespread industrial economy, to today's economy during the past 124 years, 82 of which I was schooled and have experienced in my 88 years.

THE VALUE OF A CLASSICAL EDUCATION

March 15, 2018

Throughout history, it has been common for students to study subjects that have no direct relationship to their line of work or profession in later life. A classical education centers on philosophy, history, art, and music that exercise a creative mind, does not clearly define answers to questions, and helps us appreciate uncertainty as to interpretation in the world.

Such courses nurture disagreement among students and help them develop the ability to make sound and compelling arguments in support of defensible positions. The ability of a person to use effective and persuasive language, logical reasoning, and business skills is the practical benefit of a classical education.

To express a viewpoint verbally and then articulate it in writing is a skill that will serve individuals whether they're promoting a business plan or writing a business report. A classical education offers a person the necessary background and freedom to lead and participate fully in civic life.

The classical curriculum outlined below was set-up in 1827 by Yale College and adopted in 1828 by Georgetown College, Kentucky. Admission to the freshman class required exams in Latin and Greek grammar, Caesar's *Commentaries, Virgil's Aeneid*, English, geography, and algebra.

> First Year. Ovid and Latin Grammar, Latin Composition, Xenophon's *Anabasis*, Ancient Geography, Plane Geometry, Livy and Latin Syntax, Latin Composition, Greek Mythology, Xenophon's *Memorabilia*.

> Second Year. Cicero's *Senectute and Amicitia*, Latin Composition, Roman Antiquities, Homer's *Iliad*, Solid Geometry, Greek Antiquities, Plane and Spherical Trigonometry, Horace and Terance, Sophocles's *Antigone* and Plato's *Gorgias*, Analytical Geometry, Engineering.

> Third Year. Demosthenes' *Corona*, Greek Literature, Logic, Literary Criticism, Mechanics, Juvenal and Tacitus, Roman Literature, Chemistry, Natural Philosophy, Botany.

> Fourth Year. Political Economy, Constitution of the United States, Mental Philosophy, Geology, Physiology, Zoology, Moral Philosophy, Analogy of Religion and Nature, Evidence of Christianity, Astronomy, International Law, Hebrew (Optional).

Albert Einstein said, "*The value of a classical education is not the learning of many facts but the training of the mind to think something that cannot be learned from textbooks.*"

People today are filled with wonder and astonishment when they look back at what our forefathers accomplished. I'm talking about not just those men who came-up with the Federalist Papers and the U.S. Constitution but their forefathers as well, men like Plato and those responsible for designing and building, without modern tools, the Parthenon between 447 and 432 BC.

Those men were **<u>educated</u>** in the classics, which provided mental and moral growth that stimulated their minds to think critically about something that can't be learned from textbooks. Today, we are **<u>trained</u>**, not educated, either to acquire knowledge in a field of study using textbooks and specialized instruction or to develop manual dexterity in practical crafts using small reference manuals with special instruction and actual practice.

Constructing arguments based on historical evidence or studying the use of effective language to improve one's ability to persuade an audience has obvious applications today. Computers and software permeate nearly everything and interdisciplinary approaches to problem solving are crucial to addressing modern challenges. This includes cultivating relationships in an increasingly digital world and creatively integrating new technologies into different sectors of the economy.

Though no one knows exactly how the workforce will operate ten or twenty years down the road, it's certain that critical thinking will still have value. And in that world, so will a classical education.

Our Thanks Go out to Big Corporations

November 22, 2019

A number of colleges are beating Democrat Socialists Elizabeth Warren and Bernie Sanders to the punch when they talk about the high cost of a college education. Cornell University's Medical School (located in New York City) has announced a $160-million scholarship program to eliminate education debt for all its students with financial need.

The fund is backed by the kind of Wall Street achievers Warren and Sanders love to openly assault. Most money for the scholarships came from the Starr Foundation, which is affiliated with Hank Greenberg, CEO of AIG, and from Sanford Weill, former CEO of Citigroup.

Last year, New York University announced $450 million from private donors to cover tuition for all its medical students. In late 2017, Columbia University unveiled a $150-million scholarship fund, endowed by former Merck CEO Roy Vagelos and his wife, to mitigate medical students' debt.

Such assistance isn't only for future medical doctors. Late last year, Johns Hopkins University accepted $1.8 billion from Michael Bloomberg for undergraduate financial aid. This past spring Robert Smith, chief executive of Vista Equity Partners, told Morehouse College's class of 2019 that he would pay-off their college debt.

These donations defy the stories about big bad corporations, so it's no surprise that the Democrat Socialists have reacted sourly.

Bernie Sanders said that Robert Smith's gift was "extremely generous" but added that the "student crisis will not be solved by charity. It must be addressed by governmental action."

On the contrary, private generosity has an advantage in that it's more accountable than public policy. Donors give to institutions they love and trust, and colleges find the students they believe are most needy or deserving.

Federal subsidies have inflated college prices, but private giving may be creating ethical competition. Columbia University applications for the 2019–2020 school year increased five percent after it announced their scholarship program in December 2017.

Given this trend, other medical schools may need to sweeten their own offers to stay competitive. This is America's civil society at its finest. These private-sector donors deserve much praise for helping so many students without burdening the middle-class with higher taxes.

American Schools Need to Teach Cursive Handwriting and American History

December 5, 2017

Cursive handwriting has not been taught in many, if not most public elementary schools since 1957. Today, cursive writing is pretty much gone except for those American adults who are in their sixties or older.

After producing three generations of students who know only keyboarding, texting, and block printing their words in longhand, cursive penmanship is coming back into elementary schools. Finally, it's now realized that fluent cursive writing prepares students brains to master grammatical tasks such as spelling and sentence construction partly because they don't have to think about forming block letters.

It's a good skill to have, especially when it comes to everyday life. Your signature is needed for all legal documents such as driver's license, voter registration, credit cards, etc., etc. Learning cursive goes beyond ordinary life. It also can help to distinguish the literate from the illiterate.

Similar programs, such as "iCanWrite" and "iWriteWords," can help parents create cursive writing lessens for their elementary school children. The program "ABC Cursive Writing" turns iPads into writing tablets, allowing students to practice uppercase, lowercase, whole words, and cursive sentences at home.

Failure to teach American history in our public schools is demonstrated by similar failure in our colleges and universities. American history is important! It's our heritage, it's who we are, and we should be proud.

The most widely used history textbook in U.S. public schools is *A People's History of the United States* by the late Howard Zinn, published in 1980 It is required reading in many high schools, colleges, and universities.

This history textbook by Zinn is a Leftwing version of U.S. history, full of multicultural, feminist, racial, and class-war propaganda. It's based on the thesis that America is not a republic but an empire controlled by a few white men. Its heroes are the antiestablishment protesters. The book debunks traditional heroes, such as George Washington, Andrew Jackson, and Dwight Eisenhower, and doesn't mention great Americans such as Thomas Edison.

Zinn's textbook deprives young readers of the opportunity to learn that they are part of the great story of American exceptionalism. His book inspires guilt and the belief that success comes only through exploitation. He belittles patriotism, never allowing pride in America.

Before his death in 2010, Zinn told one interviewer that his goal in writing this textbook was to start a "quiet revolution" of people taking power from within the institutions. Although when alive, Zinn publicly lied and denied his Communist Party membership, the FBI indeed did confirm his longtime Communist Party membership. His textbook was specially written to present a Marxist version of U.S. history based on the Communist strategy of "class war."

For years, liberals have imposed their revisionist history on our nation's public school students, completely removing important facts and historic figures while loading textbooks with liberal propaganda, distortions, and repetition. It's easy to get a quick lesson in the malignant leftwing bias by checking the index and noting how textbooks unfairly describe President Ronald Reagan and Senator Joseph McCarthy.

When parents object to leftwing inclusions and omissions, claiming they should have something to say about what their own children are being taught and how their taxpayers' money is spent, they're usually vilified as "book burners" and belittled as uneducated primates who ought to allow the "experts" to make all curriculum decisions.

The self-described "experts" are alumni of liberal teachers colleges and/or members of the leftwing teachers union. In most states, the liberal education establishment has total control over the state's board of education, department of education, and curriculum committees.

*****

Texas is different, the State Board of Education is elected, and the people (even including the parents) have a voice. Texas is uniquely important in textbook content because the state is the largest single purchaser of textbooks. Publishers can't afford to print different versions for other states, so Texas curriculum standards have nationwide influence.

The review of social studies curriculum (covering U.S. Government, American history, world history, and economics) comes up every ten years, and 2010 was one of those years.

The unelected education "experts" proposed their history revisions such as eliminating Independence Day, Christopher Columbus, Daniel Boone, Thomas Edison, and Neil Armstrong, and replacing Christmas with Diwali (the Hindu festival of lights celebrated every year). After a public outcry, the Texas State Board responded with common-sense improvements. Thomas Edison, the world's greatest inventor, will be again included in the narrative of American history.

Schoolchildren will no longer be misled into believing that capitalism and the free market are dirty words and that America has an unjust economic system. Instead, they will learn how the free-enterprise system gave our nation and the world so much that's good for so many people.

Liberals don't like the concept of American exceptionalism. They want to teach what's wrong with America (masquerading under the code word "social justice") instead of what's right and successful. The Texas State Board voted to include a description of how American exceptionalism is based on values that are unique and different from those of other nations.

The Texas State Board specified that teaching about the Bill of Rights should include a reference to the right to keep and bear arms. Some school curricula pretend the Second Amendment doesn't exist. Texas curriculum standards will henceforth accurately describe the U.S. government as a constitutional republic rather than as a representative democracy. Secularist liberals tried to remove reference to the religious basis for the founding of America, but that was voted down.

The Texas Board rejected the anti-Christian crowd's proposal to eliminate the use for historic dates of BC and AD, as in before Christ and Anno Domini, and replace them with BCE (as in Before the Common Era) and CE (as in Common Era).

The deceptive statement that the United States was founded on a "separation of church and state" gets the ax and rightfully so. In fact, most of the original thirteen colonies were founded as Christian communities with much overlap between church and state.

History textbooks that deal with Joseph McCarthy will now be required to explain "how the later release of the Venona papers confirmed suspicions of Communist infiltration in U.S. government." The Venona papers are authentic transcripts of some three thousand messages between the Soviet Union and its secret agents in the United States.

Discussions of economics will not be limited to the theories of Karl Marx and John Maynard Keynes. Textbooks must also include three champions of free-market theory, Adam Smith, Milton Friedman, and Friedrich von Hayek.

History textbooks will now be required to cover the "unintended consequences" of Great Society legislation, affirmative action, and Title IX legislation. Textbooks should also include "the conservative resurgence of the 1980s and 1990s."

Texas textbooks will now have to mention "the importance of personal responsibility for life choices" instead of blaming society for everything and expecting government to provide remedies for all social ills.

*****

It's no secret that the people who control public schools are at war with our nation's history, culture, and achievements. Since taxpayers foot the bill, it's long overdue for state boards of education to correct many textbook myths and lies about our magnificent national heritage.

Pulitzer Prize winning historian David McCullough believes that the ignorance of American history among U.S. high school teachers and students is a threat to national security. He told a Senate committee that "we are raising a generation of people who are historically illiterate." **Thomas Jefferson said, "If a nation expects to be ignorant and free, it expects what never was and never will be."**

College and university American history courses now deemphasize great people and events, often ridiculing them as DWEMs (Dead White European Males). The professors, many of whom are less than forty years old, want to teach history the way they wish it had happened instead of the way it did happen.

Students should learn about the accomplishments of America, its ingenuity, its freedom and abundance. We want our young people to become informed and optimistic, grateful to our ancestors, respectful of our values and institutions, proud of our heroes, and patriotic so they can pass this knowledge along to the next generation.

Most elite colleges no longer require students to study American history. Students are often allowed to take worthless classes to satisfy core curriculum requirements. For example, students at California State University, Monterey Bay can count the history of rock and roll as their required course in American history. Emory University allows students to choose among six hundred courses to fulfill the history, society, and culture requirement, including one called gynecology in the American World.

America's Public School System Needs Correcting

May 24, 2018

As usual, the politics of public education lately is all about grown-ups—teachers and teachers unions—instead of students. Crafty schemes by the teachers unions, including recent walkouts in states like Arizona, Kentucky, and Oklahoma, are leading America's public education system to a disastrous end.

Because they have resorted to **unionizing**, which is defined as a **labor** union, teachers are incorrectly called trained professionals. Unionized teachers are trained **blue-collar** workers. The most ill-prepared college students, sadly, are education majors today. When SAT scores are ranked by major, those majoring in education place twenty-sixth on a list of thirty-eight.

Schools of education, with but few exceptions, tend to be home for students with the lowest college entrance exam scores and also represent the academic slums of colleges. Teacher certification exams contain questions that a good eighth- or ninth-grader can answer.

How did our public education system get to its current state? Progressive reformers bureaucratized public education in 1933 by requiring certification for teachers and principals. Small schools that once reflected their local communities became rule-bound educational factories, in which mostly female teachers processed students under the watchful eyes of mostly male school principals and male school boards.

Though certified, the teachers were poorly trained, poorly paid, and managed in a manner not unlike that of Dilbert in the comic strips. This system functioned adequately so long as women and minorities had few other job opportunities.

Today, however, most of the brainy people who once might have been teachers instead become trained professionals—doctors, dentists, lawyers, professors, or engineers. The share of teachers who scored in the top ten percent on their high-school tests fell from twenty-four percent in 1971 to eleven percent in 1992, even as teacher salaries remained roughly constant in real dollars.

Because the evidence is clear that teacher quality hugely affects student learning, significantly increased teacher pay might reverse the brain drain of the past several decades. Higher teacher compensation might attract talented college graduates who have other employment options but may prefer to teach.

Liberals believe that higher pay for teachers is a matter of social justice. Even though it's established that increased teacher pay fails to improve teaching, it's seen by liberals as a matter of gender equity and economic fairness. Conservatives believe teachers are relatively privileged government bureaucrats with great benefits, fat pensions, summers off, tenure, reasonable pay, and working conditions far superior to what most other **blue-collar** jobs provide.

Both of these ways of thinking about teacher pay are inadequate. A better approach would start by recognizing three very conservative facts: history matters, teachers matter, and you can't get something for nothing. Together, they point to a policy of higher teacher pay but only in exchange for real reforms to improve teacher quality.

Unfortunately, teacher pay is only part of the equation. What will taxpayers get for teacher raises? Not much, if the conventional teacher certification requirements and teachers unions, both imposed by state governments, remain in place. Current standards for public schoolteacher training and recruitment are alarmingly low.

In contrast to the trained professions, studies show that certification has little to no effect on teacher performance. Instead, it provides the mere appearance of professionalism. Top-notch college prep schools such as Phillips Academy, Sidwell Friends, Punahou

School, Hillsdale Academy, and Oldenburg Academy, to list only five, hire uncertified teachers.

Teacher pay should be significantly increased only if teacher certification is made significantly more competitive. Public schools should be recruiting the most talented college graduates instead of only education majors.

Public schools also need more power to fire ineffective teachers. Teacher unions fear that such power would be misused by authoritarian school principals. Recruiting more talented teachers will result in better school principals down the road.

Most parents of public school students and public school board members want to restore teaching as a trained profession, but substantial pay hikes will get them only part-way there.

Corruption among Many of Today's Academics

November 19, 2015

The concept of white privilege, along with diversity and multiculturalism, is part of today's college and university campus craze. Millions of dollars are spent on conferences and other forums teaching students about the horrors of white privilege. A Vanderbilt University sociology professor even said white privilege is to blame for the Baltimore riots and looting.

I wonder how one goes about determining whether a person is privileged? White privilege can't be based on median income. Why? It turns out that Asian-American households had the highest median income ($68,686) in 2012. Median income for white households was $57,000. Maybe our academic elite should condemn Asian privilege instead of white privilege. But there's another problem.

If those who condemn white privilege would recognize the dark brown skin color and wealth of some professors and coaches, they would have to condemn them for white privilege. The bottom line to this campus nonsense is that "privilege" has become the new word for "personal achievement."

Obama has often said the wealthiest Americans must make sacrifices to better the lives of poor people. Earlier this year at Georgetown University, Obama said, "If we can't ask from society's lottery winners to just make that modest investment, then really this conversation is for show."

Let's take a look at the "lottery winner" nonsense. A *lottery* is defined in my dictionary as "an activity or event regarded as having an outcome depending on luck, chance, or fate." The question before us is whether wealth is something that's obtained by luck, chance, or fate. Did Bill Gates acquire his wealth by luck, chance, or fate? He produced something that benefited his fellow man, causing people to voluntarily reach into their pockets to pay.

Gale Cook founded a medical device company using a spare bedroom in her apartment as a factory. Her company specialized in stents and antibiotic catheters. Now Gayle Cook has a net worth in the billions of dollars. Was she a winner in the lottery of life, or did she have to do something like serve her fellow man?

Are those who work hard, take risks, make life better for others, and become wealthy in the process the people who should be held up to ridicule and scorn? And should we make mascots out of social parasites?

Obama talked about asking "from society's lottery winners to just make that modest investment." Congress doesn't ask people for money. Through intimidation, threats, and coercion, it takes people's earnings. If people don't comply, the agents of Congress will imprison them.

It's important to realize that Obama's remarks were made at a university. Not a single professor has said anything about his suggestion that people accumulate wealth by winning life's lottery. That's just more evidence about the level of corruption among today's academics.

ACADEMIC FRAUD IS AT EVERY LEVEL OF AMERICAN EDUCATION

April 1, 2014

In early April, The Nation's 2017 Report Card was released—our high school graduation rate is higher than 80 percent. That means public high school diplomas, which attest that these students can read and compute at a 12th-grade level, are conferred when 63 percent aren't proficient in reading and 75 percent aren't proficient in math. For blacks, the news is far worse. Roughly 75 percent received diplomas. However, 83 percent couldn't read at a 12th-grade level, and 93 percent couldn't do math at that level.

It's grossly dishonest for the public educational establishment to boast about graduation rates when the high school diplomas, for the most part, don't represent academic achievement. At best, they certify attendance.

Fraudulent high school diplomas aren't the worst part of the fraud. The greatest fraud occurs at the college and university level. In 2016, 70 percent of white high school graduates enrolled in college, and 58 percent of black high school graduates enrolled in college.

If only 37 percent of white high school graduates test as college-ready, how can colleges admit 70 percent of them? And if roughly 17 percent of black high school graduates test as college-ready, how can colleges admit 58 percent of them?

It's inconceivable that the liberal college and university administrators are unaware that they're admitting ill-prepared students who can't perform at that level of education. They provide remedial courses, for which students must pay for at college-level cost, rather than receiving the same "for free" in public schools.

More than two-thirds of two-year community college students take at least one remedial course, as do 40 percent of 4-year college students. The Liberal College professors dumb-down courses so that ill-prepared students can get passing grades.

Colleges also set-up majors with few analytical demands so as to accommodate students with analytical deficits. Such courses often include the term "studies"—ethnic studies, cultural studies, gender studies, and American studies.

The major for the most ill-prepared students, sadly enough, is education. When student SAT scores are ranked by intended major, those with an education major place twenty-sixth on a list of thirty-eight. With but a few exceptions, schools of education represent the academic slums of colleges. Techniques in the art of teaching can be learned through short formal training, coaching, and experience. They tend to be home to students who have the lowest academic test scores when they enter college, when they graduate or choose to take post-graduate admissions tests—the GRE, the MCAT, and the LSAT.

Following are some questions on a teacher certification tests:

- Janet can type 250 words in 5 minutes, what is her typing rate per minute?
  a) 50wpm, b. 66 wpm, c. 55 wpm, d. 45 wpm.
- Find the verb in the following sentence: The interior temperatures of even the coolest stars are measured in millions of degrees.
  a) coolest, b. of even, c. are measured, d. in millions.
- You purchase a car making a down payment of $3,000 and a monthly payment of $225. How much have you paid so far for the car?
  a) $3225, b. $4350, c. $5375, d. $6550, e. $6398.
- Which of the following is the largest?
  a) ¼, b. 3/5, c. ½, d. 9/20.

- A town planning committee must decide how to use a 115-acre piece of land. The committee set aside 20 acres of the land for watershed protection and an additional 37.4 acres for recreation. How much of the land is set aside for watershed protection and recreation?
  a) 43.15 acres, b. 54.6 acres, c. 57.4 acres, d. 60.4 acres.

My thinking is that these are question that a good eighth- or ninth-grader ought to be able to answer. Such test questions demonstrate the low bar that states set in order to become a certified teacher.

How necessary is college anyway? One estimate is that one in three college graduates today have a job historically performed by those with high school diplomas. A 2012 study found there were 115,000 janitors, 16,000 parking lot attendants, 83,000 bartenders, and nearly 35,000 taxi drivers with a bachelors' degree.

I'm not sure what can be done about education. But the first step toward any solution is for the American people to be aware of this academic fraud.

COLLEGES DON'T TEACH
TODAY—THEY INDOCTRINATE

December 18, 2018

Benjamin Franklin (1706–1790) wrote, "Whoever would over-throw the Liberty of a Nation must begin by subduing the Freeness of Speech." Many years later, Supreme Court Justice Potter Stewart (1915–1985) said, "Censorship reflects a society's lack of confidence in itself. It is a hallmark of an authoritarian regime."

From the Nazis (1933–1945) to the Stalinists (1941–1953) to the Maoists (1949–1969), tyrants have always started-out support-ing free speech, as did America's Leftists in late 1960s. Their support for free speech is easy to understand because free speech is vital to the realization of Leftist goals—command, control, and confiscation.

The right to say what they please is a tool used by Leftists to indoctrinate, propagandize, and proselytize. Once they gain control, as they have at many American universities, free speech becomes a liability, and they undertake to suppress it.

This is the case on university campuses, and much of the off-campus incivility seen today results from what a college back-ground has done to Americans younger than about age fifty. Take for instance the highly publicized recent examples of incivility and attacks on free speech mentioned below.

- Members of Congress such as Paul Rand, Susan Collins, and Andy Harris have been physically attacked or harassed by Leftists.

- Senate Majority Leader Mitch McConnell and his wife, Transportation Secretary Elaine Chao, were accosted and harassed by a deranged Leftist mob as they were leaving a dinner at Georgetown University.
- Senator McConnell was harassed also by Left-wing protesters at Reagan National Airport, as well as at several places in Kentucky.
- Senator Ted Cruz and his wife were harassed at a Washington, DC, restaurant. Afterward, a group called Smash Racism DC wrote: "No, you can't eat in peace. Your politics are an attack on all of us. Your votes are a death wish. Your votes are hate crimes."
- A Leftist group showed-up one night at Fox News political commentator Tucker Carlson's house, damaging his front door and chanting, "Tucker Carlson, we will fight! We know where you sleep at night! Racist scumbag, leave town!"

The infliction of violence on people with different political points of view is considered by Leftists to be hate speech. Let's take a look at some examples of this violence. Enterprise Institute scholar Charles Murray discovered this when he was shouted down at Middlebury College, and the professor escorting him was sent to the hospital with injuries. Students at the University of California at Berkley shut-down a controversial speaker and caused riot damage costing the university $100,000. Protesters at both UCLA and at Claremont McKenna College disrupted scheduled lectures by Manhattan Institute scholar Heather MacDonald.

Universities expressly set their sights on prohibiting constitutionally protected speech. Left-wing "bias response teams" have been set-up on hundreds of American college campuses. These teams report, anonymously, to campus officials, and sometimes law enforcement officers, any speech they consider may cause "alarm, anger, or fear" or to be offensive.

It was recently reported by the Brookings Institution nearly half of college students believe that hate speech is not protected by the

First Amendment. That's nonsense; it is. Fifty-one percent (51 percent) think they have the right to shut-down a speaker with whom they disagree. Nineteen percent (19 percent) think it's acceptable to use violence to prevent a speaker from speaking. Over fifty percent (+50 percent) agreed that colleges should prohibit speech and viewpoints that might offend certain people.

As a college student, 1949–1953 and 1956–1958, professors taught an understanding of American culture and values. Today, many professors and the college bureaucracy teach students that they are victims of American culture and values.

AMERICANS MISEDUCATED

December 12, 2018

According to a survey released in October 2016, many Americans born since about the mid-1970s have little understanding of socialism. The survey, conducted by the Victims of Communism Memorial Foundation, reveals just how badly the minds in this segment of our population have been indoctrinated.

Seventy-one percent (71%) agreed more with statements by socialist Senator Bernie Sanders than statements by capitalist and economist Milton Freidman. Fifty-eight percent (58%) agreed more with statements by Milton Freidman.

Forty-five percent (45%) of those people age 16 to 56 said they would vote for a socialist, and twenty-one percent (21%) said they would vote for a communist. Fifty-five percent (55%) of those below age 36 felt that communism is a problem, compared to eighty percent (80%) of those above age 36.

Fifty-one percent (51%) of these people said they would rather live in a socialist or a communist country than in a capitalist country. Only forty-two percent (42%) said they prefer living in a capitalist country.

Twenty-five percent (25%) of those who knew that Vladimir Lenin was the first premier of the Union of Soviet Socialist Republic viewed him favorably. Almost a third of them actually believe that former U.S. President George W. Bush killed more people than Soviet Dictator Joseph Stalin (Lenin's successor) who killed 62 million.

Fifty percent (50%) of these individuals had never heard of communist Mao Zedong, ruler of China from 1949 to 1976. Mao was responsible for the deaths of forty-five million Chinese.

Even worse, most of the people in this survey were not familiar with brutal communist dictators through history. The percentage of those familiar with the listed mass murderers follows:

- Vladimer Lenin. 33%
- Joseph Stalin. 18%
- Mao Zedong. 42%
- Chi Guevara. 40%

Although not included in the survey, Adolph Hitler and his National Socialist German Workers' Party killed about twenty million. The Nazis came-in as a poor third in terms of history's most prolific mass murderers. My research finds the twentieth century to be humankind's most brutal. Two hundred sixty-three million (263,000,000) people's lives were destroyed at the hands of their own governments.

This survey's results are reflective of other surveys that show a growing tendency of more than fifty years of young Americans warming to socialism. This is what happens when the Left seizes power in all levels of academia, the media, and Hollywood.

Millennial and some Gen-X folks have become indoctrinated in the progressive ideology, which necessarily requires the concealing of the horrors of Karl Marx's destructive philosophy. Unless they're presented the truth about Marxism, America's freedoms are in danger.

We older Americans must wait no longer for the world to change, now is the time that we change ourselves before the Leftist segment of our population grows to rule America. This starts with teaching of the truth about socialism at home, at school boards, by K-12 administrators and teachers, and higher level academia administrators, teachers, and professors. It means changing adults whose minds at an early age were indoctrinated with socialist ideology, rather than taught American History and American values.

Those who weren't alive during WWII or not old enough to understand its Cold War aftermath might be forgiven for not knowing the horrors of socialism. Most of America's socialists, communists, and Marxists today have little knowledge of socialist history.

They don't realize socialists and fascists have always been "kissing cousins."

When the tragedies of socialist regimes such as Venezuela, Cuba, USSR, China, and many others are pointed-out to America's Leftists, they hold-up Sweden as their role model. Sweden's experiment with socialism lasted about twenty years, ending in disillusionment and reform.

Sweden began rolling-back government in the early 1990s and recaptured the spirit of entrepreneurship that made it a wealthy country to begin with. It's now a nation of free trade, school vouchers, light business regulation, no minimum wage laws, and open immigration.

School vouchers and no minimum wage are offensive to America's Leftists. Are Americans who admire the world's most brutal regimes miseducated, just plain stupid, or do they have an agenda of devious character?

Students Yesteryear
Versus Students Today

June 21, 2018

About fifty-million Americans are sixty-five years of age or older, and I belong to that fine group of citizens.

Ask any one of those fifty-million Americans if there were any discussions about the need to hire armed guards to protect students and teachers against school shootings or how many students or teachers were shot to death during the time they were in school. For me and those other Americans sixty-five or older, when we were in school, a conversation about hiring armed guards and having police patrol hallways would have been seen as lunacy.

What's the difference between yesteryear and today? The logic of those people who argue today for stricter gun control laws is that something has happened to guns. Guns themselves are the problem because guns today behave more poorly and have become evil.

The duty for those of us sixty-five and older is to disclose the fact that guns were far more available and less controlled when we were in school. We know guns themselves can't change. Therefore, something else is the problem.

It's people who have changed. Behavior that's accepted from students today was not accepted during the period from 1930 to early 1970s. For example, in 2010, an average of four teachers and staff members were assaulted each school day in Baltimore, and more than three hundred school staff members filed worker's compensation claims in a year because of injuries received through assaults or altercations on the job.

In Philadelphia, 690 teachers were assaulted in 2010, and 4,000 were assaulted during a five-year period. In that city's schools, according to *The Philadelphia Inquirer*:

- *"On an average school day 25 students, teachers, or other staff members were beaten, robbed, sexually assaulted, or victims of other violent crimes.*
- *That doesn't even include thousands more who were extorted, threatened, or bullied in a year."*

Gun accessibility in America has never been as restricted as it is today. Until the 1960s, New York City public schools had shooting clubs. Students carried their rifles to school on the subway in the morning and turned them over to their homeroom teacher or a gym teacher to keep them centrally stored and out of the way. The rifles were retrieved by the students after school for target practice.

Prior to the early 1970s, people could simply walk into a hardware store or sporting goods store and buy a rifle. Buying a rifle or pistol through a mail-order catalog was easy. Often, a father would give his twelve-year-old son on his birthday a 22-caliber rifle or a shotgun for sport hunting.

With greater accessibility to guns in the past, why wasn't there the kind of violence seen today when there is much more restricted access to guns? When a murderer uses a bomb, truck, or car to kill people, we fully recognize that such objects are incapable of acting on their own, and we blame the perpetrator.

However, when the murder is done using a gun, we do call for control over the inanimate instrument of death—the gun. Do I smell a hidden anti-gun agenda?

Undermining America

November 6, 2017

Our nation's political Leftists have long sought to undermine American values expressed in the Declaration of Independence and Constitution. Though some Democrats don't have this leftist hate for America, they are willing accomplices in undermining the most basic value the Founding Fathers promoted—limited government.

Leftists have had their greatest successes in undermining American values on the nation's college campuses. Derelict and dishonest college administrators, boards of trustees and professors have given the institutions of higher learning unconditional authority to act at their own discretion.

Students at the University of Virginia desecrated the statue of Thomas Jefferson, founder of the university. University of Missouri students want Jefferson's statue gone because he was a slave owner.

Many in the college community supported Senator Bernie Sanders' presidential bid. They welcomed his belief that the United States was founded on "racist principles."

There have also been calls for the removal of George Washington's and Abraham Lincoln's statues. Some have called for the renaming of schools that honor Washington, Jefferson, and eleven other slave-owning presidents.

Leftists have called for the renaming of streets named after slave-owning presidents. There have been many leftist calls for the elimination of Columbus Day. Their success at getting Confederate statues taken down has emboldened them.

Many patriotic Americans don't understand the true significance of America's Leftists attacking the founders. If leftists can delegitimize the Founders themselves, it goes a long way toward their agenda of delegitimizing the founding principles of our nation.

The average parent, taxpayer, and donor have absolutely no idea of the strikingly unconventional and far-fetched lessons that college professors are teaching students.

A couple of examples follow: "Whether or not your individual ancestors owned slaves, you as a white person have benefited from slavery and are complicit in it." Patriotism is "drenched in whiteness," and patriotism implies "that black people are un-American."

These types of attacks on American values have reached one of our most prestigious institutions of higher learning—the U.S. Military Academy. West Point administrators knew of one particular student's disqualifying insubordination, extremist political views, and regulation-breaking online activity.

They also knew as early as 2015 that the student was an avowed communist and that he held Marxist anti-American beliefs. Despite the student's conduct and demonstrated hatred of America, the Military Academy's administration allowed him to graduate in 2016.

The rot of America's premier military academy goes beyond the traitorous ideas of this particular student. A retired former West Point professor wrote a letter exposing widespread corruption, cheating, and falling standards at the academy, to which the administration has turned a blind, politically correct eye.

In response to the retired professor's letter, the superintendent of the academy wrote a standard bureaucratic letter saying: The administration will investigate the revelations that it not only managed to graduate the student but also sent him on to Army battlefield units, thus enabling him to spread his anti-American ideas.

Patriotic Americans need to lead efforts in putting a halt to the undermining of our nation that is taking place in our institutions of higher learning.

FINANCIAL LITERACY
A REQUIRED COURSE
IN HIGH SCHOOL

April 3, 2019

There's a trend of state governments seeking to help individuals get their financial lives in order. An estimated forty-two percent of private sector workers don't have access to retirement-savings plans at work, and many of them don't save at all. To help these workers, some states are enacting programs that require or encourage companies without these plans to offer them and, in some cases, automatically enroll employees.

Some states are turning to financial-literacy programs to educate high school teenagers before they form bad spending and payment habits. They're doing this hoping to save taxpayers money over the long term by reducing public assistance, including Medicare.

Nineteen states currently require that high school students study financial literacy before they receive a diploma. That's up from seventeen states in 2018 and thirteen states in 2011. Lawmakers in states including Rhode Island, Florida, Texas, and South Carolina are now considering expanding financial-literacy mandates in their schools. New Jersey and Wisconsin recently added financial-literacy instruction requirements for lower grades.

Additionally, a growing number of companies have begun offering programs that teach employees basic financial literacy and money management skills. This reflects concern over the impact money problems are having on employees' stress and productivity levels.

A researcher at George Washington University says that the trend is occurring at schools because surveys show that "financial literacy can be hardly taught at home given the low financial knowledge of many parents."

Americans often struggle to manage their money. According to the Federal Reserve, forty-four percent of adults lack the funds to cover a four-hundred-dollar emergency. The median household headed by a person age fifty-five to sixty-four has little more than $100,000 in retirement savings. Furthermore, eleven percent of borrowers who started paying federal student loans in 2015 had defaulted within three years. Research has found that students from states that require financial-literacy instruction have: lower credit card balances, pay for college with more grants, and lower-cost student loans than students from states without such mandates.

The mind of a senior at Elizabethtown (KY) High School who planned to attend Western Kentucky University after graduation was changed by a financial-literacy class. He said the class brought home the long-term costs of attending a four-year college away from home. It also taught him how best to divide his income between his expenditures and saving for college and repairs on the used car his grandfather gave him.

This eighteen-year-old now aims to continue living at home, keep his very good part-time job, attend a local community college for two years, and transfer to a four-year state university. The young man says, "After finding-out the costs, I knew the extra spending might hurt me later in my life."

This was precisely what three of my fellow high school graduates and I did seventy years ago (1949), except none of us had a car. Each of us has been professionally successful, and each of us still lives as I write today.

What Is a College Degree Worth?

November 22, 2019

The fact that a college degree is among the most expensive investments many Americans will ever make is one reason they have accumulated $1.5 billion in student-loan debt. The U.S. Department of Education hasn't made the price go down.

In spite of that, Department of Education Secretary Betsy DeVoss relaunched a website several days ago that will help students get a better idea of what they're buying. The website is CollegeScorecard.ed.gov, and it's been around a few years.

Before this very recent relaunch, however, students could only look-up the earnings and debt for colleges as a whole. Given the large difference between what an electrical engineer major and an English major can expect to earn, this has been a crude and usually unhelpful measure.

The good news is that the website now offers a much fuller picture that enables students more ways to compare. A student choosing a field of study, for example, at Iowa State University might want to know that while a civil engineer can look forward to earning $60,700 the first year after graduation, a history major can expect to earn $30,600.

The relaunched website also compares the median monthly earnings and loan payments for, say, computer science at Duke University ($8,300/$82), Rutgers University ($5,858/$221), and

Florida State University ($4,233/$231). The same can be done for the debt a student accumulates before graduation.

Colleges should be offering students more of this information on their own. Transparency won't solve all the problems. But more information will help students learn what they can expect in exchange for all that debt they're taking-on.

College Is Not for Everyone

September 14, 2017

There's absolutely no shame in a high school graduate learning a trade. Doing so may make that person happier and better off financially than many peers with bachelor degrees. The fact is that colleges admit a far greater number of students than those who test as being college-ready.

Why should students be admitted to college when they aren't capable of academic performance at the college level? Admitting such students gets America's high schools off the hook, allowing them to deliver grossly fraudulent education.

They can continue issuing diplomas that attest their students can read, write, and compute at a twelfth grade level when they may not be able to perform at even an eighth or ninth grade level. Only twenty-five percent of students who took the ACT in 2012 met the test's readiness benchmarks in all four subjects (English, reading, math, and science); **history** isn't considered. Anywhere from twenty-eight to forty percent of first-year students enroll in at least one remedial (high school level) course. At community colleges, studies have found remediation course rates surpassing fifty percent.

Many college students who manage to graduate don't have much to show for their time and money. A New York University study shows that more than a third of students demonstrated no improvement in critical thinking skills after four years at a university. That observation is confirmed by the many employers who complain that lots of recent graduates can't write an email that will not embarrass the company.

In 1970, only eleven percent of adult Americans held college degrees. Today, over thirty percent hold college degrees. A significant portion of today's graduates aren't demonstrably more intelligent or more disciplined than the average American. Declining academic standards and grade inflation confirm employer perceptions that college degrees say little about job readiness.

What happens to many of these ill-prepared college graduates? If they manage to become employed in the first place, their employment has nothing to do with their degree. According to a study at Ohio University in 2012, there were 115,000 janitors, 16,000 parking lot attendants, 83,000 bartenders, and about 35,000 taxi drivers with bachelor's degrees.

Post-Election Chaos in Colleges and Universities

November 29, 2016

Donald Trump's victory in the recent presidential election has provided additional clear evidence regarding the steep decay of academics in America's colleges and universities. Let's look at the response to Trump's win, not only among college-age students still wet-behind-the-ears acting like kindergartners but also among the professors and administrators.

Distressed students at University of Michigan were provided Play-Doh and coloring books as they sought comfort and distraction. A professor postponed an exam at UM after many of his students complained about their "serious stress" caused by the election results.

Cornell University held a campus-wide "cry-in" while officials distributed tissues and hot chocolate to the students. One of Cornell's foreign students told others, "I'm looking into flights back to Bangladesh right now so I can remove myself before Trump repatriates me."

A dormitory at University of Pennsylvania reportedly hosted a post-election "Breathing Space" for students stressed out by election results. This included cuddling cats and a puppy, coloring and crafting, tea, and chocolate snacks.

University of Kansas reminded its stressed-out students that its therapy dogs, a regular campus feature, were available.

A Yale University professor made his midterm exam "optional" in response to "many heartfelt notes from students who are in shock over the election returns." Also at Yale, students had "teary eyes, bowed heads, and cries of disbelief" and had an opportunity to participate in a post-election group primeval scream "to express their frustration."

Students at Columbia University petitioned professors to cancel classes and postpone exams because they feared for their lives and they couldn't take an exam while crying. Officials did not entirely cave but said, "We are, however, leaving decisions regarding individual classes, exams, and assignments to the discretion of our faculty." "The faculty is well aware that you may be struggling, and they are here for you."

Regardless of political affiliation, the readers of this writing should be deeply concerned about the future of our nation based on the response to an election outcome of so many of our young adult college students, and professors and administrators who sanction the coddling of these students.

There are students at Brown University who claim that freedom of speech doesn't confer the right to express opinions they find distasteful.

A Harvard University women's group advised female law students that they should not be pressured to attend or participate in class sessions focusing on the law of sexual violence if they feel it might be traumatic. Such students, who may be practicing law professionally later in life, will be useless to rape victims and should not be a student in any law school.

My firm belief is that no person belongs in a college or university if that individual can't handle or tolerate differing opinions. It is such intolerance of different opinions that lies at the heart of multiculturalism, diversity, and political correctness.

An American Institute for Research study reveals that seventy-five percent of two-year college students and fifty percent of four-year college students can't complete everyday tasks. Thirty percent of two-year college students couldn't progress past elementary arithmetic while twenty percent of four-year college students demonstrated only basic mathematical ability. Fortune five hundred companies reported that they spend three billion dollars annually to train employees in "basic English."

My conclusion is that many of today's college students are both emotionally and academically incompetent and should not be there. How can these college snowflakes and their intellectual professors view themselves as superior to ordinary American people?

A Sad Occurrence

December 21, 2018

The political controversy about Donald Trump's win over Hillary Clinton in the 2016 national election was at its peak in January 2017. Earlier this year, a college professor began the first class-day of his political psychology course by asking students in the lecture hall a series of questions.

He ended the series with the following two questions: How many of you feel that liberals are safe walking across campus expressing their political views? Every hand was raised. How many of you feel that conservatives are safe to walk around campus expressing their political views? The room was filled with laughter as nobody raised their hand.

While most of the students thought little of the exercise, this would have been a very frightening experience for me and fellow students during our college years ending in 1953 and in 1958. Here was an entire lecture hall full of young adults laughing at the recognition of political suppression at a university founded 1819 on the principles of free thought and discourse.

My-oh-my, how the attitude of America's young adult college students have changed in fewer than sixty years!

College Students and Their Free Speech Today

October 11, 2017

Benjamin Franklin wrote: "Freedom of speech is a principal pillar of a free government. When this support is taken away, the constitution of a free society is dissolved." A new Brookings Institution survey shows that America's college students have no clue what the First Amendment to our Constitution means.

More than fifteen-hundred college undergraduates were surveyed, and the findings are as follows: most American college students don't know that even hate speech is conditionally protected; fifty percent agree that it's okay to shut-down a speaker whose views they don't agree with; and nearly twenty percent believe it's acceptable for a student group opposed to a speaker to use violence to keep the person from speaking. Some of the answers vary by political identification, but overall, the findings indicate much confusion.

The conclusion of the survey is that "Freedom of expression is deeply imperiled on American college campuses." Given that a functioning democracy-in-a-republic rests on free expression, what does the results of this survey say about America's future when these students leave school and begin to take their places in public life?

It's easy to ridicule the students for their ignorance. What about the people responsible for teaching them? The failures of our current education system are beginning to have terrible consequences for America's civic life.

The Name of the College You Attend Doesn't Really Matter

March 29, 2019

The method colleges use to select students is not a reliable predictor of student outcomes, particularly when it comes to learning. The selection process typically considers SAT and ACT scores, high school GPA and class rank, and the college's acceptance rate. As common sense suggests, students who study hard at college are the ones who end-up learning the most, regardless of whether they attend an Ivy League school or a local community college.

A recognized 2014 study of more than thirty thousand college graduates found no correlation between college selectivity and future job satisfaction or well-being. The study showed that graduates were just as likely to score high or low on a scale measuring their thriving whether they attended community colleges, regional colleges, or highly selective private and public universities.

There is a modest financial gain from attending a highly selective school if students are the first in their families to attend college or come from underserved communities. Nonetheless, the difference in financial outcomes between the low-earning and high-earning graduates of top-ranked colleges is greater than the difference between graduates of highly ranked colleges and graduates of non-selective colleges, including community colleges. The fact that smart, ambitious, persistent students who graduate from elite colleges also do well in life doesn't mean that the college caused the graduate's success.

It seems to me that the American society today is too hyper-focused on achievement, credentials, and status. According to recent surveys of more than 145,000 students, more than 80 percent of students at high-achieving colleges cheat in one way or another.

Three-quarters of high school juniors and seniors list planning for college as a top source of stress and worry in their life, well above relationships and family issues. More and more of these students are reporting sleep deprivation, anxiety, depression, and thoughts of suicide as they struggle to meet expectations imposed upon them.

Students who benefit most in college are those engaged in learning, including higher levels of subject matter competence, curiosity, initiative, and better course grades. Looking back on my own college life, I find the following five key experiences correlate with my own professional fulfillment, initially as an employee and later in private professional practice. Study courses with professors who make learning exciting. Work with professors who personally care about students. Make friends with individual professor who encourages you to pursue personal goals. Work on a project spread over two or more semesters. Participate in an internship that applies classroom learning.

It's critical that students enter college with an engagement mind-set. Make the most out of the time. Invest in relationships, try new things, study hard, reach out to peers and adults, build empathy, and take appropriate risks. College years are short relative to the rest of a student's life.

The Norm at Some Colleges

January 30, 2019

During late April of this year, some shocking professorial and student behavior came to light. None of this behavior is new in the nation's colleges. It's part of the Leftist agenda that dominates our colleges.

In the wake of Barbara Bush's death, California State University female professor Randa Jarrar took to twitter to call the former first lady an "amazing racist." "I'm so happy the witch is dead, can't wait for the rest of her family to fall to their demise the way 1.5 million Iraqis have."

At the City University of New York School of Law, students shouted down a guest lecturer for ten minutes before he could continue his remarks. When Duke University President Vincent Price was trying to address alumni, students commandeered the stage shouting demands and telling him to leave.

According to U.S. World News and World Report, the political affiliation at 51 of the 66 top liberal arts colleges are Republican-free with zero registered Republicans on their faculties. As for Republicans within academic departments, seventy-eight percent of those departments have no Republican members or so few as to make no difference.

The faculty Democrat-to-Republican ratio by academic department doesn't offer many surprises. Engineering departments: 1.6 Democrats for every Republican. Chemistry and economics departments: 5.5 Democrats for every Republican. Anthropology departments: 133 Democrats for every Republican. Communications departments: 108 Democrats and zero Republicans. Not one Republican appointment was found in fields like gender studies,

African studies, and peace studies. Many professors spend class time indoctrinating students with their views. For faculty members who are Democrats, those views are Leftist, Socialist, or Communist.

It's cowardly for a professor to take advantage of student immaturity by indoctrinating pupils with their opinions before the students have developed the maturity and skill to examine other opinions. It's also a dereliction of duty of college administrators and boards of trustees to permit the continuance of what some professors and students are doing in the name of higher education.

These findings suggest biases in college research and academic policy, where Leftist political homogeneity is embedded in the college culture. The Leftist bias at most of the nation's colleges is in stark contrast to the political leanings of our country.

According to a number of Pew Research Center surveys, most Americans identify as conservative. These Americans are seeing their tax dollars and tuition dollars going to people who have contempt for their values and seek to indoctrinate their children with Leftist ideas.

Chapter IV
To Val from Jim

Our forty-sixth is drawing near
Oh, how the time does fly!
Your hair is gray; my head is bare;
And wrinkles skirt our eyes.

You watch our diets closely now
And meals are not so rich.
Your gout does kick-up somehow
My esophagus changes pitch.

But just so long as you can see,
So long as I can hear.
I think we just might make it,
Down the road a few more years.

While I can cast my line and lure,
And you can play a tune,
Let's stay on board and paddle on,
And listen for the loon.

During our years I will walk with you,
In deep green forests, on shores of sand,
And when our time on earth is through,
In heaven too, you will have my hand.

August 10, 2002

American Heritage

Get on your knees each day, my friend
Give thanks that you are here,
Then raise your eyes, look to the skies,
And see if you can hear
The Force that's calling all of us
To share our rightful load
And work to steer America
Back to the honor'd road.

Our fathers left this land to us
To cherish and to love,
To mold by hand as best we can,
To mirror heav'ns above.
So do your share, then say a pray'r,
Protect her with your might.
It is our final hope, my friend—
No other land's in sight.

The plan that we must use right now
Is still the very same,
The plan that gave our fathers strength
To strive and to attain.
So listen, all America,
The benefit is clear.
The benefit is freedom, yes—
The freedom we have here.

Music by
Valeska M. Hough
Lyrics by
James E. Hough
© 1981

WOODLAND INSPIRATION

Often have I started out
No thought in my noodle,
Wandered here and thereabout
Where trees made me doodle;
Feeling childlike in my joy
I wrote some happy lines,
Returning joyfully saying oh boy,
A poem from tree mines.

Squatting on a fallen oak
With vast of woods about me,
I scribbled on an envelope
Rhymes the trees do shout me;
Couplets the birds would call
The songs that breezes proffered...
I didn't think at all,
Just took what Nature offered.

That's the way I need to write,
Without a touch of trouble;
Supercharged with great delight
Allow the words to bubble;
Voice of trees, dale, and stream
Without a plan or proem:
Aroused from out of drowsy dream
Then find I've writ a poem.

I'll go forth with mind a blank
The trees and stream they charm me;
While resting on a flowery bank
Make notes of what they tell me;
As Mother Nature speaks to me
Her words I'll merely docket,
I'll come singing home for tea
A poem in my pocket.

May 27, 2014

My Oak and Hickory Woods

I have an oak and hickory woods,
The trees are ten thousand fifty,
They give me shade and solitude
For they are tall and hefty.

Every day to me they bring
With riches underlying,
Food'an shade to make me sing
And keep my face aglowing.

Go buy an oak and hickory woods
When you have cash for spending,
Where you can dream in mellow mood
With serenity unending.

Where you can cheerfully retreat
Beyond all religious teaching,
And make yourself a temple sweet
Of enraptured abiding.

Silence has a secrete voice
That claims the soul as portal,
And those that hear it can rejoice
Since they are more than mortal.

Standing in my oak and hickory woods
When soft the owl is winging,
By granite stone still as I stood...
Only sound! The stars are singing.

September 2, 2013

My Buddy Rascal

b. 6/30/94, d. 12/30/05

My years numbered sixty-four;
Rascal was a little tyke.
With my buddy, just a pup,
In the forest I did hike.

With my Rascal in the lead,
Many's the day that we did run.
Over slopes and creeks and hills,
Chasing deer and yod'ling fun.

Chain saw slipped and leg I cut,
Skin and muscle but no bone.
To the rescue. Rascal came,
Val in tow and not alone.

Then one day on icy ground,
On my shoulder down I dropped.
Buddy Rascal was right there,
Kissing, licking, got me propped.

Though I thought my buddy clear,
That old van rolled on ahead.
Then old Rascal gave a howl,
'Neath the van; I thought him dead.

Once again, our strolls resumed,
Seldom then did Rascal run.
Faithful Aussie with his pal.
Watching deer, still yod'ling fun.

As the years did roll along,
Rascal's eyesight did grow dim.
From the Vet the message came,
"Nothing can be done for him."

Rascal knew he was to go,
Reaching out, he licked my hand.
He looked up as if to say,
"Sorry, but you understand."

Cried a lot and could not see,
God did call my old pal home.
Faithful dogs a heaven have,
My friend Rascal can't be gone.

A Dog Owner's Prayer

August 23, 2016

Lord, I know grown men don't cry. But when I looked at Freedom's front right paw and saw the deep fresh gash in the pad, I had to fight hard to keep the tears from falling. Freedom had trotted ahead of me, as usual, on our four-mile walk in my forest and wildlife preserve this morning. He didn't limp a single time.

When I knelt down to rub Freedom's head and neck, there was a long honey locust thorn embedded deep in his right shoulder muscle. And there was another one too. I didn't feel him flinch when I pulled them out, not once.

But when I saw the hole in his right hip and the dried blood where something had jabbed him, I couldn't hold back the tears any longer.

Lord, I ask you to bless Freedom and me and take his pain away until we get to the vet. If you have only one blessing left for today, give it to Freedom. He means more to me than I can express at this time, and I love him.

Thanks, Lord, and amen.

Chapter V
Colors That Only Bees and Birds Can See

April 10, 2019

My ticket, to live full-time in a wonderfully soothing symphony of cicadas and chorus of numerous spring and transient birds of the forest, was punched twenty years ago. Now I can hardly wait for April 30 when Wood Thrush and Hermit Thrush arrive with their piccolo calls and the redbud and dogwood trees around my lake bloom in mid-April.

Spring has arrived. Pinkish-white spring beauties hide many acres of a deeply leaf-laden forest floor, and wild Myrtle with its blue flowers thickly carpets the floor in a couple of acres. Beneath the leafless forest canopy, new green leaves are pushing themselves into sunlight on undergrowth and saplings as they build solar panels that will fuel them until late October. This bright showcase of cheerful color is rapidly replacing the brown-and-gray palette of late winter.

Each sighting of new colors makes me wish for some sort of expanded vision that could show me all the colors these early flowers have to offer. I can see some of them, but birds and bees can see more. The potential range of invisible colors (to humans) is mind-boggling, and science is getting a grip on it.

Human color vision is neatly summed-up in our perception of a rainbow, sweeping from red, the longest wavelength of light our eyes can detect, to violet, the shortest. Our eyes can't detect each shade individually. In order to make sense of this continuous spectrum of colors, our eyes have three types of cone cell that respond to red, green, and blue. Our brain figures-out how much of the light we see that falls into each category, and it recombines that information to construct the myriad of colors that we register.

Bees have a different set of priorities. They feed on nectar, and they need to find flowers as efficiently as possible. The eyes of bees split their color vision into three categories, green, blue, and ultraviolet, a wavelength human eyes can't detect. As a result, bees see flowers differently than we do.

Many flowers advertise themselves with a bull's-eye pattern; the center of the flower has a pigment that looks dark in the bee's ultraviolet vision as the outer parts of the petals look light. Bees use this distinctive pattern to find flowers to visit.

Birds also see in the ultraviolet range, although bird-pollinated flowers seem not to have the pattern that bees use. But even the birds can't see every color there is.

This method of perceiving three or four broad categories of color works well in nature, but it lumps lots of different light wavelengths together. Scientists split the entire spectrum into very thin slices, producing hundreds of distinct color categories that stretch well beyond limits of the rainbow. It's called hyperspectral imaging.

Different types of molecules have very distinct color signatures, making it possible to detect the colors of different cell components of a plant—proteins, cellulose, and micronutrients. Water also absorbs light strongly in the infrared wavelengths, and these infrared colors indicate whether the plant is dehydrated.

Furthermore, infrared light can indicate the temperature of a leaf and whether it is drawing-up new water from its roots. All this means that it's becoming possible to use a hyperspectral image to determine the species of plant, whether it's diseased or malnourished and the part of its life cycle it's in.

As I wander about my forest in the springtime, I absolutely appreciate the richness and beauty of everything I can see. But I also wonder about how much more the colors have to offer. Each plant tells its own story, written in color and broadcast to the world in plain sight. Just imagine being able to read those plant biographies; that's surely a superpower worth having.

Geophysics of Swaying Trees in My Forest Preserve

November 26, 2019

On mornings after a night of howling wind, I find small and sometimes large broken tree branches on my mile long unpaved driveway, casualties of the wind's violent pummeling. The leafy top of each deciduous tree acts like a sail, and the force on the trees is enormous as they are caught by gusts of strong wind.

Yet those splintered boughs are the exception since most trees manage to withstand the storm. Trees sway when pushed. A completely rigid tree would snap in a strong wind, but because live hardwood is flexible, trees behave like upside-down pendulums.

The base is fixed, and the top rocks from side to side. Trees will mostly sway at a fixed rate, just like the pendulum in a clock. In both cases, the rate depends on their structure. A longer pendulum will swing at a slower rate and so will a taller tree.

The amount of time it takes for the top of a tree to bend to one side, swing away, and then come back again can vary from half a second to twenty seconds. If you were to walk through my forest where each tree would be labeled with its own natural sway rate, you would quickly notice patterns.

Height is the dominant variable, but other parts of a tree's complex internal structure also play a role. A slender tree will sway more slowly than one with a thick trunk because the slender trunk provides less resistance to the force of the wind.

That means it can be pushed further before it bounces back, making each oscillation take longer overall. A top-heavy tree swings at a more sedate pace than one with its heaviest branches lower down because it takes more time to reverse the direction of the heavy crown. If I could measure tree sway rate throughout the year, I would be able to track those changes.

As new leafs burst out on deciduous trees each spring, they make the top of the tree heavier, increasing the time for a single oscillation. The sway rate slowly declines until fall when the tree sheds its leaves and returns to its stripped-down winter state.

A tree's sway rate can vary over the course of a day based on the dryness of the weather. Water flows from soil into the tree roots, up the trunk, and out to the leaves where it evaporates. But the evaporation happens only during daylight, and if the water supply from the roots can't keep-up with the water lost at the leaves, the tree dries-out in the middle of the day.

Without as much water inside it, the tree has less mass (weight)—it's also less rigid because the water pressure in its internal plumbing has dropped. The result is that trees sway more slowly in the middle of dry days and then speed-up as they recover water in the afternoon and overnight.

Most people assume that the inside of a deciduous tree can't be investigated without damaging the tree. But the internal structure of each tree is so tightly tied to the way it bends in the wind that the tree is broadcasting its status almost constantly.

Prophesy and Apocalyptic Prophesy

October 19, 2019

All sorts of prophesies, most of which turn-out to be false, have been around more than four thousand years. Even the world's greatest genius, Albert Einstein, is not exempt. My point in the following twenty bulleted items is to say we've listened the past 120 years to experts and others in the know but should take what they say publicly with a grain or two of salt.

- Charles H. Duell, the commissioner of U.S. Patents in 1899, said, "Everything that can be invented has been invented."
- The president of Michigan Saving Bank in 1903, advising Henry Ford's lawyer not to invest in Ford Motor Company, said, "The horse is here to stay, but the automobile is only a novelty, a fad."
- Confidence in the staying power of the horse was displayed by a 1916 comment of Field Marshal Douglas Haig at a tank demonstration: "The idea that cavalry will be replaced by these iron coaches is absurd. It is little short of treasonous."
- Irving Fisher, a distinguished Yale University professor of economics in 1929, predicted, "Stock prices have reached what looks like a permanently high plateau." Three days later, the stock market crashed, causing the great depression.

- Listening to its experts in 1936, *The New York Times* predicted, "A rocket will never be able to leave the earth's atmosphere."
- In 1939, the U.S. Department of the Interior predicted that American oil supplies would last for only another thirteen years. In 1949, the Secretary of the Interior said the end of U.S. oil supplies was in sight. Having learned nothing from its earlier erroneous claims, in 1974, the U.S. Geological Survey said that the United States had only a ten-year supply of natural gas. The U.S. Energy Information Administration estimated in 2017 that there were about 2,459 trillion cubic feet of dry natural gas in the United States. That's enough to last us for nearly a century. The United States is the largest producer of natural gas worldwide.
- Albert Einstein predicted, "There is not the slightest indication that nuclear energy will ever be obtainable. It would mean that the atom would have to be shattered at will."
- Regarding money spent on the Manhattan Project, Admiral William Leahy in 1945 told President Truman, "That is the biggest fool thing we have ever done. The (atomic) bomb will never go off, and I speak as an expert in explosives."
- Stanford University biologist Dr. Paul Erhlich in 1969 warned: "The trouble with almost all environmental problems is that by the time we have enough evidence to convince people, you're dead. We must realize that unless we're extremely lucky, everybody will disappear in a cloud of blue steam in twenty years."
- Peter Gunter, a professor at North Texas State University, predicted in 1970: "Demographers agree almost unanimously on the following grim timetable: by 1975, widespread famines will begin in India; these will spread by 1990 to include all of India, Pakistan, China, the Near East, and Africa. By the year 2000, or conceivably sooner, South and Central America will exist under famine conditions. By the year 2000, thirty years from now, the entire world,

with the exception of Western Europe, North America, and Australia, will be in famine."

- Ecologist Kenneth Watt's 1970 prediction was, "If present trends continue, the world will be about four degrees colder for the 1990 global mean temperature, and eleven degrees colder in the year 2000." He added, "This would be twice what it would take to put us in to an ice age." He also said, "We will be using-up crude oil at such a rate that there won't be any more crude oil in the year 2000."

- Harrison Brown, a scientist at the National Academy of Sciences, published a chart that looked at metal reserves and estimated that humanity would run out of copper shortly after 2000. Lead, zinc, tin, gold, and silver would be gone before 1990.

- In 2000, Dr. David Vinar, a senior research scientist at University of East Anglia's climate research unit, predicted that in a few years winter snowfall would become "a very rare and exciting event. Children just aren't going to know what snow is."

- The Pentagon in 2004 warned President George W. Bush that major European cities would be beneath rising seas, and Britain will be plunged into a Siberian climate by 2020.

- In 2008, Al Gore predicted that the polar ice cap would be gone in a mere ten years.

- A U.S. Department of Energy study predicted the Arctic Ocean would experience an ice-free summer by 2016.

- Former U.S. Treasury Secretary Larry Summers predicted that if Donald Trump were elected, there would be a protracted recession within eighteen months.

- Listening to its experts a month before the 2016 election, *The Washington Post* published an editorial with the headline "A President Trump Could Destroy the World Economy."

- A Democrat financier and former head of the National Economic Council, Steve Rattner warned, "If the unlikely event happens that Trump wins, you will see a market crash of historic proportions."

- When Trump's election to the presidency became apparent, Nobel Prize-Winning economist and *New York Times* columnist, Paul Krugman, warned that the world was "very probably looking at a global recession, with no end in sight."

*****

Dating from the second century BC to second century AD, the Bible contains the oldest prophesies—apocalyptic. I refer herein to the one prophesy regarding the eminent destruction of the world. Those scriptures today are read with literalness by Christian fundamental "born again" evangelists who claim biblical infallibility and assert the Bible to be the work of God.

In 1988, United Nations' international politicians, who had already committed themselves to "global warming," anointed a group of sixty so-called scientists to serve on the Intergovernmental Panel on Climate Change (IPCC). It's the duty of the IPCC to tell the people living in 195 UN-member nations what to believe.

The Russian Academy of Sciences in 2004 published a report concluding that the 1997 Ktoto Protocal has no scientific grounding at all. Between 2006 and 2014, IPCC issued five different reports. The IPCC has been misleading humanity about climate change and sea levels by publishing information that has been discredited.

They use incorrect "correction factors" in their data to make it appear that seas are rising worldwide. Rising sea level data were exaggerated due to measurements in Hong Kong and Shanghai where land has been naturally subsiding for many years.

IPCC has admitted many of its predictions are based on inaccurate data; for example, that Himalayan glaciers will disappear by 2035, and forty percent of the Amazon is endangered. They further admit that the percentage of the Netherlands currently below sea level was doubled in a report, and the effects of solar and cosmic activity and volcanic eruptions were not at all considered.

The ClimateGate scandal began in late 2009 after British "scientists" admitted they had manipulated temperature data to support claims of "unequivocal global warming." Along with collapse of the case for "global warming, the top UN climate change official, Yvo de Boer, resigned in early 2010.

Many scientist at Harvard, MIT, Columbia University, and many other reputable American and foreign higher education institutions that supported IPCC earlier have withdrawn further support. ConocoPhillips, BP, Caterpillar, Xerox, and a big number of other large corporations have refused to renew membership in Climate Change Partnership (CAP).

Coastal cities such as Miami, Florida, will not be flooded due to sea-level rise caused by alleged man-made global warming. According to observable data, there is no rapid sea level rise going on today, and there will not be; on the contrary, if anything happens, the sea will go down a little. Paleo-geophysicists and geodynamicists have proven that a new solar-driven cooling period is not far off.

In fact, even speaking of something called "global sea level" is highly misleading. It is different in different parts of the world. Sea levels can rise in one part of the world and decline in another depending on a variety of factors.

Solar activity and its effects on the globe have been the "dominant factor" in what happens to both the climate and the seas. Meanwhile, the politically backed IPCC claims that current changes in climate and sea level are attributable to human emissions of carbon dioxide (CO_2) are totally untrue. Human emissions of this essential gas required by plants and exhaled by humans makes-up a fraction of one percent of all so-called gasses present naturally in the atmosphere.

As for the man-made global warming hypothesis, eighty-five percent of the world's physicists know the hypothesis is wrong. And among the world's geologists and astronomers, at least eighty percent know it's wrong.

Shady tactics used by climate alarmists and the UN lobbyists they work with to suppress the real facts demonize those real scientists who contradict the alarmist narrative. The IPCC is blacklisted by publishers of real science documents.

Scientists who are deserving of public trust apply scientific objectivity and present their information openly for others to weigh the evidence on which policy decisions can be made. In trusted science, scientists discuss; the IPCC "scientists" forbid or neglect discussion.

I believe there are behind-the-scenes United Nations promoters of the man-made CO_2 hypothesis with dark, ulterior motives. They want the UN to be the One World Government, at U.S.A.'s expense, and that's a dangerous thing.

The so-called exhaustive study of CO_2 performed by a number of politically biased Duke University professors is full of altered and twisted facts of science. The emphasis on climate alarmism and the alleged dangers of CO_2 has diverted resources and attention away from all the real problems in the world that really do exist. The world is full of real problems such as hunger, starvation, diseases, killings, natural disasters, and so much more. Yet because of the incessant focus on demonizing CO_2 and trying to "control climate," those very real problems get ignored.

President Trump did the right thing to withdraw from the highly controversial UN Paris Agreement. CO_2 levels today are unusually and extremely low by historical standards. More CO_2 would be a very good thing.

When the next cooling phase begins, the world will be going into a so-called grand solar minimum, and that will occur in the middle of this century, maybe even as early as 2030. I express sympathy for all those people who don't know what they're talking about and have been duped into believing they're saving the world by fighting CO_2.

Human efforts cannot save God's creation; science proves that the perfect harmony of God's universe will prevail.

The most dangerous and frightening thing about the United Nations IPCC is how such a group has been able to fool the whole world. I compare it to how National Socialists in Germany and communists in both Russia and China were able to deceive their populations and seize power.

I'm shocked that the UN and member governments would parade children around at the 2017 climate summit in Katowice, Poland. What do the children know? They should be outdoors playing, not talking at the United Nations. It's evil to use children as propaganda props.

News media reached-out to the IPCC for comment repeatedly during the Climate Change Conference in Poland. However, IPCC didn't respond to e-mails, phone calls, or visits to the IPPC booth seeking comment.

Today in America, Leftist Democrats predict the world will end in 2030. These politicians, like the IPCC "scientists," refuse to debate it. Main media "journalists" continue to exhibit themselves as fools by covering new reports from the United Nations IPCC and the political left.

They claim global CO_2 emissions must fall forty-five percent by 2030, twice as much as earlier forecast, and the world must wean itself entirely off fossil fuel. That catastrophe is predicted to include underwater coastlines, widespread drought, and disease.

The truth is: any journalist with a fifth-grade education could have made that calculation last week, last year, ten years ago, twenty years ago.

All they would have to do is apply the same standard climate-sensitivity estimate (in use in 1979) to the standard emissions forecast.

The IPCC people with supposedly superior knowledge about climate are more focused on a report due in 2022. They don't yet know what the report will say about the then forty-three-year-old unsatisfying climate-sensitivity model that underlies the fuzzy past reports made as fact by the main news media. The IPCC today is silent but does acknowledge specifically two studies in 2018 that greatly play-down the likelihood of catastrophic climate outcomes.

The virtuous benefit of President Trump's administration is that it will turn away from policies that are costly and produce no benefit. Modification of the forecasted "climate warming" could be accomplished simply by injecting reflective particles into the earth's atmosphere.

Unraveling the case for "global warming" has left people worldwide uncertain about what to believe and whom to trust. Any idea of a static and unchanging climate is foreign to the geologic history of planet Earth. Hysteria over "global warming" simply represents international scientific illiteracy and people's susceptibility to the constant repetition of false information as the replacement for truth.

Levels of CO_2 have often been many times higher and earth surface temperatures much higher than today. Indisputable evidence contained in 4.54 billion modern years of observable geologic conditions and geologic history establishes that global climate change is a cyclical natural phenomena. Arctic and Antarctic ice cores reveal that CO_2 levels rise and fall for hundreds of years following earth surface temperature change. The saltwater Arctic ice and the freshwater Antarctic ice both have frozen and melted, and sea levels have risen and fallen many times for millions of modern years. Greenhouse gasses, in addition to CO_2, consist of water vapor from clouds, methane, and nitrous oxide.

The 2010 volcanic eruptions in Iceland, in just four days, negated every human effort worldwide in the previous five years to "control man-made" CO_2 emissions. When Mt. Pinatubo in the Philippines erupted in 1991 and was active for more than a year, it spewed more greenhouse gasses into the atmosphere than Homo sapiens have caused in 195,000 years on planet Earth. Approximately two hundred active volcanoes are spewing out CO_2 at any time, every day.

The CO_2 that humans are trying to suppress is a vital chemical compound required by every plant to live and to grow and to synthesize into oxygen for humans and other animals to breathe. The effect of solar and cosmic activity and an eight-hundred-year global heating-and-cooling cycle continues despite human efforts to "control" CO_2 emissions.

Forest fires across the United States and Australia in 2016 alone, not considering the California fires 2017 through 2019, negated all human efforts to reduce CO_2 for the following two to three years.

Some governments in the world are trying to impose carbon taxes on the basis of bogus "human-caused" climate change.

Planet Earth cooled 0.7 degrees Centigrade from 2014 to 2018, while the Unites States warmed slightly because of salinity reduction in the gulf-stream, due to freshwater ice melt in the Antarctic, and the effects of El Nino and El Nina. Undoubted scientific evidence shows global climate change is far too complicated to be caused by a single factor such as CO_2.

Today's predictions about climate doom are likely to be as true as were the apocalyptic and yesteryear's predictions. The major difference is many people worldwide, especially in America, today are far more gullible and more likely to spend trillions fighting global climate change. And the only result is that the world, especially Americans, will be much poorer and America less free.

Your Amazingly
Plastic Brain

February 12, 2015

Our most important organ, the brain, is not a machine doomed to breakdown as was thought not long ago. Exercising the brain, like exercising the body, keeps it fit and able to recover mental capacities lost to nonuse, trauma, or both. Exercise, both mental and physical, is the best way to offset the natural wasting process and damaging influence of our unnaturally sedentary way of life today. Our brain, like our body in general, is far more likely to waste away from underuse than to wear down from overuse.

Until sometime in the past ten to fifteen years, many physicians and scientists generally believed the brain could not repair or restore itself with replacement parts, as is possible with other organs such as the skin, liver, and blood. Rapidly growing recent research shows that the brain's circuitry changes microscopically with experience and activity and that the most accurate rule for the brain, as for the other body organs, is "**Use it or lose it.**"

Neuroscientists have shown the living brain to be actually "neuroplastic." This means our brain's "circuits" are constantly changing in response to what we actually do out in the world. As we think, perceive, form memories, or learn new skills, the connections between brain cells also change and strengthen.

This capacity is the foundation for the brain's distinctive way of healing. If an area is damaged, new neurons take over old tasks. Our memories and experiences are encoded in the patterns of electrical energy produced by the brain cells, like a musical score. As with an orchestra, when one member of the violin section is sick, the concert can still go on if a replacement has access to the musical score.

Dementia and Alzheimer Disease

The most detailed study ever done on the effect of lifestyle and exercise revealed, in 2013, that the risk of experiencing dementia is lowered 60 percent by doing the following five things:

- consistently eating a healthy diet (at least three to four servings of fruits and vegetables a day);
- maintaining a normal weight, with body-mass index of 18 to 25;
- limiting alcohol to a glass of wine a day;
- not smoking; and
- (the activity having the biggest impact on risk reduction) walking at least two miles a day, biking ten miles a day, or engaging in some other regular, vigorous physical exercise.

If there were a drug that could reduce dementia by 60 percent, it would be the most talked-about drug in history. Yet this astonishing finding has been fairly quietly received. One reason is that many people assume Alzheimer's disease to be "all in our genes." But expert neurologist and dementia researchers point-out that environmental factors "interact with genetic makeup to eventually allow or deny dementia a foothold."

Ten other studies that preceded the 2013 described above showed that regular exercise in midlife correlates with lower rates of dementia; and that lack of regular exercise corresponds with higher rates of dementia. Exercise triggers the growth of new brain cells in the hippocampus, which is the brain region that turns short-term memories into long-term memories, and is often the first to degenerate in Alzheimer's cases and with age in general. Exercise also triggers the release of "neurotropic growth factors," which are a kind of brain fertilizer that help the brain to grow, maintain new connections, and stay healthy.

Parkinson's Disease

Recent studies have also found that exercise can reduce the symptoms of Parkinson's—a degenerative disease that causes patients to gradually lose control of their muscles. Parkinson's treatment to date has primarily focused on medication with exercise as something of a distant runner-up.

Parkinson's patients are caught in a tightening noose. Fast walking can help them but fast walking is precisely what they can no longer do. And the Parkinson's patient who cannot walk does not "stay still"—the disease gets worse. Because our plastic brains are "use it or lose it" organs, when walking becomes more difficult, walking less will cause whatever walking circuits the patient still has to wither and become dormant from nonuse.

Stroke

For people who have suffered a stroke, their brain circuits have been killed by a blood clot or a bleed that cuts-off the blood supply and oxygen to the brain tissue. When people with dormant brain circuits try to walk, they "learn" that they can't walk and stop trying. This is called "learned nonuse."

After a stroke, the brain enters a state of shock. Neurons die, chemicals leak-out of some cells and harm others, inflammation is very active, and blood flow around the dead tissue is interrupted. All these events disrupt functioning not just where the stroke occurred but throughout the brain.

The basic neuroplastic principal of "use it or lose it" and the benefit of forming new brain connections through intensive learning also apply to people without brain problems. Physical exercise produces some new cells in the memory system, but mental exercise preserves and strengthens existing connections in the brain and gives a person "cognitive reserve" to fend-off future losses and to perfect skills.

People who have done certain brain exercises—called Brain HQ—showed benefits ten years later. They didn't just improve on the brain exercises; their cognitive function improved in everyday life. The exercises increased a person's mental sharpness so they could process information with the speed and accuracy they had when they were ten years younger.

Although a lot is yet to be learned about the brain and its powers of recovery, evidence to date enables the medical profession to conclude that they have been seeing our brains the wrong way for too long. One day, the medical profession may well marvel at how odd it was that, for several centuries, it chose to view our ever-changing, activity-craving, animate brains as fixed, passive, inanimate machines or computers.

The foregoing is a brief summary of *"Brain, Heal Thyself"* by professor and researcher Dr. Norman Doidge, appearing in *The Wall Street Journal*, February 2, 2015, issue.

THE CONTINUING
DEVELOPMENT OF
MODERN SCIENCE

January 30, 2009

Robert Hooke (1635–1703) identified irrefutably three stages in the formation of a typical fossil in the coalfields of England. Observers noted that many of the petrified fossils represented plants and animals that didn't exist at the time. If indeed the plant and animal fossils were relics, they were relics of life that was no longer around and had become extinct.

These newly formulated natural laws of science brought questions to the minds of numerous observers in the mid-1700s. Since the Bible (King James Version, 1611) clearly indicated that God had created land before life, many considered it impossible for fossil remains to be infiltrated deep inside the newly created rock strata because there was no life in existence to be inserted. Could it be that maybe, just maybe, the old beliefs rooted in the blind acceptance of churchly teachings might not be wholly true?

Among the observers, chemist Joseph Priestly (1733–1804) and physician Erasmas Darwin (1731–1802) took a muscular and skeptical approach to the wisdom of the church. Priestly discovered oxygen in 1774, and Darwin's *Zoonomia* (1794–1796) anticipated the evolutionary theories of his grandson, Charles.

Gradually, from the world of fossils emerged the ideas that eventually lead Charles Darwin (1809–1882) and Alfred Wallace

(1823–1913) to reach their profound conclusions about the origins of species in 1859 and 1876 respectively. This year marks the 150th anniversary of the most incendiary book in the history of science and the 200th birth year of the mild-mannered Englishman who wrote it.

Charles Darwin didn't invent the idea of evolution any more than Abraham Lincoln, who shares his February 12th birthday, invented the idea of freedom. What Darwin provided in *The Origin of Species* was a powerful theory of how evolution could occur through purely natural forces.

The book gave scientists freedom to explore the glorious complexity of life, rather than merely accept it as an impenetrable mystery. At the time of Charles Darwin's death, evolution was generally accepted by scientists, but not the notion that mankind descended from apes.

Measurements of radioactive decay, about 1906, revealed the Earth to be more than four hundred billion years old, countering claims that there hadn't been enough time for species to evolve through natural selection. After decades of pursuing often-conflicting paths of research, by 1940 biologists, population geneticists, paleontologists, and field naturalists reached accord in a "modern synthesis" of Darwinism. Evolution at the time was seen to proceed through natural selection and other random mechanisms, with new species originating through the gradual accumulation of mutations or changes in isolated populations.

Discovery, in 1953, of the double helix structure of DNA unlocked the mystery of how genetic information is passed from one generation to the next. A series of East Africa fossil discoveries in the 1960s and 1970s climaxed in 1974 with "Lucy," a 3.2-million year old hominid, which helped define a new species considered to be the base of the human lineage.

Geneticists agreed in 1976 that "nothing in biology makes sense, except in the light of evolution." The tree of life was redefined in 1977 by classifying organisms according to their genetic rather that their physical similarities, showing that life is composed of three bacterial domains.

Sequencing of the human genome, completed in 2003, found a close similarity between the human and chimpanzee genomes, underscoring their descent from a common ancestor. Scientists continue to expand on Darwin's insights, incorporating much new genetic, paleontological, and behavioral evidence.

Variation among species today is seen to be in part the result of mechanisms controlling how genes are switched on and off during an organism's development. That light, which began as a glimmer in the mind of a field naturalist, today casts a beam so bright the very text of life can be read by it. It's astonishing to see how much Darwin didn't know and how much modern science has yet to learn.

What Science Tells Us about Preventing Dementia

November 25, 2019

There are no instant, miracle cures. But according to a recent wave of scientific studies, you have more control of your mental health than previously thought. In fact, around 35 percent of dementia cases might be prevented if people would exercise and engage in mentally stimulating activities.

The following factors contribute to your risk of dementia and they are within your power to control. Social isolation, Low education level, Physical inactivity, Midlife obesity, Type 2 diabetes, High blood pressure.

Following is a brief close look at what these scientific studies tell about common sense ways to help reduce your risk of dementia.

- Eat a diet of leafy green and other vegetables, nuts, berries, beans, whole grains, fish, poultry, olive oil, and wine (in moderation).
- Do aerobic exercise to increase the flow of blood to your brain because it improves the health of blood vessels and raises the level of good (HDL) cholesterol, which together help protect against cardiovascular disease including high blood pressure.
- Increase your brain's ability to compensate for neurological damage through reading, hobbies, walking, social activities such as visiting friends and relatives, attending religious services, and volunteer activities.
- Do not deny yourself of ample sleep. Sleep washes toxic substances out of your brain.

CHAPTER VI
A Crime against Humanity

November 15, 2019

Every year worldwide, 262,800 children die of malaria; that's 720 each day or 5 every two minutes. Nonetheless, radical environmentalists are mobilizing against an important measure to stop the female mosquitoes from spreading that disease.

The Gates Foundation organized and financially supports **Target Malaria**, which is a research effort to develop genetically modified sterile mosquitoes. Its approach is to drive modified genes through a mosquito population to produce sterile females or cause the breading production of only males. The goal is to reduce mosquito populations so much that the malaria parasite cannot be spread from person to person.

Target Malaria conducted a carefully controlled experiment this past spring in Burkina Faso, West Africa. This test followed years of research and similar successful releases in Latin America and the Caribbean.

None of that mattered to the coalition of forty leading environmental and "civil society" organizations demanding the project be shut down immediately. This activist opposition to Target Malaria is part of a larger and growing campaign against all modern genetic technologies and pesticides used in disease control and in agriculture. The campaign has been promoted in recent years by United Nations agencies such as the Food and Agriculture Organization (FAO), as well as by European governments and European Union-funded non-governmental organizations.

Malaria deaths in Africa are declining thanks to insecticide-treated bed nets, spraying and better treatment, but the disease remains stubbornly persistent in much of the continent. The emergence of resistant strains of malaria and malaria parasites means public health programs need new tools.

Field releases of genetically modified mosquitoes in a Brazil trial, aimed at controlling Dengue fever, have been conducted without the dire consequences environmentalists predicted. But during the 2016–2017 Zika outbreaks in Florida and Texas, scare campaigns succeeded in blocking mosquito tests already approved by the Food and Drug Administration.

There's a long history of opposition to genetic technology with serious human costs. Consider the decades-long effort to stop cultivation of genetically modified golden rice. This effort could save two million people a year from early death and crippling blindness caused by vitamin A deficiency. A petition signed by 144 Nobel laureates calls on environmentalists to end their campaigns and accuses Greenpeace of a "crime against humanity" for its leading role.

Opposition to modern technology has deepened, and its highly politicized ideology has captured much of the development community under the banner of "agro-ecology." This radical approach to food production excludes modern farming techniques, including synthetic pesticides and fertilizers, modern hybrid seeds, and even mechanization.

Agro-ecology explicitly promotes "peasant agriculture" and the superior wisdom of "indigenous peoples." I'm reminded of America's century-long history of opposition to labor-saving machines for its agricultural society of the 1800s.

Agro-ecologists detest free markets. A leader of "Food First" asks, "How can agro-ecology help us transform capitalism itself?" One of the groups protesting Target Malaria uses abusive language against international trade and "profit at any price." This Third World Network supports worldwide socialism and blames the United States for Venezuela's economic and humanitarian crisis.

Now with little debate, agro-ecology dogma has been officially adopted by FAO and is being underwritten by European governments through their development agencies and support of environmental groups. Like other radical "social justice" movements, agro-ecology is based on a fraudulent history.

An FAO Steering Committee member describes the Green Revolution, which saved a billion people from starvation, as a "failed" project that undermined the ability to address "the root causes of hunger" and put "global food production under the control of a few transnational corporations, bolstered by free trade agreements." According to the FAO's own data, however, the Green Revolution increased the worldwide food supply from 2,253 to 2,852 calories per person from 1961 to 2013 when the global population more than doubled.

A recent study promoted by agro-ecologists acknowledges that their policies would reduce food production by 35 percent in Europe, which has not given agro-ecologists pause. It's hard to determine whether they promote their policies out of sheer nostalgia or because they would prefer a planet with fewer people.

Allowing millions to die from preventable diseases and inadequate nutrition is certainly one way to achieve that goal. The Nobel laureates are right to call it a crime against humanity.

INFECTIOUS DISEASES
AND VACCINATIONS

June 14, 2019

It wasn't long ago that advancements in medical science, which included vaccinations, had eradicated infectious diseases in America. Due to the illegal immigration along our politically uncontrolled border with Mexico, we are experiencing a return of those diseases, plus others such as Ebola from Africa.

The current outbreaks of measles in our country result from this illegal entry situation, and some parents in both America and the UK are afraid to vaccinate their children. This fear has been initiated by publication of a British medical study **falsely** linking the measles-mumps-rubella vaccine to autism.

After it was found that the study was based on only twelve children, the lead author of the study lost his license to practice medicine. But the damage had been done. Unfortunately, those parents don't know the study is false or don't believe it is false.

Born in 1930, I knew few other children who didn't have the measles, chicken pox, and scarlet fever before appropriate vaccines were developed. For infantile paralysis (polio), the iron lung was used from the late 1930s until 1955 when the Salk polio vaccine was approved. Use of Dr. Albert Sabin's oral polio vaccine began in 1961.

Many had the mumps, but I didn't. Instead, I had malaria for many years until DDT was developed about 1945 toward the end of WWII. During military service in the first half of the 1950s, there was no contagious disease anywhere for which I was not either vaccinated or revaccinated.

We've read or been advised about all sorts of changes in medicine. Hormone replacement is good; then it's bad. Vitamin E lowers the risk of prostate cancer; then it raises the risk. It's part of the ebb and flow of medical science.

Autism is a neurodevelopmental disorder starting in early childhood but not well-defined and known by that name until the last half of the 1900s.

During the 1800s and early 1900s, it's regrettable that some people with this disorder were considered insane and placed in asylums.

An Assault on America and Western Civilization

July 16, 2019

A set of philosophies that focus strongly on the sanctity of individuals and the power of logic and reason are basic elements on which America and Western civilization were founded. This belief led to a desire to trust things that could be proven to be true and legitimate from government to science.

Judeo-Christian morality has formed the basis of most American and Western ideas of ethics and behavioral standards. For that very reason, the attack on American and Western civilization has begun with an assault on Jewish and Christian religious institutions and values and the undermining of the family unit.

The reason why America's political Left targets religious institutions, values, and family is they want the people's loyalty and allegiance to be to a (socialist) state. Jewish and Christian religious institutions, values, and the family unit stand in their way.

While criticizing sexual assault, Joe Biden said, "This is English jurisprudential culture, a white man's culture. It's got to change." Our American and Western culture is not perfect, but the lives of women are better under it than any other culture.

If I were a woman, in which of the following countries would I prefer to live? Would it be Saudi Arabia, other Middle Eastern countries, China, or African countries? Women encounter all kinds of liberty restrictions in those countries, including in at least thirty countries on the African continent, the Middle East, and Southeast Asia, where female genital mutilation is practiced.

I would like to personally ask Joe Biden what part of the "white man's culture" needs to be changed.

The greatest efforts to downplay the achievements of American and Western civilization today start with the curricula-and-teacher-attitude in most of our K-12 public school systems and most colleges and universities. Results of a recognized 2016 study showed that "the overwhelming majority of America's most prestigious institutions do not require even the students who major in history to take a single course on United States history or government." It's because of this ignorance our young people fall easy prey to fraudulent people, quacks, and liars who wish to downgrade our founders and the American achievement.

In 2012, 2014, and 2015, a commissioned survey of college graduates found that fewer than twenty percent could accurately identify the effect of the Emancipation Proclamation. Less than fifty percent could identify George Washington as the American general at Yorktown.

A third of college graduates were not aware that President Franklin D. Roosevelt introduced the New Deal. More than a third could not place the American Civil War in its correct twenty-year time frame. Nearly half could not identify correctly the term length of U.S. representatives and of U.S. senators.

America's political Left often claims that people who stand-up for Western civilization are supporting racial hierarchy. World history tells us that arbitrary tyrannical abuse and control are factual. Poverty has been the standard way-of-life for a vast majority of mankind.

America has become the exception to what life is like. That condition of being exceptional inspired imitators, and our freedom and liberty spread to what has become known as the Western world.

Many Americans don't appreciate the fact that freedom and competition in the marketplace and in the arena of ideas unleashed a level of entrepreneurism, risk-taking, and creativity heretofore unknown to mankind. For example, the Nobel Prize has been awarded to 860 people since its 1901 inception. Americans have won 375, United

Kingdom 131, Germany 108, France 69, and Sweden 32. That's 83 percent of the Nobel Prizes won. Japan has 27 Nobel Prize winners, but their first winner was awarded in 1949, after the end of WWII led Japan to become westernized.

America leads the world in terms of scientific innovation, wealth, and military might because of our environment of freedom in the marketplace for goods and in the idea market. Rigorous competition brings out the best in mankind. Political Leftists and would-be tyrants find American values offensive.

MULTICULTURALISM AND DIVERSITY ARE A CANCER ON OUR SOCIETY

September 15, 2016

History tells us that tyrants, the Nazis and Stalinists for example, have always started by supporting free speech. Why they did that is easy to understand because speech is vital to realization of their goals of command, control, and confiscation.

The tools of indoctrination, propagandizing, and proselytization are basic to their agenda. Once they gain power, as leftists have at many U.S. universities, free speech becomes a liability.

In 1964, Mario Savio was a campus leftist who led the free speech movement at the University of California, Berkeley. Savio played a vital role in placing American universities center stage in the flow of political ideas, no matter how controversial, unpatriotic, and vulgar.

It was the free speech movement that gave birth to the hippie movement of the 1960s and 1970s. The longhair, unkempt hippies of that era have grown up, and we often find them as being university professors, deans, provosts, and presidents.

An update on the university campus attack of free speech and different ideas was in the May 7, 2014, *Wall Street Journal* editorial titled "Obama Unleashes the Left: How the Government Created a Federal Hunting License for the Far Left."

One of the nations most accomplished women, Condoleezza Rice, former secretary of state, graciously withdrew as Rutgers University commencement speaker after two months of campus protests about her role in the Iraq War. Some students and professors said, "War criminals shouldn't be honored."

Brandeis University officials were intimidated into rescinding their invitation to American Enterprise Institute scholar Ayaan Hirsi Ali, whose criticisms of radical Islam were said to have violated the school's core values. Brandeis decided that allowing her to speak would be hurtful to Muslim students.

A private west coast Christian university canceled a planned address by distinguished libertarian scholar Charles Murray out of fear that his lecture might upset "faculty and students of color." Western values of liberty are under ruthless attack by the academic elite on college campuses across America.

These people want to replace personal liberty with government control; they want to replace equality with entitlement. As such, they pose a far greater threat to our way of life than any terrorist organization or rogue nation. Multiculturalism and diversity are a cancer on American society.

Immigration That's in Our National Interest

November 10, 2017

On November 7, 2016, for the first time in our nation's history, the American people elected as president a person with no high government experience. That person was not a senator, not a representative, not a governor, not a cabinet secretary, not a general.

We did this because we had lost faith in both the competence and the intentions of the governing class in Washington—of both political parties. Our federal government now takes nearly half of every dollar we earn and bosses us around in every aspect of life yet can't deliver basic services in a good and proper manner.

Our working class, the forgotten people, has seen its wages stagnate while the four richest counties in America are located inside the Washington, DC beltway. The sons and daughters of the working class are those who fight our seemingly endless wars and police our streets, only to be criticized too often by the governing class that sleeps under the blanket of security our military and police provide.

Immigration has emerged in recent years as a kind of acid test for our governing class—a test they've mostly failed. Our cosmopolitan governing elite, in both parties, has pursued a radical immigration policy that's inconsistent with American history and American political tradition.

They've celebrated the American idea yet undermined the actual American people of the here-and-now. They've forgotten that the Declaration of Independence speaks of "one people" and the Constitution of "We the People."

At the same time, they've enriched themselves and improved their quality of life while creating a new class of forgotten people.

There's probably no issue today that calls more for an "America first" approach than immigration. After all, the guidepost of our immigration policy should be putting America first—not foreigners and not a tiny group with superior intellect, training, or wealth.

As James Madison (1751–1836) said in that first Congress, our immigration policy should serve the "strength and wealth" of our people. It should not divide our nation, impoverish our workers, or promote hyphenated Americanism (which suggests that those so designated are not fully American as unhyphenated citizens).

Citizenship is the most cherished thing our nation can bestow, and our governing class in Washington ought to treat it as something special. I know this firsthand because my daughter-in-law was a foreigner who after eight years and much study of American history became an American citizen in 2016.

The interests of our citizens ought to come first and welcome those foreigners best prepared to handle the duties of citizenship and contribute positively to our country. When our leaders do that, American citizens will begin to trust Washington.

Be Aware! Immigration Lies and Hypocrisy

February 6, 2018

Our president recently asked why the United States is "having all these people from s***hole countries come here." The language he used is rather indelicate, but it's a question that should be asked and answered.

President Trump's question sounded to me a lot like something I remember President Truman would have said. How many Norwegians, Swedish, Finnish, Welsh, Icelanders, Greenlanders, and New Zealanders have illegally enter our nation, committed crimes, and burdened our prison and welfare systems?

The bulk of our immigration problem is with people who enter this country criminally from Mexico, Central America, the Caribbean, Africa, and the Middle East. Illegal immigrants from those countries have committed crimes and burdened our criminal justice and welfare systems.

A large number of immigrants here illegally are law-abiding in other respects and have fled oppressive, brutal, and corrupt regimes to seek a better life in America.

*****

In the debate about illegal immigration, there are questions not explicitly asked but can be answered with a straight "yes" or "no."

Does everyone in the world have a right to live in the United States?

Do Americans have a right to decide who and under what conditions a person may enter our country?

Should we permit foreigners landing at our airports to ignore United States border control laws the same as some ignore our laws at our southern border?

The reason those questions aren't asked is that an American would be deemed and idiot for saying: everyone in the world has a right to live in our country, Americans don't have a right to decide who lives in our country, and foreigners landing at our airports have a right to ignore U.S Customs and Border Protection agents.

Immigration today, even when legal, is quite different from immigration at Ellis Island in the late 1800s and much of the 1900s. People who came here in those years came to learn our language, learn our customs, and become Americans.

There was a guarantee that immigrants came to work because there was no welfare system; they worked, begged, or starved. Today, there's no such assurance. Because of our welfare state, immigrants can come and live off taxpaying Americans.

There's another difference between today and yesteryear. Today, Americans are taught multiculturalism throughout their primary, secondary, and college education. They're taught that one is no better or worse than another. To believe otherwise is criticized at best as European cultural influence and at worst as racism.

As a result, some immigrant groups bring to our country the cultural values whose failures have led to poverty, corruption, and human rights violations in their home countries that caused them to flee. As the fallout from President Trump's remarks demonstrates, too many Americans are afraid and unwilling to ask which immigrant groups have become a burden to our nation and which have made a contribution to the greatness of America.

Very unfortunate for our country is the fact that we have political groups that seek to use illegal immigration for their own benefit. They've created sanctuary cities and states that openly harbor criminals—people who have broken our laws.

The whole concept of sanctuary cities is to give aid, comfort, and sympathy to people who have broken our laws. Supporters want to prevent them from having to hide and live in fear of discovery. For the sake of equality before the law, I ask, should we apply the sanctuary concept to Americans who have broken other laws, such as robbers and tax evaders?

We shouldn't fall prey to people who criticize our efforts to combat illegal immigration and who pompously say, "We're a nation of immigrants!" The debate is not over immigration, stupid. The debate is over illegal immigration.

My sentiments on immigrants who are here legally and who want to become Americans are expressed by the sentiments of Emma Lazarus's words on the plaque inside the Statue of Liberty that in part say, "Give me your tired, your poor, your huddled masses yearning to breathe free."

PERSONAL LIBERTY

March 23, 2017

Most Americans, regardless of their political thinking or affiliation, don't seem to have much of an understanding or respect for the principles of personal liberty. The behavior of our political leaders simply reflects the values of we the people who elected them to office. Consequently, we the people are to blame for excessive government control over our lives and a decline in personal liberty.

We each own ourselves. I'm my private property, and you're your private property. Since we accept self-ownership, certain of our acts can be deemed moral or immoral. Theft, rape, and murder are immoral because those acts violate private property. Most of us agree that rape and murder are immoral but are ambivalent about theft.

Theft is defined as taking the rightful property of one person and giving it to another to whom it doesn't belong. It's also theft to forcibly use one person to serve the purposes of another.

There is notable contempt for liberty—free speech—on many college campuses today. In fact, colleges lead the nation in attacks on free speech. The true test of a commitment to free speech doesn't come when a person is permitted to say things with which students agree. Instead, the true test comes when a person is permitted to say things with which students disagree.

It's been reported that more than fifty percent of college students want restrictions on speech they find offensive. Many colleges have complied with the student wishes through campus speech codes.

It takes a bold person to favor personal liberty because you have to be able to cope with people saying things and engaging in voluntary acts that you deem offensive. Liberty isn't for "snowflakes" and wimps!

NOTABLE INFORMATION
DATED EARLY 2004

October 8, 2019

A Pentagon report to President Bush appeared in *London's Observer* February 21, 2004. It says that climate change over the next twenty years could result in a global catastrophe costing millions of lives in wars and natural disasters.

The secret report suppressed by U.S. defense chiefs warns that major European cities will be sunk beneath rising seas as Britain is plunged into a Siberian climate by 2020. Nuclear conflict, mega-droughts, famine, and widespread rioting will erupt across the world.

The document predicts that abrupt climate change could bring the planet to the edge of anarchy as countries develop a nuclear threat to defend and secure dwindling food, water, and energy supplies. The few experts privy to its contents say the threat to global stability vastly eclipses that of terrorism.

The Pentagon analysis concludes that disruption and conflict will be endemic features of life. Once again, warfare would define human life. As early as 2005, widespread flooding by a rise in sea levels will create major upheaval for millions.

Our Nonpolitician "Outsider" President

October 10, 2018

President Donald J. Trump is an extremely wealthy seventy-two-year-old unusual man, habitually works eighteen to twenty hours every day, has made many mistakes in past years, and continues to do so. He's also human and has spent his life learning. Some of his businesses have gone bankrupt, and he's learned from those experiences not to let it happen again.

The president has wisdom, intelligence, and is a deliberative, tough negotiator. He knows how to evaluate an opponent and is skillful and adept at managing difficult situations. It doesn't matter what he may say publicly about an opponent, it's what the results are months later that matters.

In his first twenty months in office, President Donald J. Trump:

- turned around the failing American economy,
- brought nearly full employment,
- reduced welfare and food-stamp lines,
- eliminated ISIS in Raqqa,
- moved our embassy to Jerusalem,
- launched massive deregulation of the economy,
- opened oil exploration in Arctic National Wildlife Reservation,
- is massively rebuilding the U.S. military,
- walked-out of the Paris Climate Accords,

- exited the nonfunctional Human Rights Council of the United Nations,
- convinced Mexico and Canada he'll walkout of NAFTA if they don't pay-up,
- convinced Europeans he'll walkout of NATO if they don't pay-up,
- slashed income taxes,
- expanded legal protection for college students falsely accused of crimes,
- taken steps to protect religious freedoms and liberties under the First Amendment,
- taken on the legislative mess on immigration inherited from Regan-Bush-Clinton, Bush-Obama, and has appointed a long line of conservative federal judges to sit on district courts, circuit appellate courts, and two justices to the U.S. Supreme Court.

President Trump sees opportunity and a solution in every problem. If he doesn't see a solution without delay, he creatively finds a solution.

Popular Misunderstandings and Unpopular Truths

August 15, 2017

The deplorable happenings in Charlottesville, Virginia, last Saturday causes much concern about popular misunderstandings and unpopular truths some Americans still hold today. Misunderstandings can be old or new; but truths are as old as the universe. There's no such thing as new truth.

I'm reminded of the monument on Maryland Street in Indianapolis, three blocks from Monument Circle. This monument praises *The Indianapolis Times* for "winning the Pulitzer Prize" and for exposing the Ku Klux Klan.

Except for this monument, the terrible 1920–1925 period of Indianapolis history is invisible on its landscape. By not portraying the KKK in a negative sense, this brief mention of unpleasant history doesn't begin to tell the story of the Klan in Indiana.

A coal dealer residing in Indianapolis was Grand Dragon of the Ku Klux Klan in the state of Indiana. From 1922–1924, Indianapolis was the unrivaled bastion of KKK in Mid-America, and it practiced vigilante violence against black Americans, Roman Catholics, and Jews.

The Indiana Klan's newspaper, *The Fiery Cross*, had a circulation of 125,000 in late 1923, and the Indianapolis Klan chapter had 28,000 members, making it the largest in America. Its women's auxiliary enrolled another ten thousand, and many Protestant Clergy in Indy openly lauded the Klan.

Klansman Ed Jackson won the office of governor in 1925. KKK candidates won the sheriff's office, an office in Congress, and the Klan elected a majority of the state legislature. It's been more than ninety years, and some groups of American people today are still displaying their ignorance.

An example of popular misunderstandings is the notion that because Thomas Jefferson owned slaves, nothing good could come from him. Jefferson's Declaration of Independence provided for all Americans unpopular truths for political progress: "that all men (humans) are created equal," "that they are endowed by their Creator (not by the government) with certain unalienable Rights," "that among these are 'Life, Liberty and the pursuit of Happiness,'" "that to secure these rights, Governments are instituted among Men."

Our Constitution doesn't distinguish between citizens on account of skin color but provides justice and fair play with no favor. Race pride of any form in America, including Black Lives Matter, is a positive evil and a false foundation for progress. The only racial minority is a minority of one—the individual.

The politics of identity makes the present a prisoner of the past with individuals viewed mainly through a lens of race or other impulsive reason. America is a nation founded on human brotherhood and the self-evident truths of liberty and equality. There are no rights of race superior to the rights of humanity.

In Abraham Lincoln, the American people should see a full-length portrait of themselves with better qualities represented, incarnated, and glorified.

The Decline of
Patriotism in America

July 14, 2018

The avowed socialist, Bernie Sanders, was chosen by seventy-two percent of young voters, age 17 to 29, in the 2016 Democrat Party primary. Sanders advocated massive new progressive government programs that would nearly double America's debt to a staggering and unsustainable forty trillion dollars.

The Far Left, Progressive teaching in America's public schools and colleges has influenced young people to vote for Bernie Sanders and his big government agenda.

The large number of young Americans who have anti-American views is a result of two very significant factors: the teaching of absolutely no American History in public schools, and Far-Left, Progressive indoctrination in public schools and some colleges.

Two widely recognized 2016 polls reported the following: 55 percent of millennials said they had a "positive view" of socialism, and 45 percent of millennials would prefer to live in a socialist country over a capitalist democracy like the United States. This anti-American sentiment is extremely dangerous to the future of liberty.

The key to reversing the support for socialism among our nation's youth is to strongly encourage high school students of all ages to **learn** about the Constitution and our American heritage. TELL students and they **forget**. TEACH students and they **remember**. INVOLVE students and they **learn**.

A free online course—**Constitution 101**—on the meaning and history of the Constitution, made available by Hillsdale College, Michigan, is open to all Americans. Free copies of our Declaration of Independence and the Constitution are also available. The **Declaration of Independence** beautifully makes the case for liberty.

America must rid itself of Far-Left, Progressive, anti-Constitution politicians like Chuck Schumer, Elizabeth Warren, Cory Booker, and a number of others, each of whom **lied** when they took the **oath** to uphold the Constitution. Schumer now says, "Time and time again, we find progressive laws getting struck down. And it's always—always—the ones the Constitution is against." Warren now says, "We need judges to be advocates of progressive laws, not people who will bow to the whims of the Constitution." Booker now says, "We're sick and tired of the Constitution sitting in the National Archives, manipulating everything we do."

In addition to the lying and collusion of elected politicians Hillary, Obama, Schumer, Warren, and Booker; political appointees Huma, Mueller, Comey, Rosenstein, and McCabe; and FBI employees Strzok, Page; further lying and collusion is rampant among congressional members of the Democrat Party itself, as well as the politically appointed supposedly neutral leaders of the Department of Justice, Central Intelligence Agency, and National Security Council.

Medicare and
"Medicare for All"

August 2, 2019

Medicare is a national health insurance program that began in 1966 under the Social Security Administration to provide health insurance for American citizens aged sixty-five or older, younger people with some disability status as determined by the Social Security Administration, people with end stage renal disease, and people with Lou Gehrig's disease. It is abundantly clear that Medicare is intended for neither noncitizens nor able-bodied citizens below age sixty-five. It's intended mainly for the old and the retired citizens with limited income.

On average, Medicare covers about half of healthcare expenses of those enrolled and is funded by a combination of payroll tax, beneficiary premiums and surtaxes from beneficiaries, co-pays and deductibles, and U.S. Treasury revenue. Almost all Medicare enrollees cover remaining out-of-pocket costs by taking supplemental private insurance by joining a public Medicare health plan or both.

Although Medicare is popular, it is already unsustainable as is, even without expanding it to include everyone. As the American population ages, the taxpayer-base financing Medicare is dramatically shrinking.

Nearly four million citizens turn age sixty-five annually; by 2040, that population will reach eighty-seven million, twice what it was in 2012. Medicare trustees predict that Medicare's Hospitalization Insurance fund will be depleted in 2026.

As of 2014, Medicare was also fraught with error, fraud, and waste in the amount of sixty billion dollars. Massive taxation would be needed to expand "Medicare for All."

*****

Democrat rivals for the party's candidacy for president are falling over each other as each tries to outdo the other to abolish private health-care insurance in favor of "Medicare for All." Joe Biden announced his plan last week by reviving the **discredited** Obama slogan: "If you like your health-care plan, your employer-based (private insurance) plan, you can keep it."

The public option—"Medicare for All"—is a **bad idea**. Rather than provide coverage to the uninsured, government insurance options erode or "crowd-out" private insurance. The MIT economist who designed ObamaCare, Jonathan Gruber, showed in 2007 that when government insurance expands, six people go off private insurance for every ten people who go on public insurance. Those costs are shifted onto other taxpayers.

Only seven months after Hawaii offered Keiki Care in 2008, the only statewide child health care insurance, the state **ended** its optional program. Approximately eighty-five percent of those who signed-up already had private insurance. Those costs were suddenly shifted onto other taxpayers.

Even those Democrat Socialist presidential candidates calling for "a public insurance option" have openly admitted that it would inevitably lead to a single-payer-dominated system. The inevitable consequence would be the **death** of affordable private health insurance.

The public insurance option would further stratify America's healthcare system, as it has done in other countries, where only the lower and middle classes suffer the full brunt of inferior single-payer care. Margaret Thatcher observed thirty years ago that "socialists don't like ordinary people choosing, for they might not choose socialism."

That's why the Democrat Socialist Party's presidential hopefuls insist on simply outlawing private insurance. It's these "big ideas" of Democrat Socialists that will re-elect President Trump in 2020.

Never Underestimate the Power of Stupid People in Large Groups

May 14, 2016

Eight reasons why Hillary Rodham Clinton **must not** become president follow.

"Yeah, I got him off. So what? Who cares? We got the evidence thrown out, so he walked, (laughs) I mean, sure, we knew he did it, (laughs) but it didn't matter." Audio recording of Hillary discussing the child rapist she defended when a criminal lawyer in Arkansas, 1982.

"I don't give a f*** about them. Get them out of here and away from me." Hillary talking about her Secret Service Agents during Bill Clinton's first term (1993–1997) as president. Taken from Ron Kessler book, *First Family Detail.*

"I believe the primary role of the state is to teach, train, and raise children. Parents have a secondary role." Taken from Hillary's book, *It Takes a Village*, 1996.

"What the hell are we doing here? There's no money here. Get me the hell out of here." Hillary's comment while she was being driven through Upstate New York during her first term as NY Senator (2001–2005). Taken from Ron Kessler book, *First Family Detail.*

"Look, the average Democrat voter is just plain stupid. They're easy to manipulate. That's the easy part." Hillary's opinion, as told to Dick Morris, included in his book, *Rewriting History*, 2005.

"The Benghazi thing will fade, the public isn't interested." Hillary's comment, reported in *Time Magazine*, July 2014.

"I will get the NRA (National Rifle Association) shut down for good if I become president. If we can ban handguns, we will do it." Hillary interview with Des Moines Register, Iowa, August 2015.

"Maybe Mr. Stevens (Ambassador to Libya) should have contacted me if he wanted to live, if he wanted security. He should have thought about that." Hillary's comment, Benghazi Committee hearings, October 2015.

ABUNDANT DISPARITIES
FLOOD AMERICA

January 14, 2019

Much commotion or stir is made about observed differences between sexes and among races. Academic and legal minds try to convince us of their notion that men and women and people of all races should be proportionately represented socially and economically.

They make statements such as, though African Americans and Hispanics comprise about thirty-two percent of the U.S. population in 2015, they constituted fifty-six percent of all incarcerated people in 2015, twenty percent of Congress is women, and only five percent of CEOs are women. These differences are frequently referred to as disparities or conditions of being unequal.

Legal professionals, judges, politicians, academics, and others often operate under the assumption that we are all equal. Therefore, inequalities and disparities are seen as serving to prove injustice.

Thus, government must intervene, find the cause, and engineer a policy or law to eliminate the injustice. Such a vision borders on insanity relieved intermittently by periods of clear-mindedness.

There is no evidence anywhere or at any time in human history that shows where for some kind of social injustice, people would be proportionally represented across a range of social and economic identities by race and sex. In fact, if there is a dominant feature of mankind, it's that we differ significantly over a host of social and economic characteristics by race, sex, ethnicity, and nationality.

The differences have little or nothing to do with any sort of social injustice or unfair treatment. With an eye toward finding the injustice involved, I prefer to take a look at some racial, ethnic, and sex disparities.

We might also consider with thoroughness and care what kind of policy recommendation is necessary to correct this condition of being unequal. What would Congress or the United Nations do to "correct" the following?

- As of 2017, Nobel Prizes had been awarded to 902 individuals worldwide. Jews constitute no more than three percent of the U.S. population but are thirty-five percent of American Nobel Prize winners.
- Though Jews are less than two percent of the world population, 203 (22.5 percent) of the Nobel Prizes were awarded to Jews.
- Proportionality would have created 18 Jewish Nobel laureates instead of the "unfair" 203. Blacks are thirtyteen percent of the U.S. population but, in some seasons, have been as high as eighty-four percent of NBA players.
- To add to that "injustice," blacks are the highest paid basketball players and win nearly all the MVP prizes.
- Blacks are also guilty of taking sixty-seven percent, an "unfair" share, of professional football jobs. But how often do you see a black NFL kicker or punter?
- Women from Laotia, Samoa, and Vietnam have the highest cervical cancer rates in the United States.
- The Pima Indians in Arizona have the highest reported prevalence of diabetes of any population in the world.
- Tay-Sachs disease favors Jews of eastern European decent. Cystic Fibrosis haunts white people.
- Blacks of West African origin have the highest incidence of sickle cell anemia.
- American men have the highest prostate cancer rates of any racial or ethnic group in the United States. Black males are

also thirty percent likelier to die from heart disease than white men.

- Sharks are nine times likelier to attack and kill men than they are women.

There are many other disparities based upon physical characteristics, but it would take a fool to believe that we are all equal and any difference between us is a result of some kind of social injustice that takes without proof a societal remedy. The only kind of equality consistent with liberty is equality before the law, which doesn't require that people in fact be equal.

A Medical Academy
Wrongly Considers
Discipline to Be Abuse

May 13, 2019

A fairly recent news article said that the American Academy of Pediatricians (AAP) has expressed opposition to "all forms of corporal punishment." The article defined corporal punishment of children to include: "spanking, kicking, shaking, or throwing;" "scratching, pinching, biting, pulling hair, or boxing ears;" "forcing to stay in uncomfortable positions; burning, scalding, or forced ingestion (for example, washing-out a child's mouth with soap or forcing [him] to swallow hot spices)." Child abuse is a serious crime and should be punished as such.

The AAP is also right to oppose verbal punishment that "belittles, humiliates, denigrates, scapegoats, threatens, scares, or ridicules the child." But I believe the academy oversteps when it lumps spanking in with these harsh, heinous acts.

I know very few people who were not disciplined corporally as children and who know the sting of bare legs that are switched and the taste of Ivory Soap. As adolescents and adults, these flourishing, loving, wise, and nonviolent people admire and respect their parents and attribute much of their success in life to the discipline they received and learned as children.

I believe there is a proper and loving manner to spank a child. The child should be old enough to understand why he/she is being punished. Spanking should be a last resort after other disciplining methods and verbal warnings are exhausted and only to punish clearly and willfully disobedient acts. Spanking should never be done in public. Limit spanking to not more than three swats with a wooden spoon. Discipline should come as soon as possible after the offending behavior, followed by a reflective moment parent and child review the reason for the discipline, then reconcile and hug.

Disciplining children properly is time-consuming and unpleasant. But I believe parents who do so consistently and conscientiously will find that spanking becomes rare because their children learn to respect them and obey their words.

It's unreasonable to demand that Jews and Christians dismiss clear teachings like the one in Proverbs 22:15: "Folly is bound up in the heart of a child, but the rod of discipline will drive it far away." Ancient rabbis weren't fools. They understood human nature and recognized that children have wills that need to be quelled. Spare the rod, spoil the child.

I fear that the American Academy of Pediatrics policy may be an invitation for lawmakers to enact spanking bans, urging the government to intrude into intimate family affairs. Proper spanking is highly effective in shaping a child's character and behavior. It should continue to be an option for loving parents to employ when disciplining their children.

THE VALUE OF WORK

October 19, 2018

Work ennobles the human condition. When we refer to someone being a productive member of society, the connotation is that the person works at a meaningful vocation. Not only does such work benefit society at large, it also fulfills the individual worker's inborn desire to provide a useful product or service to mankind.

At all levels of government, public servants should strive to enact policies that respect the significance of work. Such policies include work requirements for able-bodied people receiving aid through public assistance programs aimed at lifting no-income and low-income individuals from poverty.

Last April, the Trump Administration issued a document aimed at systemizing this very principle. It's called the "Executive Order Reducing Poverty in America by Promoting Opportunity and Economic Mobility." It's online and worthwhile reading.

The document praises the bipartisan welfare reforms between Democrat President Bill Clinton and a majority-Republican Congress. The purpose of the order is the promotion of "further reform and modernization in order to increase self-sufficiency, well-being, and economic mobility." This document deserves more attention that it has received for the positive policy goals it sets forth.

Although unemployment is low almost everywhere in America today, welfare enrollment among able-bodied adults is at a record high. It's troubling that while organizations have difficulty filling available jobs, about sixteen million able-bodied adults receive food stamps and fifteen million of them don't work.

President Trump's order instructs "departments of Health and Human Services, Housing and Urban Development, and six others to review programs of Medicare, Section 8 Housing, and others." The departments are then supposed to "propose new regulations that will require most recipients to work or enter a serious job-training program."

Some politicians depict work requirements as somehow cruel; the truth is that putting reasonable demands on able-bodied people provides them tangible and intangible benefits. By either working, going to school or participating in training programs while receiving assistance, welfare recipients are more likely to develop the skills and work ethic needed to obtain permanent jobs and ultimately transition into the workforce.

The best thing life offers is the opportunity to work hard at work worth doing. Work shapes us. Work is innately good for human beings to experience. This is why so many unemployed people on welfare find it difficult to become the best they can be.

Work enables us to express ourselves in exchange for money, to identify and groom our talents, and to cultivate healthy self-esteem because we are adding value to others. From a purely spiritual standpoint, it's a divine gift. Work can be an act of worship to our Creator. Work is about more than money. It's about meaning.

SUFFERING FROM GENDER DYSPHORIA

April 14, 2017

Eighteen years ago when I retired at age sixty-eight from my own consulting engineer practice, my determination of a prospective employee's sex was a simple matter of appearance; they looked male or looked female. If there was uncertainty, which never happened in my experience, I could have asked for a birth certificate. Assuming that a birth certificate could not be produced, determination by a medical laboratory of the prospect's chromosomes could have been obtained—XX marks a female, and XY marks a male.

If I were to use those same tried-and-true methods of sex identification in today's society, I'd be scornful and abusive and accused of contempt for homosexuals. Nowadays, a person is male or female based on what he or she chooses to be.

This new "liberty" applies also to race. In the state of Washington, Rachel Dolezal was born Caucasian but chose to be black. She has become president of the Spokane NAACP and instructor of African studies at Eastern Washington University. She now has a new legal name, Nkechi Amare Diallo, which means "gift of God." Another beneficiary of racial fakery is politician Elizabeth Warren, who claims Cherokee Indian ancestry. That helped her obtain a one year $430,000 job as a professor of law at diversity-starved Harvard University. Since both Diallo and Warren are politically Leftist, learned college professors and their snowflake students praise their racial behavior.

Let's take a closer look at this idea of people freeing themselves from what, in their minds, is oppressive biological determination. If a male student says he's a female, how tolerant would the high school or college administrators be of that student going into the female restroom or showering facilities? Would male students claiming to be female be eligible for tryouts to play on the women's basketball team?

Suppose a high school or college honored its students the right to free themselves from biological determination and allowed those with XY chromosomes to play on the women's basketball team formerly designated as an XX team. Any opposing women's team would refuse to play against a mixed-chromosome team with a starting five consisting of three 6-foot 6-inch, 220-pound XYers, and two 5-foot 11-inch, 130-pound XXers.

What about allowing XYers claiming to be female compete in the Women's International Boxing Association or the Women's Olympics? They could qualify by just swearing that they feel female or suffer from gender dysphoria.

Femininity and Masculinity

January 21, 2019

Over the past fifty years, ideas about femininity and masculinity have evolved in America. Psychologists today think that traditional masculinity is a disease. They believe that traditional masculinity—marked by indifference to pleasure or pain, competitiveness, dominance, and aggression—is harmful and the cause for the oppression and abuse of women.

My belief is that masculine traits such as aggression, competitiveness, and protective alertness not only are positive but also characteristically have a biological basis. Boys and men produce testosterone, which is associated biologically and behaviorally with increased aggression and competitiveness. They also produce more vasopressin, a hormone originating in the brain that makes men aggressively protective of their loved ones.

The same goes for feminine traits such as nurturing and emotional sensitivity. Women produce more oxytocin than men when they nurture their children, and the hormone affects men and women differently. Oxytocin makes women more sensitive and empathetic while men become more playfully and tactually stimulating with their children, encouraging the ability to recover quickly from illness, change, or misfortune. These differences between men and women complement each other, allowing a couple to nurture and challenge their children.

American society is also too often derisive toward women who embrace their biological tendencies, labeling them abnormal or unhealthy. Women who choose to stay home with their children can feel cruelly judged, which contributes to conflict, anxiety, and depression shortly after childbirth.

What's unhealthy is not masculinity or femininity but the demeaning of masculine men and feminine women. Psychologists today believe that masculinities are based on social, cultural, and contextual norms, as if biology had nothing to do with it. They also show scorn, in my mind stupidly, at binary notions of gender identity as tied to biology.

From a mental-health perspective, it's beneficial for women to embrace masculine trait and for men to express feminine ones. Every person will have some mix of the two. But that doesn't change the reality that women tend to be feminine and men tend to be masculine.

Why can't psychologists acknowledge biology while seeing femininity and masculinity as characteristics? To be sure, manhood can be harmful when taken to extremes. Teaching boys, or girls for that matter—that they should always be indifferent to joy, grief, pleasure, or pain, and keep their feelings inside, and never allowing themselves to be vulnerable—is a recipe for mental illness. But so is telling boys that aggression, competitiveness, and protectiveness are signs of sickness. The same is true of telling girls that their desire to nurture children is shameful.

American society may not ever return to rigid sex roles. But it's wrong to devalue the important and positive differences between men and women that have complemented and enriched our relationships for tens of thousands of years.

Are You Fit for Military Service?

March 31, 2018

No individual human being has the right to serve in the United States Military, and the military is not an equal opportunity employer.

The military has one job: war. Anything else is a distraction. War is very unfair, and there are no exceptions made for being a special or challenged or socially unusual individual.

An individual changes self to meet military standards. The military does not change standards to accommodate any individual with special issues.

The military regularly and consistently uses prejudice to deny individuals who want to join for any one of the following standards:

- low IQ.
- too young or too old
- too skinny or too fat
- too short of too tall
- flat feet
- missing fingers or thumbs
- poor eyesight
- bad teeth
- bad back
- hearing damage
- crippled or other physical disability or malformation
- malnourished

- cannot perform required number of pushups
- cannot run required distance within required time
- criminal history
- drug addiction
- anxiety
- phobias
- refuse to follow orders,
- any individual issues that detract from readiness for war or causing death
- self-identification as homosexual or transgender

Avoid Legalizing Marijuana

November 7, 2018

Many people in the United States believe that legalizing marijuana is the answer to America's opioid crisis. They ignore the 2017 study published by the American Journal of Psychiatry showing marijuana users are more than twice as likely as the general public to abuse prescription opioids.

Or perhaps they're unaware that in 2015 the Centers for Disease Control found that people addicted to marijuana are three times more likely than the average person to become addicted to heroin.

Let's take a look at Colorado—America's "poster child" for legal dope. Colorado fully legalized marijuana in 2014, and pot continues to blossom into big business. The Rocky Mountain State now has more than 513 "medical marijuana" centers, more than 491 recreational marijuana shops, and roughly 700 cultivation facilities.

There are far more marihuana businesses in Colorado than its 394 Starbucks locations and 208 McDonald's restaurants combined. In the city of Denver alone, licensed "medical marijuana" centers outnumber pharmacies 210 to 108.

Occurring at the same time with marijuana legalization in Colorado, certain other trends have taken place. In 2016, 147 driver/operators involved in fatal crashes tested positive for marijuana, more than double the total in 2013 when 71 tested positive. Between 2013 and 2016, violent crime in Colorado increased 18.6 percent. Anyone who doesn't see a link between the disturbing trends must be smoking something.

Colorado now is ranked first in the nation in marijuana use among twelve- to seventeen-year-old adolescents. The usage rate for youth in this age group, in fact, is fifty-five percent higher than the national average. Homelessness has increased in the state of Colorado tremendously. Young people are without jobs; they just sit and use dope. There's nothing good in what they do for society.

There's the story about a successful high school student-athlete who made the mistake of smoking a joint before getting behind the wheel of an automobile. The vehicle struck and killed a little girl. Among the multiple lives ruined were those of the young driver and his family.

America is the most medicated country in the world. Do we really need to legalize another drug? The United States consumes eighty-five percent of the world's opioid painkillers. Another study shows that kids who use marijuana are five times more likely to use heroin.

In 2013, those between twelve and seventeen who smoke marijuana are ten times more likely to use other illicit drugs than their peers who don't smoke marijuana.

Other states would do well to pay heed to the experience of Colorado and some other states stumbling into the same mistakes. Legalizing marijuana is a road to nowhere good.

Important Statistical Data

July 22, 2018

The June 2016 population of the United States was 324.06-million people. Annual gun-related deaths undisputedly totaled 30,000.

- 19,500 deaths by suicide,
- 5,100 deaths by gun violence or criminal activity (gangs, drugs, mentally ill),
- 4,500 deaths by law enforcement, in line-of-duty,
- 900 deaths were accidental.

Annual death by **gun violence** was only 5,100, with 1,276 (25%) occurring in the following four cities, each of which has strict gun laws:

- Chicago. 480 homicides
- Baltimore. 344 homicides
- Detroit. 333 homicides
- Washington, DC. 119 homicides

Annual death by **gun violence** in the remainder of this nation was 3,824.

- California. 1,169 homicides (has strictest gun laws, by far, of any other state),
- Alabama. 1 homicide,
- forty-eight other states. 2,654 homicides.

*****

Annual death by heart attack is 710,000.
Annual death by medical errors is 200,000-plus.
Annual death by drug overdose is 40,000-plus.
Annual death from flu is 36,000.
Annual death from traffic accidents is 34,000.

In light of the foregoing data, why focus on guns? The founders of this nation knew that regardless of the form of government they might choose, those in power may become corrupt and seek to rule. The British knew that before their standing army could rule, they must first disarm the populace of the thirteen colonies.

The Founders understood that a disarmed populace is a controlled populace. That's why the Declaration of Independence was signed July 4, 1776, and the 2nd Amendment was proudly and boldly included in the U.S. Constitution. It must be preserved at all costs. The next time someone tries to convince you that gun control is about saving lives, assuming, of course, they're literate and rational, show them the foregoing factual data.

Is There Another Agenda or Just Glaring Ignorance?

March 12, 2018

According to government records, nearly thirty Americans die each day in motor vehicle crashes that involve drunk driving. Should there be federal background checks in order for an individual to obtain a license to drive or to purchase a motor vehicle?

The 2015 FBI Uniform Crime Report reveals that the number of shotgun and rifle deaths totaled 548 and that nearly three times as many people (1,573) were stabbed or hacked to death. Should there be federal background checks and waiting periods for knife or machete purchases?

For most of our history, virtually anywhere in the United States, a person could buy a shotgun, rifle, or pistol at any hardware or department store. When I was a child in the 1930s, the Sears & Roebuck Catalogue had thirty pages of firearm advertisements. Private transfers of guns to juveniles were unrestricted.

My father gave me a new 1942 Stevens 12-gauge single shotgun for my twelfth birthday. It was exactly like his 1905 Stevens 12-gauge single shotgun. I still have both shotguns. I hunted bob-white and Mexican quail with my dog, Dan, and sometimes with two close neighbor friends who had two good pointer dogs until I graduated high school.

Any mature and reasonable adult would argue that, just as the general public and courts do, motor vehicles, knifes, machetes, and guns are inanimate objects and can't act on their own. It's plain folly, therefore, to focus on guns in the cases of shooting deaths.

Today, there is far less availability of shotguns, rifles, and pistols than any time in our history. That historical fact raises a question: Despite the greater accessibility of guns in previous decades, why wasn't there the kind of violence we see with today's far less access to guns?

Have guns changed their behavior from yesteryear, and are they now committing mayhem and evil? An answer in the affirmative can be dismissed as lunacy. If guns haven't changed, it must be that people have changed. Half-witted reasons such as stopping children from playing cowboys and Indians or cops 'n' robbers won't do much. Calling for more gun restrictions, gun-free zones, and other measures have been for naught. Schoolteachers have enough on their plates; they don't need to carry a concealed gun.

Americans must own-up to the fact that laws and regulations alone can't produce a civilized society. Morality is society's first line of defense against uncivilized behavior. Moral standards of conduct have been under siege in our country for more than a half century.

Moral absolutes have been abandoned as guiding principles. We've been taught not to be judgmental, that one lifestyle or set of values is just as good as another. We no longer hold people accountable for their behavior and we accept excuse-making.

Problems of murder, mayhem, and other forms of antisocial behavior will continue until we regain our moral footing.

Mainstream Media Journalists

March 9, 2017

There are no journalists who are independent and free today in America's mainstream news media. You know it, and I know it.

If any dared to express their honest opinions, they would know beforehand that it would never be aired or appear in print. They're paid to keep their honest opinions to themselves.

Any mainstream news journalist who would be so foolish as to air or write honest opinions would be out on the streets looking for another job.

If any allowed their honest opinions to be aired or appear in print, their occupation would be gone the next day.

The business of the mainstream news journalist is to: destroy the truth, lie outright, corrupt, debase, vilify, bootlick for material gain, and sell his country and race for his daily bread.

They are the tools and slaves of George Soros (behind the scenes). They are the jumping jacks. Soros pulls the strings, and they dance.

Their journalistic talents, careers, and lives are all the property of another individual. They're intellectual prostitutes.

Immigrants and Diseases

September 4, 2018

All legal immigrants and refugees undergo a medical screening to determine whether they have an inadmissible health condition. This screening is mandated by the United States of America Immigration and Nationality Act.

The Centers for Disease Control and Prevention (CDC) provide technical instructions for medical examination of prospective immigrants in their home countries before they're permitted to enter the United States. They're screened for communicable and infectious diseases such as tuberculosis, malaria, hepatitis, polio, measles, mumps, HIV, and sexually transmitted disease.

The CDC medical screening guidelines for refugees are performed thirty to ninety days after the refugees arrive in the United States.

*****

Regarding illegal immigrants crossing the U.S./Mexico border, the CDC specifically cites the possibility of cross-border movement of HIV, measles, whooping cough, rubella, rabies, hepatitis A, influenza, tuberculosis, shigellosis, and syphilis. What's coming over into the United States could harm everyone. In south Texas, they're starting to see the spread of scabies, chicken pox, methicillin-resistant staphylococcus aureus infections, and different viruses.

Some of the children illegally entering our country are known to be carrying lice and suffering from various illnesses. Because there's no medical examinations of illegal immigrants, we have no idea how many are carrying infectious diseases that might endanger American school children when these immigrants enter schools across our nation.

The CDC reports that, in most industrialized countries, the number of tuberculosis cases and the number of deaths caused by TB steadily declined from mid-1885 to mid-1985. Since mid-1985, immigrants from countries where the disease is prevalent have reversed this downward trend.

In 2002, the CDC said, "Today, the proportion of immigrants among persons reported as having TB exceeds fifty percent in several European countries, including Denmark, Israel, Netherlands, Norway, Sweden, and Switzerland. A similar proportion has been predicted for the United States." The number of active TB cases among American-born citizens declined from an estimated 17,725 in 1986 to 3,201 in 2015. That's an eighty percent drop.

The National Tuberculosis Surveillance System reports the TB-incidence among foreign-born people in the United States (15.1 cases per 100,000) is roughly 13 times the incidence among U.S.-born people (0.2 cases per 100,000). Those statistics refer to immigrants who are legally in the United States. There's no way to know the incidence of TB and other diseases carried by illegal immigrants because they're not subject to medical examination.

This public health issue is ignored by all those Liberals supporting sanctuary cities as well as those Liberals clamoring for open borders. In the late 1800s and early 1900s, when masses of European immigrants were trying to enter the United States, those with dangerous diseases were turned back from Ellis Island.

In addition to diseases, there's the greater threat of welcoming to our shores people who have utter contempt for our values and want to import anti-Western values, such as genital mutilation, honor killings, and the oppression of women. Libertarians argue that we would benefit from open borders when it comes to both people and goods. This ignores the fact that imported goods don't demand welfare benefits.

My essential point is that we Americans have a right to decide who enters our country and under what conditions. If we relinquish that right, we cease to be a sovereign nation. But that's unimportant to Liberals.

A Better Way to Determine
Minimum Wage

August 25, 2018

America should have a minimum wage that provides roughly the same standard of living across the country. This means that minimum wages should be based on the cost of living, which varies regionally.

Let's take a look at three widely different regions, for example, Spokane, Washington. a 2,700-square-foot, 4-bedroom home with two baths sells for $165,000, with a $600 monthly mortgage. New York City. $600 monthly will pay rent for a parking space in Manhattan. Selma, Alabama. the median home is around $90,000. The idea that Spokane, New York City, and Selma should share the same minimum wage is stupid and unfair to low-wage American workers everywhere.

Based on half the median hourly wage of non-supervisory employees, according to the Bureau of Labor Statistics, the minimum hourly wage should be, Spokane. $11.30, New York City. $12.70, Selma. $9.80. These hourly floors would then rise with inflation.

The current minimum hourly wage of $7.50 is too low and practically impossible to raise, but there's a reason Congress hasn't voted to raise it. Legislators representing low-cost areas are blocking a $15.00 minimum wage not because they're stingy but because it isn't right for their constituents.

Americans have a choice. We can keep our stupid and unfair national minimum wage and hope that the stars align every ten years when Congress votes to raise it, or we can remake the minimum wage to accommodate the nation's vast economic differences.

The Major Barrier to Racial Progress Today Is Not Discrimination

April 20, 2018

Many black people think that black political power is necessary for blacks to be better off economically and socially. Let's take a closer look at that supposition.

Between 1970 and 2012, the number of black elected officials rose from 1,500 to more than 10,000. And in addition, a black man was elected to the to the U.S. presidency, not for just one term but for two.

A study by the Manhattan Institute explains how this surge in black political power has had minimal positive impact on the black community. The study shows how wrong the conventional thinking was when based on the notion that only black politicians could understand and address the challenges facing blacks.

After the 2014 Ferguson, Missouri, riots much ado was made of the small number of blacks on the city's police force. If the racial composition of the police force is so important, how are the Baltimore riots in 2015 explained after Freddie Gray died in police custody?

Baltimore's police force is forty percent black, the mayor is black, and most of the City Council is black. This black political power in Baltimore is seen also in Cleveland, Detroit, Philadelphia, Washington, DC, Cincinnati, Atlanta, and New Orleans.

Blacks have been mayors, police chiefs, city councilors, and superintendents of schools in these cities for decades. By contrast, when blacks had very little political power, they made significant economic progress.

During the 1940s and 1950s, black labor force participation rates exceeded those of whites and black incomes grew much faster than white incomes. Also, during that time period, the number of blacks in middle-class occupations quadrupled, and that was long before affirmative action programs.

After the 1960s, government began pouring trillions into various social programs that undermined the work ethic and discouraged marriage through welfare programs that kept poor people poor.

The Manhattan Institute study found that political success is not required for economic and social success and indeed may have the opposite effect. Black political power means nothing.

It's true that the black experience in America has been very different from that of all other racial groups. But none of those difficulties undermines the proposition that skills and education are far more important than political success.

The formula for prosperity is the same across the human spectrum, and traditional values are immeasurably more important than the color of your mayor, police chief, representatives, senators, and president.

The challenge for blacks is to reposition themselves to take advantage of existing opportunities. That involves correcting the antisocial, self-defeating behaviors and habits and attitudes that characterize the black underclass.

African-Americans Versus Police Officers

November 30, 2018

A new perspective is needed concerning the millionaire black National Football League players who show disrespect for the American national anthem and flag. Ask any ten of them, in private, why he's "taking a knee" and there will be ten different answers. One may say he's protesting against racial discrimination, another may say he's protesting against police treatment of blacks. Each of the remaining eight will have a different answer. How much sense do any of the protests make? This is some kind of stupid.

At the end of September this year, 737 people had been shot and killed by police in the United States. Of that number, there were: 329 whites (45%), 165 blacks (22%), 112 Hispanics (15%), 24 other races, and 107 unknown race.

In 2016 when Colin Kaepernick started taking a knee, Chicago had witnessed 806 murders and 4,379 shootings, and most of the murder victims were black. When a black person is murdered in Chicago, the perpetrator is found and charged with the murder less than 13 percent of the time.

Similar statistics regarding police killing blacks versus blacks killing blacks apply to predominantly black urban centers, such as Baltimore, Oakland, Philadelphia, St. Louis. Most white Americans see the black NFL player protest of police brutality as pathetic, useless showboating. These players have made no open protest against the thousands of blacks being murdered and maimed by blacks. They stupidly view them as trivial in comparison with police killings.

Black NFL players aren't alone. Black politicians, black civil rights leaders, and liberal whites give no attention to the merciless black homicides in our cities? You hear none of them condemning the fact that most black murderers get away with murder. They wouldn't be as silent if it were the Ku Klux Klan committing the murders. What is to blame for this havoc?

If you ask a Leftist college intellectual or academic in a sociology or psychology department, you'll be told it's caused by poverty, discrimination, and a lack of opportunities. But the black murder rate and other crime statistics in the 1940s and 1950s were not anywhere near as high as they are now.

The Leftist intellectuals or academics would not explain that there was less black poverty, less racial discrimination, and far greater opportunities for blacks during that earlier period. If any one of them did explain it, that individual would be considered by their associates to be an unrepentant idiot. Black people need to find new heroes. Right now, their heroes are criminals such as Baltimore's Freddie Gray, Ferguson's Michael Brown, and Florida's Trayvon Martin.

Black support tends to go toward the criminals in the community rather than to the overwhelming number of the people in the community who are law-abiding. That needs to end. What also needs to end is the lack of respect for, and cooperation with, police officers. It's true, some police officers are crooked. But blacks are more likely to be victims of violent confrontations with police officers than whites simply because blacks commit more violent crimes, per capita, than whites.

If something good is to be done about these unflattering crime statistics, we can't play the blame games that black politicians, black NFL players, civil rights leaders, and white liberals want to play.

THE COP-KILLER "EPIDEMIC" IS FICTION

January 13, 2016

To hear or read the media tell it, America is in the grips of an unprec-edented orgy of merciless murder in which heavily armed thugs ran-domly gun down innocent people, some of them teens, as an active pastime, except that these homicidal goons are wearing the blue and badges of American police departments.

It's the narrative that's given rise to the protest "Black Lives Matter" and to a growing public mistrust of the police in general. From Michael Brown in Ferguson, Missouri, to the recent shooting of a middle-aged woman and a teen in Chicago, the body count seemingly keeps rising, exacerbating racial tensions, and keeping the nation on edge. And each incident is breathlessly reported by a media determined to show that America remains deeply, irredeem-ably racist.

The problem is, it's simply not true.

The last week of December 2015, a study of police shootings that took place in 2015 was published in *The Washington Post*. It's likely they intended the story to be shocking. As of December 24, police had killed 965 people! Instead, the report quells the notion that trigger-happy cops are out hunting for civilian victims, espe-cially African-Americans.

Among its key findings:

- White cops shooting unarmed black men accounted for less than four percent of fatal police shootings.
- In three-quarters of the incidents, cops were either under attack themselves or defending civilians; in other words, doing their jobs.
- The majority of those killed were brandishing weapons and suicidal or mentally troubled or bolted when ordered to surrender.
- Nearly a third of police shootings resulted from car chases that began with a minor traffic stop.

The moral of these findings is don't point a gun at the cops and don't run when they tell you to stop. Since America's population is about 318 million people, 965 deaths at the hands of police is about 1 in 318,000. You have a better chance of being killed in a violent storm (1 in 68,000) or slipping in a bathtub (1 in 11,500) than being shot by a cop, no matter what color you are.

But even these figures are deceptive. Of those 965 killed, only 90 were unarmed, and the majority of those were white.

And that doesn't take into account other extenuating circumstances besides a weapon that would have caused a police officer to fire.

Still, the "killer cop" narrative refuses to die, and *The Washington Post* decided to throw fuel on the racial fire with context-free statements like this: "Although black men make-up only six percent of the U.S. population, they account for forty percent of the unarmed men shot to death by police this year."

This ignores the fact that black violent-crime rates are far higher than those of whites. The Department of Justice reports that blacks committed 52.5 percent of the murders in America from 1980 to 2008 when they represented only 12.6 percent of the population.

Certainly, this doesn't excuse cases of police misconduct. Bad cops should be investigated and tried. The death of the South Carolina black man last spring who was shot in the back while fleeing a white police officer after a routine traffic stop resulted in the indictment of the cop, who is now awaiting trial. And the killing of Quintonio LeGrier and Bettie Jones in Chicago last December 26, after a troubled LeGrier allegedly became "combative" with officers, certainly needs further investigation.

But these incidents don't prove that the "real problem" is cops. This isn't an "epidemic." And it isn't racist to suggest that some perspective is warranted here. Most, if not all, cities where real problems exist are led by democrats and have been for many decades.

Yet encouraged by liberal politicians and a liberal media, the rhetoric of protesters has become more heated, poisoning relations between local police and the folks they serve. Most tragically, it's resulted in the murders of police officers, such as the two NYPD Officers killed in a Brooklyn ambush a year or so ago.

Against the numbers cited by *The Washington Post*, what about this one: the worst neighborhoods in Chicago—say, West Garfield Park, where gangs run rampant—have a higher murder rate (116.7 per 100,000) than world murder capitals like Honduras (90.4 per 100,000).

Enough Is Enough

August 22, 2018

Before last weekend's Chicago Mayhem, 1,718 had been shot since the beginning of the year, and 306 had been murdered. In more than 206 of Chicago's homicides, no suspect is charged. Chicago is by no means unique in this lawlessness. Detroit, Baltimore, Philadelphia, St. Louis, and some other major cities share high rates of homicides.

It's not just shootings and homicides that negatively impact the overwhelmingly law-abiding black residents of these cities. In addition, there are high rates of burglaries, rapes, and property destruction. The public schools are notoriously bad. City budgets face shortfalls. Residents deal with deteriorating city services. All this causes mass exoduses from these cities by their most capable people.

Ordinary decency demands that something be done to address the horrible conditions under which so many black Americans live. White Democrats and white Liberals and black politicians and black sports figures focus most of their attention on what the police do, but how relevant is that to the overall problem?

Would electing more Democrats and blacks to political office help? It turns out that of the Chicago City Council's fifty aldermen, only one is Republican. One is an Independent. Forty-eight are Democrats, and nineteen of those are black. In fact, most of the cities where large segments of their black citizenry live under horrible conditions have been controlled by Democrats and blacks for fifty years or more, and there are many blacks on the instruments of control, such as police chiefs, school superintendents, and city council members. If Democrat and black control meant anything, these cities would be paradises.

The leader of the movement to impeach President Trump is Rep. Maxine Waters. Her congressional district suffers from high crime rates and failing schools. She, like most other black politicians, claims that she is helping her constituency by doing all she can to fight to get more taxpayer money for her district.

More taxpayer money could not fix the problems of these communities. Over the past fifty years, more than sixteen trillion dollars has been spent on poverty programs. The majority of those programs have simply made poverty more comfortable by giving poor people more food, health care, housing, etc.

What's needed most is to get poor people to change their behavior. Most important among the modifications is reducing female-headed households. Female-headed households produce most of the prison inmates, the highest crime rates, and disproportionate numbers of high school dropouts and suicides.

These devastating factors are far beyond the capacity of Washington, DC to fix. The only people who can fix these problems are black people themselves. Black athletes could be far more productive by going to schools and community centers to encourage constructive behavior and shaming self-destructive behavior.

If you look at many of the NFL players who take a knee, their records on out-of-wedlock children show that they contribute significantly to the problem against which they're protesting. Antonio Cromartie has twelve children by nine different women. Apparently, an NFL team had to shell-out $500,000 before he could even play football for them.

Travis Henry has eleven children by ten different women. Willis McGahee has nine children by eight different women. Derrick Thomas has seven children by five different women. Bennie Blades has six children by six different women. Ray Lewis has six children by four different women.

Marshal Faulk has six children by three different women. Adrian Peterson has eleven children by seven different women. Before these guys take a knee, they should take a good look in the mirror. The cause of their problem is themselves.

Citizenship and Immigration

August 11, 2018

Donald Trump appealed to the importance of citizens and borders in the 2016 presidential campaign. He took his stand on behalf of the nation-state and citizenship. He was against the idea of a homogenous world-state populated by "universal people."

Donald Trump succeeded in defeating both of the political parties, the media, pollsters, political professionals, academics, and bureaucrats. For too many years, all these groups formed part of the bipartisan cartel that had represented the entrenched interests of the Washington establishment. Although defeated in the election, the cartel has not given-up. It is fighting a desperate battle to maintain its power.

Throughout history, constitutional government is found only in the nation-state, where the people share a common good and are dedicated to the same principles and purposes. The homogenous world-state, which is the European Union on a global scale, will be neither a constitutional democracy nor a constitutional republic using democratic principles.

It will be government by unelected, unaccountable bureaucrats much like the burgeoning administrative-state that is trying today to expand its reach and magnify its power in the United States of America. Rights will be superfluous because the collective welfare of the community, determined by the bureaucrats, will have superseded the rights of individuals.

The Democrat Party and its progressive liberalism no longer views self-preservation as a rational goal of the nation-state. Instead, it insists that self-preservation and national security must be subordinate to openness (uncontrolled immigration) and diversity ("who we are as Americans").

American citizens can consent to allow others to join the compact that has created our nation-state. However, American citizens have the sovereign right to specify the terms and conditions for granting entry and qualifications for citizenship.

Qualifications for the entry and naturalization in America are whether those who wish to enter demonstrate a capacity to adopt the habits, manners, independence, and self-reliance of republican citizens, and devotion to the principles that unite the American people. Furthermore, it would be unreasonable not to expect that potential immigrants possess useful skills that will ensure they will not become victims of the welfare state.

Immigration policies should serve the interests of the American people and of the nation; they should not be viewed as acts of charity to the world. Putting America first is a rational goal. It is the essence of sovereignty. And the sovereign nation-state is the only home of citizenship; as it is the only home of constitutional government.

America's Changing Form of Government

July 16, 2018

America's original Constitutional Republic has undergone gradual change to yesterday's (Constitutional) Democracy to today's (Representative) Democracy. *The Federalist Papers, Essay 10*, written in 1787 by James Madison, follows: "*Democracies have ever been spectacles of turbulence and contention; have ever been found incompatible with personal security of the rights of property; and have in general been as short in their lives as they have been violent in their deaths.*"

At the 1789 signing of the Constitution, Alexander Hamilton said: "*We are now forming a Constitutional Republic form of government. Real liberty is not found in the extremes of democracy, but in moderate government. If we incline too much Democracy, we shall soon shoot into a Monarchy, or some other form of Dictatorship.*"

John Adams declared: "*Remember, Democracy never lasts long. It soon wastes, exhausts, and murders itself.*"

Edmond Randolph stated: "*In tracing these evils to their origin, every man had found it in the turbulence and follies of Democracy.*"

As John Adams emerged from the signing of the Constitution, he was asked by a lady: "*What have you given us?*" Adams answered: "*A Republic, madam, and I hope you can keep it.*"

Was the "Battle Hymn of the Republic" incorrectly titled when written in 1861? Did Rev. Francis Bellamy, of the National Education Association, use the wrong word when, in 1892, he wrote: "*I pledge allegiance to the flag of the United States of America and to the Republic for which it stands."*

The 1928 War Department manual 2000-25, used for training military personnel, defined a democracy as: *"A government of the masses; authority derived through mass meeting or any other form of direct property expression; results in mobocracy; attitude toward property is communistic, negating property rights; attitude of the rule of law is that the will of the majority shall regulate, whether it be based upon deliberation or governed by passion, prejudice, and impulse, without restraint or regard to consequence; results in demagogism, license, agitation, discontent, anarchy."*

America's Constitutional Republic form of government uses the democratic process to elect members of Congress. Our Constitution limits the powers of government, spells out how government is structured, creates checks on its power, and balances power between the legislative, executive, and judicial branches.

Before 1933, the idea of a democracy was foreign to citizens of the United States of America. In 1933, Democrat President Franklin D. Roosevelt took office; humanism entered the public school system; and politicians, political talking heads, false academics, counterfeit historians, and news media began calling America's historic political system a (constitutional) democracy.

This new form of government, a democracy for eighty-five years, has spread like a contagious disease and infected the public mind throughout America. It has been repeated often enough, over a period of many years, to persuade the public mind to believe it.

Corrupt activity is prevalent today among many of the 535 members in Congress, the Department of Justice, the Federal Bureau of Investigation, former President Obama's Deep State, and Obama's current Organizing for Action group of more than 32,500 demonstrators. America is the country for which many of us veterans spilled our blood, the nation I feared before the November 2016 election was on the fast track to becoming a hopeless cause.

Under our new (outsider), President Trump, in office since January 21, 2017, the principles that define a Constitutional Republic are being emphasized and America's original form of government is returning. The Constitution is being upheld together with the God-given liberties enshrined in our Declaration of Independence, including the unalienable right to life, liberty, and the pursuit of happiness. America is again filled with promise, which is being reestablished by President Trump on the basis of individual freedom and personal responsibility.

Funding Our Infrastructure Highways and Bridges

February 28, 2017

President Trump, the new transportation secretary, and Congress should give attention to something important that's happening now in the states of Colorado, Oregon, and Washington.

Thousands of drivers in each of these states are participating in pilot-test programs for mileage-based user fees. It's anticipated that our nation's transportation infrastructure (highways and bridges only) can be financed using this financial resource.

That money can replace the **shrinking fuel taxes** collected now for the virtually defunct Highway Trust Fund. Under a mileage-based system, people would pay a fee for the miles they travel rather than a per-gallon tax paid at the gasoline pump.

The ability to implement such a system using cell phones, GPS, or other technologies and make payment simple already exists. The biggest problem is how states will standardize their systems to provide a perfectly consistent experience for those who regularly drive across state lines. But the U.S. Department of Transportation can help in that regard.

The main objection is that more data and more tracking usually equal bigger government. And of course, there will be winners and losers under a mileage-based user fee, as there are with the gasoline tax and any other method.

While gasoline use declines, the national odometer keeps on spinning. Americans drove a record 3.1-trillion miles in 2015. If a system is wanted that can continue to pay for our roads and bridges and make our infrastructure great again, a mileage-based user fee appears to be a good way to do it.

Predictable Spending on Infrastructure Would Vastly Improve Its Quality

June 23, 2018

A report card published last year by the American Society of Civil Engineers gave our United States an overall D-plus. The ASCE, of which I've been an active member since 1959, recommends spending $4.59-trillion by 2025 on repairs and improvements.

A lack of understanding, good sense, and foresight has caused politicians to consider infrastructure spending largely as something to act upon or not act upon as economic conditions or political impulses warrant. This creates not only inefficiency but also the temptation for politicians to pick favorites, like the Bridge to Nowhere in Ketchikan, Alaska.

My viewpoint, as a licensed professional geologist and licensed professional engineer specializing in geotechnical (a discipline of civil engineering), is that true reform means consistently supporting an extensive ecosystem for rebuilding infrastructure. It would be filled with skilled engineers, well-trained civil servants, and many other workers involved in planning, monitoring, and executing projects.

Forming such an ecosystem requires the promise of continuing contracts. Few qualified personnel, for example, would choose the specialty of bridge engineering as a career without the expectation of consistent work. Sporadic opportunity similarly reduces incentives for entrepreneurs to develop new and better technologies to build sewers and tunnels, and it discourages incumbents from innovating.

Meanwhile, municipalities can't make long-term plans without a dependable flow of funding. They can't afford to hire teams of expert civil servants to manage construction contractors and keep projects on track. Instead, they end-up relying on costly arrangements, leading to poor results.

An excellent example is New York City's Second Avenue subway project. For almost one hundred years, the need for this new line was obvious. The first attempt to build it ended in the 1970s when funding disappeared, leaving wasted tunnel underground.

Last year when the first phase finally opened, about 1.6 miles long, the final price tag was more than $4-billion. Ultimately, the price was so high, the work so slow, the disruption so great, and the funding so unpredictable, it's doubtful subsequent phases will be built during the next twenty years.

When a project does make it to completion, there's an awful lot that can be learned from the work. In science and technology, learning through repetition is a core value. Building additional copies of something almost always lowers unit costs. Unfortunately, most projects in America, due mainly to geologic conditions, are effectively one-offs like the Second Avenue subway work.

The United States is constantly reinventing the wheel as new projects come due. Building a strong infrastructure ecosystem would require a shift in thinking. Instead of spending in fits and starts, we would think of building projects to undertake consistently as a matter of national interest.

Bridges, roads, dams, and other public works decay at a steady rate. The need for new infrastructure to support population growth is readily calculable. Rather than going on periodic spending binges, Congress should decide what percentage of gross domestic product to invest year-in and year-out. Americans spend about 18 percent of GDP on health care. Surely, there's a way to increase the 2.4 percent of GDP spent on infrastructure. It isn't near enough.

Adopting a more constructive way of thinking about infrastructure would bring many benefits. State and local governments would be able to develop more workable and effective building plans.

Engineering firms would invest more confidently in their employees and in state-of-the-art technologies. Students and entrepreneurs would increasingly see one of the many disciplines of civil engineering as a viable career path. In the end, the rewards would be even greater American innovation, opportunity, and economic growth.

CAPITALISM AND SOCIALISM

June 4, 2018

Polls concerning the Democrat Party primary in 2016 demonstrate the popularity that avowed socialist Bernie Sanders had among young democrats; they prefer socialism to free market capitalism. That preference is a result of their ignorance and indoctrination during their school years, from kindergarten through college. Neither they nor many of their teachers and professors know the differences between free market capitalism and socialism.

Free market capitalism, in which there is peaceful voluntary exchange, is morally superior to any other economic system. Each of us own ourselves—you are your private property, and I am my private property. Theft, murder, rape, and the initiation of violence are immoral because they violate self-ownership. Similarly, the forcible use of one person to serve the purposes of another person is immoral because it violates self-ownership.

Somewhere between two-thirds and three-quarters of the federal budget can be described as Congress taking the rightful earnings of one American to give to another American, using one American to serve another American (or illegal alien). Such acts include business bailouts, farm subsidies, food stamps, welfare, Social Security, Medicare, Medicaid, and many other programs.

Free market capitalism is disfavored by many Americans and threatened not because of its failure but ironically because of its success. Free market capitalism in America has been so successful in eliminating the traditional problems of mankind—disease, hunger, and poverty—that all other problems appear both unbearable and inexcusable.

The desire by many Americans to eliminate these "unbearable and inexcusable" problems has led to the call for socialism. That call includes equality of income, sex-and-race balance, affordable housing, medical care, orderly markets, and many other socialistic ideas.

What are the differences between capitalism and socialism? Let's take a look at some areas in our lives where we find the greatest satisfaction and those areas in which we find the greatest dissatisfaction. Seldom are we upset with clothing stores, hardware stores, and supermarkets. The motivation for these retail businesses is profit. If you're not satisfied with their services, you can "fire them" by taking your business elsewhere.

It's a different matter when we're upset with the services of motor vehicle bureaus, boards of education, and police departments. They aren't motivated by profit at all. If you're not satisfied with their service, it's costly and, in many cases, even impossible to fire them.

A much, much larger, and totally ignored, difference between capitalism and socialism is the **brutality of socialism**. In the twentieth century, the one-party socialist states of the Union of Soviet Socialist Republics, Germany under the National Socialist German Workers Party, and People's Republic of China were responsible for the murder of 118-million citizens, mostly their own (USSR 62-million, Nazi Germany 21-million, and PRC 35-million).

Consequences of
Muslim Inbreeding

July 6, 2017

There's a huge genetic problem in the Middle East; it's caused by 1,407 years of Muslim inbreeding since Muhammad founded Islamism in AD 610. The problem is marriage of first cousins, for seventy consecutive generations, in order to keep the wealth within the family. A town in Saudi Arabia, for example, has only two last names for all its citizens.

The disastrous results of such inbreeding will never disappear in the Muslim world since Muhammad is the ultimate example and authority in all matters. This massive inbreeding has done virtually irreversible damage to the Muslim gene pool, including intelligence, sanity, and health.

Roughly half of all Muslims in the world are inbred: 70 percent in Pakistan; 67 percent in Saudi Arabia; 64 percent in Jordan and Kuwait; 63 percent in Sudan; 60 percent in Iraq; 54 percent in United Arab Emirates and Qatar, and 40 percent in Denmark.

In 2014 England: 5.4 percent of the total population was Muslim; 9 major cities (including London) had a Muslim Mayor; 15 major cities had large Muslim populations; 1,740 mosques; 130 Sharia Courts; 50 Sharia Councils; and 63 percent of Muslim men didn't work but had free benefits and housing; 78 percent of Muslim women didn't work but had free benefits and housing; and all schools served only *halal* meat.

While Pakistani Muslims are responsible for only 3 percent of births in the United Kingdom, they account for 33 percent of children with genetic birth defects. The risk of disorders such as cystic fibrosis or spinal muscular atrophy is eighteen times higher, and death due to malformations is ten times higher. Other negative consequences of inbreeding include a 100 percent increase of stillbirths and a 50 percent probability that a baby will die during labor.

Lowered intellectual capacity is another devastating consequence of inbreeding; the risk of having an IQ lower than 70 (the official "retarded" level) increases by 400 percent. In the past 1,200 years of Islamism, just 100,000 books have been translated into Arabic, which is about the number Spain translates in a single year.

Only nine Muslims have ever won the Nobel Prize, and five of those were for the "Peace Prize."

In Denmark, 64 percent of schoolchildren with Muslim parents are still illiterate after ten years in the Danish School System. Mental illness is also a product of inbreeding; the closer the blood relative, the higher the risk of schizophrenic illness. This increased risk of insanity explains why more than 40 percent of patients in Denmark's largest ward for clinically insane criminals have Muslim backgrounds.

I conclude that Islamism is a dark and dangerous movement for world conquest. It's not simply a benign and morally equivalent alternative to the religions of Judaism and Christianity. Simple Jewish and Christian compassion for Muslims and the common-sense desire to protect our civilization from the ravages of Islam dictate a vigorous opposition to the spread of the Islamic way of life in our country.

The opposition to President's Trump's ban on immigration by the two Judges of the Left-leaning 9th District Federal Court was not just stupid, it was anti-American. Call President Trump Islamophobia if you wish, but he was right in doing what he did and the Supreme Court agrees.

Europe Provides a Valuable Lesson, but America Is Not Listening

June 7, 2016

America's leftists and progressives believe that the United States should become more like Europe. I wonder whether they want to also import the European policies that created barbaric extremism among its Muslim population.

The tragedies in recent years in France aren't surprising, given some of its policies that aren't widely publicized abroad. France has "no-go zones," officially called "sensitive zones," where police are reluctant to go because the zones are dominated by Islamic extremists. There's hardly a city in France that doesn't have at least one NGZ. It has been estimated that there are more than 750 such zones in France.

According to one of America's leading newspapers, "France has the largest population of Muslims. And some of these Muslims talk openly of ruling the country one day and casting aside Western legal systems for harsh, Islam-based Shariah."

Most of France's Muslim population has no intention of joining the French culture. They are hell-bent on importing the failed components of their motherland, such as Shariah (the subjugation of women, suppression of free speech, and honor killings). France isn't alone in tolerating people who have little desire to abandon the culture from which they fled.

Sweden's Ingrid Carlquist says, "Once upon a time, there was a safe welfare state called Sweden, where people rarely locked their doors. Since the Parliament decided in 1975 that Sweden should be multicultural and not Swedish, crime has exploded. Violent crime has increased by over 300 percent, and rapes have increased by an unbelievable 1,472 percent."

The Swedish police say, "The situation is slipping from our grasp," referring to some no-go zones like Tensta and Rinkeby. "If we're in pursuit of a vehicle, it can evade us by driving to a no-go zone where a lone patrol car simply can't follow because we'll get pelted by rocks." As a result of the increasing danger, Swedes are arming themselves in unprecedented numbers and sales of home alarm systems are booming.

The Belgian government admits that it has lost control of the no-go zone in Brussels—Molenbeek, which is referred to as "Europe's jehadi central." Terrorist plots connected to this neighborhood include:

- the assassination of anti-Taliban leader Ahmad Shah Massoud;
- the 2004 Madrid train bombings, which killed 191 people;
- the 2014 attack on a Jewish museum in Brussels;
- the attack on a Kosher grocery in Paris after the Charlie Hebdo shootings; and
- the attack on a Paris-bound train, in which an Islamic terrorist was overpowered by three Americans.

There are zones where the government has lost control in Germany, England, and most other European countries too. The prime minister of Hungary explained the situation confronting Europeans. "For us today, our stakes are: Europe, the lifestyle of European citizens, European values, the survival or disappearance of European nations and, more precisely formulated, their transformation beyond recognition. Today, the question is not merely in what kind of a Europe we would like to live but whether everything we understand as Europe will exist at all.

At the time of this writing, Dearborn, Michigan, is America's no-go zone. For those of you who don't believe me, I challenge you to drive there in your own car. Most Americans welcome people to our country who come here to become Americans, as immigrants have in the past. In fact, two days from today, my own beloved daughter-in-law whom my son married and brought to America eight years ago will become a naturalized American citizen.

We don't welcome people who wish to import the failed culture from which they fled. We could extend the welcome mat further if we abandoned the welfare state. We have far too many Americans living off the earnings of others and don't need to encourage others to do the same.

Interesting Factual Information

CAUSES OF DEATH IN USA, JANUARY 1–JUNE 15, 2016

1. Abortion: 501,325 her body, her choice
2. Heart Disease: 282,038
3. Cancer: 271,640
4. Tobacco: 160,680
5. Obesity   140,939 healthy at every size!
6. Medical Errors: 115,439
7. Lower Respiratory Disease: 65,623
8. Accident (unintentional):   62,460
9. Stroke: 61,106
10. Alcohol: 45,908
11. Hospital Associated Infection: 45,449
12. Alzheimer's Disease   42,942
13. Diabetes: 35,114
14. Influenza/Pneumonia   25,394
15. Kidney Failure: 19,631
16. Blood Infection: 15,363
17. Drunk Driving: 15,521
18. Unintentional Poisoning: 14,580
19. All Drug Abuse: 11,479
20. Prescription Drug Overdose: 6,886
21. Murder by Gun: 5,276 we need gun control!

The strictest gun laws in America are in Chicago. During the month of September 2019, 57 people were killed by guns, and 273 were shot. Murder is illegal. Attempting murder is illegal. A felon owning a gun is illegal. Shooting people indiscriminately is illegal. Criminals do not go through background checks when purchasing guns.

Explain how criminals will follow new laws. Explain how new laws will make us safer. Explain how restricting law-abiding citizens even more will make us safer. Oh, you can't? Then your argument is invalid.

Poor children of every color or race picked cotton. Open a history book and gain some knowledge.

Florida has had 119 hurricanes since 1850, but the most recent one—August 2019—was caused by climate change?!

President Trump Is Also a Skilled Military Strategist

November 9, 2019

In early October 2001, United States military forces invaded Afghanistan in retaliation for the September 11, 2001, Twin Towers tragedy in New York City. Later on, the Middle-East governments of Syria (excepting the Kurds), Iran, and Turkey—each of which was influenced by Russia—became allies.

On October 8, 2019, in order to end U.S. involvement in this eighteen-year-long war, President Trump pulled U.S. troops out of Syria because history shows middle-east wars are **"<u>endless</u>."** The next day, October 9, Turkey military forces assaulted the Kurds in northern Syria, causing Iran to send their military forces to Syria's border with Turkey.

As long as U.S. military forces were in Syria, the coalition of Syria, Iran, Turkey, and Russia were united against them. One of the consequences of President Trump's 10/8/19 decision is that it has pitted these former allies against each other.

Furthermore, the decision has brought unity between Syria and the Kurds, division between Turkey, Iran, Syria, and Russia, and causes Iran to focus on defending its interests instead of harming Israel. President Trump understands the nature of God, the laws of nature, the nature of history, the nature of humankind, and the nature of the many Islamic factions. He uses this knowledge to solve problems created in the past by U.S. politicians.